UNKNOWN9

REVELATION™

UNKNOWN9
REVELATION™

Book Two of the Genesis Trilogy

BY LAYTON GREEN

 REFLECTOR

Published by Reflector Entertainment
Montreal, Quebec www.reflectorentertainment.com

Distributed by Greenleaf Book Group
For ordering information or special discounts for bulk purchases, please contact Greenleaf Book Group at PO Box 91869, Austin, TX 78709, 512.891.6100.

Cover design by Pascal Hamelin
Interior book design by The Book Designers

Publisher's Cataloging-in-Publication data is available.
Print ISBN: 978-1-9992297-9-5
eBook ISBN: 978-1-9992297-8-8

Part of the Tree Neutral® program, which offsets the number of trees consumed in the production and printing of this book by taking proactive steps, such as planting trees in direct proportion to the number of trees used: www.treeneutral. com

Printed in the United States of America on acid-free paper
21 22 23 24 25 26   10 9 8 7 6 5 4 3 2 1
First Edition

Between the idea
And the reality
Between the motion
And the act
Falls the Shadow

—T. S. ELIOT

PROLOGUE

Broken glass and discarded wrappers littered the sidewalk as the veil of night settled on the Lower East Side of Manhattan. Now the streets belonged to the pushers and addicts, muggers and gang members. For a man such as Dr. James Corwin, professor of theoretical physics at Columbia University, a lone figure in a fedora and tailored linen suit, an outfit that screamed for attention in the rough neighborhood, trouble seemed inevitable.

Yet his environs did not bother him. Dr. Corwin had come of age in a slum in Kingston, Jamaica. He had survived much harder streets, had traveled the world and back again.

What bothered him was the puzzle of the abandoned building across the street.

Only thirty-one years old, Dr. Corwin had received tenure at Columbia a year earlier, a most impressive feat. He was also a member of another organization, the Leap Year Society, which he considered even more prestigious—but which he still knew precious little about, despite his recent induction.

Earlier that morning, Dr. Corwin had arrived at his office to find a manila envelope delivered beneath his door. Inside was a calling card bearing the ouroboros seal of the LYS. Printed on the back of the card was a clock set to midnight above the address that had led

7

him to this abandoned building on Canal Street.

The message was clear.

He checked his watch. 11:30 p.m. A graffiti-stained, roll-up aluminum barrier covered the ground floor of the building. How to get inside? Was the lack of an obvious entrance a precaution against prying eyes? A hidden message, a challenge?

Knowing the Leap Year Society, it was probably all three.

This suited Dr. Corwin just fine. He loved intellectual puzzles, searching for the hidden meaning of things, uncovering the patterns and enigmas strewn about the world like the pieces of a broken pearl necklace.

In theory, a society of driven, intelligent individuals from around the globe searching for esoteric knowledge was a perfect fit for him. Yet the reality was a serpentine road that wound through a dark and tangled wood, leading to an unknown terminus that gave him a shiver of anticipation.

Whatever lay in store, he was prepared to take it on. Best to stay the course for now, rise through the ranks and discover the tantalizing secrets of the upper echelons of the Society. Secrets which the elder members dangled like ripe mangoes before their inductees.

He took a closer look at the abandoned building as steam drifted out of a sewer grate beneath his feet. Decades of neglect had left the exterior stained with soot and grime, but the architecture was exquisite. Pillars in bas-relief flanked three arched faux windows high above the street. Heavy ornamentation rich in mythology framed the windows and decorated the cornice. The white terra-cotta resembled marble at first glance, and the elaborate design—Spanish Baroque, if he wasn't mistaken—implied an abandoned theater or museum.

No address was visible, yet the red-brick apartment buildings on either side, both fronted by fire escapes and AC units sagging in the windows, bore street numbers above and below the one he was seeking.

This had to be the place—but what was it? All he knew for certain was that he was supposed to get inside before midnight.

He leaned on his ironwood cane and studied his surroundings. The smell of garbage and reefer and fried grease. Sirens in the distance, the rattle of the subway underfoot, the shouts of an angry husband drifting through a window.

Down the street, a few drunks were heckling an old woman walking her dog. All the shops were closed except for a bar with a blinking neon sign missing letters. The Brooklyn Bridge loomed in the distance. The intrigue and danger of Chinatown lurked just around the corner. Getting involved in a shady altercation on the Lower East Side would not be a good look for a young professor. He needed to get off the street.

Could one of the sewer grates lead to an underground entrance? Perhaps, though he rather hoped it didn't, since he loathed tight spaces. He approached the building to study the aluminum barricade. If he cut the padlock securing the bottom, he could roll up the gate. Yet this seemed too obvious a solution, and lifting the noisy barrier would alert the neighbors, along with every ruffian within earshot.

He turned and crossed the street behind him, eyeing the building from a new perspective. Now he could see, set farther back on the flat rooftop, a boxy structure secured by an iron cage. It was too dark to tell exactly what it was.

His gaze roamed to the fire escapes of the adjacent apartments. A set of iron stairs on the taller building ran very close to the roof of the derelict building to which he had been summoned.

The drunks had moved on. No one else was in sight. He approached the taller apartment building, attached his cane to the custom-made loop on his belt, jumped to grab the ladder of the fire escape, and pulled himself up. A sinewy man just over six feet tall who kept himself in shape with squash and a daily exercise regimen—he was a champion cricketer in his youth—scampering up the fire escape proved to be an easy task.

Within moments he was balancing on a short iron railing high above the street. He checked to ensure no one was watching, then leaped across six feet of empty space to land atop an ornamental para-pet on the roof of the abandoned building. His foot slipped on a patch of fresh bird droppings, and he teetered precariously on the edge, but he regained his balance and dropped lightly onto the level rooftop.

He studied his new environment in the privacy of darkness. Adjacent buildings on three sides walled him in. He now realized the iron cage on top of the building enclosed a rusty ventilation system, as well as a wooden trapdoor that provided access to the roof.

He glanced down and saw a new pair of drunks staggering up the street.

Enemy spies in disguise?

Perhaps, though in recent years the Ascendants preferred more direct confrontation. Or at least he was told. He had never actually met a member of the rival organization. But it was a troubling trend that could endanger everyone.

Once the drunks had passed, Dr. Corwin checked the padlock securing the cage. Unlocked. He took that as a sign. After slipping inside, he shut the door and pocketed the lock. He didn't want any-one sneaking up behind him and trapping him inside.

In case of trouble, he gripped his cane, which doubled as a weapon in a pinch. He approached the wooden trapdoor set into the floor and pulled on the handle. It creaked open, releasing a stale odor and revealing a spiral staircase that wound through a service shaft. Dr. Corwin grimaced at the claustrophobic passage and took out a penlight. Motes of dust floated in the stream of illumination as he tested the stairs.

He closed the hinged wooden door above him. Except for a few spiders watching from the safety of their webs, there was no sign of life as he climbed down the long stairwell. At the bottom loomed a coffered wooden door, stripped of paint and streaked with moisture stains. Dr. Corwin gently twisted the knob.

Also unlocked.

He eased the door open and found himself in a wide hallway with patches of exposed brick framed by frescoes faded to obscurity.

On his left was a series of oval archways. After letting his eyes adjust, he peered inside the first archway and saw a set of carpeted steps descending into a tiered auditorium.

He checked his watch. Five minutes to midnight.

Moldy air leached out of the vast hall. The penlight was too dim to reveal the far walls or ceiling, yet with his first step onto the stairs, a spotlight flooded the auditorium, causing him to gawk at the remains of a movie theater from a grand and bygone era. The fabric had long been stripped from the seats, plaster was peeling off the walls and ceiling, and a ruined chandelier hung over the theater like a giant bag of bones. All the rot and decaying beauty left a surreal impression, like being inside a melting painting, or trapped inside Miss Havisham's nightmarish fever dream of jilted love.

A trio of people emerged from the wings and walked onto the stage below him. All three wore full-length white robes and square beige masks that disguised their age and gender. Red markings with logographic and syllabic elements, a combination of hieroglyphs and runes, covered the surface of the masks.

The trio regarded him in silence from the stage as he walked calmly down to the first row and took a seat. He understood the message imparted by the visceral power of the setting.

You might have joined us, Dr. James Gerald Corwin, but you're still on the bottom rung of the ladder, granted an audience in an abandoned building to a trio of faceless superiors.

An audience before a stage where all the world's a play . . .

A stage where the curtain is thick and ancient and has yet to be pulled, and in the wings and under the deck lurk hints of secret knowledge, waiting just below the surface, layers on layers on layers.

"Welcome," said a deep female voice, though he could not tell which of the three had spoken. "You did well to arrive here."

Dr. Corwin crossed his legs as he eased back into the seat. "You could have made it easier, but that's not how this thing works, is it? Is this a safe-house location? A typical meeting place?"

"It is just an old theater."

Dr. Corwin flashed an amused grin. "Is it, now?"

An older male voice said, "Many of us are in agreement that you're one of our most promising adepts."

"Obliged."

"One who, if the course is stayed, possesses an extremely bright future."

"If I may be so bold as to ask, with how many people am I in competition?"

"There is no competition. Only collaboration," the man said. "All will be revealed in due course, but for now, we have a task for you."

"An extremely important task," the woman chimed in. "You've heard of Ettore Majorana?"

Dr. Corwin blinked. "I'm a professor of theoretical physics. Of course I have."

"Have you studied his work?"

"Yes and no. I'm aware of his contributions, but I'm hardly a Majorana scholar."

"Ettore was once a member of the Ascendants."

Dr. Corwin whistled. "That could explain some things."

Decades ago, the sudden disappearance of the brilliant Italian physicist had shocked the world. Yet from what Dr. Corwin understood, many members of the Leap Year Society chose to withdraw from public life, or even disappear altogether, in order to fully commit their lives to the organization. He did not consider himself any less dedicated to the Society by remaining in his profession. Perhaps one day he would have to choose between the two, and perhaps not. In his opinion, seceding from the world did not serve a greater cause.

In any event, he did not have a trust fund, and no one had offered him one. So the issue was moot for the moment.

"On the contrary," the woman said, "the Ascendants were just as shocked by Ettore's disappearance as the rest of the world. In fact, they were furious."

"Why?"

"He was working on a top-secret project for them. One of utmost importance."

"An atomic weapon," Dr. Corwin guessed, thinking about the time period when Ettore had vanished at sea. 1938, if memory served.

"What Ettore was developing . . . was something greater than a mere destructive device. He was pursuing no less than the theory of everything: a theorem uniting micro and macro physics."

"Aren't we all," Dr. Corwin said dryly.

"He might have been successful. Or at least partly so."

"I'm afraid I don't understand. Are you implying research beyond that which we have today?"

"Perhaps."

Dr. Corwin uncrossed his legs and sat up straighter in the chair. He had joined the Society because of a shared ideal to solve the most profound mysteries of the universe, because the other members had impressed him—and because of the secret knowledge in the possession of the Society. So far, he had been given only a taste, a collection of curios from the past with no easy explanation. While the Society promised much more as he rose through the ranks, in truth he had his doubts. "I'm listening."

"We don't really know how successful he was. No one does. But Ettore made a device for the Ascendants, which they believe crossed new borders. They also believe he took it with him when he disappeared."

"What sort of device?"

"Should you choose to accept, you'll be given a file with more details."

"Choose to accept what?"

The woman paused before she spoke. "Recently, knowledge has surfaced that suggests Ettore Majorana might still be alive."

Dr. Corwin regarded each of the beige masks in turn. "How very intriguing."

"Our sources tell us the Ascendants think so too. In fact, they're actively seeking to find him."

"And you want me to do what? Try to locate him before they do?"

"Exactly that. You're one of the top physicists of your generation. If you find Ettore, you can speak his language, appeal to his scientific sensibilities. You are not yet known to the Ascendants, at least to our knowledge. Both of these attributes weigh in your favor. It is increasingly apparent that technology will decide not just the outcome of our struggle with our former brethren, but the Cold War raging across the globe, and all future wars. We're not convinced—in fact, we have our doubts—that Ettore, if still alive, possesses knowledge that we do not. But if he does, and if the Ascendants reach him first . . ."

"I understand."

"We are not sure that you do. Our enemies do not share our ideals, our basic humanity. They will do *anything* to achieve their aims. Even worse, they believe they are all the nobler for it."

"True believers," Dr. Corwin muttered. "Always the most dangerous adversaries." He toyed with a silver ring on his left index finger, imprinted with a barely visible spiral pattern. "What do I need to get started?"

"If you choose to accept, then all the background information we possess is contained in the attaché case."

"What attaché case?"

"The one beside you."

Dr. Corwin looked down and started. In plain sight on the seat to his left was a slender black briefcase he was sure had not been there when he sat down.

One hundred percent sure.

"Neat trick," he said.

"This is an excellent chance for you to make your mark on the Society," the woman said. "We apologize that we cannot send a more senior member with you, but the Ascendants are exerting pressure around the globe, and our resources are stretched thin. Should the situation change, we can reevaluate."

"As in, don't come asking for help unless I'm successful."

"Some say it's a curse to live in interesting times. We believe it's the only way to advance the human narrative. Will you help us find Ettore, James?"

With an easy grin that belied the intensity of his stare, Dr. Corwin laced his fingers behind his head and leaned back in his chair again. "It just so happens I'm on summer break."

Bologna, Italy
Present Day

1

From the back seat of the silver Alfa Romeo sedan speeding through the Italian countryside in the deep of night, Andie felt as if they were driving through cotton, the pervasive fog a veil of mystery separating the starry sky from the fecund brown earth of the Po River Valley. Cal was sitting beside her, glancing nervously out the rear window. When the fog cleared, bursts of heat lightning illuminated the flat landscape, jagged tongues of raw energy that added to her unease.

Had anyone seen them leave the Venetian cemetery?

Had Zawadi survived?

Could Andie and Cal trust the sedan's driver—the tall blond-haired man who had saved them from Omer less than two hours ago? Due to the driver's accent, aquiline nose, and strong jaw, Andie had guessed he was Scandinavian, but so far he had said very little other than providing a name—Henrik.

Earlier, when fleeing across the Venetian lagoon in a cigarette boat, Henrik had veered away from the airport and toward a collection of squat manufacturing buildings pockmarking the shore. Barely slowing as they entered an inlet that cut through the buildings, Henrik had guided the boat through a nest of canals to a slip outside a shuttered warehouse. He had tied the vessel off, jumped onto the creaky aluminum dock, and led them to the front of the warehouse, where the Alfa Romeo was waiting like a diamond in a coal mine of industrial blight.

Henrik had driven among the buildings with his lights off until they reached a small road, which merged with a succession of larger ones until it joined Autostrada A13 outside Padua.

So far, Henrik had refused to answer questions. Sensing the urgency of the situation, Andie had kept quiet, knowing they had little choice in the matter and letting him concentrate.

But now it was time for some answers.

"Thank you for saving us," she said.

Henrik gave a curt nod.

"Any word from Zawadi?" she asked.

"Not yet."

"Is that a bad sign?"

"It could mean any number of things. With Zawadi, I've learned not to assume the worst."

"Why not? Who is she?"

"I'll let her answer that question."

"Where are we going?" she asked.

"To a safe house in Bologna. It's not far."

Cal finally turned away from the window. "A safe house provided by who?"

Henrik's penetrating gaze slipped to the rearview mirror. "I would think by now you know."

"The Leap Year Society? It'd be nice to hear you say it."

Henrik's attention returned to the road.

Bologna, Andie thought. The same city where Dr. Corwin was shot and killed—unless, as she fervently hoped, he was somehow still alive.

"Is the city safe?" she asked.

"It used to be," Henrik said darkly. "Times have changed."

"Because of the Ascendants?"

"I'm afraid so."

Cal said, "There's something I've been wondering—if the CEO of Aegis International is an Ascendant, why did he have the symbol of the Leap Year Society on his computer?"

"Because the usurpers cling to the delusion they represent the true spirit of the Society."

Andie asked a few more questions that Henrik refused to answer, which annoyed the hell out of her. Though exhausted by the ordeal, she forced herself to stay awake on the drive through the uninspiring outskirts of Bologna and into the softly glowing historic center, where a handful of slender stone towers dominated the skyline. They passed countless piazzas and basilicas, street after street of elegant buildings with wide arched porticos.

Henrik turned onto a quiet avenue and pulled to a stop. The empty porticos lining the street resembled corridors of Roman ruins in the darkness. Henrik hustled them out of the car, stepped beneath a portico, and approached a fifteen-foot wooden door with iron studs and a brass knocker in the shape of a snake eating its own tail. *Another ouroboros.* Andie had seen a similar symbol used by the Leap Year Society on numerous occasions along her journey.

Henrik handed her a pair of keys. "These unlock this door and the apartment at the top of the stairs. Someone will come for you tomorrow night."

"You're not staying?" she said.

"I have other duties."

"Who's coming for us? Where will they take us?"

"Goddammit," Cal said, "you can't just leave us here like this."

Henrik hesitated. "You'll be given more information tomorrow, I promise. You're not prisoners and are free to leave at any time. Though with the threat level so high, I'd advise staying in the building."

"What happens tomorrow night?" Andie said. "Have you heard from Dr. Corwin?"

"No one has, and I have to go. There's plenty of food in the apartment. Are you carrying any electronics besides Dr. Corwin's device?

"We were prisoners in a medieval torture chamber a few hours ago. So no."

"Keep it that way. And good luck."

As Henrik drove off in the Alfa Romeo, Cal touched her arm. "Come on," he said. "We should get out of sight."

Frustrated, Andie opened the heavy door to the building and made sure it locked behind them. Inside, an unlit hallway led past an interior courtyard dotted with marble statues and plants in huge terra-cotta pots. The salmon-pink plaster was flaking off the walls, and the plants looked starved for attention. Despite its shabby condition, the building evoked a grander era and felt oversize, similar to much of the architecture they had seen on the drive in. As if Bologna were built for a race of aristocratic giants.

Just past the courtyard, a stairwell led to the upper stories. They climbed six floors to a door at the very top. Andie caught her breath as she tried the key, half expecting someone to jump out at them, but the key worked on both latches and no shadowy forms emerged from the darkness.

Cal flicked a light switch as Andie locked the door behind them. The light revealed a cozy, wood-floored apartment with an open layout and a sloping ceiling that reminded Andie of her childhood attic. Directly ahead was a sitting area and a dining table with chairs. The kitchen was off to the right. Bookshelves, framed prints and cinema posters, and a few curios were interspersed throughout the room. The prints were Klimt and van Gogh, the posters from classic Italian cinema.

A hallway past the kitchen led to a modest bedroom suite. Except for a terrace that overlooked the city off the main living area, that was it. No ancient secrets or mysterious furnishings or radical technology. Just a top-floor apartment they might have found on Airbnb, and which looked as if it belonged to a middle-aged Italian bohemian. Though a bit disconcerting, it was a welcome haven of normality after everything they had been through.

Before they relaxed, they inspected every nook and cranny of the apartment, searching for hidden cameras, listening devices, false doors, or anything else suspicious. For good measure, Andie even did a walk-through with the Star Phone, wondering if the device would reveal any secrets when trained on the walls or objects.

Nothing.

No one.

As boring as central Kansas.

"First things first," Cal said as he rummaged through the fridge and pulled out a block of cheese, a mortadella roll, and a Peroni. "If someone's coming to kill us tonight, I'd prefer to die on a full stomach."

Andie grabbed a couple of plates and another beer, and joined him in the sitting area. She was too tired to bother with the bottle of red wine on the counter. "I suppose they wouldn't bring us all this way just to poison us."

Through a set of French doors that opened onto the terrace, she glimpsed a flash of lightning. The ghostly aura of the backlit city mirrored her state of mind. Ever since she had left Durham, the journey to find her mentor had felt like a harried swim through fathomless dark waters, illuminated at times—and all too briefly—by flashes of enlightenment. She was reminded of the legend of the blind men who had never encountered an elephant before, and who conceptualized its form based on which part of the pachyderm they touched. This of course led to wildly different opinions as to the true nature of an elephant.

What was the Leap Year Society? When had the group started, who was chosen for it, what were its aims?

How did the Ascendants fit in, and who the hell was the Archon?

What was the Enneagon that Dr. Corwin had invented?

Most mysterious of all, what was the place called the Fold, which the LYS and the Ascendants seemed to know about, and which Andie might have glimpsed in her strange visions throughout her life?

"I wonder if we'll get some answers tomorrow," Cal said, reflecting her thoughts.

She sat with her back against the side arm of the sofa, her knees propped in front of her, sipping her beer. "You know what I think?"

"Lay it on me."

"I think this apartment may belong to the LYS, but has nothing else to do with them. I think this is where they keep the outsiders."

Cal lowered a piece of cheese he was about to nibble. "What if tomorrow night isn't about helping us at all? What if they want to interrogate us like the Ascendants did? What if they have someone..."

Andie knew what he was thinking. *What if they have someone like the Archon who can toy with our minds?*

"Why leave us in this cozy apartment if that was their intention?" she said. "You're being too paranoid."

"Are we really free to go? Maybe they're watching us right now and plan to trail us when we leave."

"They could have left us to rot in the dungeon or locked us up tonight. I think it's worth the risk. And I'm not sure we can survive on our own."

He muttered a reply under his breath. They ate in silence, letting the alcohol calm their nerves. Cal's eyes were less hollow than when they had arrived, which relieved Andie, though her own exhaustion and emotional turmoil had left her feeling like a dishrag wrung out by a sumo wrestler. She could only imagine how he was feeling, after countless hours imprisoned behind a brick wall with no food or water.

"Nightcap?" he said after a while.

"Sure."

He rose and returned with two more beers, then hunched forward on the sofa. "I agree we should hear them out. If we don't like what they say, or if they don't show tomorrow night, then we get the hell out of Dodge."

Andie was facing the patio. The intensity of the heat lightning had increased, etching patterns of fading light into the sky. "Agreed."

Andie slept like the dead.

As light slanted through the bedroom window the next morning, she stared at the thick wooden beams on the ceiling and wished it were all a bad dream.

Dr. Corwin shot in cold blood in this very city, either dead or imprisoned.

Her mother—who, until Venice, Andie had not seen since she was a child—trapped in some cultlike secret society, so terrified of their mysterious leader she had let them take her own daughter away.

Andie had refused to turn over the Star Phone, and perhaps her mother hadn't had a choice. Still, Andie knew if it were her decision, *her* child, she would fight like a cornered wolverine before letting those bastards win.

Just like she was going to do for her mother—and for Dr. Corwin.

She couldn't shake that last haunting image of her mother's eyes. She was crying out for help. Andie knew it in her bones. Maybe the Archon controlled her mother to such a degree that she was no longer making her own decisions. Maybe her mother had risked life and limb to contact Andie in the first place and *would* do anything to help her, if given the chance.

Or maybe her mother had the safety of someone else to consider. Maybe *that* was why she had left in the first place, forced to make a terrible choice between Andie and her children by another marriage, who were also at risk.

That was a dangerous road to go down, Andie knew, because she wanted so very much to have a Hollywood ending, for none of this to be her mother's fault, for the two of them to walk hand in hand into the sunset.

Despite everything that had happened, her years of silent suffering and rage at the world, Andie still gave her mother the benefit of the doubt.

Why? she wanted to scream. *Why does she deserve that?*

Except Andie knew.

No matter what had happened all those years ago, for better or for worse, she had only one mother. Samantha Zephyr was her flesh and blood, her creator. Andie didn't know if she could ever truly forgive her, but she would always love her—and she was going to do everything in her power to secure her release.

In Andie's mind, the math was simple. The Ascendants wanted the Enneagon above all else, and Dr. Corwin's enigmatic invention was the only thing she could barter for her mother's and her mentor's safe return.

According to Dr. Corwin's journal, and from everything she had witnessed, the Star Phone puzzle led to the Enneagon. She didn't know why the Ascendants wanted it—was it a weapon, an explosive new technology?—and it didn't really matter. Because no matter the cost, no matter where it led her, she was going to follow the Star Phone to the bitter end. Unless and until a better avenue presented itself, that was the only plan she had.

After a deep breath, she stretched like a cat and rolled out of bed. Through the closed bedroom door, she heard Cal snoring. He had fallen asleep on the couch before he finished his second beer.

Outside the bedroom window, she saw a street with flowerpots on the windowsills, and orange blossoms sprinkling the sidewalks. A server was setting up tables outside a trattoria. After a long shower, Andie threw on a silky blue bathrobe she found in an armoire, and carried her filthy clothes to the bathroom sink. She left them to soak as she made scrambled eggs and toast.

"Ahh, waking up to the aroma of breakfast that someone else is cooking," Cal said, sitting up on the couch with a yawn. "How about some bacon?"

"How about kissing my ass? Put your dirty clothes in the sink, and the rinsing is on you. There's another bathrobe in the armoire."

He pushed to his feet. "Yes, drill sergeant Andie."

By the time he returned in a silk bathrobe with black trim, Andie had carried two plates to the table.

Cal rolled back the sleeves of his robe. "I look fairly ridiculous."

"I won't disagree. This is hardly my natural habitat."

"The eggs are delicious," he said, "and I was just kidding. I love to cook."

"I loathe it. I had to cook for my dad almost every night growing up. I'd be happy with takeout the rest of my life."

"My dad didn't lift a finger at home either. Not unless it was to smack me."

"Mine is a gentle guy. He's just an alcoholic who can't fend for himself and had no business raising a child."

"Ah, the good old days."

"What about your mom?" Andie asked. "Was she around?"

Cal took a moment to answer. "She was there. And she was awesome. We split from my dad and took off for LA when I was fifteen." He averted his eyes, leaving a story untold. "There's something I've been thinking about."

"Yeah?"

"The Ascendants and this Enneagon thing. I get that human beings crave answers to the big questions. And I understand this technology could be groundbreaking, or might access this Fold place—if it really exists. But even with all of that . . . is it really worth the lengths they're going to? Am I just being dense?"

"I think some of these answers only the Ascendants and the Leap Year Society can give us," she said slowly, "especially concerning the Fold. But in terms of groundbreaking technology, these very same questions were raised in the early twentieth century, when relativity and quantum mechanics had just been discovered. Why pour all of these private and government resources into these bizarre theories, everyone wanted to know? How relevant are they to our everyday lives?"

"Exactly. Who the hell cares if a theoretical cat is alive or dead at the same time? Or if a black hole might swallow our planet fifty trillion years in the future?"

"The desire for knowledge is reason enough for me. What's more worthy than developing a better picture of the universe in which we live?"

"Feeding hungry children? Peace on Earth?"

"You're right," she said. "But those aims aren't mutually exclusive.

Where do you think we got nuclear energy and the transistor? CDs and DVDs? Nanotech, lasers, GPS, MRIs? Modern computers and the *internet*, Cal. All in less than a century. Billions of lives improved, children saved, average life spans extended. Theoretical physics isn't science fiction. It's quite literally the world in which we live."

He scratched at his stubble. "That does put it in perspective."

"The next leap in physics won't just be a cool idea. It will be the *future*. Even if the theorems or the technology inside the Enneagon is a small piece of the puzzle, the value could be incalculable."

"That's not even considering the potential for weapons, is it? Nuclear energy was the first thing you mentioned. A new super-weapon could make hydrogen bombs look like hand grenades."

"You're getting the picture," she said quietly. "Apart from the economic impact, the next frontier will affect the balance of power for generations. Imagine if Hitler had managed to split the atom before the Allied powers."

He chewed on his lip, and they finished eating in silence. After breakfast, he hung their clothes to dry on the patio while she paced the living room. Now that she was rested, she was itching for a long run or a heavy bag to pummel. An outlet for her stress and mental energy.

"Have you thought any more about the Star Phone clue we found in Egypt?" Cal said from the couch. "The zero inside the double helix?"

"Thought about it? Yes. Made any headway beyond what we've already discussed? No. I'm tempted to take a cab to the nearest internet connection and do some research."

"Do they still have cybercafés in western Europe?"

"I doubt it. There's got to be something. A library, maybe."

"I don't think we should go out today. It's too dangerous."

Andie knew he was right, and it made her furious at the valuable time lost. They were stuck until they figured out the next destination on the Star Phone. She ran a hand through her hair as she continued to pace, hating the fact they were virtual prisoners.

"First thing in the morning," she said, "no matter what happens tonight, I'm researching that clue."

Cal crossed his arms, his face still wan from his ordeal in the dungeon. "I'll be right beside you."

11:30 p.m.

Still no message, still no sign of anyone from the Leap Year Society.

Andie had begun to give up hope, feeling bitter they had wasted an entire day. Why bother to save her and Cal if the Society was just going to abandon them?

She thought of Zawadi, wondering if she had survived the flight through the lagoon, and remembering her final imperative before she left them at the gate to the island cemetery.

Whatever you do, keep the Star Phone safe.

Would the Society take the device from them? Andie knew worrying about it wouldn't change anything, but she had never been good at sitting back and letting life happen. She had spent the day conducting a more thorough search of the apartment, looking for a hidden compartment or more clues to the LYS, even checking behind the artwork and moving the appliances. When that failed, she flipped through the books on the shelves in the common room. Most of the titles concerned either world history or biographies of famous scientists, inventors, explorers, and other luminaries who had shaped the boundaries of the world.

Is there a theme? Were all these people members of the Leap Year Society?

Andie stepped through the French doors to the terrace and leaned on the wrought-iron railing, absorbing the towers and steeples rising above the jigsaw puzzle of terra-cotta rooftops. Cal was asleep on the couch. Earlier, he had impressed her by whipping up a red sauce with fresh Roma tomatoes, herbs, onions, and peppers. The aroma still lingered, mingling with the flowers on the terrace and the dusty stone smell of the rooftops.

Her eyes roamed to the heavens. The night was mild and clear, the moon still below her sight line. Stargazing had always calmed her, given her a sense of belonging that she had never found anywhere else. As a teen, whenever she felt as if her father and the rest of the world had failed her, she would drive to a nearby field and sit alone on a blanket. As the crickets chirped around her, she would feel absorbed by the stars, drawn into that infinite dark as if her soul were drifting upward, merging with the universe, becoming part of something greater.

She still got that same peaceful feeling, except now she knew vastly more about outer space, and it enriched the experience. The Hubble Telescope—orbiting above Earth right that very moment—could peer so far away that it took snapshots of the residual light of galaxies colliding more than ten billion years in the past, drawing closer and closer to the beginning of the universe.

Those images were mind-boggling, an entire undiscovered country. Yet Andie preferred using her own two eyes on a moonless night in the countryside. Unaided by a refracting lens, she could look up and pinpoint star clusters, nebulae, comets, other galaxies and planets, the eerie star-birthing glow of the Milky Way.

It was nothing short of a miracle. There it all was, outer space itself and swarms of distant stars, right above us every single night, a direct conduit to the boundless beauty and mystery of the universe.

Where stargazing had once made her feel grounded, she now knew that perspective was an illusion, that if she raised her arms above her head an observer from far enough away would observe her spinning like a top on the Earth's surface at one thousand miles per hour, racing around the sun at sixty-seven thousand miles per hour, and hurtling through the Milky Way at nearly five hundred thousand miles per hour. Nothing was static. Nothing alone. Andie was born in the furnace of those stars, and she was passing through life like a celestial whirling dervish with mind-bending velocity—reaching, searching, absorbing, exuding, both infinite and mortal.

She closed her eyes and held them shut, feeling strangely unmoored by the night sky that evening, trying to center herself amid the madness that had consumed her life since Dr. Corwin was attacked.

When she opened them again, she glimpsed a shadowy human form standing in the corner of the patio less than ten feet away.

2

Andie gasped and whirled, confused as to how an intruder had entered the apartment and reached the terrace without making a sound. Fear drowned any further thoughts, and she rushed forward, prepared to lash out with a snap kick, when a familiar voice broke the silence.

"It's okay, Andie. It's me. Zawadi."

The figure in the shadows clarified into a six-foot-tall woman with ebony skin, a tight-lipped oval mouth, cheekbones like knife cuts, and a lithe body with the grace and power of a professional athlete. Her fade haircut made her seem even taller.

Andie let her fists uncurl. "Thank God you're alive." Still unsure how the woman had snuck up behind her so quietly, Andie glanced through the French doors and exhaled when she saw Cal roll over in his sleep. For a moment, she had thought Zawadi might have killed him.

Except for her brown combat boots, Zawadi was dressed all in black, from her leather pants to the microfiber shirt that draped her waist. A bulge in the shirt when she moved suggested a concealed weapon.

"How did you get up here?" Andie asked. "Do you have a key?"

Zawadi ignored the question. "Are you ready to go?"

"Go where?"

"To the meeting."

"Can you be less cryptic?"

"I'll explain more on the way. We don't have much time."

"Yeah, we never seem to."

Zawadi checked a forest-green polymer watch on her left wrist. "We're due at midnight."

"How far is it?"

"Not far. Quickly now. You should wake your friend."

Though annoyed by all the secrecy, Andie was glad their mysterious protector was alive and that events were in motion. She swallowed her questions and went inside to rouse Cal. His eyes widened when he saw Zawadi. When he jumped up to embrace her, she took a step back, though her eyes were warm.

"What happened in the lagoon?" he asked. "How did you get away?"

"I went someplace they couldn't follow. Come now, both of you. I realize you have questions, but we mustn't delay."

Andie and Cal had already changed back into their clothes. They had no other possessions, so after Andie grabbed the keys to the apartment and the Star Phone, they followed Zawadi down the staircase and out into the warm night.

Lanterns hung from the sides of the buildings in iron cages, illuminating the street with a soft glow. No one was in sight. The tall wooden shutters on the windows were all closed. After Zawadi glanced in both directions and scanned the rooftops, she ushered Cal and Andie into the back seat of an Alfa Romeo sedan, similar to the one Henrik had driven.

"Where are we going?" Andie asked as Zawadi pulled away from the curb.

"The Archiginnasio."

"The what?"

"The first home of the University of Bologna. Now it's a municipal library and museum."

"There's something to the libraries, isn't there? They're meeting grounds of some sort."

"I'll tell you right now I'm not a member of the Society and unable to share details. The very fact this meeting is happening is . . . unprecedented."

"Wait," Cal said. "*You're* not a member? What about the escape, your connection to Dr. Corwin..."

"I have some knowledge and connections, yes, but my loyalty is to Dr. Corwin—not the LYS. Even if I was authorized, I know very little about the inner workings of the Society. I'm almost as in the dark as you are."

"I doubt that," he said, "but whatever. Can you at least tell us *what* it is?"

There was a long silence in which Andie could sense the other woman debating how much to reveal. "The Leap Year Society," Zawadi said finally, "is an organization of like-minded individuals around the world. They're agnostic to race and culture. All that matters is intelligence, talent, vision, and, above all else, the dedication to seeking out and preserving knowledge."

Andie snorted. "You mean scientists?"

"They accept members from all disciplines, as long as the level of achievement is extraordinary."

"What happens when you join the club?" Cal said. "And what kind of knowledge do they have? Because we've seen some things . . . It's almost like they have access to a different supply of information than the rest of the world."

"Maybe they just know where to look," Zawadi said. "I've seen things too—and I don't have any answers for you."

"So what do they do?" Cal pressed. "How old is the society? Where do they meet, what do all the symbols mean, how deep does it go?"

"As I said, I'm in the dark too, and I took an oath not to reveal what little I know. I've told you nothing I suspect you haven't already figured out, or that I believe will help us find Dr. Corwin. In any event, you can ask them yourself tonight."

"I plan on it," Cal said. "And the Ascendants? Who are they?"

"Some time ago, a splinter faction arose in the Society. One that believes the future of humanity depends on obtaining knowledge at all costs—no matter the price, no matter who they hurt—before it falls into the wrong hands and destroys us all."

"And the Leap Year Society disagrees?"

"They believe the acquisition of advanced knowledge obtained without wisdom, without ethical consideration, is dangerous. A simple example is distributing the plans for a weapon of mass destruction online, such as a pathogen or a nuclear weapon."

"Dr. Corwin was important to them, wasn't he?" Andie said quietly.

Zawadi's face tightened. "Not *was*, I pray. *Is*. I do not think the Ascendants would have killed him. At least not until they find the Enneagon."

"That's some relief."

"Perhaps, perhaps not. There are rumors about the Archon . . . But in answer to your question, I've gathered that James's standing in the Society is complicated."

"How so?"

"My job is to protect him. We almost never discuss Society matters. But I know he has radical views that are quite unpopular. He and a few others—he thought Dr. Rickman was one of them—shared a similar ideology."

"Which was?" Andie asked.

"Not to be so removed from world affairs. Not to let the Ascendants continue to grow in power and hunt the Society down. James believed in a proactive stance and was ostracized for it. Not to mention the nature of my own association. Working with outsiders was . . . unprecedented."

"Why did he do it?"

"Because of my skill set, because he trusted me—and because he was making a point."

"What did Dr. Rickman do?" Andie asked. "Why did you have

to kill him?"

"I don't know what the Ascendants offered him, but the filthy rat betrayed James and Lars Friedman. Now both are dead or imprisoned. For that alone, he deserved to die."

"Says you," Cal said.

"Yes," she said. "Says I. But I was only going to interrogate him. He tried to resist and forced my hand."

"How did you know?" Andie asked.

"James has a mole deep within the Ascendants. Not even I know who." She eyed Andie in the rearview. "It was Professor Rickman who misled the Ascendants about your visit. He told them you were coming at midnight, not eight, which was why I arrived so early—and why Omer was so surprised to see you."

"Why would he mislead them?"

"My guess is he planned to milk your knowledge for himself, then kill you before the Ascendants found out."

Andie's hand tightened on the seat rest. "To learn what I know about the Enneagon? So he could get it first?"

"That's right."

"He would have been disappointed," she said. *And I would have died for nothing.* She shuddered at the level of violence, deceit, and desperate behavior surrounding the search for Dr. Corwin's invention. "What do you know about the Enneagon?"

"Only that it was a top-secret project of utmost importance. I was given no details."

"Do you have any idea where it is? Why it's tied to the puzzle on the Star Phone?"

"Absolutely none."

Frustrated, Andie absorbed the new information as they drove into the heart of Bologna. Many of the byways were off-limits to automobiles, forcing Zawadi to take a circuitous route. The city at night was a maze of cobblestone streets, flower-draped balconies, towering wooden doors, and ornate iron gates that tantalized with glimpses of inner courtyards. The larger streets had raised sidewalks sheltered by the city's signature porticos: miles and miles of covered walkways supported by painted round columns.

Bologna also gave the impression, with its ancient corridors of silent, handsome buildings and courtyards tucked away from view, of a city that had long harbored secrets—and continued to do so.

The perfect place to shelter a group like the Leap Year Society.

"If they don't talk to outsiders," Andie said, "why did they agree to meet? Because we have the Star Phone?"

"*They* didn't call for this meeting. *I* did—to convince them I need help finding James."

"Why wouldn't they help?"

"Because they're not sure he's alive, and they don't like to interfere."

"Don't they want the Enneagon as much as the Ascendants?"

"Perhaps," Zawadi said with a touch of scorn. "But they do not take what is not theirs, or force others down a path they do not wish to travel."

"Seems like good policy," Cal said.

"What about you?" Andie said, slipping her hand inside her pocket and letting it rest against the cool metallic surface of the Star Phone. "Since you don't share their philosophy."

Zawadi gave her a sharp glance in the mirror. "Dr. Corwin loved you dearly, and he guided you to the device. That's enough for me. If you're intent on keeping it—"

"I am."

"Then I'll assist as best I can, as long as it involves helping James. I agree that, for now, using the Star Phone to find the Enneagon is our best chance to secure his release."

"And if he's dead?"

"Then none of this is my concern."

Zawadi parked the sedan in front of a *prosciutteria* with plate glass windows, revealing cheese wheels and cured meats hanging from wooden beams. She turned in her seat and said, "You're certain about this path? Even with the threat to your lives it poses?"

"The Ascendants have my mentor and my mother," Andie said. "It's the only way I see to help them."

Cal looked Zawadi in the eye. "The Ascendants stole my life, and I'm committed to exposing the truth and getting it back. Besides, I have a feeling we're in danger no matter what we choose."

Zawadi coolly met his gaze. "I have a feeling you're right." She opened the door. "Follow quickly and don't make a sound."

After easing the doors shut, Andie and Cal stayed close to Zawadi as she hurried down a winding street, her feet a whisper on the worn paving stones. Beside her, Andie felt like a rhinoceros crashing through a glass house, and began to understand how Zawadi had arrived on the terrace unseen.

Halfway down the street, Zawadi ducked into an alley so tight Andie thought she could spread her arms and touch the buildings on either side. Thirty feet down, Zawadi used a key to unlock a door that proved to be the rear entrance to a courtyard filled with pungent flowering vines, alabaster statues, and a gurgling fountain. The depths of the courtyard were shrouded in darkness, and its high brick walls felt as quiet as a tomb.

Zawadi approached one of the statues and stepped hard on the base, causing it to depress and then swivel on some type of track. She shone a penlight into the darkness, revealing a stone walkway six feet beneath the surface of the street. The walkway hugged an algae-covered wall as it ran alongside a sluice of dark water.

"I'll be right behind you," Zawadi said, waving them forward.

"Make sure of that," Cal muttered. He lowered his body into the opening, hung on to the lip of the hole, and dropped down to the walkway. Andie followed close behind. Once Zawadi joined them and resealed the passage, she led the way alongside the subterranean channel.

The walkway was slippery in places, as if a boat had come through and sloshed the sides. The feeble illumination from the penlight barely pierced the gloom, and Andie had to force herself to remain calm and not jump at shadows.

"Modern-day Bologna sits atop miles of waterways," Zawadi said, illuminating the ribbed ceiling and the stagnant green water in the canal.

"But it's inland," Andie said.

"In the Middle Ages, the city built a sophisticated network of canals and locks to facilitate trade. This allowed large ships to come and go on the nearby rivers, greatly enhancing Bologna's wealth and status."

"What happened to it all?"

"You're looking at it. The canals are still here. As time went by, streets and new buildings were built right on top of them."

"An underground Venice right under everyone's feet," Cal said, looking nervously behind them. "Creepy."

The mention of the floating city, along with the slimy floor of the walkway and the steady plop of water, gave Andie flashbacks to their dank Venetian prison. With a shudder, she pressed forward until Zawadi stopped at an intersection of canals, reached up, and pushed against a block of stone on the ceiling that looked like any other to Andie.

A trapdoor hinged open above them. Zawadi leaped up to grab the edge of the opening and pulled herself through. "There are easier ways to get to where we're going," she said, peering down at them, "though not as safe. After our escape from Venice, the Ascendants might suspect we're in Bologna."

Zawadi stuck a hand down. Andie declined the offer and pulled herself up, though not as gracefully. Cal had an even harder time. They emerged in a concrete room with a musty odor and piles of wooden crates stacked along the walls.

Zawadi consulted her watch. "We're right on time. Come."

Still using the penlight, she led the way to a door that opened onto a cement hallway. After navigating a few twists and turns through the basement corridor, they took a flight of stairs to a wooden door two floors above. Zawadi unlocked the door and entered a hall-way. Andie gasped at the thousands of hand-painted coats of arms covering the walls and high concave ceiling, each a unique display of symbols, colors, and heraldic beasts.

"This is the Archiginnasio?" Cal whispered.

"Yes."

On their left, a closed iron gate protected a room full of wooden cabinets with glass doors. Shelves and shelves of ancient manuscripts were tucked behind the glass, but Zawadi ignored the gate and started down the hallway.

"We're not going to the library?" Andie asked.

"The meeting is at the Anatomical Theater, an early medical school used for dissection. Now it's a museum."

As their footsteps echoed in the wide hallway, Andie noticed the other woman seemed a shade more at ease.

Not far down the hallway, Zawadi opened a door and shepherded them into a room made from wood the color of a light-roast coffee bean. Rows of tiered pews surrounded a marble-topped table in the center of the room, and a succession of carved wooden scholars gazed down from alcoves recessed into the walls beneath the coffered ceiling.

Across the room, two gruesome, skinless human carvings supported the canopy above the lecturer's chair. Andie could imagine the dissections that must have taken place on the marble table under the watchful eye of the professors, probing the mysteries of the human body all those centuries ago.

At first Andie thought they were alone, but a quick glance to her left, opposite the lecturer's chair, revealed the familiar face of their driver sitting in the highest row, wearing dark clothing and a newsboy cap.

"You're on time, Zawadi," Henrik said as they entered. "A remarkable occurrence."

The comment was delivered in a droll tone, which allowed Andie to relax a fraction. *At least they have a sense of humor.*

"Where are the others?" Zawadi said, checking her watch.

"No one else is coming."

Zawadi grew very still. "What do you mean? I received notice—" She took a deep breath, seeming to come to a realization. "Then both the threat and the level of disassociation are worse than I suspected. Do they understand nothing?"

"Your pleas have not gone unheard," he said. "They agree the situation is grave. They just have a different philosophy on how to combat the threat."

"A philosophy that will get them all killed."

"Why do the Ascendants care about the Leap Year Society if they don't want to be involved?" Andie said.

Zawadi and Henrik exchanged a glance. "Because the Ascendants believe the Leap Year Society harbors certain knowledge," Zawadi said.

"About what?"

"The Fold and the Nine, principally—but other things as well."

"The nine what?"

"That's enough, Zawadi!" Henrik warned.

She scoffed. "These two know as much about the Fold as I do. What I do know is that if Dr. Corwin's warning is not heeded, the Ascendants will hunt the Society down one by one, and they'll die with their precious knowledge."

Cal was staring at Henrik with a greedy expression. Andie, too, was eager to learn what else he knew about the Fold and her visions.

"We've agreed to help you in two ways," Henrik said, "one of which is monetary support."

Zawadi stiffened. "Funds."

"You'll find a large deposit in your account this morning."

"And the other?" she said, her voice low and venomous.

"Protection." He gave a little bow. "As in, my personal services."

"I don't need a bodyguard."

He tilted his head toward Andie and Cal. "They will."

"What about access to safe houses?"

"I'm afraid that's not on offer. It puts our members at risk."

"James was right," Zawadi said, seething. "Their isolation will be their downfall."

"Or the insurance to survive the coming storm. You don't know the full picture."

As Zawadi gave him a withering look, Andie stepped forward and said to Henrik, "Is Dr. Corwin still alive?"

"All evidence points to the fact that he is dead."

"But the message—"

"A single line of text delivered from an unidentified source? That's more likely a lure than a plea for help."

Zawadi snarled. "A lure? For what purpose? It didn't request anything!"

"The Ascendants lay their traps well in advance, in layer upon layer. You know this better than most."

"You're blind. You're all blind."

Andie's curiosity about the true nature of the Leap Year Society was a distant second to her desire to help her loved ones. She had no patience for covert games, god complexes, and hidden agendas. "What do you know about the Enneagon?" she asked Henrik.

"Almost nothing," he said bitterly. "James hid the project from everyone but his inner circle."

"Seems pretty smart," Andie said, "since one of you betrayed him."

Henrik leveled a stare at her. "In any event, we believe returning the Star Phone to us is a wise choice."

Andie tensed. "I bet you do."

Both Cal and Zawadi took a protective step closer to Andie, causing Henrik to hold his palms out. "We won't take it by force."

"I know you won't," Zawadi said calmly.

Henrik turned to Andie. "Please understand we are much better equipped to locate the device."

"Maybe so," she said. "But I have no idea whether finding him is your priority, or whether he wanted you to have the Enneagon at all. He came to me, not you. So if you want to help me, then just do it."

"We're wasting time here," Zawadi said. "We should go."

"Go where?" Andie said.

"Back to the apartment for now. Unless that, too, is off-limits?"

Henrik spread his hands. "It's yours for as long as you wish to stay."

"Then I suggest we use it as a base to determine our next destination."

"I'll need to use the internet," Andie said. "From a secure location."

"We'll arrange it first thing in the morning," Henrik said.

Cal ran a hand through his hair in frustration. "Who *are* you people? Why all the secrecy? What are you really hiding?"

"History has proven time and again that knowledge dispensed without the proper safeguards can be disastrous," Henrik said. "Would you want a true open-source society? I think not."

"Who made you the judge and jury?" Cal said.

"Who gives you the right to question us?"

"It's called freedom of the press, pal. The mark of a healthy democracy."

"Hush," Zawadi said softly, putting a finger to her lips and pulling out a compact black handgun.

A similar weapon sprang into Henrik's hand, and he crept down the aisle to join them by the dissection table. "What is it?" he whispered.

"I heard a faint creak. Perhaps the door to the library."

Henrik looked startled. "No one else should be here. We should go. Now."

Zawadi took a step toward the door. "If we encounter resistance, I'll clear the hallway while you get them out."

Henrik grabbed her arm. "I know a better way."

He hurried to the lecturer's chair and leaped on the wooden balustrade. While balancing between the pair of skinless carved figures, he reached up to depress the eye of the one on the left. Andie noticed movement and turned to see one of the ancient robed statues in the alcoves swinging outward, revealing a hidden nook.

"Where *don't* you people have secret passages?" Cal said.

Even Zawadi's eyes widened in surprise. Without a word, she led the way up the stairs to the base of the alcove, climbed onto the balustrade, and stepped into the opening.

Andie and Cal joined Zawadi in a sliver of a stone passage that led between the walls. The statue started to swing shut as Henrik rushed to join them. Almost as soon as they were sealed inside the claustrophobic passage, they heard a door in the Anatomical Theater burst open—as well as a voice issuing a harsh command to search the room.

Asheville, North Carolina
Summer 1970

The bug-eyed convertible, a midnight-blue Austin-Healey Sprite with supermodel curves and cognac leather seats, hugged the serpentine mountain passes of the Blue Ridge Parkway as it sped toward Asheville, North Carolina.

The night before, Dr. Corwin had made a snap decision after leaving the abandoned theater on the Lower East Side. After checking flight schedules in his apartment and realizing it would be just as fast to jump in his beloved British roadster and drive south, rather than take a connecting flight the next day through Atlanta, he had packed a valise, slept for three hours, and left before the sun rose.

And why not? It was summer, he preferred the wind in his hair to the cramped confines of an airplane, and he had never driven on the famed Blue Ridge Parkway or visited the American South. He wanted to know more about this sprawling country he now called home.

The trip had lived up to his expectations. Once he cleared the congested Northeast Corridor and entered Virginia, tracing the spine of the Appalachians, he drove through a panorama of emerald-green slopes and rounded peaks softened by eons of erosion, the lungs of the continent living and breathing all around him, a temperate rain forest that cradled the sky in its bosom.

Dr. Corwin loved a variety of music, especially swing and the Rolling Stones, but he preferred jazz while driving. Together, he and Thelonious Monk had solved many a thorny physics problem driving in the Berkshires or along the New England coast.

On this particular journey, traffic was so light Dr. Corwin was able to hold the file on Ettore Majorana against the steering wheel and digest it as he drove. The dossier was over a hundred pages long: a summary of Ettore's work, as well as facts and speculations on his final days and his ties to the Ascendants. Many years ago, a spy within the rival organization had provided excellent details of the entire sad affair, days before the mole was caught and executed by Stefan Kraus.

When Dr. Corwin had finished reading, fascinated by the narrative, he congealed the information in his mind as he crossed the border into North Carolina.

In the 1930s, a splinter faction of the Leap Year Society led by a German scientist and soldier named Stefan Kraus—a Nazi—had recruited Ettore Majorana and revived the Ascendants, igniting a civil war inside the Society. Believing Ettore's hypothetical tower of infinite particles was the key to marrying macro and micro physics, Stefan forced him to construct a device he believed was a weapon of mass destruction—but which might access another plane of reality called the Fold. Or perhaps it was both.

No one knew, because Ettore had vanished with his device in 1938, never to be seen again.

His research lost forever.

That was, until a neuropsychologist named Waylan Taylor submitted an article to an obscure psychiatric periodical less than a year ago, claiming to have met a disciple of Ettore while traveling in South America.

If Ettore *was* still alive, huge questions loomed. What was the true nature of his device? How had he escaped on the open sea, and where had he gone? Maybe the answer was prosaic—maybe Ettore had wanted to break free of the iron grip of Stefan Kraus, and carried out an elaborate plan of escape.

Yet this explanation did not jibe with Ettore's character profile. At the time of his disappearance, the Sicilian physicist was a depressed loner, who had alienated everyone around him. How had he summoned the chutzpah to defy Stefan and flee Europe right under the thumbs of the Ascendants?

Dr. Corwin did not give the alternative explanation the file had proffered any credence—that Ettore's device had worked, and he had disappeared into some unknown dimension or realm, perhaps even later to return.

Was there a third option?

Something no one was seeing?

There had been alleged Ettore sightings over the years, all over the world, some more credible than others. As for Waylan Taylor, his journal article had mentioned a man named only as X, who claimed to have been Ettore Majorana's disciple. According to the article, the goal of Dr. Taylor's recent sabbatical was to expand the limits of psychiatric knowledge by probing the shamanistic practices of indigenous cultures, in order to apply experiential knowledge of psychedelic drugs and phenomena, such as dreamwalking and ritual possession, to accepted psychiatric norms.

It was all very intriguing, yet what had caught the Society's eye was a drawing of a runic symbol shown to Dr. Taylor by X. The symbol would look nonsensical to most people, but the Leap Year Society used a secret language called Sahin, and the symbol in Dr. Taylor's paper was the first letter of the Sahin alphabet, surrounded by a simple ouroboros.

Without doubt, a reference to the LYS.

According to the article, X had seen the symbol in Ettore's notes and asked him about it. Ettore left town the next day, and X never saw him again.

The Society kept a close watch on scientific journals. They had pulled strings to quash the mention of the mysterious X and the Sahin letter when Dr. Taylor's article was submitted. The reason given to Waylan by the journal's editor—a fair one—was uncertain source material.

Consumed with questions, Dr. Corwin urged the Austin-Healey up a ridge through a dense evening fog that swallowed the tops of the mountains. The fog thickened to the point where it threatened visibility of the road. Clutching the wheel with a white-knuckle grip, weaving in and out of tractor trailers, he felt as if he were driving through a cloud until he finally pulled into Asheville, where the buildings of the modest downtown, smudges of white stone rising through the mist like statues in an overgrown garden, allowed him to navigate.

His destination was the Grove Park Inn, an exclusive hotel that had housed an endless roster of luminaries: presidents, monarchs, magnates, musicians, artists. Tricky Dick Nixon had visited just last year. Various members of the Society, including Helen Keller and Harry Houdini, had also conducted business at the inn.

But that night, the only guest of importance to Dr. Corwin was a young psychologist from Boston by the name of Waylan Taylor, recently returned from a sabbatical in South America.

Wispy entrails of fog curled around the long driveway as Dr. Corwin approached the inn, a red-roofed granite monolith surrounded by ancient firs and spruces, sitting proudly on a western-facing slope of the Blue Ridge Mountains. It was a breathtaking sight, a Bavarian châteasu supersized by American industry, though not in a gauche manner.

He parked the car and stepped out, inhaling the fresh air, stretching the long legs that had earned him the nickname of Stork as a boy. The cool, damp slopes in the distance reminded him of the verdant landscapes of his Jamaican youth.

Inside the main lounge, the ceilings soared high overhead, supported by stacked stone pillars as thick as castle walls. Oversize leather chairs and sofas swallowed their occupants, and the stone hearth was wide enough to park his Austin-Healey inside. He strode through the lounge and saw that it opened onto a tiered outdoor terrace with stunning views of the mountains.

After securing a room that overlooked the golf course, Dr. Corwin took a hot shower, ordered a warm Grand Marnier from room service, and relaxed in an armchair while he debated how to find Waylan Taylor. Though possessed of one of the finest intellects of his day, Dr. Corwin had another gift that was all too rare among the academic elite: common sense.

Yes, he might be able to sweet-talk the cute receptionist with the pixie cut into giving out Waylan's room number. Yes, he could probably contrive a way to peruse the spa register or examine the tee times, in case the psychologist had anything scheduled the next day.

But why complicate matters?

Waylan Taylor was a single male staying in a glamorous hotel away from home. Unless he was ill or there were extraordinary circumstances in play, Dr. Corwin was betting he knew exactly where to find him.

Later that night, after a scrumptious meal of pecan-crusted trout and roasted potatoes on the candlelit terrace, Dr. Corwin carried his Macallan single malt to a leather sofa in the lounge. Lanterns suspended from the ceiling on iron chains cast a spell of rustic sophistication on the room.

The clientele was a mixture of stuffy southern aristocrats and long-haired young professionals dressed in polyester trousers and waist-hugging pantsuits. Dr. Corwin had opted for white pants that flared at the ankles, a lime-green cotton dress shirt with a wide collar, his trademark blue trilby, and the same model of Omega Speedmaster that had adorned the wrist of Buzz Aldrin when he stepped foot on the moon.

Though not poor by any stretch, Dr. Corwin was a college professor with no family money to fall back on, and very little savings. After paying the rent on his Manhattan apartment each month, he believed in spending his remaining income on the finer things in life, and in living fully in the present. A mindful capitalist he was. The Society had allotted him a per diem for the assignment, which he planned to use in full.

Just a bachelor enjoying his nightly tipple, he kept his eyes alert, scanning every patron who entered the lounge for a resemblance to the photos of Waylan Taylor in the file.

A man glanced at Dr. Corwin from the bar. By itself, this was nothing out of the ordinary. Almost everyone in the lounge had given him a surreptitious, or sometimes direct, look at some point: he was the only black person in the room, excluding the staff. An unfortunate reality, since it made his face easy to recall, but a reality nonetheless. He did not like to dwell on such matters. It was not that he was unsympathetic to the racial issues plaguing America; he was simply preoccupied with other things.

In his view, true change would remain elusive until a radical dissemination of knowledge and technological advancement equalized the wealth and opportunity gaps and engendered mutual empathy among all people. In short, the sort of global step forward that the Leap Year Society espoused.

And that was very much his concern.

Yet the look from the handsome man at the bar with blond hair and a sharp Teutonic nose had been different from the rest of the rather ovine glances. Brief. Direct. Purposeful. A moment of attention from someone such as a policeman, a dictator, or even a successful entrepreneur—someone who lived apart from or above societal norms.

The man seemed familiar, which bothered Dr. Corwin. He rarely forgot a face. Maybe it was nothing, a resemblance to a colleague he had met at some conference abroad.

The blond man returned to his drink, so Dr. Corwin continued to watch and wait, letting his mind drift. He was still processing the Ettore Majorana file. To a layperson, much of it would have read like speculative fiction, even the part that was established science. To a professor of theoretical physics, such wild conjecture on the nature of the cosmos was a matter of daily routine. What was the quantum realm if not another layer of reality? Less than a century ago, the composition of an atom was an undiscovered kingdom, a fantastical tale that would have elicited disbelieving chuckles in science labs and universities around the world.

Dr. Corwin was not hopeful that science would soon uncover more hidden realms and dimensions—he was convinced of it. Only a fool thought the present age of discovery was the last.

Still, what was this place called the Fold? He had been told nothing beyond what the file contained. Who else in the Society knew of it? Did they take it seriously?

Could Ettore's theorems truly make inroads into the so-called theory of everything?

He had to know more.

As soon as he got time, he planned to ask the Society about the Fold, and research everything he could about Ettore Majorana and his theories. For the moment, he would focus on following the ball of string that led to the center of the labyrinth where the answers to these questions, and possibly Ettore himself, might reside.

As if on cue, Waylan Taylor walked into the lounge.

Just like the photos, the young neuropsychologist possessed an unassuming round face, thick sandy hair pushed back at the forehead, a mustache that turned down at the corners of his mouth, sleepy eyes, and the doughy hands of a desk jockey. What the photos did not show was the burnished skin from his travels, the slight hitch to his gait, and how his eyes burned behind his glasses with a detached intensity.

Though he wore a brown suit with a loosened tie and patent leather shoes—a criminally boring ensemble—there was something about him, perhaps the peach-colored tint of his glasses or the lack of press on his suit, that lent him a slightly unscrupulous air.

Dr. Taylor had degrees from Stanford and Harvard, a residency at Johns Hopkins, and papers published in the most respected journals of his field. What had led such an accomplished man to the fringes of his discipline, and more importantly, to a physicist in South America who claimed to be a disciple of Ettore Majorana?

Waylan purchased a glass of red wine from the bar and made his way to a chair near the stacked stone fireplace. Despite the season, a fire crackled inside the hearth. Dr. Corwin rose and followed him over. "Mind if I join you?"

Waylan agreed without meeting his gaze, strengthening the notion the psychologist was a slippery cat in some way. "Do I know you?"

"If I'm not mistaken, are you Waylan Taylor?"

He blinked in curiosity. "I am."

Dr. Corwin offered a hand. "James Corwin, professor of physics at Columbia University. I'm familiar with your work."

Waylan accepted the gesture. "I'm both surprised and flattered. Please, sit."

He never flinched at my color, Dr. Corwin thought, *or looked around to see who was watching.*

Dr. Corwin sat to Waylan's left, closer to the fire, so he could keep an eye on the room. The man with the hawkish gaze at the bar seemed to be paying them no attention.

"I'd like to think my publications are more well-known," Waylan continued, "but I'm afraid they're rather obscure. How is it you recognize my face?"

Waylan spoke in a soft and slow voice that, despite his lack of eye contact, commanded attention. He radiated a self-absorbed charisma that seemed to siphon off energy as they spoke, the rapacious magnetism of a cult leader.

It made Dr. Corwin uneasy.

"I'm a rather obscure reader, I must admit," Dr. Corwin said. "And I believe we have something in common."

"Oh?"

"We're both unafraid to risk contempt by exploring the outer limits of our professions."

Waylan swirled his wine, his expression indecipherable, waiting for the professor to continue.

"I'm especially intrigued by your recent article in the *Journal of International Psychotherapy*. The one influenced by your experiences among the shamans of the Amazon basin, which reexamined certain cornerstones of your profession."

A faint smile lifted the corners of Waylan's lips. "And the fall of which shibboleth did you most enjoy?"

"The prevailing wisdom among neuroscientists that the brain itself is the source of human consciousness."

Waylan's gaze slid to meet his, making contact for the first time. "Indeed an *en vogue* position. My colleagues believe they have it all figured out," he said softly, and with disdain. "That the only remaining mysteries lie within the architecture of the brain itself."

"And you disagree?"

"Oh, very much, sir. Very much indeed. Though I admit the brain is a wondrous enigma."

"Correct me if I'm wrong," Dr. Corwin said, "but the theme of your conclusions is twofold. One—and forgive my lack of technicality—is that if consciousness had arisen purely from evolutionary factors, there would not be such commonality among our mores, dreams, myths, and thought processes."

"Exactly. I've studied indigenous societies on six continents, and what I've found is a remarkable . . . confluence . . . of the subliminal. One unexplainable by current models of the brain."

"So you're a Jungian?"

He chuckled. "Certainly not a Freudian. Jung was a genius—of that there was no doubt. Still, I believe we have evolved from that position, though not in a deconstructive, so-called progressive manner."

"But what is it? From where does this strange confluence stem?"

"That's the seminal question. A god, a parallel universe, a dream world, a higher reality, an alien mind—perhaps we can never know. But I plan to spend my career applying modern science to ancient practices in an attempt to codify the common elements." He took a long drink of wine. "And I won't stop at dreams either."

"You've a very brave mind."

"Thank you. I'm afraid the establishment doesn't agree."

"They never do." Dr. Corwin leaned forward. "What if I told you I share a similar research interest—and can say with some certainty that I believe science *agrees* with you?"

Waylan regarded him closely for a moment. "Then I would say your colleagues might be even more surprised than mine. It's difficult to find a physicist these days who believes the universe is not self-contained."

"Indeed." Dr. Corwin pursed his lips, contemplative. "I read about your consultation with the physicist in South America."

"But how could you? That portion was never published." Waylan's eyes narrowed, and he stood. "At this point, I must ask if you're a reporter seeking to discredit me. Because if so, I warn you this conversation—"

Dr. Corwin flashed a charming grin and reached for his wallet. He withdrew his Columbia ID and handed it to Waylan, who studied it carefully before easing back into his seat. "It appears you are who you say."

"Since your unnamed source was a physicist," Dr. Corwin continued, "the journal's fact-checkers consulted a professional organization of which I'm a member. I was tapped to investigate the claims."

"It was a fair decision not to publish," Waylan said slowly. "The source preferred to remain anonymous. But I'm afraid you've misinterpreted the article. I never spoke to the source firsthand."

Dr. Corwin sipped his Scotch as the fire crackled in the hearth beside him. He enjoyed the aroma of woodsmoke, but he was uncomfortably warm. Why had Waylan chosen to sit so close to the fire on a summer evening? Dr. Corwin had the sudden irrational thought that the psychologist had an inhuman reptilian nature that needed warming.

"To be honest," Waylan said, "I doubt if the source used a real name."

"This is starting to sound more like a spy novel than a research trip."

"I'm afraid there are certain resemblances."

"Was he connected to a college or institution? If so, I can understand the secrecy, since claiming to be a disciple of Ettore Majorana might not be the best career move. My curiosity is piqued. If you didn't meet with the source firsthand, then who did?"

"A mutual acquaintance in Cartagena."

"That's not exactly on Main Street!"

Waylan looked distracted for a moment, lost in the past. "He's a former *curandero*, who once helped me approach a shaman in the Darién Gap."

"Curandero?"

"An indigenous healer, a witch doctor. Except this particular one is also a trained psychiatrist. Due to his unique background—not many curanderos engage with modern medicine—he has a similar interest in supplementing theories of the mind with tribal wisdom. In any event, he claimed there was someone in Cartagena, a physicist, who shared our viewpoint. Since I always seek to bolster my theories with cross-disciplinary research, I inquired about their conversation."

"And what did you learn?"

Waylan ran the tip of his tongue over his mustache. "Something I did not include in my article. Not even the redacted portion."

"I'd love to hear it."

Waylan glanced at the fire. "This physicist—X—claimed to be helping Ettore Majorana conduct experiments to prove the existence of the soul."

Dr. Corwin crossed his legs. He thought he had caught the blond German at the bar watching them, though the man had already looked away.

Where had he seen that face?

"The soul," Dr. Corwin repeated.

"According to X, Ettore thought if the soul existed—and he

believed that it did—then it must be provable by physical laws. Perhaps the soul exerts gravity at the quantum level, or in another dimension altogether."

"How very interesting. And what did they conclude?"

Waylan rubbed a thumb against the unloosened knot of his tie. "Ettore disappeared without sharing the results of the experiments."

"X must have been quite disappointed."

"As was I." Waylan's voice grew agitated. "He also said Ettore claimed to have personal evidence of the soul, that he had seen something for himself he couldn't explain—which was exactly why he was trying to prove it."

"This is getting odder and odder—what did Ettore see?"

"X said he never told him. I think he might be lying." Waylan's eyes darted upward, a sudden movement that caught Dr. Corwin off guard. "It's quite a coincidence that we both happen to be staying in the same hotel."

"One might find it quite curious, I agree."

"You don't deny it then? That you sought me out?"

"Oh, it's nothing of the sort," Dr. Corwin said quickly. "Though I do not believe in coincidence, luck, or chance. In fact, I can disprove their very existence with simple logic."

Waylan chuckled. "Is that so?"

Dr. Corwin raised his glass. "And in the same fell stroke, speak to that common source of all things I mentioned."

A new voice startled them both. "That's an enticing prospect, gentlemen. One which I would very much like to hear."

Dr. Corwin had been so involved in the conversation he had lost track of his surroundings. He turned his head to find the blond man from the bar standing beside them, holding a White Russian. Though a few inches shorter than both Dr. Corwin and Waylan, the newcomer was broad-shouldered and muscular. His polyester blue pants and matching sport coat fit him snugly, and the casual beige shirt beneath the jacket had two buttons undone, exposing a thick neck and a peach fuzz of chest hair.

"I couldn't help overhearing talk of a common source," the new-comer said with a slight German accent, confirming Dr. Corwin's guess. "Do you mind if I join you?"

Waylan adjusted his glasses. "And you are?"

"Dr. Hans Riess. I'm a physician in town for a conference."

James couldn't stop staring. He *knew* this man. He kept searching his brain, digging for a neural connection from the past . . . and then it hit him like a heavyweight blow to the chin.

Blond, Teutonic features.

Piercing blue eyes.

Handsome and square-jawed, with a cleft chin.

Dr. Corwin had seen a dozen photos of the infamous Stefan Kraus, the legendary leader of the Ascendants. While the face he was staring at now was fuller and less hard, as well as a few decades younger, the features were almost an exact replica.

He was sure of it.

3

Andie's chest tightened in fear as the secret passage inside the Archiginnasio became so constricted that she and the others had to put their hands on the rough stone walls and shuffle sideways to pass through. Henrik was in the lead, followed by Andie, Cal, and then Zawadi. If the Ascendants found them, there would be no chance of escape.

"Where does this lead?" Zawadi whispered.

"To a side street a block from the Archiginnasio," Henrik whispered back. "Not the most secure location."

"They must have followed us through the canal."

"It's the only explanation. The courtyard entrance is secure."

"What happens next?" Andie asked.

"We leave Bologna," Henrik said. "It's no longer safe."

The floor sloped gently downward as they walked. The surface of the pitted gray walls felt as old as the foundation of the city, causing Andie to wonder who had built the ancient passage. The night before, she had read that Bologna was settled around 500 BCE. As with most European cities, the power dynamic in Bologna had shifted countless times over the millennia. Not to mention, Cal had added when they had discussed it over dinner, the murky cabals and conspirators whose names and agendas went unrecorded in the history books, the puppet-master elites who had played a role in shaping the world order.

In the past, Andie would have scoffed at such speculation, despite Cal's ability to rattle off a startling array of networks and connections.

Now she wasn't so sure.

She caught her breath when the passage dead-ended at the bottom of the slope. Without pause, Henrik approached the stone wall and heaved on it with both hands. A seamless door opened with a groan that caused them all to crouch in alarm.

The door had only moved a few feet, exposing a cobblestone street. Henrik put a hand on the door and slipped his head out, then stepped all the way through and waved everyone forward. The door was invisible from the street after he shoved it closed.

The canvas shades on the buildings were all drawn. Not a soul in sight. The medieval towers of central Bologna loomed above a shuttered *osteria* across the street.

Henrik started walking to his left. "I'll warn the sentries in the courtyard of the security breach. We can leave in my car."

"What if the Archiginnasio is compromised?" Zawadi asked.

"The exits are secure, and they won't dare step into the courtyard."

Despite his confidence, Henrik gripped his gun in both hands and held it chest-high as he crept toward the intersection a hundred feet away. Zawadi was on high alert, her eyes sweeping the balconies and rooftops. Andie and Cal huddled close behind and tried not to make a sound. The scuff of Andie's shoes on the cobblestones sounded to her like a ringing fire alarm.

As they neared the intersection, they noticed a homeless person sleeping under a blanket in a doorway. Henrik and Zawadi exchanged a glance. She signaled for him to approach the prostrate form, of which only a handful of dark hair was visible beneath the soiled cover.

It was strange for someone to be buried under a blanket on such a warm night. As Zawadi leveled her gun, Henrik bent to get a look at the person's face. Andie held her breath, waiting for a shot to ring out or the person to jump up, but instead Henrik took a step back and turned, his face pale. "It's one of our sentries. His throat was cut." He swept an arm for everyone to follow, then hurried back the way they had come.

"What does this mean?" Andie said, trying not to panic. "Where are we going?"

"They're expecting us to leave through the courtyard. We have to get away from here."

"I thought you said the courtyard was secure?"

"What it *means*," Zawadi said, "is the situation is far graver than any of you realized."

Instead of disagreeing, Henrik balled his fists as they hustled toward the next intersection. "Everything could be compromised. Everything! Zawadi, you took one of our cars tonight—how far away is it?"

"Don't be absurd," she said. "We don't know how they found us. Perhaps they hacked the interface."

"Impossible."

She gave a harsh laugh. "And still, in your hubris, you underestimate them. James told you this would happen! You know what they want—and they'll do anything in their power to get it."

"I don't care what anyone wants or thinks right now," Cal said in a harsh whisper, "unless it involves getting us the hell out of this city.

"We'll have to try for a safe house," Henrik said. "The closest is half a mile away."

"It's foolish to assume anywhere is safe tonight," Zawadi said.

"Then what do you propose?"

"Improvisation."

The narrow street curved like a snake toward the intersection of a wider one. Headlights swung into view, forcing everyone to flatten against the side of a building, but the car passed by.

When they reached the intersection, Zawadi took a moment to scan their surroundings. Andie figured it was only a matter of time before the Ascendants began sweeping the streets. She felt terrified and weak and helpless, and she hated it.

Hated that these people had taken so much from her.

Hated that her life hung in the balance of their next decision.

Hated that all she could do was run.

"Come," Zawadi said. She glanced at the parked cars on their right as they fled down the street, past a cathedral with marble steps. Andie assumed she was looking for a car to hot-wire, but Zawadi surprised her by stopping not at one of the speedy BMWs or Alfa Romeos, but beside an older, rusting Fiat hatchback.

Zawadi tried a door and found it unlocked. "Get in." She slid into the driver's seat and began tugging on the panel beneath the steering wheel.

Andie and Cal jumped into the back seat. Henrik sat up front, rolled down the window, and trained his gun on the street. After one of the longest minutes of Andie's life, the engine began to rumble.

"Why'd you pick the slowest car on the street?" Cal asked Zawadi. "To throw them off?"

"Because the electronic ignitions on newer cars make them hard to hijack."

"And now?" Henrik asked. "Won't the routes leaving the city be watched?"

"That's why we're not leaving by car."

"Then how?"

"Take the wheel," she said.

With a frown, Henrik leaned over to steer the car while she took out a phone and sent a hurried text.

"Who was that to?" Henrik asked.

"Our only chance at escape. He's already on standby."

"You don't trust me."

"If I didn't trust you, you'd be dead."

Henrik started to say something, thought better of it, and slammed a fist into the dash.

Zawadi switched into a higher gear and whipped the Fiat through the living museum of Bologna, past hulking cathedrals and ancient towers and moonlight-washed piazzas, the endless porticoes a blur of concentric arches.

"Someone's coming," Cal said, keeping an eye on the side window.

"You're sure?" Zawadi said.

"I've spent the last three years looking over my shoulder. SUV with its lights off, pacing us on a parallel street to the left. I've seen them twice through a courtyard."

Zawadi swore and threw caution to the wind, ramping the curb and racing down pedestrian-only byways. The car's suspension rattled Andie's teeth on the rough cobblestones as Zawadi careened around tight corner after tight corner, pushing the car to its limits on the serpentine alleys. They exited the center and turned onto Viale Aldini, a much wider artery. Moments later, the headlights of a black SUV appeared behind them.

Cal grimaced. "That's the car."

"And they're getting closer," Andie added.

Henrik had his handgun poised by the open window. Two vehicles separated them. If either side got a clear shot, Andie wondered how well their abhorrence of public exposure would hold up.

"For God's sake," Henrik cried, "where are we going? How far is it?"

Zawadi overtook a white van as she tried to outpace their pursuer, but the speedy SUV kept gaining ground. "Basilica San Luca."

"You're aiming for the hill? Higher ground?"

Zawadi gave a wordless nod.

"That's ten minutes, at least. We'll never make it."

Zawadi swerved onto Via Saragozza at the last second, then veered so hard onto a deserted side street Andie thought for sure they would end up flying off the road and crashing into one of the angular brick townhomes.

It was dicey for a moment, but the Fiat held, tires screeching as it evened out. Zawadi made two more turns before entering a tree-lined residential neighborhood. Andie felt queasy from the ride—she had always succumbed easily to nausea.

Henrik had a palm thrust against the dash. "Where are you going now?"

"I told you," Zawadi said.

"But this isn't the way."

"We'll use the portico. It's far more direct."

"If you're on foot, yes. Surely you don't mean to run four kilometers uphill, with armed gunmen at our back?"

"You wish to help me? Let me know—all of you—when you see a pair of motorbikes."

"That just might work," Henrik said slowly, "*if* we can find the bikes."

Andie was helping Cal watch the road during the exchange. "They're behind us again!" she said.

"Too soon," Zawadi muttered. "Too soon."

"There!" Cal pointed out the window. "The street we just passed, halfway down. Three motorcycles."

She cut hard to the left at the next intersection. "We'll have to make a stand, before more join them."

Andie felt panic clawing at her throat. "Make a stand?"

"Stay behind with Henrik while he covers us. I'll start the bikes. Cal, you ride with me to distribute weight."

"This could be suicide," Henrik said.

Zawadi turned left two more times, circling back to the deserted commercial street Cal had pointed out. A trio of weathered cruisers, two black and one red and royal blue, were parked on the street. Each was chained to a metal U-bar on the sidewalk.

Zawadi raced forward, whipping the Fiat sideways at the last second to block the road twenty feet away from the motorbikes. Someone shouted in Italian from a balcony and slammed a door shut.

Zawadi killed the engine, reached underneath the dash with a pocketknife, and sliced off a wire. "Stay in the car until I call you," she said to Andie and Cal. "Henrik, watch the road."

As Zawadi leaped out of the car and sprinted toward the bikes, she stuffed her handgun in the back of her leather pants and pulled out a six-inch metal rod from beneath her shirt. After a few manipulations, the rod became a pair of bolt cutters in her hands, allowing her to snip the chains on the bikes with ease.

"That's handy," Cal said.

From the back seat beside him, Andie was the first to spot the headlights of the black SUV. "They're here!" she shouted through the lowered window.

Instead of continuing down the street, the SUV disgorged a tall red-haired woman and then roared away.

"They're circling around for a crossfire," Henrik said. "Hurry, Zawadi!"

A gunshot shattered the driver's-side mirror. As Henrik opened the door and took up a defensive position, Andie and Cal huddled low in the back seat. Andie risked a glance out the rear windshield and saw the red-haired woman taking cover behind a forest-green Volkswagen Golf. In the opposite direction, Zawadi had returned the metal rod to her belt and was bent over the nearest motorcycle, fiddling with the ignition.

"We have to do something," Andie said to Cal.

"We'll just get ourselves killed."

"If we don't get off this street in time, we're dead anyway."

After Henrik rose to return fire, keeping their attacker at bay, Andie opened the door and slid out of the car, then ran in a crouch to Zawadi. Both men yelled at her to stay put, but she ignored them.

"How can I help?" Andie said. "I know bikes."

Without looking up, Zawadi said, "Find the ignition wires. Follow them to the connector."

Moving in a crouch to the next bike over, Andie found the three ignition wires and traced them to the little plastic box on the underside of the engine. "Got it."

"Pull it off."

Andie tugged as more shots rang out. Down the street, the black SUV swung into view again, hemming them in. Shadowy figures were visible through the dash.

"It won't come off!" Andie said.

"Twist it in half and then pull."

Andie tried that, and it worked. An arm holding a gun leaned out of the SUV. Just as Zawadi got the red-and-blue bike to start, a bullet hit the ground inches from her exposed leg. Andie cringed as Zawadi fired back, shattering their pursuers' windshield, then ducked behind the bike and tossed Andie a piece of loose wire with stripped ends. "Connect two ports with the wire."

"Which ones?"

"Any two!"

Sirens whined in the distance. Andie's adrenaline spiked so hard she dropped the wire and had to waste a precious second leaning over to pick it up. As feared, their attackers had them in a crossfire, and Andie could almost feel a bullet ripping into her. But Henrik and Zawadi were firing back, covering her, so Andie did her best to calm her shaking hands as she twisted the ends of the loose wire onto the ignition wires.

The windshield of Andie's bike shattered. "Hurry!" Zawadi urged.

Someone screamed behind them. Andie thought it was a woman but wasn't sure. *Please let it not be Cal or Henrik.*

Finally the ends of the wires connected. Not daring to take the time to look up, Andie begged the bike to start as she reached up to press the ignition.

Smooth as silk, the engine came to life.

Relief surged through her. Before she had to time to call out, a number of things happened at once.

Zawadi spun around. She'd been shot in the chest. Though her face scrunched in pain, she didn't cry out, instead dropping to a knee to return fire, forcing the occupants of the SUV to stay low.

As Andie realized Zawadi must be wearing a vest, Henrik ran towards Zawadi, shouting that he had killed the red-haired woman.

And Cal had turned the Fiat around and started driving down the street right toward them. "Go!" he cried to Andie and Zawadi, accelerating toward the parked SUV, though the car didn't have much time to gain speed. Cal rolled out of the door as soon as he passed the motorcycles.

Zawadi was already seated on the red-and-blue bike, grimacing in pain. She waved Cal on behind her as the runaway Fiat forced the SUV to back up before ramping the curb and crashing into a tree. Andie crouched behind the black motorbike as Henrik raced toward her, yelling at her to get on and drive.

Gunshots rang out from both sides. As Zawadi and Cal drove by, Zawadi turned to fire, trying to cover them. Henrik, ten feet away, was also laying down gunfire.

The sirens drew closer. The chaos and gunshots rang in Andie's ears, making her feel dizzy and strangely unmoored.

Shake it off, Andie. You have to get out of here.

There was a lull in the gunfire. With any luck, the people in the SUV had to reload. Andie took the opportunity, rising from her crouch to throw a leg over the purring motorbike. Henrik climbed on behind her. If they made it off the street, it would be easy to evade the SUV.

As she knocked the kickstand back, a bullet zinged right by her cheek. When Henrik returned fire, the sound exploded in her ears and the muzzle flashed in her eyes. The acrid stench of gunpowder stuffed her nose. All of a sudden, her limbs felt heavy and she had the sensation she was floating even though the ground was right beneath her—

And then she was inside the shadow world, the old buildings lining the street now smudges of haze in the darkness, the street a ribbon of charcoal that twisted and curled like smoke beneath her.

No! I can't be here right now. I'll die.

Henrik was motionless behind her, so faded he resembled a shade more than a person. Same with the motorbike, and the cars floating in slow motion. She called out, but Henrik didn't respond. Something rippled in the gloom, a streak of silver light coming her way. She stepped to the side to avoid it. As the object passed her by, about the speed of a slow-pitch softball, she got a better look and noticed the core was shaped vaguely like a pellet.

Was that a bullet? How is that possible?

Or am I dreaming?

Despite the ephemeral nature of the place, it felt suffocating, as if the gloom itself had weight. As always, shapes drifted through the murky recesses of the void, sentient things aware of her presence, causing chills of unease to creep down her spine.

You have to snap out of it, Andie. You have to wake up.

When she tried to pinch herself, her hand sank weirdly into her flesh, horrifying her. There was a gun battle going on in the real world. She had already spent far too long inside. Sensing a presence behind her, she whipped around and saw, about a hundred feet away—distance was hard to judge—a spectral figure approaching. It was dressed in some type of clothing, frayed at the edges, that looked almost Renaissance. She couldn't make out any features; the figure seemed made of shadow like everything else.

Whoever or whatever it was, the figure knew Andie was there, and it was watching her. Andie could sense it. She turned to search for an escape, but all she could see were endless vistas of gray and those awful silhouettes, those *things*, hovering on the edges of her vision.

The figure kept drifting in her direction, slow at first and then faster. Andie backed away but couldn't seem to move as fast. She had never felt so lost, so hopelessly lost, trapped in a maze with no rational borders, maybe trapped forever if she didn't wake up. The figure drifted ever closer, reaching out for her now. Andie lurched to get away, never so terrified of anything in her life—

The world returned in a flash of color and sound: the glow of streetlamps, the roar of a motorbike, a gunshot nearby.

She tumbled off the motorcycle, which was idling in the same place she'd gotten on. It was as if she had been under the spell of the shadow world for only a moment, a blip in time in the real world.

Henrik, still on the bike, was startled by her fall. "Andie, get up!"

Zawadi, noticing they had stalled, stopped her bike near the end of the street, and laid down cover fire to help them escape. Andie was so woozy she tripped and fell when she tried to stand. Henrik jumped off the bike and yanked her to her feet. "We have to go before—"

A bullet slammed into his back, causing him to lurch into Andie. She caught him, warm blood oozing onto her hands.

She screamed. "Henrik!"

Another gunshot. Out of the corner of her eye, she saw one of the people in the SUV slump as if hit.

"Go," Henrik managed to gasp. "You have to drive."

Adrenaline spiked inside her, snapping her fully awake. A lull in the gunfire allowed her to jump onto the bike, and she helped Henrik climb on behind her. Though his grip felt weak, he was able to hold her around the waist.

"Hang in there!" she said as she wheeled the bike around. Zawadi fired again as Andie jammed her wrist forward and took off down the street in the opposite direction from the SUV.

Henrik didn't respond. When she glanced back, his head was bobbing as if he couldn't hold it up. Zawadi and Cal caught up and zoomed past them, turning left at the corner. Andie followed. She knew the best way to help Henrik was to get the hell out of there.

The SUV roared down the street behind them, then fell farther and farther behind as the nimble motorbikes raced deeper into the neighborhood. Andie guessed the Moto Guzzi she was driving was at least twenty years old, with only a few hundred ccs. But that was more than enough power to eviscerate an SUV in tight quarters. She had no idea what had happened to the police sirens, but she suspected the Ascendants had something to do with that.

Soon they emerged onto a larger street, which spilled into a circle of pavement fronting a medieval gate flanked by a pair of squat barbicans. The road led straight through the gate. Zawadi cut to the left, barely slowing as she zipped through a smaller archway at full speed. This archway signaled the entrance to a succession of covered arcades, which extended up the hill as far as Andie could see in the light from the headlamps.

Andie clutched the handlebars as she followed Zawadi, at once seeing the wisdom of the decision. Composed of ancient paving stones worn smooth over the centuries, the roofed colonnade was not wide enough for a car and ran straight up the long hill, which must have lead to the basilica.

At first a succession of darkened houses and shops flanked the colonnade, but after a mile or so the tunnel of painted archways left the city behind as it climbed higher and higher into the forested hillside.

Henrik's grip on Andie's waist grew weaker. Beside them, a paved road wound up the hill in circumspect fashion. Soon Andie glimpsed lights near the bottom that surely belonged to their pursuers. The situation grew worse when the paving stones turned into a staircase for the final portion of the climb. It took all of her strength and balance to manage the jarring ride up the incline while reaching back to grip Henrik by the shirt, keeping him steady.

They emerged from the colonnade into a courtyard at the base of a domed basilica high above the city. Stone walkways and manicured green spaces dissected the ancient piazza. Zawadi parked her bike and left it running as Cal jumped off and dashed over to help Andie ease Henrik to the ground.

After a glance at her wristwatch, Zawadi joined them, checking Henrik's pulse as he lay unmoving on the stone pathway. Andie had never felt so helpless. They didn't even have a bottle of water for him.

"They mean well, but they're wrong," Henrik murmured. "We were all wrong." Blood bubbled at the edges of his mouth, a worrisome purple color.

"Hush," Zawadi said. "Save your energy."

His breathing was very shallow, and Andie took his hand as his eyes closed. He started to whisper something, and she bent down to listen. "Find Dr. Corwin," he whispered. "He's our only hope."

"We'll find him together," Andie said. "Stay with us. You're going to make it."

"Zawadi," Cal warned. "Lights on the hill."

Andie turned to see a pair of headlights approaching on the paved road that led to the basilica. The road spilled out on the opposite end of the courtyard, in a parking area beneath a retaining wall. She also heard the distinctive thump-thump of a helicopter approaching from the distance.

Cal cringed as a wasp-shaped copter swooped into view. "Who

the hell's that? More Ascendants?"

"Our ride," Zawadi replied. She was cradling Henrik's head in her arms when Andie turned back around. Zawadi checked his pulse one more time, then gently let him go.

A lump rose in Andie's throat. "Oh my God. He's dead? We can't just leave him here."

"We must, and we will."

Zawadi ushered them into the safety of the colonnade as Andie suppressed the urge to vomit. Zawadi might be right, but Andie hated the logic of the situation. Henrik had risked his life to get them out of Bologna. Not only that, he had risked his life to help her after she slipped into the shadow world—and now he was dead because of it.

Because of *her*.

As the vehicle neared the top of the hill, powerful searchlights swept the base of the basilica. Above them, the ultralight copter began to descend into the courtyard. The SUV was out of sight beneath the retaining wall, though someone was shouting instructions in Italian, and gunshots started pinging off the body of the copter.

"As soon as it lands," Zawadi said, "run for your lives."

"You're not coming?" Cal said in disbelief.

"That was never my intention." She reached beneath her shirt and lifted a small gray pouch off a utility belt, then tossed it Andie. "Funds and documents and a secure phone are inside. Only texts, no calls."

Andie felt a stab of desperation as Zawadi raised her gun and stepped away. "When will we see you again?"

"Soon."

"How?"

"Go! Now! Follow the Star Phone!"

The helicopter hovered just above the ground, whipping the air around them. Zawadi grabbed Henrik's gun and began firing to distract their assailants, racing toward the retaining wall at the edge of the courtyard. As she drew nearer, she ducked behind benches and potted trees, anything she could find as the spotlights swept the grounds. Two Ascendants tried to run up the stairs on either side of the wall, but Zawadi drove them back. She had the higher ground, but it was only a matter of time before someone flanked her.

The pilot opened a door to the cockpit and threw out a rope ladder. With Cal right beside her, Andie hunched over and dashed across the courtyard, flinching at each spurt of gunfire and waiting for a bullet to pierce her in the back. She sprinted for the ladder with everything she had, outpacing Cal. She jumped to grab a rung above her head, scrambled up like a monkey, and turned to give him a hand.

"Pull the ladder!" the pilot said as soon as they were up, and the helicopter began to ascend.

"What about Zawadi?" Andie said. She and Cal had squeezed into a pair of tight folding seats behind the cockpit. "We have to help her!"

"She told me not to wait," the pilot said.

"I don't care!"

"She gave orders. I'm sorry."

No amount of cajoling would change his mind. As they climbed higher and higher above the copper dome of the basilica, the lights of Bologna a million lanterns blazing far beneath them, Andie could only watch in horror as the staccato muzzle blasts in the courtyard grew fainter and fainter.

"Look!" Cal said, gripping Andie's arm as he pointed to their left. Behind the basilica, at the edge of the courtyard, a single headlight could be seen, just barely, weaving down the forested slope at a break-neck pace. "That's got to be Zawadi—she doubled back on them."

Andie gripped the back of the pilot's seat as she watched the lone figure disappear into the trees. The last thing they saw before soaring out of range was the SUV at the bottom of the courtyard, whipping around to race back down the long drive.

"I hope she has a plan," Andie said.

Cal slumped into his seat and let his shoulders sag in exhaustion. "I hope our pilot does too."

Asheville
Summer 1970

"What sort of doctor are you?" Dr. Corwin said casually, though he was staring at Hans in the cozy lounge of the Grove Park Inn, analyzing every detail of the broad-shouldered German man. He cut quite a handsome figure, with his fashionable thin mustache, cleft chin and dimples, beige shirt with two buttons undone, and the most piercing blue eyes Dr. Corwin had ever seen.

The man had to be a close relative of Stefan Kraus, quite possibly his son. Yet to Dr. Corwin's knowledge, no such person existed. The Society did not have a full record of all the Ascendants, or even most of them, but a child of Stefan Kraus . . . they should have known about this.

He had to assume Hans's identity, his very existence, had been kept a secret. Yet why surface now? The Ascendants must have seen Waylan's journal article and decided to send their own promising young member to investigate the rumors of Ettore Majorana's reappearance.

"I'm a pediatric oncologist." Hans held Dr. Corwin's gaze as he took a seat in a leather armchair across from Waylan Taylor. Dr. Corwin caught the faint aromas of dark rum and a crisp citrus cologne wafting off the German. "And you?"

If Hans was an oncologist, then Dr. Corwin was a peach farmer. But it was a smart choice. No one in polite company would question the credentials of someone saving the lives of children.

Does Hans know of my true allegiance? "I'm a theoretical physicist at Columbia. I'm afraid I must be off, though. I've quite an early flight." Though intrigued by the conversation with Waylan, Dr. Corwin had gained the information he needed.

"How disappointing," Hans said. "I'm highly curious as to this common source of all things and the demystification of chance."

"Yes," Waylan said. He was looking warily at both men, aware of strange dynamics in play. "I'd be most keen to hear this myself before you go."

After a moment's hesitation, Dr. Corwin held up his palms. He might need to consult with Waylan in the future. "Why not?" he said, then reached into his pocket and withdrew a quarter. "I often make this argument with a deck of cards. But a coin will suffice. Let me start with a question: How do you believe the universe began? By design or by chance?"

Hans crossed his legs, revealing white suede loafers, and threw an arm over the back of his chair. "I'm of the opinion that the sooner we distance ourselves from superstitious beliefs, the better."

"You reject design in the universe then?"

"Design by a white-bearded deity? Absolutely. Do you not?"

"Religion is irrelevant to my argument. Chance, then, is your answer? The luck of the draw? A big bang followed by a random confluence of celestial events that led to the miracle of life on Earth?"

"If you put it that way," Hans said, "then yes. Unless there is another choice?"

"I'm not aware of one," Dr. Corwin said. "Random chance, or a design of unknown origin. There is no middle ground."

Waylan folded his arms as Dr. Corwin held the quarter in his palm for both men to observe. "At first blush, it would seem that luck and chance are everywhere. Take a coin flip—would you posit the outcome is simply a matter of fortune?"

"As long as you're not a sleight-of-hand artist," the German said.

"That, too, is irrelevant. In fact, no matter the medium, chance has *nothing* to do with the outcome of a coin toss."

Hans was bristling. "I'm dying to hear your explanation."

"The problem is, chance has become synonymous with probability. Playing the odds. I grant you there is close to a fifty-fifty mathematical probability that, on the average toss, a coin will land on heads." Dr. Corwin wagged a finger. "But every single time, the outcome is predetermined long before the coin lands. For starters, we have to consider the strength and motion of the wrist, the atmospheric pressure, the landing surface, and the effect of gravity. Moving backward in time, one could argue for an almost infinite number of factors."

"It's a logical trap," Hans said.

"Oh? How, then, would you ensure a random flip?"

"I'd hire someone to write a computer program that negated the effect of the environment in determining heads or tails."

"And how would you exclude the influence of the computer circuits involved and the design of the program itself? Pure chance is still nowhere in sight. More equal probabilities perhaps, but not chance."

"Yes, I understand the effect of the observer on an experiment can never be removed. But did Bohr and Heisenberg not prove the inherent uncertainty in the quantum realm?"

"A common misconception. All they proved was that quantum events operate in a manner *in which we do not yet understand.*"

Waylan sipped his drink. "'God does not play dice,' I believe Einstein said."

"No," Dr. Corwin said. "He does not." He could not tell where Hans himself stood in these matters, or his goal in joining the conversation. Dr. Corwin turned to Waylan. "While it may sometimes appear that two people meet out of nowhere, their union is attributable—always—to a host of factors that happened to converge in that particular location in time and space. Chance has nothing to do with causal power. Events only appear to be irrational from our limited perspective. The probability of spontaneous, chance creation of the universe or anything else with ontological existence is precisely zero."

"Bold words," Waylan murmured. He was now staring at Dr. Corwin with disturbing intensity. "Are you arguing against free will?"

"Just because a particular choice results from a confluence of factors doesn't mean it wasn't free. It just means it wasn't random."

"You seem to have lots of answers," Hans said. "So what was it, then, which brought into being the whole of reality? An omnipotent deity? A simulation by an advanced society? Surely, if you've thought this much about it, you have an opinion."

Dr. Corwin finished his Scotch, fluffed the collar of his shirt, and rose to leave. "I've no idea, gentlemen. But the popular scientific opinion that the universe came into being by sheer random chance is a myth on the order of Zeus and Mount Olympus."

On the walk back to his room, Dr. Corwin did not feel tipsy at all. He had a high tolerance for alcohol and had only knocked back two Scotches.

Instead he felt intrigued and energized by what he had learned from Waylan Taylor.

Next stop: Cartagena. The psychologist was a disconcerting man in many ways, an obsessive man, but Dr. Corwin did not think he was a liar. The information would need to be verified, but he felt in his bones the trail to Ettore led to South America. It was, after all, the continent where the most rumors about Ettore's appearances over the years had occurred.

In terms of finding the mysterious physicist called X who was supposedly a disciple of Ettore's, how many native healers turned psychiatrists could there be in Cartagena, or even in all of Colombia? Rather than asking Waylan directly and tipping off Hans, Dr. Corwin knew it should be a simple matter to track down Waylan's contact.

Now, whether the curandero or X truly knew Ettore—or where to find him—was another matter.

He had wanted to ask Waylan about the appearance of the LYS symbol in Ettore's journal, but with Hans involved, he couldn't risk drawing attention to the Society. He planned to ask X directly.

As Dr. Corwin exited the elevator and entered his hallway on the second floor, he saw a woman in a slinky violet dress and long brown hair parted in the middle—he had noticed her in the bar, quite a looker—hurrying down the hall in the opposite direction.

After a moment of confusion, he understood.

The Ettore files. Why didn't I lock them in the safe?

Cursing his carelessness—he had no idea the Ascendants would strike so soon—he sprinted down the hall as the woman turned the corner.

She must be working with Hans. He realized I was leaving the lounge and joined the conversation as a diversion.

Dr. Corwin hesitated as he passed his room. Should he check to see if she stole the file? *I'll never catch her if I do. And if she did steal it, then it's on her person.*

He whipped around the corner and saw her disappear into a stairwell, which bolstered his suspicions. Guests walking alone at night, especially female, did not take the stairs. They used the elevator.

With a burst of speed, he reached the stairwell and bounded down to the first floor. He banged the crash bar open and scanned the hallway.

Nothing. No one.

Either the woman had slipped into one of the rooms—in which case she was out of reach—or she had continued down the stairs. Left with little choice, he hurried to the basement level and exited the stairwell. There she was, at the end of a short hallway!

The woman pushed through a set of double doors marked as leading to the spa. Dr. Corwin followed. The doors opened onto a carpeted hallway that spilled into a foyer with a tile floor and potted plants exposed to a skylight. Moonlight flooded the foyer, and a miniature waterfall inset into the wall emitted a pleasant trickle.

A wall of frosted glass obscured the spa from view. He tried the door and was surprised to find it unlocked. It made him wonder if the woman had set up an escape route beforehand. Wishing he had his ironwood cane in hand, he opened the door and stepped into an otherworldly scene.

Rock walls and a cavernous ceiling surrounded a rectangular basin of water with steam wafting off it. The air smelled of chlorine; the hotel must treat the water at night. Fluorescent pool lights glowed eerily beneath the water and spread shadows on the ceiling. A dozen or so alcoves, separated by stacked stone pillars, lurked in the darkness surrounding the steam basin. Except for the dim red glow of a few emergency lights in glass cases, this could have been the pleasure grotto of a Roman emperor, a subterranean hot spring illuminated by natural phosphorescence.

There had to be an exit on the far side. If Dr. Corwin didn't find it quickly, he knew he would lose the woman. Avoiding the darkened alcoves, he stayed close to the edge of the pool as he hurried through the room, unable to run on the marble floor that was slick with moisture from the steam. Nearing the far side of the basin, he noticed a door closing, set into a wall of frosted glass. As he rushed forward, a black-clad figure jumped out of the last alcove on the left. Before Dr. Corwin had time to react, the figure slipped behind him, wrapped a leather cord around his neck, and drew it tight.

The strangling cord bit deep into his flesh. Dr. Corwin jerked and bucked, slipping on the wet floor, unable to free himself. The assailant's grip was enormously strong. In the back of Dr. Corwin's mind, he caught the aroma of rum and citrus.

How did Hans arrive so quickly? He must have entered from another direction.

Clawing at the cord, Dr. Corwin tried to bend at the waist and flip the German over his back. Hans resisted by lowering his weight and bending his quarry backward, keeping him off-balance. Dr.

Corwin tried to twist his torso and sweep one of his assailant's legs out from under him, but Hans kept dragging him backward, relentless, tightening the cord with each step.

Dr. Corwin had some limited training in boxing and Okinawan karate, but more importantly, he had engaged in countless brawls on the streets of Kingston as a youth. Though a skinny and cerebral child, he had never backed down, and suffered a beating on many an occasion.

Which taught him how to deal with pain and not panic—invaluable skills in a real fight.

Yet nothing he did seemed to work. Hans knew how to hold a strangle, and Dr. Corwin was starting to see black. He kept trying to insert his fingers beneath the leather cord, but it was drawn too tight.

To his left, one of the blinking red lights drew his attention. He might have one last play. Summoning a burst of adrenaline, he jerked to that side, bringing them both closer to the wall. When Hans leaned him over even farther, Dr. Corwin didn't resist. Instead he gave in and threw his legs high on the wall. Hans jerked him back down—but not before Dr. Corwin managed to lash out with a foot, kick the red emergency light, and shatter the glass case.

An alarm sounded at once.

Hans cursed under his breath and tried to retighten his grip, but Dr. Corwin had managed to slip his fingers beneath the cord, allowing him to catch a precious few breaths and relieve the pressure of the strangle. When Hans noticed and tried to rip Dr. Corwin's fingers away, Dr. Corwin bucked so hard they both fell to the ground. Quick as a cat, Hans leaped to his feet and drew the cord taut in his hands.

A door slammed nearby. Shouts emanated from the outside hallway. Hans took a step forward, thought better of it, and backed away with a snarl.

Still gasping for breath, barely able to feel his legs, Dr. Corwin slumped on the floor as Hans fled into the murky recesses of the grotto.

Shanghai, China
4

As thin and delicate as a lotus stalk, her straight black hair streaming to her waist, Daiyu walked with a hunch through the crowded nightclub, the contorted posture a product of her lifelong battle with scoliosis.

Black lights strobing the club exposed a psychedelic range of colors on the painted walls and ceiling. A former slaughterhouse built in the 1920s, rivers of blood had once flowed in the vast concrete hall, pouring through grated canals lining the floor. The slaughterhouse had been discovered in a forgotten corner of Shanghai and resurrected by a tribe of urban worshippers called biohackers—a tribe to which Daiyu and her brother, Jianyu, belonged.

Biohackers. Grinders. Upgraders.

Synonyms for adherents to a group who believed in augmenting the human body through the use of machines and technology.

The world was full of biohackers, though most people cringed at the term. Anyone who used a pacemaker, voice modulator, implanted electrodes to treat Parkinson's disease, or even a hearing aid belonged. Contraceptive coils and prosthetic limbs counted as well.

Yet true biohackers took the practice much further, surgically implanting chips and magnets and other devices beneath their skin that could do all manner of things: connect to PCs and cell phones and voice assistants, give directions to personal robots, fire smart-guns, even detect seismic tremors. Major companies aiming to connect the human brain to a computer interface had already surfaced. The movement was in its infancy, and the possibilities were endless.

Wincing at the pain shooting down her back and through the sciatic nerve, Daiyu approached one of the raised daises near the center of the room, where her brother held court. In their religion, Daiyu was the high priestess, and Jianyu her warrior protector. Though born only a few hours ahead, Daiyu's beloved twin dwarfed her in size. He was tall, handsome, and blessed with a narrow waist and muscular physique that could have graced the cover of a body-building magazine.

No, not *blessed*, Daiyu knew. *Given*.

The twins had a special status among the biohacker community. In addition to their talents—Daiyu was a computer specialist, and Jianyu a living weapon—their parents were geneticists who had dreamed of gene editing long before it had become a reality. They were among the earliest adopters of IVF in human beings, and the Chinese government supported their ambitions. Jianyu's biological father was a world-class gymnast whom the government had ordered to submit to the procedure. Daiyu's DNA stemmed from a genius nuclear physicist. She was grateful for her intelligence, but bitter about her physical deformity, and blamed the limitations of science at the time. Oh, what she wouldn't give for a perfectly aligned spine!

At the time, the twins' birth was the most sophisticated body modification available. Now CRISPR and other gene editing techniques made IVF seem as sophisticated as a videocassette recorder. A Chinese scientist had already engineered the DNA of a human embryo. Soon computer chips would enter the DNA in vitro. The transmogrification of humankind was not the future: it was the present.

A beast of a man with steel horns implanted in his head and a fleet of nose rings scurried out of Daiyu's way. Bombarded by flashing light and color, she stepped onto a bronze dais with a love seat and a wraparound railing. The acid house playlist was constructed by an artificial intelligence DJ, who punctuated the music with spoken words.

Move.

Create.

Shining star.

Transform.

Her brother, Jianyu, was lounging on the love seat with a striking Japanese woman. She had fitted the left half of her face with wires and thin metal plates to resemble a cyborg. Daiyu waited in silence while Jianyu sent the woman away.

When they were alone, Jianyu lifted a cocktail smoking with liquid nitrogen, which drifted into a chiseled face framed by black hair. His soft brown eyes tempered the hardness of his features. Both their complexions were as white and smooth as alabaster.

"Sister," he shouted above the din, unperturbed by the intrusion. Jianyu never seemed to resent his sibling's quirks and cold demeanor. "What brings you out of your lair?"

Take out the earplugs, she mouthed, touching a hand to her ear.

"What? I'm listening to—"

She lifted a palm, and he complied. The people dancing with frenetic energy around the dais observed the twins with surreptitious glances. They always observed them.

Daiyu took a step forward, close enough to lean down and whisper in her brother's ear, careful not to let her face contort in pain. She had sat in her chair too long and did not want her brother to know how much she was suffering. His pity was the one thing she could never bear. "I received a text."

Jianyu stilled. He knew that only one source, one entity, would cause Daiyu to relay such an ordinary message in person.

As all human beings are committed to various tribes—family, friends, political organizations, religions—Daiyu and Jianyu belonged to another group, in addition to the biohackers. An elite society. Unlike the general population, who typically viewed biohacking with revulsion, the Ascendants—almost all of them powerful and influential people—embraced transhumanist beliefs as a natural evolution of the species.

Not many Ascendants were biohackers in the true sense of the word.

But they understood that one day everyone would be.

"They want to see us," she said. "They've requested a meeting."

"Where?" he asked. "Venice? London? Singapore?"

"Here. Tonight."

"*Tonight?*"

"We have to leave. Now. And Jianyu—it's not just anyone." She nervously fingered a black jade key that hung from her neck on a platinum chain. "The Archon is in Shanghai."

The twins left the club and stepped into the sultry night air, the Shanghai skyline a neon throb in the distance. Daiyu wore turquoise boots and skintight clothing made of silver microfibers.

Unlike her brother, who concealed his weapons and augmentations beneath his clothing—tonight he wore a black leather trench coat—Daiyu possessed only one true body mod: a micro-bracelet implanted beneath the palm of her left hand. It exuded an eerie phosphorescent glow and gave her access to the small PC she carried with her at all times in her geometric-patterned handbag.

"Why would the Archon come in person?" Jianyu asked as they hustled—as fast as Daiyu's stooped gait would allow—to his Suzuki Katana motorcycle. The location of the meeting was an unusual library in the Changning District, a common meeting spot under Ascendant jurisdiction.

"I don't know," Daiyu replied.

"Surely it concerns the war. How many others are attending?"

"I don't *know*," she snapped.

When they reached the sport bike, he stopped to put his hands on her shoulders. "What's bothering you? Is it your back?"

"No!" she said, with more heat than she intended.

Daiyu had never been comfortable around others. Most people thought she was cold and unfeeling, and in truth, except for Jianyu, she rather was. She preferred the company of machines, and was happiest when plugged into that beautiful realm that spoke in bytes instead of words, where imagination became reality.

Maybe her social alienation stemmed from knowing her parents had grown her in a test tube from a stranger's DNA. She was a child of science, and to science she felt the most kinship.

Jianyu didn't share her intolerance for others. He was a true believer in technology, complicated and enigmatic in his own way, yet he was a soulful, charismatic, fiery person who embraced life in all its facets. Especially those of the female variety.

Whatever the origin of Daiyu's social anxiety, the mysterious leader of the Ascendants made her more uncomfortable than anyone else on Earth. Daiyu had twice attended a meeting over which the Archon had presided—once in Singapore and once in Venice—and she did not want to be within a thousand miles of their leader again.

Yet she could not speak of this with her brother. He revered the Ascendants. Daiyu had passed their tests and joined them mostly to please Jianyu. Now, she feared that if she tried to leave, she would never see him again.

She also had the strange feeling the Archon knew this about her.

Could see into her true soul.

"Daiyu," he said. "What is it?"

"Nothing."

"Is it the Archon?"

"What do you mean?"

"I noticed how you looked after Venice," he said. "The same look you have now. Please, try not to show fear. Fear is weakness to them."

"It isn't fear," she lied.

"Then what is it?"

She struggled for something to say. "I . . . don't know. The Archon has a different aura. I can't read it."

"You know what I think of your belief in auras."

"You don't have to believe in something for it to exist."

Jianyu shook his head. "As much as we're alike, I've never understood how you can embrace the technological and the mystical in equal measure."

As ancient Greeks once visited the shrines of oracles, Daiyu consulted corridors of terabytes and digital architecture, and she believed in their power. Were the answers she received or the source of the responses, the mysterious origin of the laws that governed the physical universe, any less miraculous?

In modern times, humankind had simply put a name to the unknown: science.

And Daiyu bowed at its altar.

"I've told you before," she said. "It's all one and the same."

He helped her mount the bike. "I think the Archon might agree with you. You've heard the things they say. That the Archon can make you see and do things."

"Words mean nothing."

"Or they mean everything, Daiyu!" he said sharply. "Are you as dedicated to this cause as you need to be? The Archon will sense if you are not. You know this."

She squeezed his muscular wrist. "I am," she whispered. "But first I'm dedicated to you, and I don't want them to send you away again."

He revved the bike as he turned to meet her eyes, both warmth and understanding in his gaze. *Yes*, they would probably send him away. *Yes*, he would miss her too.

She tied her hair back and slipped on her face mask to mitigate the pollution. As the motorbike roared out of the factory district and onto the superhighways of Shanghai, Daiyu clutched her brother's waist, closed her eyes, and rested her head against his broad back.

Half an hour later, with the city asleep around them, the twins entered the library through a rear entrance in the shadow of a multistory megamall. The door of the library was unlocked, the security cameras disabled.

No one was inside to greet them. Strange. Normally the Archon traveled with a security contingent. They navigated a short hall and pushed through a set of doors into the main reading room. Daiyu had not visited in some time, and she caught her breath at the sight.

Designed to evoke an M. C. Escher woodcut, the four-story room was an open square stacked floor-to-ceiling with mahogany bookshelves. There were no tables or chairs in the room. Stairways zigged and zagged along the perimeter and up and down the walls, leading to short walkways that gave access to the shelves. The steps were arranged in patterns that repeated throughout the room. A mirrored floor and ceiling added to the effect, giving the illusion of stepping into an infinite maze of books.

"Welcome."

Daiyu turned, startled. Though the lights were on, they had seen no one when they entered the room—yet now the Archon and a pale thin woman with curly red hair were standing in the middle of the mirrored floor. How could that be?

As always, the Archon's golden mask and white robe hid all flesh from view. Daiyu knew the woman by reputation: Chelsea Rose Lancaster, a Brit who often accompanied the Archon to assist with affairs. Chelsea was wearing designer glasses and a dark-gray pantsuit, and carried a sleek aluminum briefcase. Daiyu knew more Ascendants were deployed in and around the building.

"Black jade, if I'm not mistaken?" the Archon asked, noticing the key nestled in Daiyu's bosom.

Her hand moved to grasp the talisman.

"Your namesake, of course," the Archon continued. "The meaning of Daiyu."

"Yes."

"According to lore, black jade creates a barrier to intrusion from psychic attack. I've heard you believe in such things, child. Is this true?"

Surprised by the Archon's knowledge of this esoteric fact, Daiyu gave a hard swallow and hesitated to answer.

Her brother interjected. "She believes there are unexplained powers of the mind. Science, not magic."

"I see," the Archon said, turning to Daiyu. "Is this so?"

"Yes," Daiyu whispered.

The Archon's gloved hands unfurled in front of the robe. "A wise position. What about you, Jianyu? In what do you believe?"

Though her brother looked tense and off-balance, he answered without hesitation. "In the advancement of humankind through the acquisition of higher knowledge."

The Archon began to pace, the gloved hands now clasped behind the robes. "I've heard many optimistic reports about you and your sister. That she is our most accomplished computer expert, and you are perhaps our most formidable asset in the field."

Jianyu bowed. "Thank you."

"I have a task for you together, if you choose to accept."

When Jianyu looked at Daiyu, she gave a barely perceptible nod. "We accept," Jianyu said. "Whatever it is."

"Loyalty is a commendable trait. Unquestioned allegiance, however, bears the stamp of tyrants. It is also the mark of an unhealthy organization. One that does not look inward to flourish and evolve."

"I apologize if I was rash. I only meant—"

The Archon raised a hand. "I do not wish to lead by fear. I wish to lead by respect."

"Understood."

After a long moment that made Daiyu even more uncomfortable than she already was, the Archon said, "Before I have Ms. Lancaster impart the necessary information, there is something we need to discuss. A lack of faith that concerns me."

The leader of the Ascendants looked right at Daiyu, causing her throat to feel dry, making her wonder if the stories about the Archon were true.

The Archon continued to stare at her as if conveying a silent message. Daiyu wanted to clutch the jade talisman and flee the room, get as far away as she could, but she corralled her emotions and said nothing.

"She believes," Jianyu said quietly. "The Ascendants mean everything to her. She's just not as vocal as I am."

The Archon turned to face him. "It is not your sister's lack of faith that concerns me."

Jianyu's stoic expression faded.

"I do not doubt your belief in our mission," the Archon said. "But I do not think you are fully aware of the scope. Though possessed of her own doubts, your sister understands the possibilities of human potential far better than do you. You are young, Jianyu, for an Ascendant. There is much to which you have not been introduced. But for this particular mission, and for the war in general, I need mature believers. The winds of change are blowing. There are events and adversaries for which you need to be prepared. It is why I have come myself to recruit you."

"How can I convince you?"

"You can observe."

The Archon's hands flashed in front of the white robe, releasing twin sprays of blinding colored lights. When Daiyu's vision cleared, she saw movement around the perimeter of the room. With a gasp, she spun and realized that hundreds of people were walking up and down the steps of the reading room like automatons, back and forth, up and down, reaching for books and carrying them elsewhere and placing them on different parts of the shelves. She whirled and saw the same scenario playing out all across the room. It was as if someone had recorded all the activity in the library over a week and was playing it back with live actors at double speed.

She blinked a few times, but that failed to dispel the illusion, or the altered reality, or whatever it was. It looked as real as anything she had ever seen.

Jianyu was turning uneasily in a circle. "How is this possible?"

The Archon waved a hand, and the people disappeared. "Technology is wondrous, but we have the most amazing machine of all inside our heads. Though we understand very little of the human brain, I have spent a lifetime unlocking its potential."

As the twins watched in silence, the Archon paced around them in a wide circle, one palm held downward, the gloved hand emitting a ray of light that inscribed a golden ring on the floor.

Suddenly Daiyu wondered whether the Archon was even in the room at all. How much of this was digitally enhanced illusion, and how much was real?

By the time the circle was complete, Chelsea Lancaster had stepped outside the ring of light. Both the twins were still inside, which made Daiyu anxious—but she dared not move.

The Archon continued to pace the perimeter. "A poet once said that if you draw a circle a hundred feet in diameter any place on the planet, even in a desert, that within the circle are one hundred things no one has ever seen and one thousand that no one understands. I believe those numbers are vastly underestimated—and we are just one planet circling one sun, in a universe of a billion trillion stars."

Daiyu cringed when the Archon turned to face her. "Consider: your laptop, cell phone, the futuristic cityscape of Shanghai, your country's sophisticated rockets and satellites that probe outer space—all of these wonders derive from a very small group of primitive hominids that emerged from the jungle and began to flourish less than two hundred thousand years ago. A speck of dust in the geological eye. We are not even children in the eyes of the universe. We are embryos. Zygotes. Imagine, just imagine for a moment, that which our species has achieved in comparison to all others. We have not just made progress or evolved—we have made vast and unexplainable leaps." The Archon stopped to face the twins. "And yet our journey has barely begun."

As the line on the floor dissolved into motes of golden light, the Archon lifted both arms and began to move them in small circles, whipping the motes into a frenzy, concealing the twins from view behind a wall of illumination.

Oddly, Daiyu began to taste dry air on her tongue. A sound like the whining of a teakettle arose, softly at first and then louder. She whipped her head back and forth, straining to see outside the wall. When the motes of light dissipated, the library had disappeared, and she and her brother were surrounded by hundreds of ziggurats dotting a vast arid plain. The steplike pyramids were made of smooth stones in dozens of brilliant hues—obsidian, sandstone, limestone, granite—and looked recently constructed. They reached hundreds of feet high, proud sentinels framed against an azure sky. Gardens and stone dwellings were interspersed among the ziggurats, an entire city which resembled nothing Daiyu had seen in a history book. The whining sound became the whoosh of a hot sere wind rushing into her face—she could *feel* it—and she noticed hordes of people moving up and down the ziggurats and through the gardens like a colony of human ants.

When Daiyu turned, she was startled to find the Archon—but not Chelsea Lancaster—standing behind them inside the circle. The eerie voice behind the mask rose above the fierce wind. "Human potential is unlimited, but our achievements thus far are parlor tricks. Scraps at the table of the gods, fallen to Earth like feed for domesticated animals. Yet we will never settle for scraps. We will become gods ourselves and plumb the depths of reality and grab the source of all things by the throat. We will save humanity and advance it. Perfect it. Those insipid fools who dare call themselves the Leap Year Society have long withheld knowledge from us, but they have failed to grasp the enormity of the indications we found in Dr. Corwin's lab. It is my firm belief the Enneagon can open doors of science that have never been unlocked."

The gloved hand lowered, and all at once it disappeared: the dusty ziggurats, the vivid sensation of dry earth in Daiyu's mouth, the people, and the howling wind.

Stunned by what she had witnessed, Daiyu realized she was gripping her black jade key so hard it bit into her palm. The Archon must have set up the illusion beforehand, using hidden XR equipment. Even so, how had it felt so real? How had she smelled the smoke of cooking fires on the wind? And what *was* that place? Reeling, she glanced at her brother, who had a wild and strained look in his eyes.

"Do you believe now, Jianyu?" the Archon said quietly.

When her brother found his voice, asking what the Archon needed them to do, his words no longer resonated with ingratiating concession, but with the power of conviction.

5

Andie and Cal were squeezed into the rear of the helicopter, flying low in a moonlit sky, sitting side by side on fold-down plastic chairs behind a cockpit with the faint odor of a well-used gym bag. The towers of Bologna had receded from view, and they had seen no signs of pursuit since escaping the basilica. *Thank God no bullets pierced the fuselage,* Andie thought.

The pilot sitting right in front of them was wearing a baseball cap and beige fatigues. Andie could tell he had a lanky build, and the hands gripping the controls were freckled and white.

"Will they follow us?" Cal asked, glancing nervously out the window.

"This baby has anti-radar curves and is coated with RAM." The pilot tapped a flat silver box, about the width of a Rubik's Cube, attached to the control panel. The box had a short antenna sticking out of each side. "And this little jammer is the best in show. If we stay low and out of sight lines, we should be fine."

Andie was surprised by the man's American accent, which reminded her of a Carolina twang. "What about the Bologna police?" she asked. "Wouldn't they notice a helicopter?"

"Zawadi pulled some strings."

"What kind of strings?"

"That's above my pay grade. But my guess would be metro police or aviation control."

"Don't tell me you don't know who she works for," Cal said, after exchanging a glance with Andie. "The Leap Year Society?"

"Don't know 'em," he said nervously. "I could take you back to Bologna if you like. Maybe someone there could answer your questions."

She shot Cal a warning look. "Of course not," she said. "Thank you for saving us."

"I won't say it's a habit when I'm working with Zawadi. But let's just say I earn my keep."

"Can you tell us where we're going?"

"Funny," the pilot said. "I was supposed to ask you that."

"What do you mean?"

"Zawadi gave me three instructions: keep you alive, don't ask questions—well, that's a standing order—and take you where you need to go."

Cal leaned in close to Andie and spoke as quietly as he could above the noise of the copter. "Your best guess is India, right?"

"Yeah, but that's obviously too broad, and I'm not even sure it's right."

"What do you need to decide?"

"The internet."

Cal raised his voice. "Any chance this bird has Wi-Fi?"

"Sure, but the jammer blocks it. And in my humble opinion, shutting the jammer down right now would be a very bad idea."

"No arguments here. The problem is, we need to get online before we decide where we're going. And it may take a while."

"How long?"

"Maybe hours, maybe a day or two."

Andie looked at Cal and mouthed, *I hope.*

After a moment, the pilot said, "There's someplace safe I can take you. Wi-Fi, food, and lodging. It's only a couple of hours away."

"Where is it?"

The pilot hesitated. "Sicily."

When Cal looked at Andie, she shrugged and said, "Let's go."

The pilot changed course, veering to the left and then straightening out. Now that they had a short-term destination, Andie decided to inspect the contents of the gray pouch Zawadi had flung at her before they parted ways. Inside they found two Canadian passports and driver's licenses with photos of Andie and Cal under false aliases: Kimberly Smith and David Hill.

As anonymous as names get.

"How the hell did she get those?" Cal said.

"Is it even worth asking?"

Zawadi had also left them two Visa debit cards bearing the same false names. A sticker with a four-digit PIN was attached to the back of each card. Andie wondered how much money was on them.

Finally she pulled out a phone charger and a metallic-blue cell phone with *QL* engraved on the back in silver font. Andie pushed a button on the side, and a touch screen appeared with four icons: a clock, a phone, a camera, and smaller *QL* letters inside the orbital swirl of electrons around an atom. When she touched the *QL* icon, an internet browser popped up.

"Quasar Labs, I presume?" Cal said, with a frown. "There's bound to be a tracker in there."

"Maybe we need one. Zawadi has saved our lives twice already."

"And for that I'm eternally grateful. It's not about her. We don't know the full story behind the fire at Quasar Labs. What if their technology is compromised and Zawadi doesn't know it?"

"They would have found her by now, if that was the case."

"Probably. I'm just . . ."

"Paranoid?"

"Yeah. I guess so. You aren't by now?"

"Sure, but since we have no other ID or way to get money or a secure browser, I don't see much choice, unless you're prepared to rob a bank or wash a lot of dishes."

Cal muttered something unintelligible and turned away from her, trying to get comfortable. He ended up with his knees folded awkwardly against the side of the copter. After a minute, he closed his eyes as Andie turned to stare out the opposite window, too wired to fall asleep. Soon the sporadic lights of the countryside fell away, and they flew south above the inky expanse of the Tyrrhenian Sea.

Just hours earlier, with Zawadi and Henrik by her side, she had felt a modicum of security for the first time in weeks. Now she and Cal were on their own again in a deadly and uncertain world, running for their lives, their only hope the enigmatic Star Phone puzzle she wasn't sure they could solve.

Fearing the onset of another vision, she took long, slow breaths to control her stress, letting her thoughts drift, hoping to catch some needed rest.

Breathe in, Andie. Breathe out.
Breathe in, breathe out.

Breathe in, breathe out.
Breathe in, breathe out.

The evening before Dr. Corwin was shot, Andie had taken one of her solo runs through the woods, the crickets providing a cadence to her steady exhalations.

Like the constellations of a starry sky, the trails behind her house were a familiar thing, comforting and peaceful. It was her fourth run that week, one of countless since she had arrived in Durham.

She doubted the tattoo artist she had met would call her back. He didn't look like the type of guy who made the effort to dig numbers out of his pockets and set up formal dates. It was now or never, baby. Or, if he did manage to call, it would be a short-lived fling.

Which was okay. She dug flings.

Something she didn't have to think about too hard.

Someone she didn't have to trust.

She hadn't always run alone. When she first moved to Durham, Andie had joined a running club to try to make friends. The family of one of the club's founders, Matt Stevenson, owned a farm just outside Hillsborough. A number of footpaths on his property connected to a nearby trail system. Every now and then, on a nice Saturday afternoon, the running club would take to the woods and end up at picnic tables in the backyard of Matt's bougie farmstead, drinking rosé and craft beer and talking college basketball and southern politics.

It wasn't Andie's scene. Not even close. But when she had started at Duke, she figured it was a new chapter in her life and she should make an effort to fit in. Not because she wanted the things these people had for their intrinsic value, but because it might be nice, for the first time in her life, to belong.

One day, Matt asked her if she wanted to go on a morning run. Just the two of them. She knew he was attracted to her, and he was definitely handsome: wavy blond hair, easy smile, broad shoulders. Again, not her type. But maybe he should be. Maybe it was time for her to conform. She had never tried that and didn't really want to.

Then again, she had never truly been happy.

So she decided to give it a shot, just this once.

With Matt.

After a jaunt through the woods, he led her on a new route that swung by a root cellar which had been in his family for two hundred years. Just past the cellar, beside a curve of the Eno River, was a glade covered in wildflowers. It was early October, the leaves starting to turn, the air dry and pleasant.

"It's pretty," Andie had said.

"Want to take a break?"

"You don't want to finish the route?"

He grinned. "Five miles isn't enough on a Sunday morning? C'mon, I'll show you the root cellar."

"I don't really like to stop . . . but sure, why not."

He slowed to a walk and removed the bar on the wooden door set into the hillock. After using a stick to clear away a cobweb, he led her inside the stone-and-mortar cellar. Wooden shelves stocked with cloudy mason jars lined the walls. A dozen barrels took up space in the rear, and a set of garden tools rusted away in a corner.

Just inside the door was a wine rack full of dusty bottles. On top of the rack, she noticed a pair of sparkling glasses and a picnic blanket.

"Why don't we skip the last mile and call it a day?" Matt said. "Grab a bottle of wine and cool off by the river."

"Wine before brunch?"

"After that run, I think we deserve it. You pushed me hard."

To Andie's left was a trash can. She glanced inside and saw, nestled among the discarded wine bottles, the edge of an empty box of condoms.

"Maybe I'll just finish the run," she said.

"Really?" he said, reaching out to touch her arm. Both of them reeked of hard-earned sweat.

"Really."

"I think we could have some fun together, Andie."

She took his hand off her arm. "Do you take all the girls in the running club here? Is this the girl-of-the-month club?"

His charming grin remained locked in place like a birthmark. "We both know you're not like the other girls."

"Is that right?"

"I can tell you like to have a good time."

"What the hell does that mean?"

"The way you dress, the way you talk, the way you run. I know you like to. . . " He smiled at her as he trailed off.

"Like to what, Matt?" she said sweetly.

His grin broadened as his arm slipped around her waist this time, then moved down to give her butt a gentle squeeze. "Like to fuck."

"You can tell, huh? It's that obvious?"

"From the first time I saw you."

She kneed him in the groin, doubling him over. "I like lots of things, Matt. Things like stargazing and watching foreign flicks and eating Thai food on my couch with a cold beer. Maybe you should have tried for one of those first, asshole."

He was holding his groin and gasping for breath. She swept out his legs for good measure, and he crashed to his back on the floor.

"Oh, and I like to kickbox too. Don't come near me again—and don't ever touch a girl like that without asking."

She quit the running club the next day.

From then on, she ran alone.

"Andie? Hey Andie, you with us?"

She realized Cal was gently shaking her.

"We're about to land," he continued. The sun had just breached the horizon. Directly ahead she saw a stone villa perched on a golden-brown hill dotted with shrubs.

"I guess I fell asleep."

The copter continued past the villa, touching down on a dusty landing pad abutting a vineyard. As the whirring blades came to rest, Andie looked out on the palms, coastal firs, and gnarled cork oaks that surrounded the property, shielding it from casual view.

The pilot had a craggy, deeply tanned face and short blond hair. He shouldered a duffel bag as he exited the copter and helped Andie and Cal climb down. Everyone shook out their limbs after the long ride, and Andie inhaled draughts of fresh air that smelled of sage and lavender.

"I never got your name," Andie said to the pilot.

"There's a reason for that. Call me Steve if you like."

"Who owns this place?" Cal asked.

The pilot shrugged. "Same answer as before, partner. Zawadi or her people. It's a pit stop for me, and let's just say people don't ask questions around these parts." He pointed to a guest cottage on their right, thirty yards from the main villa. "There's toiletries and spare clothes in the guesthouse. As far as I know, we can stay as long as we need."

Andie had seen no sign of activity. "Where is everyone?"

The pilot lifted his palms as he started walking toward the cottage. "You'll probably see a gardener or two, and that's about it. Don't ask me how it works."

Andie kept glancing at the shuttered villa as they made the short walk to the cottage, which was made of pebbled stone and smothered in ivy. Inside, the ceiling was so low Cal barely had clearance. Rustic furniture dotted a common room that opened straight into a kitchen and dining area.

"Bedrooms are down the hall," the pilot said. "You two can take the larger one on the right."

Cal held up a hand. "We'll need two of those."

"Then the second one's a couch."

"Sold."

"The place is always well stocked," the pilot continued, "so help yourself. I've never been told not to wander around . . . but if it were me, I'd stay put."

"What about the internet?" Andie asked.

"There's a desktop in the office at the end of the hall. That's the only connection you're allowed to use."

"Is it secure?"

"I'm told it is."

Andie and Cal exchanged a glance. Andie wondered if it was safer to try using the cellular device Zawadi had given them, but decided not to raise the issue. "Fair enough."

"I'll leave you to it then. I'm going to grab a beer and catch some shut-eye. We'll leave when you're ready. Just knock if you need me."

After the pilot disappeared into his bedroom, Andie yawned and said to Cal, "We should get started. But I'm taking a hot shower before I do anything."

"First on my leaderboard is caffeine. How about I scrounge around for some coffee and breakfast and meet you in thirty?"

She agreed with a weary nod. She didn't trust this place, and didn't plan to rest until they figured out where to go next. "Deal."

In the kitchen, Cal found an unopened canister of Illy coffee and a French press. The fridge was stocked with the basics. He pulled out some eggs, cheese, and peppers for an omelet.

Cooking was his happy place. As he puttered around making breakfast, taking his time to dice the peppers just right, he tried to live in the moment, something he was normally good at. But he couldn't stop thinking about the shitshow of the present, and the black hole of his future.

Cal considered himself an even-keeled guy. Lighthearted even. But ever since his article exposing the black-site facility belonging to PanSphere Communications had been discredited, and he was blackballed from respectable journalism, his life had felt like it was circling around a drain with no bottom.

And that was *before* the Ascendants tried to kidnap him in LA, and he went on the run with Andie.

He tried to stave off his depression with the aroma of ground coffee and the simple pleasure of farm-fresh eggs and grated cheese, but his thoughts kept spiraling. Before he fled LA, he was living month to month, eking out a living by scrounging for bottom-feeder articles, writing crap for pennies for whomever would pay. He never slacked in his research. His journalistic integrity would never allow that. But it didn't take much work to rewrite an Associated Press report for some third-rate network or to repurpose some old articles for the conspiracy theory of the day.

Losing his job had cost him his convertible, his girlfriend, and his nosebleed Clippers tickets. His credit cards were maxed. No more little pleasures in life. A beer or two after work at the bar had turned into a six-pack at home, sometimes a twelve-pack. Leon's dog food got cheaper and cheaper.

And by now, he would have missed the payment on his house for the third time that year. He was going to lose it, though he was upside down on the mortgage anyway. His 401(k)—what he hadn't pulled out—had fewer zeros than an NBA score.

Worst of all was the knowledge that his career was ruined. Cal lived for being an investigative reporter. He loved everything about it: the coffee-fueled days and nights during a story, the beauty and economy and power of the written word, the clever disguises and the research trips and the fast-talking seat-of-his-pants interviews with a source. Most of all, though he would never admit to it on a first date, he loved pursuing justice and righting wrongs through the dogged pursuit of truth, imposing order on a chaotic world that had broken both his parents in different ways, and which he longed to make sense of.

Losing his livelihood did something terrible to a man, stripped him of dignity and self-confidence in a way that nothing else could. He had learned that from watching his dad implode when the airline went bankrupt. Cal had vowed never to follow in his footsteps—and now the same thing was happening to him.

But now, for the first time in years, he had a spark of hope. His mood began to lift as he realized he would choose that spark—terrifying and life-threatening as tracking the Ascendants had been so far—over a slow death in LA.

All he had to do was finish the story. He knew from breaking into Elias Holt's house and seeing his own background file on a laptop that Aegis International and the Ascendants had targeted him because of his work on PanSphere. These were the bastards who had destroyed his life.

Now he just had to prove it.

As he cooked, he found a pen and a napkin and wrote down the principal facts and resolutions, preparing for the article or even the book that would clear the record and become the ticket back to his former life. He always started a story like this, outlining the essentials in his head, and often in the kitchen. Every reporter had a different method. He called his "Cal Sous Vide." During a big story, he worked in a vacuum, ignoring everything else until the temperature was right, when he would send his fingers flying across the keyboard.

What he knew

- PanSphere Communications owned the black-site lab in Bolivia that Cal had uncovered.
- Elias Holt's company, Aegis International, provided online security for the Ascendants.

- Aegis/the Ascendants had a huge file on Cal that started the day he published the exposé on PanSphere.
- The Ascendants almost certainly orchestrated the disappearance of Cal's source, discredited his article, and wrecked his career.
- Although the Ascendants lived in the shadows, they wanted the Star Phone and the Enneagon bad enough to risk exposure.

Objectives
- Find proof to verify his story on PanSphere
- Go public with that proof, and with as much corroborating info on the Ascendants (and the LYS if needed) as he could find: names, dates, government and business connections, illegal activities, etc.

The best way forward
- Follow the money trail behind PanSphere, Aegis, and Quasar Labs.
- See where the Star Phone puzzle led.

The rest of it, this business about the Fold and the Enneagon and the ultimate aims of the Ascendants, the true nature of the LYS, and how deep this conspiracy reached—all that was gravy. If he tried to wrap his head around the enormity of it, the historical mysteries and the wild technology, his head just started to hurt.

He had learned, as a reporter, to keep it simple.

To follow the main thread of the story like a starving raccoon digging for a meal.

So while he had a feeling that everything he and Andie were pursuing was connected, he needed to stay laser-focused on his primary goal: finding evidence that would clear his name.

It turned out that the biggest, most important assignment of his career was the story of his own life.

6

After her shower, Andie slid her jeans back on and changed into a white V-neck T-shirt she found in the bedroom. It was hard to pull herself away from the comfortable four-poster bed, but she couldn't let herself sleep yet.

By the time she made it to the wood-paneled office with a view of the vineyard, Cal had set out two mugs of coffee, orange juice, and an omelet.

"Best I can do on short notice," he said.

She bit into the omelet and realized how hungry she was. "It's a lifesaver. And delicious."

"You know," Cal said between bites, "I hate to say this, but if the Archon did hypnotize me in some way, there's a good possibility I told them about the next clue on the Star Phone."

"I know," Andie said. "I've thought about that already."

"Which means that, unless we figure out the clue first, the Ascendants might be waiting for us at the next destination."

After that sobering thought, they ate and drank in silence, hurrying through the meal. Once the caffeine had perked her up, Andie pushed the plate aside and turned on the desktop computer, a sleek silver model with no visible manufacturer.

That figures.

Andie set the Star Phone on the desk beside the computer. She pressed the power strip on the bottom of the device to bring up the current image: a blue zero formed by two lines intertwined in a twisting spiral pattern, emulating a classic representation of a double helix.

Nested inside the open space in the center of the zero was another symbol outlined in crimson: the number 3 with a looped tail, set beneath a curved horn or claw lying on its side and cradling what could be a square or a hollow box.

"So remind this befuddled old-timer," Cal said, "what we've got so far. This is the third step of the Star Phone puzzle since you started, right? And you think there are nine in total? With the Enneagon waiting as the prize?"

"Yeah, at least according to Dr. Corwin's journal. The first step, the bust of Democritus, was in the Victoria & Albert Museum in London. The second, as you know, was a puzzle based around the Library of Alexandria."

"Wait—there was more to Egypt than that. The library, the catacombs, that weird old house."

"Yes, but all the markers in Alexandria except the first were temporary, dependent on aiming the Star Phone directly at them. Clues along the way. We've only had two new alphanumeric codes that, when entered, display a lasting image on the Star Phone. I'm guessing those permanent markers are the 'steps' the journal refers to."

"Okay, I get all that," Cal said, "but *why* did your mentor set this whole thing up?"

"That I don't know. In the journal, there was a staircase with nine steps, along with a bunch of symbols I didn't understand beside the stairs. On the first step were two words: 'Democritus' and 'Arche.' At the top of the nine steps, he wrote 'Enneagon.' Elsewhere, it was clear the Enneagon was the same weird nine-sided device he had sketched throughout the journal."

"Nine steps, nine sides to the device . . . and 'Arche'? What does that mean?"

"The beginning."

Cal put a hand to his head. "The beginning of *what*?"

"I don't really care at this point. I just know the Ascendants want it, and I have to find it first."

Cal looked down at the strange pictogram displayed on the Star Phone. "There's a clear theme of ancient knowledge. You said the zero reminded you of some genius Indian guy?"

"Aryabhata. My guess was he lived in the fifth or sixth century, but let me check right now." She pulled up the browser to confirm the dates. "Yep, his birth date is commonly accepted as 476 AD. The puzzle clues seem to be moving forward in time."

"And what did he do again?" Cal said.

"He was an astronomer and mathematician who wrote the *Aryabhatiya*—one of the classic works of ancient mathematics—when he was only twenty-three."

"Wait—he named his opus after himself?"

"Maybe it was the custom at the time. I don't know. Anyway, he made a whole host of contributions, but he's most famous for his work with the zero. He didn't exactly come up with the concept—Indian philosophers had been pondering the idea for centuries—but Aryabhata developed a counting system that made it common parlance in mathematics."

"Didn't you say the Mayans were sniffing around the same concepts?" Cal asked.

"Definitely. The Babylonians too. Both cultures understood the concept of nothing, or the absence of a measurable quantity, but they used it as a placeholder in counting systems, rather than as an actual number. I know it seems an odd thing to have to invent, but the numerical zero is the anchor for the modern calculations used in physics and digital technologies."

"I suppose it's fairly important to the binary system. Right around, oh, fifty percent."

"The other reason I was drawn to India," she said, "was the squiggly symbol in crimson. Let's just do a quick search here, for the hell of it—"

She typed "common Sanskrit symbols"' into the search bar. The three with the looped tail was the very first thing that popped up.

"That was easy," Cal said.

She read the caption. "The om symbol. Interesting. I didn't know that."

"Om? As in, chanting monks and yoga class? Ohmmm?"

"That's the one." She followed the link, summarizing as she read. "A Sanskrit syllable spoken as a mantra, om has been in circulation for thousands of years . . . considered the primordial sound . . . The exact meaning is uncertain, but most believe it symbolizes the essence of consciousness and reality . . . infinite language, infinite knowledge . . . that which is mysterious and inexhaustible."

"It's good they didn't try to do too much with it. Aimed nice and low."

"The om is all over Eastern religion: Jainism, Buddhism, Sikhism, Hinduism. I think it's clear the symbol is pointing us toward India. But where? It's an enormous country."

"The double helix has to be the key to how they all fit together," Cal said. "Is it a code, a formula, what?"

Andie slowly shook her head, and they spent the rest of the morning trying to answer that question. She started by researching Aryabhata himself, and discovered his contributions were truly vast for the time period. He was the first to calculate pi to four decimal points, deduced that the Earth rotates daily on its axis, and proclaimed that eclipses are caused not by a demon named Rahu but by shadows of the Earth and moon.

She moved on to the history of the zero and the om symbol, trying to find a common thread.

Two hours later, they still had no good leads tying everything together.

"It's got to be the double helix," she muttered to herself. "It's far more modern than the others. And the om symbol is literally everywhere."

She already knew the double-helix structure, identified in the 1950s, was present in the DNA of all known organisms, and held the key to life on Earth. By 2003, scientists had mapped the human genome, which contained over three billion base pairs—the largest collaborative biological venture in history. The Human Genome Project revealed that human beings were all 99.9 percent alike, and that our physical differences reflect environmental factors in the gene code, rather than core biology. It drove a stake into the heart of misguided race theories.

She and Cal also learned that outer space was not the sole province of vast distances: it shocked Andie to discover that unraveling the DNA of every cell spooled inside a single human being would stretch for more than ten billion miles, twice the distance of Pluto from the sun.

Exposing the secrets of DNA had led to a host of advancements, including the sort of genetic engineering that allowed scientists to play God. The possibilities were limitless. Exhilarating. Terrifying.

But those were questions for another day. Nothing they had found so far helped them advance the Star Phone puzzle.

"Break time," Cal said, cracking his knuckles. "I need a coffee refuel."

Andie started to disagree, then gave in. She could use some fresh air, and she knew from experience that taking a break from a thorny problem, such as getting a good night's sleep, gave the brain's neurons a chance to assimilate information and could lead to unexpected connections.

There was no sign of the pilot as they walked through the house. Cal headed for the coffee supplies while Andie stepped through a set of French doors onto a brick patio overlooking a hillside that sloped down to the sea. A grapevine-covered trellis provided relief from the bright sun. Here and there a scraggly wildflower had squeezed between the seams of the handlaid bricks.

Staring at the azure water in the distance caused Andie to reflect on her mother. Some of Andie's fondest childhood memories had occurred on weekend trips to the beach. Invariably, as soon as they walked onto the sand at Cape May, her father had grumbled about the humid weather before retiring to a lounge chair under an umbrella with a novel and a cold beer. Her long-limbed mother, raised on a farm in landlocked central Ohio, would kick off her designer sandals and stay in the water for hours with Andie, laughing and frolicking, bodysurfing the waves. Andie remembered her staring longingly at the historic pastel homes on the other side of the sea oats, which had looked as grandiose as a storybook palace.

She had not succumbed to these memories in years, but seeing her mother in Venice had unleashed a floodgate of emotion and remembrances Andie couldn't seem to hold back.

What happened after you left, Mom?

Where did you go?

What did they do to you?

"The coffee's black, bold, and bad to the bone," Cal said as he walked onto the patio and handed her a porcelain mug. "Reminds me of our friend and savior."

"Zawadi's fairly badass," Andie admitted.

"I have a feeling she knows more about the Leap Year Society than she's telling us, but I don't see a high probability of forcing the information out of her." He took a sip of coffee. "That reminds me: there's something I've been meaning to bring up about Dr. Corwin."

"What about him?"

"I know you think very highly of him," Cal said carefully, "but he did get you into all of this."

She bristled. "Actually, he tried to keep me out of it. He told me to take the message to Dr. Friedman and stop right there. If I hadn't gone looking in Dr. Corwin's office . . ."

"Andie," Cal said with a pointed look.

She hesitated, then looked away. Though it was true Dr. Corwin had taken steps not to involve her, he had still chosen to deliver the message, knowing there was some risk involved.

A risk that had manifested in the form of Omer and a gun.

"I can accept that he made a hard choice," she said. "Whatever the Enneagon is, Dr. Corwin believed that protecting it was more important than ensuring there was zero danger to me. He did his best, and I can't fault him for that."

"I can," Cal said quietly. "He's doing the same thing as the Ascendants. Choosing his agenda over someone else's."

"His agenda? Ensuring a device that could change the world or lead to a superweapon stays out of the Ascendants' hands? Some things are worth fighting for, Cal."

"At the cost of someone you love? We'll have to agree to disagree on that one."

"I suppose we will."

She thought Cal was being naïve, stubborn, and wrong-headed. Sometimes the ends *did* justify the means. Of course they did.

Didn't they?

Just as important to Andie was that she held no one—Dr. Corwin included—to a perfect standard. That was asking for disappointment. Everyone had flaws. She felt as if she had far more than most, so who was she to judge?

If Dr. Corwin's Achilles' heel was an overactive sense of global justice, then she could live with that.

"I just want to make sure you're seeing clearly," he said. "There're two lives at stake here, you know."

"Fair enough. We should be honest with each other."

Cal took another sip and cradled the cup between his palms. "Have you made any progress?"

"It's so frustrating. I can't figure out how the double helix fits in. What does the structure of a DNA molecule have to do with two concepts developed far earlier in time, and halfway across the world? I feel like we need to consult a biologist."

"I'm not sure we do. This smacks of symbology to me rather than science."

"And you're basing that opinion on what, exactly?"

He shrugged. "I've done enough research on the codes and methods of communication of secret societies to have a feel for these things."

She put a hand to her temple. "Yeah, except those are usually bogus and amateurish. The Leap Year Society is real and powerful, and Dr. Corwin is one of the world's most respected physicists."

"Actually, most secret societies are not bogus *or* amateurish," Cal said. "I'm not talking about the modern Freemasons or some group of rich douchebags that brings underage girls to mansions. Throughout history, some of the world's wealthiest and most influential scientists, philosophers, politicians, artists, physicians—you name it—have gathered in secret for a variety of reasons. Sometimes, sure, it was to escape domestic life and get their naughty on. But often it was to advance the spread of knowledge that the ruling authority at the time—church or state—didn't approve of. It's no different today. They're out there, both good and bad. They're in the corridors of power and the boardrooms of global corporations. On private billionaire islands and yachts in the middle of the Pacific. Lurking in the deep web and hidden in plain sight."

"I'm not a true believer like you are," Andie said, "and I never will be. But I have to admit at least one of them exists."

"The LYS not only exists, but I have a feeling it might be the granddaddy of them all. But first things first." He leaned over the Star Phone to study the image. "So far the gist of the puzzle seems to be illumination of lost, hidden or rarely known historical knowledge from a variety of cultures. I don't think we're looking for some esoteric biological clue we need a PhD to unravel—I think we're looking for a connection among these three concepts that's just beneath the surface."

"Such as?"

"You're the genius, not me."

"I'm not a genius, Cal. I know some, but I'm not one."

"Compared to me, you are. I couldn't get through college calculus. Anyway, let's do some searching and keep the big picture in mind."

Andie pressed her lips together. "Okay. And it's a valid point."

She returned to the computer and, with Cal looking over her

shoulder, veered away from a deep dive into scientific research to focus on more subjective disciplines. Philosophy. Semiotics. Numerology.

"Check this out," she said after an hour of searching. "The om symbol is often associated with the number *three*. Birth and life and death. Body, soul, and spirit. The earth, the heavens, and the underworld. The Holy Trinity. Think about the image on the Star Phone: Zero is a number. Three is a number. But that still leaves the double helix as the odd one out.

Cal laced his fingers behind his head. "You're reaching, and I'm not a fan of numerology. With a little imagination, you can find hidden numbers in anything and everything."

"Great. I've gone left of the conspiracy theorist. But, yeah, it doesn't feel right to me either."

She picked up the Star Phone and paced the room. An om within a zero within a strand of DNA. Moving inside to out, the symbols progressed from ancient to modern times.

What if that was a clue in itself?

She set the device down and returned to the computer.

"What is it?" Cal asked.

She held up a finger and started scouring the web for mentions of a double helix or DNA in India. Soon after, she sucked in a breath and thrust her palms to the desk. Cal hurried to her side, giving her a whiff of coffee breath. On the screen in front of her, Andie was looking at a globe on the front page of an organization called the Kolkata Science Institute.

The globe was the emblem of the institute, and in the center of the gold-and-blue sphere, placed side by side, were three distinct images.

A zero, an om symbol, and a double helix.

Cal whooped. "Three-pointer and the foul!"

"Listen to this description: 'The KSI is dedicated to integrated research that fosters communication and breaks down barriers among traditional disciplines.'"

"Exactly the kind of thing we're looking for," Cal said. "Plus the

India angle. It's got to be it."

Just to be sure, before they flew halfway around the world, she kept researching the same angle, broadening her search to countries and institutes on six continents.

Nowhere else did the symbols converge.

Convinced they had found the trail again, Andie ran a hand through her hair and pushed to her feet. They had no time to spare. When she entered the hall, she spotted the pilot puttering around in the kitchen.

"You look like something's on your mind," he said.

"How soon can we leave?"

"Maybe you could tell me where we're going?"

"Kolkata. Can you get us there?"

"That's out of my range, and goes through way too much dangerous political territory to risk an unauthorized flight. But I can take you to someone with a plane that won't be questioned."

"When?"

The pilot held up a baguette with prosciutto and lettuce poking out from the sides. "Can I at least finish my sandwich?"

Cartagena, Colombia
Summer 1970

Dr. Corwin whistled a tune from the recently released *Let It Be*—could the album really be the end of the Beatles?—as he stepped out of a taxi in the center of the Ciudad Amurallada, the walled Old City of Cartagena. His hotel, the Casa San Márquez, was located close to the residence of Alvaro Muñoz, who according to Society researchers was the only curandero-psychiatrist in all of northern South America.

Coming to Colombia was risky. Outside of Bogotá, the Society did not have a safe house in the country. Though tourism in Cartagena was increasing, it was still a backwater, plus a key transit point in the exploding demand for cocaine. Not to mention the guerrilla groups staging violent uprisings in rural parts of the country, and which at times spread to the cities.

In short, Dr. Corwin would be on his own in a tumultuous foreign land where the rule of law was questionable at best.

His main ally was speed. After he'd struggled back to his room at the Grove Park Inn, a nasty purple bruise blossoming on his neck from Hans's attack in the underground spa, Dr. Corwin made a few calls and grabbed his bag, jumped in his convertible, and drove straight to the local airport. He snuck in a few hours of sleep on a hard bench, took the earliest flight to Atlanta, and bought a ticket to Cartagena connecting through Miami. By the time he landed in Colombia and made a call from an airport telephone, he had verified the residence of the curandero.

The race to find Ettore Majorana was on.

Though Dr. Corwin had never visited the Caribbean port before, so far it was just as he had pictured it: bougainvillea draped like living flames over stone walls and wooden balconies; horse-drawn carriages still clacking down the cobblestones; elegant streetlamps and Spanish colonial buildings; tantalizing aromas spilling out of pushcarts with vendors hawking empanadas and *patacones con queso*.

As he approached the whitewashed facade of the Casa San Márquez, a hulking young man with a complexion as dark as his, wearing dirty trousers and sandals that looked chewed by an alligator, leaped off a stoop and hustled to help with his bag. Instead of shouting at the opportunistic porter to go away, Dr. Corwin understood he was only trying to make a buck—probably to feed his family—and let him carry his bag inside.

The hotel staff gave the porter withering looks as his dusty sandals slapped on the fancy hardwood floor, but Dr. Corwin tipped him a handsome sum and opened the door for him. With a broad smile that displayed a rotten front tooth, the man shook Dr. Corwin's hand so hard he thought his bones might crack, and thanked him for the tip.

In Dr. Corwin's practiced opinion, the rooms at the Casa San Márquez were of very high quality and laughably inexpensive. Wishing he could pour himself a Scotch, take a dip in the pool, and catch up on sleep beneath a cabana, he instead washed his face and hands in cold water, changed into a fresh pair of trousers and a breezy guayabera, grabbed his walking cane, donned his blue trilby, and headed downstairs. With any luck, he could meet with the curandero and find the physicist named X before sundown.

His luck ran out before he left the hotel.

On his way through the main lounge, which boasted a stunning parquet floor and rattan furniture, he saw a familiar square-jawed Teutonic face leaving reception and approaching the elevator, holding a room key and a butterscotch vinyl suitcase.

In the short time allotted, the Society researchers had uncovered no record of a Hans Kraus or Hans Riess that fit the description Dr. Corwin had provided. As for Stefan Kraus, no one knew for sure what had happened to the infamous leader of the Ascendants. Most thought he had died. There were rumors of a succession war, and the rise of a mysterious figure called the Archon, but the Society's spies were not high enough within the organization to know for sure. The opaqueness of their enemy—to those who prized opaqueness—was a source of embarrassment and frustration.

Hans had noticed him as well. The German smirked as Dr. Corwin walked right up to him. "It appears," Hans said, "that your theory of chance encounters is being put to the test."

"The tropics can be unkind to someone with such fair skin," Dr. Corwin replied. "It might be healthier to stay inside."

"Being indoors poses its own risks." He drew a finger lazily across his clean-shaven neck. "As you can well attest."

Dr. Corwin took a step closer and gripped his cane. "I wouldn't boast of such a thing."

"I don't boast. I act, and I succeed. That is the difference between us, *ja*? Something you'll learn soon enough."

Dr. Corwin knew he was speaking not just of the two of them, but of the philosophies of their rival organizations. As the two men stood toe to toe, neither budging an inch, both maintained the forced smiles slapped on their faces so as not to alarm any onlookers.

Finally Dr. Corwin tipped his hat and backed away. "Good luck to you."

"And you."

"A pity you have to search for something your father lost so many years ago."

Hans stood very still, a flush of anger blossoming on his cheeks.

Satisfied he had hit a nerve, and that his guess as to Hans's lineage was correct, Dr. Corwin turned and whistled as he sauntered out of the hotel. As soon as he hit the street, his demeanor hardened, and he prepared to rush to the curandero's house. If Hans showed up first, or interrupted the conversation, then he would just have to improvise.

The safe thing would be to scurry back to his room and request reinforcements, or at least the delivery of a firearm.

But Dr. Corwin had not been tasked with playing it safe. He had been tasked with finding Ettore Majorana and his lost research before the Ascendants.

"Hey, boss," the porter on the stoop across the street shouted in broken English. "Have a good day!"

Dr. Corwin hesitated, then walked over to him. "What's your name?" he asked in Spanish, a language he had learned over the years and perfected on a research sabbatical in Granada.

"Carlos. You speak Spanish?"

"*Si*, and my name is James Corwin. I appreciated your help earlier. Say, did you see a blond man in a white linen suit enter the hotel just a few minutes ago?"

Carlos spat. "That son of a bitch told me to get a job and stop bothering people. As if he knows anything about me or this city."

Dr. Corwin smiled to himself. "I wonder, my friend, if you'd be open to a little work for me today."

Carlos jumped up from the stoop. "*Si, primo.* What do you have in mind?"

"Do you have any friends nearby looking for work?" Dr. Corwin said casually, then lowered his voice. "Maybe a few who look as handy with their fists as you do?"

The porter grinned and cracked his knuckles.

With Hans close on his heels, Dr. Corwin decided to walk rather than wait for a taxi. According to the map of the Old City in his pocket, if he cut through an alley off the square with the imposing stone church looming at the end of the street, the curandero's house was only three blocks away. He would make better time on foot.

Though his Society sources had told him the Casa San Márquez was the closest hotel, he passed two others on the way. Granted, they looked quite new, and researching Cartagena from afar was a difficult proposition. But it made him suspicious of his sources. After talking to Waylan Taylor, Hans had surely gathered the name and location of the curandero. Had Hans used the same logic and booked a room in the same hotel—or had someone told him where Dr. Corwin was staying?

The Old Town was a traveler's smorgasbord of grand promenades and cobbled alleys, pastel colonial buildings, Baroque churches, and sixteenth-century mansions with trim work that looked fashioned by Renaissance masters. Lush courtyards dripping with secrets lurked behind crumbling stone walls, saturated with the rich aroma of gardenia and passion fruit vines. The proud buildings conjured up images of men on horseback with swords at their hips, courting women in bright dresses leaning over their balconies. It was a place where the past felt more alive than the present.

A place built on fever dreams of gold and adventure, wealth and beauty, slavery and genocide.

Dr. Corwin let his subconscious absorb the city as he canvassed his surroundings, watching for signs of the enemy, as a barrage of thoughts and concerns crowded his mind. He was ashamed he had lost the file on Ettore in Asheville, but it was not a disaster. He had absorbed the information he needed on the drive down from New York, and the Ascendants already had as much—or more—intelligence on the Italian physicist.

The more he considered the substance of Ettore's theories, the more intrigued he became. While the foundation of quantum theory had been laid fifty years ago, the standard model of particle interaction was a mess. No one was close to marrying macro and micro physics. Ettore's model of an infinite tower was so elegant and simple, and it predated the newly developed string theory by decades.

The Italian's original calculations had not worked out . . . but what if there was something to it?

Despite Ettore's obscurity, it was undisputed that he was a genius on the level of the very best minds in history. If he was truly alive after all this time, and had worked on perfecting his theories and developing new ones, and the research was still out there somewhere...

It was an incredibly tantalizing proposition. Even a small insight into a universal law of physics could change the world.

No one accosted Dr. Corwin as he hustled down a cobblestone street of contiguous three-story residences, built crooked to maximize shade and shorten a marauding invader's line of fire. The plaster-covered stone facades were painted with warm shades of lavender, mustard, and teal. Tropical foliage overflowed from baskets and pots on the balconies, spilling through the balustrades and climbing the walls to perfume the air.

It was late afternoon. Sweat poured down his back from the heat of the walk. According to the researchers, Alvaro Muñoz had retired some years ago. Before leaving the airport, Dr. Corwin had called the psychiatrist himself to arrange a meeting. The request had been an honest one: Dr. Corwin was a physicist who had talked to Waylan Taylor and was looking to pick the former curandero's brain on a few matters, given his unique perspective.

As Dr. Corwin knocked on a lime-green door set within a recessed archway, a pushcart vendor passed by, bell tinkling, hawking mango juice and ceviche served with fried plantains. Dr. Corwin salivated at the prospect. He had not had time to eat and was an hour early for the meeting. Worried that Hans would appear at any moment, Dr. Corwin was relieved beyond measure when a wiry bald man fitting Alvaro's description opened the door.

"*Si?*" the man asked. His ocher skin tone and teardrop eyes spoke to an indigenous heritage.

Dr. Corwin extended a hand and introduced himself in Spanish. "I apologize for the early arrival. I found myself in the neighborhood and thought I'd try you."

Alvaro had a mischievous twinkle in his eye that Dr. Corwin wasn't sure how to judge. "But of course. Please come in. Your Spanish is quite excellent, by the way."

The curandero-psychiatrist ushered him through a narrow house cluttered with books, papers, Native American art, and bric-a-brac from around South America. French doors off the dining room led to a patio enclosed by palms and flowering shrubs. A parrot chattered from a freestanding birdcage, and the creak of a hammock could be heard from a neighboring property.

"I don't mind the unexpected arrival," Alvaro said, "but you'll have to give me a moment to prepare the refreshments."

"Oh, please don't go to the trouble—"

"Tsk, tsk. This is Colombia. Hospitality is not optional."

As the old man shuffled inside, Dr. Corwin watched in frustration, knowing Hans wouldn't be far behind. To his left, a banana tree shaded two chairs and a small wooden table. Dr. Corwin took a seat and swatted at mosquitoes until Alvaro returned with a tray of coffee and pastries.

Dr. Corwin took a sip of the strong, delicious coffee. "Thank you."

"But of course. Is the patio too warm?"

"I'm Jamaican. It feels nice."

"Ah, a fellow *caribeño*! You understand me then."

Since time was of the essence, Dr. Corwin laid it all out as quickly and politely as he could: the conversation with Waylan Taylor, his search for Ettore Majorana, and his desire to meet with the elusive source called X, who claimed to have known the Italian physicist. As he spoke, Alvaro interjected here or there, but mostly he listened with the calm attentiveness of an experienced psychiatrist. Dr. Corwin found his background as a curandero fascinating, and wished they had time for a longer discussion.

A sudden noise from the street—shouting, followed by the sound of broken glass—interrupted them. Dr. Corwin rose, suspecting what had occurred, but Alvaro did not look alarmed. "I fear Cartagena is not as flawless as it appears on the surface," he said.

Dr. Corwin tensed, waiting for the sound of someone breaking through the door, but the street quieted, replaced by the languorous harmonies of the city: birdsong, the hum of insects, and the occasional cry of a street vendor. He leaned forward in his seat. "I was hoping you could pass on this physicist's name and where to find him. I'd be happy to meet him anywhere he likes, under any condition."

Alvaro refilled his coffee. "I'm happy to provide a name," he said, "but I'm afraid your other request is quite impossible."

"Is it a matter of money? I'm willing to pay a handsome sum for a moment of his time."

Alvaro chuckled. "It isn't money, and the name is Nataja Tromereo."

Despite the overwhelming percentage of male physicists, Dr. Corwin felt ashamed by his presumption. But at least he had a name! "Ah. Forgive me. The name—do I have it right?" He spelled it for Alvaro, earning a nod of approval. "It's unfamiliar," he mused. "Perhaps a Slav who married a Colombian?"

"I'm unsure, but that sounds reasonable."

"And my other request?" Dr. Corwin pressed as Alvaro reached for a pastry. Fearing the worst, he prepared for the news that Nataja was deceased, and the trail lost forever.

"I fear Waylan might have given you the wrong impression. I did not meet with Señora Tromereo recently, but many years ago, when she came to Cartagena on a short visit. I have no idea where she is now, and if she once told me where she was from, I've long forgotten. We met at the restaurant of her hotel—I believe it was the Los Claustros—and talked for several hours. That was the extent of our acquaintance."

"How many years ago was this?"

Alvaro's face scrunched as he thought. "Perhaps thirty?"

"Thirty!" Dr. Corwin said in dismay, leaning back in his chair. He pressed a hand to his temple, feeling ill at the setback. Anything could have happened in the last thirty years. Ettore could easily be dead. He blew out a breath, mollifying himself with the consideration that, even if Ettore had passed, his research might be tucked away in a trunk in some forgotten attic, waiting to change the world. "Forgive me. I assumed the meeting was more recent."

"May I ask why finding Ettore Majorana is so important to you?"

"Ettore disappeared at a young age, and left behind so little of his work. If he is still alive, then finding him could be an incredible boon to the scientific community."

"You assume, of course, that he wishes to be found," Alvaro said calmly. "Is it not more reasonable to assume that a man who has withdrawn from society for over three decades might, in fact, not desire such a thing?"

Dr. Corwin gave a tight smile. "It's very reasonable. But we don't know the circumstances. Maybe he needs protection from someone, or is mentally ill."

Alvaro's frown conveyed his thoughts on that line of reasoning.

And perhaps, Dr. Corwin thought, *a man such as Ettore Majorana should not be the one to choose whether the world needs his theorems. Perhaps it is an act of extreme selfishness to keep one's intellect to oneself, at the expense of human progress.*

"In any event," Dr. Corwin said, after failing to learn anything else useful, "I'd love to speak to anyone who once knew Ettore, and who might be able to shed light on the mystery." Dr. Corwin gripped his cane as he stood to leave, all too aware of how long the visit had taken. "If there are other details about Ms. Tromereo you can recall—a city or a name she mentioned, where she worked or what university she attended—please get in touch. I'll be at the Casa San Márquez for the next few days. It could be very helpful."

Alvaro rose with him. "I'll see you out."

"Thank you for your time. I'm sorry to cut the discussion short."

The mischievous gleam was brighter than ever. "You mentioned on the phone you were seeking my opinion. Was Ettore your sole concern, or was there something else?"

Dr. Corwin hesitated, unable to help himself. "Waylan mentioned experiments concerning the existence of the soul. I'm curious as to your thoughts on the matter."

"I am often asked this question. Both Dr. Taylor and Ms. Tromereo seemed quite preoccupied by it. Are you seeking my opinion as a curandero or as a psychiatrist?"

Dr. Corwin shrugged. "As a man."

"Whose closest companion is a parrot who repeats his thoughts back to him? Are you sure this is what you desire?" Alvaro laughed and slapped a knee. "I will give you all three. As a psychiatrist for many decades, while I've witnessed quite a number of extraordinary phenomena, I would posit the left half of the human brain—the side that generates our sense of self-awareness, or the ego—is a self-limiting barrier to higher knowledge. Neuroscience will never answer the question of the soul. Nor should it try. As a curandero, I would tell you that my forebears have known since time immemorial that the seat of the soul and the world of dreams exist in a different place than the conscious world—and that all are intertwined in ways we do not understand. And as a man, I would urge you to look, really look, into the eyes of another human being, and decide this question for yourself."

Dr. Corwin absorbed the answer as he reached for the door. "Thank you," he murmured. "I wish we had more time to talk."

"I'm retired and have plenty of coffee. You may stop by anytime."

A broken bottle on the street was the only sign of a disturbance in front of Alvaro's house. Dr. Corwin breathed a sigh of relief that Hans was not waiting for him. On the walk back to the hotel, as the onset of dusk brought swarms of mosquitoes as well as a modicum of relief from the stifling heat, the hypnotic pulse of salsa began to bubble out of bars and cafés. More people filled the street, and he caught someone slipping out of an alley to emerge right behind him. He wheeled and raised his cane, only to see the opportunistic porter from the hotel.

"Hey, boss, we took care of that business."

Dr. Corwin noticed the skin on the knuckles on the porter's right hand was torn and raw. "I appreciate that."

"It was our pleasure," Carlos said with a smirk. "Anything else you need today?"

After holding up a stack of bills that made the porter's eyes pop, Dr. Corwin said, "I need you to stay out of sight for a week. Don't go anywhere near that hotel."

"Hey, primo, he put up a good fight, but I'm not scared of that gringo."

"Out of sight, Carlos. That's my request. He's very dangerous."

The porter shrugged, and Dr. Corwin handed him the money.

Dr. Corwin spent the remainder of the day in the main branch of the local library, which stayed open surprisingly late, looking for mention of a physicist named Nataja Tromereo in books, periodicals, and microfiche. He even called his best friend, Dr. Philip Rickman, a fellow physicist and LYS inductee, to help search university rosters and scientific journals.

Still no mention of the name.

Though disappointed, Dr. Corwin understood the search could take a few days. If the information was accurate, and Ms. Tromereo was truly a scientist, there should be a record of her somewhere.

Or had the old curandero lied for some reason?

Late that evening, with no sign of Hans, Dr. Corwin opted to stay at the hotel for dinner. *Best to keep my enemies where I can see them.*

As he replayed the conversation with Alvaro in his mind, he caught a leggy brunette at the bar glancing his way. She was about his age and a real fox, with olive skin and toned calves and long brown hair parted in the middle.

Long brown hair that looked very familiar.

He stared boldly back at her. A woman alone at a bar was unusual in Cartagena, and despite how natural she looked enjoying a glass of red wine in her silver gown, she also had an adventurous air about her, as if she could just as easily be traipsing through the jungle holding a rifle.

Before she looked away, something seemed to pass between them, a frisson of mutual attraction that seemed genuine—despite his suspicion of her true allegiance.

He had never had a problem attracting the opposite sex. While he considered himself a handsome enough chap in a suit, his secret weapons were flair and the art of conversation. Still: a woman this beautiful, who just happened to be alone at the bar, and just happened to let him catch her looking?

After dinner, he sidled up to the mahogany bar and ordered a drink. A thick-bladed ceiling fan circulated the rich smoke from a dozen cigars, scenting the air with spice and vanilla. The bartender finished a line of mojitos, crushing the mint leaves and lime juice with a mortar and pestle, then poured a twenty-year Dictador, two fingers neat, into a cut-glass tumbler. Dr. Corwin picked it up, summoned a rakish grin, and laid a hand on the back of a stool beside the woman. "Do you mind?" he asked in English.

She coolly met his gaze. "Not at all."

"I've seen a lot of beautiful birds flying around this city," he said as he took a seat, "but none quite as striking as you."

An amused smile played at her lips. "Do you always begin conversations with a pickup line?"

"Life is short. I like to live it."

"I appreciate a man with confidence."

"You're not afraid to stand out yourself. Cartagena's a marvelous place, but we can't deny that machismo is alive and well in South America."

She smirked. "It's doing just fine in the north too. As is racism."

He raised his glass. "To knowledge, enlightenment, and progress."

She met the toast. "And what do you think of forward women? Vulgar, or liberated?"

He took a swallow of rum, let the spice tickle his throat, and flicked his eyes suggestively toward the stairs. "I say onward and upward."

"I don't even know your name."

He gave a seated bow. "James Corwin, though I doubt it's news to you."

"Whatever do you mean?" She offered a slender hand adorned with an emerald ring. "Pleased to meet you, James. I'm Anastasia Kostos. Ana."

"I believe I caught a glance of your ethereal beauty in Asheville, North Carolina," he said, taking her hand and giving it a lingering kiss.

"What an excellent imagination you have. There must have been someone who looked just like me."

"I don't see," he said as he returned her hand, "how that could be possible."

"Such a Casanova. What brings you to the jewel of the Caribbean?"

"I'm an overworked physicist from New York who needed some time in the sun. And you?"

"What a coincidence! I'm an overworked reporter from New York who needed some time in the sun."

"You don't sound like a New Yorker."

"I was raised in Greece, and neither do you."

"Touché," he said. "Then I have to say, indeed, what an incredible coincidence this appears to be. What are you investigating in Cartagena?"

"At the moment, a physicist."

He grinned back, appreciating the wordplay. "Wouldn't that be a pair of physicists?"

A coy smile was her only response.

He bought her another glass of wine. After a depressing examination of the My Lai Massacre and the other tragedies of the Vietnam War, they escaped to a playful discussion of free love, art, and global literature. What an intelligent and free-spirited woman this was!

When Dr. Corwin asked her back to his room, she leaned in so close her hair brushed his arm. The combination of alcohol and sun-kissed flesh, underlaid with a light rose perfume, made him dizzy. She whispered, "I prefer mine."

"I'm afraid that's impossible," he said.

"Why?"

"Because I don't trust you in the slightest. How is Hans, by the way?"

She batted her almond-shaped eyes. "Who?"

He chuckled, stood, and held out an arm. "Are you coming? Shall we 'ascend' the staircase side by side?"

After pursing her lips and affording him a lingering look he couldn't quite decipher—and which he found quite thrilling—she accepted his arm.

Upon entering his suite on the top floor of the hotel, which included a four-poster bed and a balcony overlooking the city, Dr. Corwin said, "I'll need to search you, of course."

"That's not very gentlemanly."

"I'm unsure whether you were sent to kill me or seduce me. If the former, I'll need to confiscate your weapon. If the latter, well, perhaps I'll take my chances."

As he reached for the hem of her dress, she cocked her head, bemused, and raised her arms above her head, entwining her wrists like a belly dancer. Watching for sudden movements, he lifted off her dress and set it aside. There was nothing underneath except lace underwear and smooth Mediterranean skin.

"Satisfied?" she asked in a throaty voice.

"Oh, I'm a long way from that." He placed his thumbs on the edge of her underwear, sliding it slowly down her hips as she arched into him and purred with pleasure. "I'm afraid I'm a very thorough man."

Their lovemaking was the most intense sexual encounter of Dr. Corwin's life. Like him, Ana was a passionate and experienced lover who enjoyed exploring every inch of her partner. The fact that each knew the other was an enemy, yet chose to accept the danger and vulnerability of the encounter, ratcheted his desire to new heights. It seemed to do so for her as well, though he had to wonder if she was acting. He thought not—he liked to think he could tell the difference—but that, too, was part of the excitement.

Bah, he thought, ashing a cigarette in the marble ashtray beside the bed when they were finished. He was holding a glass of rum from the minibar in his other hand, and Ana was sleeping soundly beside him in a surprising show of trust.

Or is it because the Ascendants know we're not ruthless like them and I won't kill her in her sleep?

After ensuring there was no gun planted in the bedside table or under her pillow, he lay awake and pondered the conversation with Alvaro for the umpteenth time.

And then, all at once, infused with the warmth of the rum and the high of the nicotine and that strangely lucid indolence that follows a pleasing sexual encounter, it came together in his mind.

Tromereo was a very unusual surname. So unusual, in fact, that Dr. Corwin could find no mention of the name anywhere, whether belonging to a physicist or not. He had thought it sounded Italian, but a search of phone books from New York and major European cities had uncovered no entry. Apart from that troubling fact, there was something about the name that had plagued him all day, some confluence of vowel sounds that had lodged in his subconscious.

Sitting upright in bed, he had started rearranging the letters in his mind, and discovered a shocking result.

Oh Mother Mary. It was so simple. That look of secret knowledge on the curandero's face during their discussion . . . the sly old devil had known all along.

The name Nataja Tromereo possessed the exact same letters as Ettore Majorana.

7

On the way to Dubai, where Andie and Cal were scheduled to catch a private jet to Kolkata, the helicopter pilot stopped twice during the night to refuel at semi-abandoned estates in remote locations. One was a whitewashed manor house in western Turkey; the other, a flat-roofed adobe compound somewhere in the undulating red-gold dunes of the Saudi Arabian desert.

The journey in the cramped copter was arduous. At each of the stops, Andie visited the restroom and stretched her legs before climbing wearily back into the folding seats behind the cockpit, grimly aware it might be too late to reach the science institute before the Ascendants.

She and Cal were carrying the clothes on their backs, the Star Phone, and the contents of the pouch Zawadi had given them. In particular, Andie missed her jade ring with the band of entwined silver her mother had given her the night she'd left home. The Ascendants had taken the ring in Venice. Andie felt a twinge of phantom pain, once buried as deep as an ocean trench, on the finger where the ring used to rest.

Andie had never really voiced, even to herself, her reasons for hanging on to the ring through the years. She always told herself that she liked the way it looked—which was true—but she knew the real reason was that, deep down, it represented a final tenuous thread that belonged to the tapestry of memories of her mother.

Why had the Ascendants bothered to take it? She supposed in their world, a ring could be a piece of spyware, some kind of high-tech tracking device used to infiltrate their organization. Would her mother look at the ring and think of her daughter, Andie wondered, before the Ascendants destroyed it?

Cal had been out cold the entire journey. Andie had tried desperately to rest but couldn't stop thinking about Henrik giving his life to save her. For the millionth time, she wondered where her mind went when she entered the shadow world. Was she stepping outside of her body, crossing through a gap in dimensions, entering the quantum realm? Glimpsing a new reality altogether?

Or was it nothing more, as she had always suspected, than a psychological glitch?

But if it is something, what does the Leap Year Society know about it?

Dr. Corwin, what have you done? And why didn't you tell me?

She thought about her conversation with Cal on the patio overlooking the Sicilian vineyard, and the mounting mysteries that all seemed to revolve around her mentor: the Star Phone and the Enneagon, the ink drawings of her visions, the origins and purpose of the Leap Year Society, and, most of all, the involvement of her mother.

Who was Dr. James Corwin, really?

While the story of his past beckoned, she was drawn to a different memory on the final leg of the flight. One that related to her run with that prick Matt Stevenson in Durham.

The Friday after the awful encounter, as the sun went down on the quad in front of Duke Chapel, Andie had sat cross-legged on the grass, surrounded by neo-Gothic architecture and a bower of ancient oaks. Groups of students had walked by without a second glance, laughing and chatting, planning weekend parties.

Andie went to the quad at times to center herself. It was a beautiful place, a union of architectural magnificence and natural splendor that spoke to both her rational and spiritual sides. Though she considered herself agnostic, she had always embraced the pull of the unknown. It was hard not to stare at the lattice of sheltering branches beneath the violet dusk sky, knowing the root systems of those proud sentinels were interconnected with a host of organisms beneath the forest floor, a symbiosis of mind-blowing complexity triggered billions of years ago by exploding stars, and not feel awed by the magic of creation.

Andie had always been a lone wolf, preferring to bond with a few close friends. As an undergrad, low on self-esteem and high on resentment towards her parents, she had funneled her emotions into drinking too much and pushing limits. Her college friends were products of a time and a place from which Andie had moved on by the time grad school rolled around.

She had a few childhood friends whom she cherished, but they had families and mortgages. Andie didn't want to go whining to them about her problems. Or at least not problems like Matt, who wasn't a problem at all.

He was distant history.

Hearing footsteps, she had turned to see Dr. Corwin approaching through the quad in beige slacks, a herringbone cap, and a checkered blue sport coat. Trim and dapper as ever.

"Hello there," her mentor had said.

"Hi."

"I was leaving the library and saw you. It's quite a lovely evening."

"Yup."

He studied her face. "May I join you for a moment?"

After Andie patted the grass beside her, he set down his briefcase and walking cane and eased to the ground. Despite the pain in his joints and his bad knee, every movement was elegant and sure.

She had often wondered what he was like as a younger man. A heartbreaker, no doubt.

"That look bears a curious resemblance to the one I believe you American girls refer to as 'boy trouble.' Or I should say 'man trouble.' I sometimes forget how grown you are."

"There's no trouble. And I wouldn't call him a man. Definitely a child. A prick, actually."

She had never held back around Dr. Corwin, and he had never flinched at her choice of language or her honesty.

"I'm sorry," he said.

"I don't give a damn about him. I'm just a little contemplative tonight. But thanks."

"The mysteries of the cosmos pale before the enigma of the human heart."

"Trust me—I'm not heartbroken."

"The heart is not always broken by other people," he said gently.

She sniffed and leaned back on her elbows. "Yeah. It's an annoying little organ."

"You're still new on campus. It can be a hard place to fit in."

"I've never really bothered. And I don't plan on starting now."

He chuckled. "Me either."

In the ensuing silence, she said, "Can I ask you something personal?"

He blinked. "Of course."

"Have you ever been in love?"

The question seemed to take him aback. "Many times," he said, with a sad, enigmatic smile. "When I was much younger, sometimes twice in one week."

She laughed. "You never found the right one?"

In response, his face tilted to the sky, suggesting an untold story behind the faraway gaze. "I made a choice long ago to put my work above my personal life. Don't ask me whether it was wise. I don't know. I don't believe in regret. Second-guessing your choices is like trying to pin down a quantum superposition: it's impossible to judge the outcome before you live it, and one can never replicate the conditions under which the choice was made. Every now and then, I indulge in the past with a bottle of fine Scotch and a Colombian cigar. And that is all."

Andie fingered her mother's jade ring. "That's probably wise."

"We should learn from our mistakes. But my future interests me far more than my past." He used his cane to push to his feet. "Another piece of advice. As scientific-minded as I am, I always did my best to follow my heart, including with my research."

"Really? That surprises me."

"Make of it what you will. It is not a path for everyone—especially in our profession."

She stored the comment away for further thought. "You said you were in love many times," she said with a smile. "I can't imagine any woman refusing the advances of a young Dr. James Corwin."

"Ha! Plenty have, believe me. The heart can love more than one thing at the same time, Andie, and not just other people. Don't ever let anyone tell you otherwise. Your job, should you travel the path of intuition, is to figure out who or what you hold most dear." He pointed the cane at her. "And that choice is where the true heartbreak lies."

Andie finally drifted off to sleep. When she woke, they were touching down just after dawn on a private airstrip surrounded by miles of red-gold desert. "Steve" claimed he had arranged all the details, and Zawadi would foot the bill. Andie was relieved they wouldn't have to risk using their own documents until they arrived in India.

Under a blazing morning sun, the futuristic skyline of Dubai shimmering in the distance like some high-tech mirage, Steve led Andie and Cal across the tarmac to a white microjet with a portable staircase attached to the side. The engine was thrumming, poised for takeoff.

"Who's taking us the rest of the way?" Cal shouted over the noise.

"Someone like me," he answered.

"Why can't you take us?" Andie said, her lungs choking on dust and fumes, nervous about another transfer with someone she didn't know.

"Afraid the copter's my only bird. Don't worry—he's in the network."

"What the hell does that mean?" Cal asked. "How many of you are there?"

"Once you're in India, you're on your own. I don't have contacts there."

"Are you going to answer my question?"

"I thought we discussed that. I don't do questions. Listen, you ever been to Kolkata?"

Neither Andie nor Cal had.

"Watch your back there," the pilot continued. "And not just because of what happened in Bologna."

"What do you mean?" Andie said.

"I've been through a few times on . . . other business. That city's not for tourists. There are places you shouldn't go without protection, especially at night."

She stepped onto the first rung of the movable staircase. "Isn't that true everywhere?"

"Sure, but some places more than others."

"We'll be careful," Cal said. "Thanks for your help, Steve, or whoever you are."

"Just doing my job."

Once they'd boarded, he started rolling the staircase down the tarmac without a backward glance. After exchanging a friendly but curt greeting with the pilot—an African American wearing jeans, a green polo, and a black baseball cap with no logo—the microjet stirred clouds of dust as it roared out of the desert.

The tiny plane had six passenger seats and a restroom so small Andie had to sit sideways. The pilot had set out bottled water and light snacks on their seats: peanuts, apples, and Swiss chocolate bars.

Even more reticent than Steve, the pilot refused to answer any questions except to say they were traveling on an approved flight path, the journey to Kolkata took less than five hours, and he would be dropping them off at Netaji Subhash Chandra Bose Airport to clear customs.

Andie worried the pilot wasn't who he said he was, or the Ascendants would intercept their flight, or they would be held at customs, or that some other nasty surprise awaited them in India.

But there was nothing she could do about any of that. After she and Cal devoured the snacks, she washed her face in the sink and finally managed to fall asleep.

When she woke, they were touching down in Kolkata.

After landing, the pilot told Andie and Cal to wait, then left the plane to talk with a customs official who had driven up in a grungy white van.

Andie adjusted her watch to account for the three-and-a-half-hour time difference from Sicily. It was 2 p.m. local time. The gray drizzle outside her window obscured the glass-and-concrete sprawl of the airport. On Cal's side, past a cluster of small planes and Bengali workers scuttling through the rain, she could just make out the skyline of the city in the distance.

"Well," Cal said, staring out the window. "I hope this airport and the inside of that van isn't the last thing we ever see. Because that would be depressing."

Andie felt disoriented. She had never been to India and wished she had woken up sooner, to get a feel for the geography as the plane descended.

They saw the pilot slip something to the driver of the van. Soon after, the pilot returned and said, "You're all clear."

Andie and Cal exchanged a glance. *Better not to ask questions.*

"I assume you'll want a taxi?" the pilot asked.

"Please," Andie said.

He stepped out again, shielded his eyes from the rain, then whistled and waved a hand. Within moments, a dark-blue sedan pulled away from a line of cars parked near the rear entrance to the airport. Andie guessed they serviced the private jets, and was relieved they had an easy way out.

The pilot opened the door. After checking her pockets to ensure her devices were intact, Andie climbed down after Cal. Despite the cloud cover, the outside air took her breath away, as hot and steamy as a sauna.

"I'd love some caffeine and a solid meal," Cal said, "but I vote for leaving the airport as soon as possible."

"I couldn't agree more."

The shouts of workers mingled with the cacophony of noise from the planes. Andie thanked the pilot. He replied with a nod as the driver of the sedan, a portly balding man with a birthmark splotched on his forehead, stepped out to open the door.

"No bags?" he said with a too-quick smile and a heavy Bengali accent.

"It's just a quick trip," Andie said, not wanting the driver to remember them.

"Your destination?"

"Quantum Café in Howrah."

Before leaving Sicily, she and Cal had sourced a café within walking distance of the science institute. They felt safer approaching on foot instead of being dropped in full view at the entrance.

The Quantum Café had a solid web presence—and the name seemed appropriate.

"Yes," the driver said. He closed the door and guided the private car through a maze of parked planes and utility vehicles before leaving the airport on a service road.

The inside of the sedan smelled of curry, and cottage cheese left out too long on the counter. Though the back seat was clean, clothes were heaped on the floor of the front passenger seat, and a pile of greasy discarded food wrappers cluttered the console. Attached to the dash was a bobbing goddess figurine with blue skin, six arms, pendulous breasts, inflamed red eyes, and a blackened tongue protruding grotesquely out of her mouth.

The driver must have noticed them staring at the figurine, because he patted it and said, "Not to worry, she takes no notice of Americans." He gave a high-pitched giggle. "You are American?"

"Canadian, actually," Andie said.

"Ah—very sorry. You know, they are very close."

"It's fine. How long will the drive take?"

"One or three hours."

"I'm sorry," Cal said. "Did you say one *or* three hours?"

"It is I who is sorry. The traffic in Kolkata is most unpredictable. In fact, the traditional route to Howrah is blocked, and I must drive through the city. I do hope very much to arrive at our destination as soon as is possible."

The change in route made her nervous, but they were already in the car, and there was little they could do. As they merged onto a busy freeway with flat, unkempt grassland on either side, Andie let her imagination wander to the vision the Indian subcontinent had always conjured in her mind: crowded megacities that merged into impenetrable jungles where tigers still roamed; steamy deltas rising to the snowcapped majesty of the Himalayas; a wealth of palaces and shrines and hilltop forts; devout pilgrims flocking to holy rivers reeking of human waste; a caste system that had produced both the opulence of the Taj Mahal and some of the most grinding poverty on the planet.

But most of all, more than anywhere except the beach, India made her think of her mother.

Throughout Andie's childhood, Samantha Zephyr's infatuation with the subcontinent's culture and history had registered loud and clear. Andie still remembered the mandalas her mother wore around her neck, the sacrosanct visits to the Ashtanga yogi every Saturday morning, and her mother grinding fresh spices for a curry as she regaled Andie with stories from Hindu mythology. Unlike her father's half-hearted Methodism, which seemed hopelessly dull in comparison, young Andie had the impression that Hinduism, with its thousands of deities and wildly varying practices, was a fascinating milieu that seemed to wallow in all the glorious, barbaric, insane complexities of human nature.

Her mother had been attracted to all places on Earth whose cultures she considered spiritual in an ancient way, where there was a more direct conduit from the past to the present than in Western nations. She was just as eager to teach Andie about the Incan or Siberian shamans as she was to discuss physics or astronomy. But Hinduism in particular fascinated her. This was one reason Andie had so readily accepted her father's story that her mother had left to join an ashram in India. It fit the narrative.

Because of this past connection, being in India as an adult felt strange to Andie, as if she were revisiting a familiar place she had never been, exploring memories she had never really had.

"Oh my," Cal said as they merged onto a highway with a crush of traffic unlike any Andie had experienced. The lane dividers seemed to be suggestions rather than rules, and their driver had to swerve to avoid piles of garbage and industrial waste clogging the road. "We are most definitely not in Kansas anymore."

"Have you been to India?" she asked.

"Never been east of Europe, unless you count Koreatown in LA."

Andie had done a bit of research before they left Sicily. A former capital of the British Raj, known as Calcutta until 2001, the city's name originated from the Bengali word Kalikata, which in turn meant land of Kali.

Kali, Andie knew, was a major figure in the Hindu pantheon, a complicated goddess who had become infamous in the Western imagination. Often portrayed in a similar manner to the fearsome avatar bobbing on their driver's dashboard, Kali represented the void from which all life sprang. Her lustrous hair was a symbol for the freedom of the natural world, her many limbs signified both creation and destruction. The weapons in her hands and the severed heads of her enemies spoke of her strength and cruelty as a mother goddess, a protector. She was often depicted standing with a foot on the chest of her consort, Shiva, and had long been a source of feminine strength, a slayer of demons who suckled the universe at her breast.

Andie could see what her mother once saw in the goddess.

Andie kind of admired Kali, too.

She remembered the pilot's warning about the city. Though she tended to scoff at urban legends—all cities had their unwholesome areas—she knew of the rumors of Kolkata's dark side, and not just the horrific slums. When she had spent time in the world of the occult, searching for answers to her visions, she had heard tales of Kali worshippers prowling city streets at night, looking for sacrifices among the poor and unguarded, keeping ancient traditions alive.

Which she gave absolutely no credence to.

That might have been true hundreds of years ago, when the British had stumbled headlong into a millennia-old culture it did not understand. But modern Kolkata was a city of over fourteen million people, considered by many to be the cultural heart of India, and home to countless artists, scientists, and entrepreneurs.

She believed there were about as many ritual sacrifices in the inner sanctums of Kolkata's temples as there were murders with voodoo dolls in New Orleans.

By the time they entered the city proper, the drizzle had become a monsoon, vomiting buckets of water on the windshield, limiting visibility to a few feet. Andie cringed as the driver continued at high speed along the packed highway, swerving to avoid the semis that doused passing cars with thumping sheets of rain.

Through the downpour, she got glimpses of dated skyscrapers choking the city center, entire neighborhoods made of concrete apartment buildings, chaotic markets woven among the domes and spires of the temples, slums that made her swallow in despair with her face pressed to the glass.

The rain ceased as they passed through a beautiful green space with teams of cricketers braving the weather. After the park, they crossed the gray sweep of the Hooghly River on a bridge packed with eight lanes of traffic. Two walkways on either side supported a legion of pedestrians, bicyclists, people on scooters, and rickshaws pulled by barefoot old men in grubby clothes.

Andie stared at a rickshaw driver porting two men in suits across the bridge. He was shirtless, maybe to escape the rain, and the old man's wrinkled brown skin was pockmarked with moles and unhealthy dark patches. It seemed like a cruel relic of the nineteenth century.

"Kolkata is the last place in the world where the practice of rickshaw pulling on foot has not been outlawed," the driver said with another giggle. "We are a very permissive society."

The car turned south along the river, and then east, deeper into the Howrah District. Fifteen minutes later, the monsoon ended as abruptly as if a spigot had turned off. The sun emerged as they entered a tony neighborhood with lush landscaping and swanky retail on the high street.

The driver pulled alongside a café with a smoked-glass storefront and a kaleidoscopic neon sign that kept changing shape.

The Quantum Café.

"Only a two-hour drive," the driver announced. "This is acceptable?"

"Thank you," Andie said, realizing she would have to pay with the black credit card Zawadi had given them. She held her breath as she stuck it into the handheld card reader, but it went through without a hitch. She exhaled and tipped the driver well.

"I am extremely grateful for your kindness and gratuity," he said, holding out a business card. "My name is Danesh. Please call me if you are in further need of a driver." He hesitated. "Kolkata can be a disorienting city for visitors. Please enjoy your stay, but I advise you to only solicit rides from accepted vendors."

"Gotcha."

"I am sorry but at times, unscrupulous taxi drivers have been known to charge exorbitant amounts for their services. Some have even driven their passengers to rendezvous with criminal elements, who proceed to rob and assault the passengers. I would not wish any of this to happen to you. Please, do not hesitate to call me, no matter the hour."

Andie wasn't sure if she was grateful or creeped out by the offer. After Danesh left, she and Cal stepped inside the café and hurried to the counter to order. The science institute was only three blocks away, but both of them were starving, and they had no idea how long they would be inside the institute.

The café was light and airy, divided into sections by glass partitions with math formulas etched in white marker on the surface. They each ordered coffee, bottled water, and the daily kebab platter. Soon they were pushing out of their seats and heading for the door.

"We could wait a while," Cal said as they stepped into the late afternoon heat. The sun was now so bright they had to shield their eyes. "Find disguises and make some kind of plan."

"I think our best bet is to move as quickly as we can, and pray they haven't figured out where we're going. We have to presume they know about the Aryabhata clue from interrogating you in Venice, but if we can find the next one before they get to the institute, they'll have no way of following us without the Star Phone."

"No way except for their global surveillance system and teams of assassins."

"You know what I mean."

He blew out a breath and scanned the palm-lined street. "Okay then. Either they're waiting for us at the institute or they're not. You ready for this?"

Andie clenched her fists and started walking. "Not in the slightest."

New York City

8

The body of Dr. James Gerald Corwin had finally been repatriated. When Zawadi strode into the funeral parlor, a grand marble edifice in one of the oldest neighborhoods in the city, just a few blocks off Broadway on the north end of the Financial District, almost every head turned her way.

Some of the public figures who had come to pay their respects were secret members of the Leap Year Society. They lowered their eyes as Zawadi passed, out of respect for her loss.

A few of the attendees were Ascendants. A tech entrepreneur here, a world-class surgeon there. They, too, knew of her special connection to the deceased, and of her fearsome reputation. Their hands strayed towards the weapons concealed at their sides as she passed.

Yet most of the people at the viewing were friends and family and colleagues of Dr. Corwin, normal citizens curious about the identity of the six-foot tall South African woman in the somber black dress, who seemed, both from the glossy beauty of her chiseled features and the strength and confidence of her bearing, as if she were an onyx statue come to life.

Full of soaring pillars and secluded alcoves, the enormous funeral parlor had once been a municipal library, and Dr. Corwin had requested this specific mortuary in his will.

Of course he had, Zawadi thought.

It was dangerous for her to be there. It was dangerous for every member of the Society, since New York City was in the grip of the Ascendants. They had access to the public surveillance system and had bought the loyalty of a shocking number of judges, businessmen, and political figures—some of whom they counted among their members.

Yet there were exceptions. Secret conduits and safe havens spread throughout the five boroughs. Now that she had arrived, Zawadi did not expect trouble. Dr. Corwin was a renowned scientist, and his death had garnered national attention. The presence of the Ascendants was not an overt threat but a silent message to the members of the Society in attendance: *This is our city, and we are watching.*

The brazen attacks on Dr. Corwin and Lars Friedman, accompanied by the raid on Quasar Labs in the Research Triangle and the gunfight in Bologna, had not ignited the firestorm of retaliation from the Society that Zawadi would have expected. It was just as James had feared, and the funeral felt symbolic to her. The death of Dr. Corwin, who had worked his entire life to reform the LYS and combat the rise of the Ascendants, might mark the beginning of the end of the original faction.

If he was dead—and the answer to that question was the reason Zawadi had risked her life to come to New York.

Back arched, shoulders high, her stoic gaze fixated on the coffin at the front of the room, Zawadi walked steadily forward as the organ played, the crowd parting like subjects before a queen. She enjoyed the veiled surprise on the faces of the Ascendants, who had thought she was on the run somewhere in central Europe.

Let them feel the gut-wrenching churn of uncertainty for once.

The viewing room was packed. Some of the attendees surprised her. Dean Varen, and a few other close allies of Dr. Corwin, she had expected to see. But the number of Ascendants in the room, including two feared enforcers who avoided the public eye, was troubling.

Few eyes in the room were dry. Dr. Corwin had touched many

lives. Still, Zawadi knew he was far from perfect. Throughout his extraordinary life, he had made hard choices that would turn the stomachs of most people, who would not understand the reasons for his decisions—and even some who would. Nor were all of his choices defensible, in her opinion. As brilliant as he was, her friend had let his passions drive him more than cold rationality.

Yet Zawadi loved him too. After a decorated stint in the South African Special Forces, she had become an ANC revolutionary and then a marooned freedom fighter swept up in global conflicts with dubious ideological connections. The death of a lover in a senseless conflict had sent her on a downward spiral, running from her past and unsure if she would escape. When her path had crossed with Dr. Corwin's on a fateful night in Cape Town, a chance encounter on Table Mountain, her toes inching toward the ledge, he had talked to her quietly for hours, speaking of remarkable things that made her rethink her perspective.

Helped her better understand the arc of human existence that had led to the complex realities of the present world. Sympathized with the violence and trauma in which her beloved country and her life were steeped. Spoke of the wonders of theoretical physics and astronomy in plain terms, and of his hopes and dreams for humankind. Told her he was working behind the scenes to change the narrative. Gave her a mission to believe in.

He had saved her life that night, and starting the following morning, she had worked tirelessly to protect his.

Zawadi's step faltered as she approached the body, her hands trembling at her sides, a show of emotion that was not faked.

Could he truly be gone? Discovering at last what lay on the other side of that fog-drenched mountain valley?

She could not bear the thought.

The viewing line inched steadily forward. After a weeping elderly woman wearing a lace veil moved on—perhaps an old lover—Zawadi stepped up to the raised coffin. She peered gingerly down at the body as a child peers into a closet at night, afraid of what she might find. Inhaling a deep breath through her nose, she took a good long look at the arranged corpse, so still and waxen. The sight of the familiar face caused her knees to buckle.

Yet she also discovered the absence of a faint sickle-shaped scar on the back of a hand, a scar she knew should be there but was not. Marveling at the otherwise flawless similarity of the face of the corpse, and the technological prowess of the Ascendants, Zawadi's jaw clenched for a fraction of a moment. The ruse would have fooled anyone who had not witnessed Dr. Corwin's injury firsthand and watched the wound heal, anyone not trained to notice the tiniest of details.

There's no scar, and this isn't him. He could still be alive!

In that moment out of time, hers and hers alone, Zawadi vowed to search for James Gerald Corwin to the ends of the Earth, and declared her own private war against the Ascendants.

With a little shudder, her face became an expressionless mask once more, eyes lowered and head bowed, feigning respect for the dead as she returned through the crowd.

9

Nestled in an unassuming pocket of the upscale Howrah neighborhood, the Kolkata Science Institute was a handsome four-story building made of rose-colored limestone. A spherical glass foyer extended out from the entrance, fronted by a circular drive that enclosed a green space and a fountain. Andie and Cal stood on a walkway of inlaid bricks just behind the fountain, shielding their eyes from the sun, the misty spray a welcome relief.

Emblazoned on a sign above the entrance was the emblem that had brought them halfway around the world: an embossed globe displaying the same collection of nested images from the Star Phone—an om symbol, a double helix, and a zero.

No one had accosted them so far. In fact, oddly, not a single person was in sight outside the institute. The memory of their imprisonment in the dungeon below Venice was still ripe in Andie's mind, screaming at her to run as fast and as far away as she could.

Before they had left Sicily, a quick search had revealed the Kolkata Science Institute was not a public entity, as she had surmised from the name, but a private company with very little information available online. No executives or employees were listed. The website alluded to vague descriptions of the company's goals: interdisciplinary research aiming to improve the quality of life in India and other developing countries. A collection of photos showcased projects underway in rural communities, though Andie had the distinct feeling that, while the projects might be real, the photos were staged and the people in them, actors. They were all too cheerful and good-looking to be scientists. The whole setup caused a prickle of unease to creep down the back of her neck. Was this an LYS front?

With a deep breath, she took out the Star Phone and aimed it right at the emblem, to see if it triggered the device.

"Anything?" Cal asked in a low voice.

"Not yet." Disappointed, she scanned the front of the building with similar results. "I guess we're going inside."

"Then let's get on with it," he said, looking over his shoulder. "I feel like a rabbit in a lion's den."

She pocketed the phone and led the way to a revolving door at the front entrance. Inside the plant-filled foyer, a tall Indian man rose from behind a desk to greet them. MUSEUM STAFF was imprinted on the left breast of his beige uniform.

"Can I help you?"

The man had long sideburns and a hooked nose. Though he was smiling, Andie got a vibe of wary competence, and noticed the muscularity of his hands and forearms. *This guy is a guard.*

The spherical foyer extended deep into the building. A succession of glass display cases were embedded into the mauve walls, and imprinted on the plush blue carpet, right in the center of the room, was the emblem of the institute.

Beside the guard's desk, Andie noticed a stand supporting a hardbound book describing the exhibits of the museum, next to a sign reading KOLKATA INSTITUTE MUSEUM OF ANTIQUITIES.

Museum of Antiquities? In a science institute?

"We're here for the museum," she said, wondering why that sign didn't look more permanent, and why the museum wasn't advertised on the website.

The guard held her gaze. "Yes, of course," he replied. "You'll have to dispose of your beverage before you enter."

Andie swallowed the rest of her to-go coffee, then dropped it in a trash can. The guard opened a palm to usher them forward. "Enjoy your visit."

"Is this room the entire museum?"

"I'm afraid so. It is but a sample of our region's contributions." He pointed at the glass case to the left of the revolving door. "I suggest starting your journey there and working your way around."

Journey? For a single room? What a strange choice of words. "Okay. Thank you."

"What about the rest of the building?" Cal asked. "I wouldn't mind seeing where the magic happens."

"Only the museum is open to the public."

"Do you mind if I take a few pictures?" Andie asked. "As a memento?"

The uniformed man gave her a small, knowing smile. "I would expect nothing less."

Cal eyed a clock on the wall behind the desk. It was almost 5:30 p.m. "What are the visiting hours?"

"We close when the last visitor leaves."

With that cryptic reply, the man retreated behind the desk to pick up a newspaper.

Confused by the whole scenario, Andie took out the Star Phone and pretended to photograph the room. Nothing she did affected the device.

"At least we haven't been kidnapped yet," Cal said in a low voice as they wandered over to the first exhibit, the hum of an air conditioner reinforcing the cool sterility of the room.

"Definitely a positive."

"I don't know what to think about this place."

"Me either. Let's reserve judgment for now."

"Keep trying the Star Phone," he said.

"I will. Why don't you start on the opposite side, in case something jumps out at you?"

"Sure," Cal said. "Though let's hope nothing literally does that."

Andie gave a nervous laugh, then turned to the first exhibit: a three-foot tall column made of red sandstone, displayed in accent lighting and suspended in the middle of the glass case via an unseen mechanism—she assumed invisible wires or magnets. The column had a smooth surface, topped by an exquisite carving of dragons forming a circle made of the same red stone. The bodies of the dragons were interconnected in a clever geometric pattern, leaving no open spaces. The circular shape and the serpentine motif made Andie think of an ouroboros.

She counted the dragons. There were nine—just like the number of steps from the Star Phone to the Enneagon in Dr. Corwin's journal.

Was it another sign?

She perused the bronze placard at the bottom of the case, which contained a description of the object in both English and Bengali.

Ashoka Pillar

The third emperor of the Mauryan dynasty, which dominated the Indian subcontinent from the fourth to the second centuries BCE, Ashoka is believed to have presided over 50 to 60 million subjects, making his empire one of the largest in antiquity. After seizing power circa 270 BCE, Ashoka led a bloody campaign to conquer Kalinga, a coastal kingdom in the east of India. Historians estimate that casualties ranged from 100,000 to 300,000. Aghast at the carnage, Ashoka shocked the ancient world by converting to Buddhism and vowing to treat his subjects humanely. He renounced all military conquest and transformed the Mauryan dynasty into a paragon of tolerance, charity, and nonviolence. To spread and commemorate his new policies, Ashoka erected towering sandstone pillars inscribed with his new edicts at pilgrimage sites throughout the empire, and along trade routes. The surviving Ashoka pillars

are masterpieces of Mauryan architecture and early
Indian writing. The miniature pillar in this exhibit was
commissioned for King Ashoka's personal collection
and was uncovered from his tomb in Karnataka.

At the bottom of the placard was a translation of the inscription
on the miniature pillar behind the glass. The short, curved markings
reminded Andie of cuneiform. According to the placard, the inscription was carved in Brahmi, which arose out of Sanskrit.

We pledge together at the crossroad
Devoted to the gathering of knowledge
Through immortal time and spirit.

Though an intriguing piece of history—and one which oddly
mirrored the aims of the LYS—Andie wasn't sure what to make of it.
She moved to the next display, which appeared to be a smooth bowl
made of iron, slowly rotating in midair inside the case. Again there
were ancient Brahmic inscriptions on the object, which seemed at
odds with the relatively recent appearance of the bowl. Andie would
have pegged it at a few hundred years old, maybe produced in the
heyday of the Raj—until she read the placard and learned the artifact was two *thousand* years old, and made of 99 percent iron. It was
named the Maharashtra Bowl, after the region of India in which it
was found.

A two-thousand-year-old piece of perfectly shaped iron with no
rust? And almost no alloy?

Andie knew very little about the development of iron and the
corresponding artifacts, but those claims seemed impossible. The
placard further claimed the object was similar in construction to the
famous twenty-two-foot-tall Iron Pillar of Delhi found in the Qutb
archaeological complex of New Delhi. Similar to the bowl, the pillar
was 98 percent pure and had almost no corrosion, despite standing
in open air for millennia in a subtropical climate.

Andie would have to verify the existence of the Iron pillar of Delhi. If it was real, and the bowl was of similar importance, then how the hell had the bowl ended up here?

The third exhibit went even farther back in time: two square stone seals, or stamps, as Andie discovered by reading the placard. Each stamp was about the size of a cracker. Carved on the first was the same symbol of nine dragons forming the circle she had seen on the sandstone pillar. The second seal depicted a bovine creature with a single curved horn spiraling out of its head. The perimeters of both seals were covered with plantlike markings and sharp lines and wedges that she assumed were inscriptions, and which she again found similar to cuneiform.

Wondering if the placard would claim that unicorns and dragons once existed on the Indian subcontinent, she read that the seals were companion pieces to one in the National Museum in Karachi, and that all three objects had been unearthed with the remains of a for-ty-six-hundred-year-old city in the Indus River plains. The archae-ologists who excavated the site in the 1920s were shocked. It was previously thought that Indian civilization extended only a few hun-dred years before Alexander the Great, but they now had evidence of an ancient city called Harappa that rivaled or even surpassed the sophistication of the Egyptians and Mesopotamians. Not only that: the Harappan Empire was likely twice their size.

Odd. Why had she never heard of Harappa?

The placard claimed no one had deciphered the script on the seals or any of the other pieces found at Harappan archaeological sites. Was there a rival to Mesopotamian cuneiform as the world's first written language? Or, given the similarity of the markings, was there an older common source, unknown to linguists?

She also read that, unlike with other early empires, there was no evidence the people of the Indus Valley built extraordinary monu-ments that reached for the heavens. What the Harappans did build was just as impressive: raised foundations for protection from sea-sonal floods and wastewater; grid-like street patterns of remarkable uniformity; brick buildings and houses equipped with wells and sophisticated drainage systems. All of which evidenced a high degree of city planning unheard of for the time period.

Andie thought about the lack of sanitation prevalent in so many areas of India. If the placard was to be believed, the Harappans had even provided plumbing for the houses on the outskirts of town—indeed, for every citizen within the city's walls.

I get the message loud and clear, Dr. Corwin. Some of us were better off five thousand years ago. And while humanity's technological advancements might be shinier and more sophisticated in modern day, we certainly don't have a patent on invention.

But you're glossing over a lot of dark history. What were infant mortality rates in the ancient world? Which barbarians slaughtered the Harappans so thoroughly that only scraps of their civilization remain?

And how about those women's rights? I'm thinking they weren't such a high priority.

Still, Andie understood the point. Humanity had a short collective memory. We are all too quick to think our own civilization is the pinnacle of human achievement and will never end.

Andie did not long for the good old days of patriarchy and slave labor. She put her faith in science and technology, in pasteurization and antibiotics. She loved her iPhone and her Fitbit and a working air conditioner on a hot summer day.

But she was beginning to understand there was a story untold in the history books, one forgotten or ignored by the collective hubris of so-called modern society. Not only that, but there was a treasure trove of suppressed and hidden knowledge, such as the ideas of Democritus, that might have changed the world had they taken hold with the mainstream—and that might have survived in secret. These artifacts she kept seeing in the possession of the LYS hinted at even deeper mysteries.

Someone touched her on the shoulder, and she jumped.

"Sorry," Cal said. "Find anything useful?"

"Interesting, yes. Useful, no. You?"

"Not really. You're taking a while, and I'm getting nervous."

"I'll try to hurry," she said.

"We can always double back through the exhibits if we need. Why don't you try the Star Phone again? Maybe our walk-through triggered something."

Andie put a hand to her forehead. She had been so engrossed by the peculiar exhibits she had forgotten to check more carefully with the Star Phone. She retraced her steps, and then completed the circuit.

Still no change to the device.

After an anxious glance at the revolving door and the guard, who was engrossed in his newspaper, she moved on to the next exhibit: a block of barnacle-encrusted coral from Rama's Bridge, part of a chain of shoals extending thirty miles from Sri Lanka to the southern tip of India. Seen by air, the uniform curvature of the bridge suggested a man-made origin, which some believe was evidence of the legendary Rama Empire, or even an underwater civilization akin to Atlantis. Though not a believer, Andie had never had a problem with the concept of Atlantis. Nearly all ancient cultures had a flood myth, and plenty of them had tales of ancient cities that had "fallen into the sea."

And why not? *Homo sapiens* had been present on Earth for at least two hundred thousand years, possibly far longer. While Andie did not believe in an ancient Atlantis founded by aliens and given advanced technology, a few hundred thousand years was an extremely long time for civilizations to rise and fall, for ice ages and other disasters to wipe away all traces.

The next exhibit was a reproduction of Hindu epics that spoke of mechanized beings that could move of their own accord. One recounted how King Ashoka waged a terrible battle against fierce automaton warriors guarding relics of the Buddha hidden in an underground chamber.

The placards admitted the stories were myth, but the very idea of such an ancient culture dreaming of electric sheep was shocking to Andie. It was almost as if technology and human imagination had been cast in the same cosmic forge, twinned forces lost in the prehistory of the big bang, separated at birth and slowly finding their way back together.

What would happen when they merged?

She kept moving through the dizzying exhibits, trying to find a connection. Next was a stunning replica of Nalanda, an ancient Buddhist monastery and center of learning that had rivaled the Library of Alexandria. Pilgrims to the site spoke of vast halls and colleges, jewel-adorned towers with fairy-tale turrets lost in the clouds, and beautiful observatories that glittered dreamlike in the morning fog—all displayed in 3-D miniature inside the glass case. Built in the fifth century BCE, Nalanda had served as a beacon of education and enlightenment for eight hundred years until burned to the ground during a Muslim invasion.

Eight hundred years of lost knowledge. That's longer than most nations have been in existence.

King Ashoka, the placard claimed, had erected a temple at the site of Nalanda in the third century BCE, and it was possible the site's importance dated as far back as 1200 BCE.

Why does this Ashoka guy keep popping up?

Andie moved on. She knew she had to hurry. The remaining exhibits were mostly odes to the subcontinent's amazing contributions over the millennia. Among the highlights were the counting system adopted by Arabs and then the entire world; distillation of perfumes; solutions for quadratic equations; ruler measurements; zinc smelting; chess; steel alloys used in the famed swords of Damascus; the oldest living religion and cosmology; the first iron-cased rockets, launched against the British in the eighteenth century; seamless metal globes developed in the sixteenth century that, when rediscovered in the 1980s, metallurgists had no idea how to reproduce. She was also utterly shocked to learn that Indian physicians were performing plastic surgeries, including cataract removal and rhinoplasty, in the sixth century BCE.

Jesus. I hope they had plenty of alcohol on hand.

When Andie finished with the last exhibit, she stood, contemplative, near the revolving doors at the entrance. The museum was fascinating and had transformed her view of ancient India.

Yet the Star Phone had not activated, and she had no idea what to do next.

If she was not on such a desperate mission, she would have reeled at these marvels of technology and culture, many of them developed before Roman legions had sailed to Carthage. And who knew the authors of the Vedic texts had dreamed of *robots*?

But she didn't have time to reel. Her stomach was knotted with anxiety, and she kept expecting an Ascendant to burst into the room.

"Anything?" Cal asked as he wandered over.

"Zip. I have no idea what it's all supposed to mean."

"I was hoping I was just dense and you had some inspiration."

"*Dammit*," she said. "Maybe we're at the wrong place."

"I suppose. But it feels right, doesn't it? All these weird artifacts. All this knowledge. It's definitely got that old LYS feeling."

"Yeah," she agreed. "It does."

Think, Andie. What are you missing?

She moved to the center of the room, turning in a slow circle. Was there a secret door somewhere, or some special order to the exhibits?

Her eyes roamed to the guard himself, his desk, and the stand right beside it. Out of options, she walked over to peruse the hardbound book describing the exhibits. An RFID code could be hidden in the pages of the book as easily as on a glass case.

The book was full of glossy color photographs. Over two hundred pages long, it described each exhibit in far more detail than the placards. She hardly had time to scan every single page.

As she was examining the book, the guard's phone rang. He took the call and, moments later, walked outside with a worried expression.

"What's that about?" Cal said.

"I don't know." She took out the Star Phone and quickly scanned the front and back cover of the book, and a few pages at the beginning. Nothing.

"He's walking back," Cal said, peering through the glass, "and he doesn't look happy."

Desperate, Andie flipped to the table of contents. There were eighteen chapters listed, each pertaining to one of the exhibits in the room.

All of them except one.

She thought she remembered at least the name of every exhibit, but just to be sure, she whipped around and counted the number of glass cases. There were seventeen—one shy of the exhibits in the table of contents.

Eighteen was a multiple of nine.

Did that mean something? Or was she grasping?

She turned to the last chapter, the sole exhibit that was not displayed in the museum. Titled "Yantra," it was a single page of text with no images. Very strange for such a long, colorful book.

She glanced at the guard. He had almost returned, and as Cal had said, he was hurrying forward with a grim expression.

She returned to the book and skimmed the entry. A yantra, Andie knew, was a mystical diagram in Eastern religions used as an aid in meditation. Yantras typically consisted of geometric shapes and colors arranged within a symmetrical pattern. As far as she had time to tell, the text contained a basic description of yantras and nothing more.

As Andie raised the Star Phone, the guard burst through the revolving door. "You must go! The museum is now closed!"

"You said we could stay until we're finished," Andie said.

"There is no time. I'm sorry."

"C'mon," Cal said to Andie, starting for the door. "We can come back another time."

"No, we can't." She turned her back on both of them and aimed the Star Phone at the page. Nothing happened.

Dammit.

"I urge you," the guard said, "to exit the building with the utmost haste." He hesitated, as if debating whether to keep up the charade, then said, "You're in grave danger if you stay."

"Don't risk it," Cal said, his hand on the door.

"This *has* to be it," Andie said, continuing to scan the page. The guard touched her elbow, and she shook him off. She knew she was being reckless, but if the Ascendants were here, she would never get another chance at this.

As the guard ordered them to leave again, Andie pointed the Star Phone right at the word *Yantra* written in elaborate script at the top of the page—and then her world began to spin.

Andie gasped. "It's happening."

The guard was speaking again, but she blocked out the noise and focused on the image revealed by staring through the augmented reality lens of the device: a floating representation of a square-shaped yantra outlined in black. Attached to the outer surface of all four sides of the yantra was a protruding *T* with a short stem, giving the square the appearance of having little feet. Inside the square was a red circle made of interlocking shapes that resembled puffy sultan hats, and inside the circle was a series of triangles nested within one another, all of them pointing downward, and again alternating between red and black. In the very center of the yantra, hovering within the triangle, was a single red dot.

"We have to go," Cal said. "Now!"

She shoved the Star Phone in her pocket. "Got it."

The guard herded them through the revolving door and pointed down the street to his left. "Run! Get out of sight as quickly as possible!"

Andie and Cal took off at a dead sprint in the direction the guard had pointed, wondering what in the hell was going down, aiming for a handsome commercial district lined with jacarandas. Just before they fled into the first building they came to, a supermarket right off the street, Andie looked over her shoulder and saw three black SUVs

whipping into the drive leading to the science institute.

As far as she could tell, no one had spotted them.

But she couldn't be sure.

"You see those SUVs?" she asked Cal.

His face was pale when he turned. "I think we can safely assume they'll find out we were in that museum."

Andie pulled him inside the market. "There's got to be a back exit."

Together they raced through aisles filled with exotic fruits and vegetables, drawing stares from the other shoppers and almost tripping over a stack of crates. As they burst into the employee area at the rear of the store, someone shouted at them, but they kept running, shoving open an emergency exit, which, thankfully, did not sound an alarm.

They emerged in a tight, garbage-strewn alley that smelled of cat urine. Cal looked both ways before heading for a brick side street filled with pedestrians holding purses and shopping bags.

Andie ran beside him as they navigated the crowd, pumping her arms and checking to make sure the Star Phone was secure. Despite the panic clawing at her throat, she felt a perverse satisfaction in knowing that, even if the Ascendants were on their trail and hunting them in Kolkata, they had no way to access the image of the yantra Andie had just seen.

Those bastards didn't know where to go next.

Shanghai

10

Jianyu had been summoned to his sister's office—her shrine, as she preferred to call it—on the top floor of a building connected by a skywalk to the repurposed abattoir. Though the concrete eyesore appeared derelict from the outside, the twins' living quarters possessed excellent views of the city, and were outfitted with the most modern conveniences available—and some not so available. The Ascendants owned the entire semi-abandoned block. They used the nightclub and the loose hacker collectives in the surrounding buildings as both tech incubator and recruiting tool, a place to nurture disaffected geniuses.

When Jianyu entered the room, he stood silently as his sister's fingers flew across the keyboard hologram floating above her tri-level stainless steel desk. All of her equipment—the keyboard, speakers, her custom laptop with a carbon fiber chassis, and the trio of monitors mounted on the desk—was synced to her bio-bracelet.

Daiyu's chair had a curved, elongated back that hovered above her like a praying mantis. It was an ideal fit for her hunched posture, an extension of the disorder that marred her otherwise beautiful form. Though his sister never gave voice to her pain, Jianyu knew how much she suffered. He could read her body language as clearly as the map of stars in the sky. Their nonbiological father had once told her she should accept her appearance with grace, because nature did not make mistakes. It might produce deviations from the norm, or adaptations, or even strange anomalies—but not mistakes.

Daiyu had suffered in a myriad of ways under their non-bio father, but Jianyu had been present during that particular conversation and had seen the light go out of her eyes.

She spun in her chair to face her brother, dispelling the keyboard hologram. "They're in Kolkata."

Jianyu tensed, knowing her statement meant he would be deployed. "You're sure?"

"I've already made a report," she said quietly.

He could tell she was burdened by his imminent departure. "You suspected India from the start."

"I not only suspected," she said without pride or conceit, "I deduced the correct location. It's impossible to be sure without the device, but the symbology fits, and I know from video feed that our operatives arrived less than a minute after the targets departed."

"Where were they?"

"The Kolkata Science Institute. It's a front for the LYS—another marker."

"How do you know for sure?"

"There were artifacts inside."

Jianyu whistled. "Why did we not know about it?"

Her long fingers tapped against the back of her open laptop like spidery appendages. "Maybe some of us did."

"Don't be so cynical. We're young. Our status will change after this mission."

"Perhaps. Or perhaps we will not live to see it through."

"Have faith, Daiyu."

His sister's return smile was melancholic. "How ironic that you are now asking me to believe, my brother. Were your doubts erased so quickly in the library?"

"Is that not the way belief works? Can it ever be a gradual thing?"

She answered in a near whisper, her eyes flicking past him as if searching for a golden mask. "There was never a time when I did not believe. So I do not know."

Ever since the face-to-face meeting with the Archon, Daiyu had grown more withdrawn than usual. Whenever he'd tried to discuss the astonishing illusion—or whatever it had been—of the figures swarming the library stairs and those strange ziggurats, his sister had rebuffed his attempts.

As for Jianyu, while he may not have been superstitious like his twin—in fact, he considered himself a creature of pure rational thought—he very much believed in the awesome, unexplained powers of science and the mind. He was more convinced than ever their mysterious leader had access to better technology and mental hacks than the rest of the Ascendants.

"Give me specifics," he said. "It might help me understand their methodology."

"Once I realized the science institute might be the location, I informed the team, and they sent operatives to the site. It was quite difficult to hack the security cameras—another clue about who it belongs to."

"Difficult, but you were better."

She gave a curt nod, then waved a hand over the bio-bracelet. The keyboard hologram reappeared. After typing in a command, she pulled up the recorded video of Andromeda Robertson and Calvin Miller on the central monitor. Using the bio-bracelet as a remote control, she issued voice commands and waved her forearm back and forth in sinuous motions to play the footage, pausing and enlarging the images as her brother requested.

"As soon as I took control of the system," Daiyu said, "I blocked them from terminating the feed. They knew we were watching and sounded the alarm. The targets evacuated just in time. As you can see, they were examining a book in the foyer that made a miraculous disappearance before our team entered the building."

"Did they engage?"

"The institute was too well fortified for a public disturbance."

Jianyu waved a hand. "Fine. We know where they are. It should be easy to track them, no?"

"You've never been to Kolkata—it's hardly Shanghai. Very little of the city is under CCTV. Our network has been alerted, but it will be an uphill task. And what if they have moved on to the next location, in some other country?"

Jianyu flashed a charming grin, revealing teeth as white as eggshells. "Then I am sure you will make adjustments. Tell me, sister, have you ever failed to find a target once your mind is set to the task?"

When she spun her chair around without answering, he chuckled and said, "You're too self-deprecating. I might have newfound faith in the Archon, but I've always been a believer in you."

Jianyu returned to his private suite. The plane to Kolkata was scheduled to depart in four hours, and it would take at least an hour to ride to the Ascendant-owned airstrip on the outskirts of Shanghai.

In the interim, after he packed, Jianyu ran through a quick workout. From a young age, he had trained in kung fu and chin na, and was a champion before he turned sixteen. He had joined the military at eighteen, and was quickly promoted to a special operations unit. While not as mentally gifted as his sister, Jianyu embraced all forms of technology—especially those of the military nature.

After his recruitment by the Ascendants, Jianyu had been suddenly discharged in good standing from the military. Given the twins' lineage and the resources invested in their birth, Jianyu knew the government had grand plans for them; he had no idea how the Ascendants had managed to extract them from the Orwellian reach of the bureaucrats.

While the military lifestyle had never appealed to him—Jianyu was far too creative and independent, as well as obsessed with the biohacker lifestyle—it taught him to be a creature of habit, and he never missed a workout if he could help it. The basement of his building was well stocked with training mats and every conceivable kind of hand-to-hand-combat weapon, including a blood-spattered wood-floored cage for sparring. He referred to his training area as the Monastery, since kung fu was developed in Shaolin temples. Often, the Ascendants sent new operatives to Jianyu for coaching, and this was where he held court, dispensing advice and testing his mettle against two or more opponents at a time.

In the vast soundproof hall next door was the shooting range, where Jianyu practiced with firearms ranging from assault handguns to the most high-tech weapons available: Corner Shot guns, sight-optimized rifles, PHASR rifles, digitized grenade launchers, 3-D-printed weapons of all sorts.

Jianyu started off with a hard-and-fast free-weight routine, pumping blood into his muscles until they were as red and plump as dragon fruit. As he ran through his katas and fired a few clips at center mass in the shooting range, his mind was even more focused than usual—for Jianyu knew that a very dangerous opponent awaited.

The foolish older branch of the Leap Year Society had long since lost its teeth. In response to the horror of the world wars, it had turned away from martial affairs. This was a grave mistake. Not just because of the Ascendants, but because of the inevitable incursions from the world at large. What good was knowledge if it could not be protected?

At least one sub-faction, led by Dr. Corwin, understood this. He employed a bodyguard named Zawadi who had achieved an almost mythical status among the Ascendants. She had taken many of their lives over the years.

Like any great warrior, Jianyu desired to test himself against the very best, and Zawadi's fearsome reputation only fueled his desire.

Let us see whose philosophy of battle will be victorious in the end.

While Jianyu believed he was the better fighter, the honor of battle on its own was a relic of history. He had a powerful ally he would not hesitate to use, and which set him apart: his sister. She was loyal beyond question, better and smarter than her counterparts, and always connected to him via synced chip implants.

Together, with their combination of military prowess and technological expertise, they presented a fighting duo without equal.

Relaxed and focused, he finished off with a nice stretch and a bio-cocktail from the fridge, then headed upstairs to shower. When on assignment, Jianyu's firearm of choice was a black semiautomatic pistol made of lightweight polymers, which folded to resemble a laptop battery. He also carried a serrated push dagger and a custom-made Japanese switch-sword, and wore body armor so light it barely weighed more than a pair of wool sweaters. Embedded beneath his skin were tiny retractable spikes at his wrists and ankles, which could pierce an eye or slash through a vein as a last resort, a palm trigger synced to his pistol, and a few other nasty surprises.

After assembling his gear in a tactical bag disguised to resemble a tourist backpack, Jianyu took the elevator to the garage, where his motorcycle was parked.

As the garage door opened, letting in a flood of moonlight and exposing the abandoned warehouses across the street, Daiyu stepped into view from a darkened corner.

"Sister!" Jianyu said as he strapped his pack onto the back of his bike. "What are you doing in the dark?"

"Thinking."

"About what?"

Dressed in a black leather bodysuit outlined in silver, she stepped forward to hand him a paper box wrapped with a neat red ribbon. The aromas of fresh pastry and red bean paste mingled with the bergamot and myrrh of her perfume. "Moon cakes for your journey," she said.

He accepted the treat—his favorite—with a laugh. "You take care of me just like Mother used to do."

Instead of returning his laughter, she regarded him with a stoic expression. At first he thought she was despondent—it was always a sad occasion when they separated for a mission—but then he saw the shadow behind her gaze, and understood a different feeling was in play.

He set down his helmet and cupped her narrow chin in his hand. "Of what are you so afraid, sister? Zawadi? The Archon?"

"Both." She fingered the jade key around her neck, and her eyes flicked to her bio-bracelet. "But mostly I fear the future."

"Why?" he said to humor her, for he gave no credence to her eerie digital oracle. "What did you see?"

She stared right through him, and he could never remember seeing her this concerned. "A veil, Jianyu. I saw a shadow over everything, over the sun, the moon, the stars. Over you. I don't know what any of it means. I just know the world is about to change."

Cartagena
Summer 1970

After deducing the rearranged letters in the name Nataja Tromereo also spelled Ettore Majorana, and against his better judgment, Dr. Corwin let himself fall asleep in the bed next to Anastasia Kostos, the woman he had met at the bar the night before. He was certain she was a member of the Ascendants and sent to derail him in some way. Perhaps her job was to let Hans inside the room, though the heavy wooden door to the suite had a double-sided dead bolt and a latch chain, both of sturdy design. The balcony was less secure, but a clandestine entry would require a precipitous climb in full view of the street.

So, while he knew he should have stayed awake all night or seen Ana to the door, he was in desperate need of a few hours' rest, and couldn't bring himself to part with her lustrous brown hair and honey-smooth skin.

Before he fell asleep, he hid the key to the dead bolt and set the alarm to go off at dawn. As the first rays slanted into the room and fell across Ana's high cheekbones, Dr. Corwin stirred and blinked the sleep away. He needed to get a head start on the day. No doubt Hans had talked to Alvaro by now and would soon figure out the anagram.

When he tried to extricate himself from Ana's embrace, she

stirred and curled into him, nibbling on his ear and stroking his chest with her nails. This pleasurable turn of events led to another session of lovemaking that left him just as breathless as the night before.

"I expect I'll never see you again," he said when he forced himself out of bed and began putting on his trousers.

Ana sat up and pulled the covers to her waist, leaving her full breasts exposed. "Why say such a terrible thing? A gentleman would look me up in New York as soon as he returns."

"Don't you mean to say *if* I return?"

"You shouldn't be so pessimistic."

"I don't believe you or Comrade Hans has my best interests at heart. Or even my continued longevity."

"Darling. Really. The things you say."

He was starting to get irritated, both at her casual duplicity and at his own growing attraction. "Why don't we part ways with a little honesty, and therefore dignity? I can't say I wish you success in Cartagena, but as for the two of us, I couldn't imagine a better way to spend an evening."

"It was quite dreamy, wasn't it? How long will you be staying? Maybe we could have an encore."

"Is that all you have to say?"

She batted her eyes. "What else would you like to hear?"

His fingers pushed hard as he buttoned the cuffs of his camel-brown dress shirt. "Not interested in dignity, I see."

"I don't believe in the concept. If enough suffering is endured, all human beings reach a point where dignity dissolves into the instinct for survival. Self-interest is our true nature, and where is the dignity in that?"

"And you came to this conclusion how? Through application of torture across a wide variety of subjects?"

"Through observation of world affairs."

"What do you propose then? A world where only the strong survive? A dictatorship of unfettered capital gains and rule by nuclear arsenal?"

"Isn't that what we have already?"

"We can do better."

"I agree," she said. "But I'd replace dignity with honesty. An acknowledgment that we are all human and have our limits. Abandoning the pretense of pride and self-importance."

"That doesn't sound like it came from the Ascendants' handbook."

Her mouth opened and then closed, as if realizing she might have veered off script.

"I'm afraid you'll have to get dressed," he said. "I can't leave you in here alone."

Her lips fell into a pout. "Don't I have time for a shower? You could join me if you like."

"I've dallied long enough. Which I'm sure Hans greatly appreciates."

With a sigh, she removed the covers and sat naked on the edge of the bed. "Could you close the blinds?"

After they finished dressing, he saw her out, and she started down the hallway in the direction opposite the stairs. "Where are you going?" he asked.

"To my room next door. Quite convenient, isn't it?"

He smirked. "Quite."

As he watched her insert a key into the door of the next room over, he felt a pang of remorse they hadn't had the chance to meet in another way, taking in the town as tourists rather than adversaries in a deadly game. Perhaps they would have caught each other's eye in Plaza Bolívar amid the weeping trees and fountains, strolled atop the city walls and gazed upon the domes of cathedrals rising like jeweled crowns above the terra-cotta rooftops, or dined al fresco by the sea before stumbling into a sweaty nightclub in Getsemaní, quaffing mojitos and dancing hip to hip until their bodies were electric with desire.

"Your theory on human nature is admirable in some ways," he said. "But it's also incomplete."

She paused in the open doorway. "Oh?"

"I might concede your point on dignity and honesty, but there is something even higher than those principles, which even torture cannot reach."

"Which is?"

"Love. Not for ourselves, because I agree that's unreliable, but the love of a mother for her son, a father for his daughter, a betrothed for their beloved. Our capacity to love one another deeply and truly is the hope of the human race."

Ana didn't reply, but before she entered her room, she met his gaze with a solemn, unreadable expression.

When Dr. Corwin entered the hotel lounge, he noticed Hans on the street outside, prepared to step into a black town car. A sling supported the German's left arm, dark bruises covered his face, and one eye was closed shut. Dr. Corwin felt no sympathy for a man who had tried to kill him, and when Hans glanced through a window and saw him watching, Dr. Corwin tipped his trilby. With a look of pure hatred, the German stepped into the waiting vehicle.

After indulging in a moment of satisfaction, Dr. Corwin hurried into the dining room for a quick breakfast, knowing Hans had a head start on the day.

Of course he does. You've allowed your libido to override your common sense once again.

Yes, but I beat him to Alvaro, and I didn't figure out the anagram until late last night. And there is nothing common or sensible about a woman like that . . .

He took his coffee black and dug into a stack of strawberries-and-cream arepas. As he shoved down the delicious food, Dr. Corwin pondered his course of action for the day. Now he had to reevaluate his entire line of thinking.

His gut told him the physicist called X who had visited Cartagena and met with the wily old curandero was none other than Ettore himself. Briefly, he wondered whether Waylan Taylor had lied to him or had also been deceived by Alvaro, and how much Alvaro himself knew.

Could the old curandero be persuaded to divulge more information? Perhaps. Alvaro certainly knew more than he was letting on—yet why bother with the anagram if he was prepared to be more forthcoming?

It really didn't matter. The trail to Ettore was here, in Cartagena.

It occurred to him that the Ascendants might try to force information out of the retired curandero-psychiatrist. In fact, it was almost a certainty. Deciding to warn Alvaro as well as ask a few questions, Dr. Corwin took a cab to his house, relieved not to find Hans's black town car waiting outside.

Somewhat to his surprise, Alvaro opened the door. Dr. Corwin had half expected to find an empty house. "Back so soon?"

"Nataja Tromereo," Dr. Corwin said without preamble. "Ettore Majorana. It's the same letters, a simple anagram."

Alvaro's brow furrowed. "I do believe you're right."

"Cut it. Anyone could have figured this out—so why leave it for someone to find? What else do you know? How long did Ettore stay? Why did he come here, and when did he leave? Or is he still here?" He took a step closer. "Is he alive or dead?"

Though the curandero's eyes continued to glimmer, he stuck to his original story and claimed not to know anything about Ettore beyond what he had already said. No amount of pleading or hardened tone seemed to matter, and after shaking his head in disgust, Dr. Corwin gave him a stern warning about Hans.

"Yes, he was quite worked up this morning," Alvaro said.

"You met with him? What did you tell him?"

"Why, the exact same thing I told you, of course." After thanking Dr. Corwin for his concern, Alvaro patted him on the hand and sent him on his way.

A chorus of birdsong filled the air as Dr. Corwin entered the cab again and tried to think it all through. In the end, he realized he had two suspicions, a question, and a plan of action.

The first suspicion was that Alvaro had indeed met with Ettore himself at some point, very likely to discuss experiments and philosophies concerning the soul. The narrative fit with Ettore's obsession with this place called the Fold.

Second, he did not think the curandero knew where Ettore had come from, or whether he was still in Cartagena. After eluding the Ascendants and hiding out for so long, why would Ettore reveal his whereabouts?

On the other hand, Dr. Corwin had a hunch—a strange intuition—that the idea for the anagram had come from Ettore himself, planted long ago with the curandero for some unknown reason.

Along those lines, Dr. Corwin questioned why Alvaro had given out this information. If he had kept the knowledge of his meeting with Ettore to himself for such a long time, why divulge it now?

Or had no one ever asked?

Dr. Corwin had decided where he was going next, and informed the cabdriver. In his first conversation with Alvaro, the curandero claimed he had met with Nataja/Ettore at a hotel. He had even dropped a name. Los Claustros. Translation: the Cloisters.

Fearing another anagram, Dr. Corwin had searched for the name and was surprised to find the Cloisters was an actual hotel and still in service.

In fact, it was less than ten blocks away.

A block off the sea, near the family home of the popular novelist Gabriel García Márquez, the Cloisters hotel was a converted monastery whose outer wall had once formed a portion of the city's ramparts. The arched entrance, accessed through a door flanked by hanging lanterns, sat alone at the base of a high wall that took up an entire city block.

The street view was deceiving. After he pulled on the oversize brass handle and stepped through the recessed doorway, Dr. Corwin entered a sprawling tropical courtyard, so lush it was decadent, ringed by interior balconies where guests lounged with their morning coffee and cigarettes. At least three swimming pools could be glimpsed among the foliage, along with a maze of walkways, private rotundas, and outdoor balustrades. Though opulent at first blush, a closer inspection of the hotel revealed a state of decay—peeling paint on the balconies, chipped stone on the fountains, the forest-green livery of the staff in need of a good tailor—which instead of detracting from the experience, lent a desultory charm.

With a whistle of approval, Dr. Corwin followed the signs to a brick-floored reception with antique weapons on display. Though he found it odd to have weapons in an old monastery, it was refreshingly honest, he supposed, for a city that had once served as a hub of the Inquisition. For true accuracy, maybe they should have included the torture device meant to force the brain out slowly through the ears, or the claw used to rip off a woman's breasts, or one of the saws that hacked through its victims from groin to sternum while they were hanging upside down.

He doubted the staff kept records from thirty years ago, but he was going to ask. As he waited for the line at reception to dwindle, he browsed the museum of swords, shields, muskets, plate armor, and military uniforms. Wandering closer to the front desk, he noticed a leather-bound book on display. He leaned down and saw that it was a ledger with handwritten notes from guests of the hotel over the years. He flipped to the beginning. It dated back only three years.

When his turn in line came, he claimed he was a historian researching Cartagena and asked if there were older guest ledgers lying around. *Why, yes,* he was told. *In fact there are.*

After sweet-talking the attendant, he found himself mopping sweat off his brow in a windowless office behind the lounge, poring over a stack of ledgers covered in dust. It didn't take him long to find the right time period. With the ledger open in his lap, Dr. Corwin scanned the entries one by one, nervous the enemy would appear at any moment.

Half an hour later, Dr. Corwin found it. He almost couldn't believe his eyes. It was the same handwriting he recognized from the file on Ettore, the nervous scrawl that spoke volumes about his mental state. The short missive was written in Italian, and Dr. Corwin translated as he read.

> *A toast to your wonderful hospitality that left me refreshed for the next leg of my journey. Fellow travelers would be wise to explore the hotel, as a secret bounty awaits.*

> *Nataja Tromereo, May 1939*

A frisson of excitement passed through Dr. Corwin. Ettore Majorana was still alive in May of 1939, more than a year after his disappearance.

And he had stayed at this hotel and written in this very ledger.

He realized the message could be a fake, the handwriting forged by an expert. But to what purpose? No, this possessed the ring of authenticity. He could feel it in his bones. With a deep breath, he flipped through the rest of the ledger and found nothing else of interest. He returned his attention to the handwritten note.

Ettore had known that very dangerous people were looking for him. So why leave evidence of his passage? Had he left something behind in addition to his signature? Dr. Corwin reread the note, his eyes lingering on the second sentence.

> *Fellow travelers would be wise to explore the hotel, as a secret bounty awaits.*

Before leaving the lounge, Dr. Corwin considered ripping out Ettore's entry, but couldn't bring himself to do it. It felt wrong to erase the evidence of his passage from the historical record and deter future seekers. What if Dr. Corwin himself failed and his successor was destined to succeed?

What he did do, however, was hide the ledger from Hans. He couldn't remove it without someone noticing, so he stuck it behind a file cabinet, wedged against the wall, where no one could see. It wasn't the best solution, but it was something.

After debating a return to the Casa San Márquez to gather his belongings, he decided to stay where he was and expedite the search. He booked a room for the night so he could roam the grounds with impunity. The staff informed him it was impossible to discern what room a specific guest had occupied back in 1939, so he searched the hotel for another clue.

So far there was no sign of Hans, but the German might be on his way to the Cloisters, or the Ascendants might have sent someone else. *Any of these guests could be watching me at this very moment,* Dr. Corwin thought as he strolled through the tropical courtyard, trying to appear nonchalant.

The converted monastery was unlike any hotel he had ever visited. Except for the balconies ringing the courtyard, the layout of the rooms and hallways was convoluted and illogical. Long silent corridors that seemed to stretch on forever would suddenly dead-end or lead to a section of short, stubby hallways arranged around a central staircase that wound down to the edge of the gardens. Luxury suites occupied an old bell tower, a sunken bar was built into the choir pit, and the atmospheric crypt beneath the courtyard was open for viewing.

Just before lunch, after peering into every nook and cranny he could find, he wandered into the wine cellar, a brick-floored chamber honeycombed with bottle cubbies. Black-and-white photos of musicians, politicians, and other luminaries adorned the walls, interspersed with bottles of rare vintages, displayed upright on little shelves. Off the main room was a rough-cut tunnel, lined with old casks and cobwebs, which disappeared into darkness.

A waiter with a white towel draped over his arm was servicing a tasting table. Dr. Corwin did not have to feign enjoyment as he browsed the rare vintages. A Romanée-Conti here, a Château Lafite there. He took a closer look at the photographs, most of which depicted one or more celebrities lounging in various parts of the hotel. Nothing caught his eye until one of the black-and-white photos made him gape.

The photo had been taken in the wine cellar itself. A tall, slim man with a bushy mustache and penetrating eyes was holding a glass of wine, engaged in conversation with someone very few people outside of academia would recognize: a Mexican-born physicist named Ted Taylor, who had made great strides with fission bombs and reactors, but who spent his later years campaigning against the use of nuclear weapons. Like Ettore, his intellect had been far ahead of his time.

As accomplished as Taylor was, both his fame and his contributions paled in comparison to the other man in the photo, a Serbian-born inventor and futurist whose sanity near the end of his life might have been questionable, but whose genius no one disputed.

Nikola Tesla.

The mysterious, invisible world of electromagnetic waves and radiation that permeated the universe had always fascinated Dr. Corwin, and Tesla was a virtual god in the field, making discoveries and predictions so prescient it was almost as if divine intervention had occurred.

The photo shocked Dr. Corwin because of the date—May 1939—scrawled in the bottom left corner.

Earlier in Tesla's life, he had developed the concept of the alternating current, famously feuding with Thomas Edison—who championed the direct current—over how to power American households. While both AC and DC would become integral components of the electrical grid, Tesla, a better visionary than businessman, failed to monetize his work as Edison did. By the late 1930s, Tesla was virtually impoverished, living in Manhattan at the New Yorker Hotel, with no means of support other than a small stipend from the Westinghouse Electric Company—likely paid to avoid the bad press of having their star inventor living on the street.

There was no known trip to Cartagena in May of 1939, or to anywhere at all. Tesla didn't have two pennies to rub together. In fact, by that time, he had become known as something of a quack. In 1935, he infamously claimed to have invented a cosmic death ray, as well as an earthquake machine that could destroy the Empire State Building with five pounds of air pressure. His health was in decline, his serious work in his past.

Or so Dr. Corwin had thought before seeing this photo.

So the *world* had thought.

What did this mean? Had Tesla continued his work in secret? Could his late decline have been an act?

The thought sent a chill coursing through him.

Dr. Corwin wasn't as well versed in Ted Taylor's public appearances—and it was a bit odd that he shared a surname with Waylan Taylor—but Dr. Corwin was quite sure the nuclear physicist wasn't known to have visited South America during this time. How had two men so famous managed to dodge the press?

On second thought, he realized Colombia in those days would have been an excellent place to avoid scrutiny.

In a flash of insight, he wondered if Tesla and Dr. Taylor were members of the Society. Tesla, especially, fit the profile: geniuses in their field who disappeared from public view, and sometimes disappeared altogether. As soon as Dr. Corwin returned to New York, he would make inquiries.

But he wasn't finished with the photo.

Like most of the others on the wall, the date was handwritten, though no signature was attached. Strange. Dr. Corwin couldn't tell who had written the date, and he didn't think it was Ettore—but May 1939 was the same month and year that Ettore had signed the ledger.

Something else: in the upper right corner of the photo, part of another man could be seen. Someone with a slight build, dressed in a conservative brown suit and holding a wineglass in his left hand. The man's face was not in view, as if he were deliberately leaning out of the photo. He was standing just inside the entrance to the rough-hewn corridor housing the wine casks, and his right hand was resting, almost suggestively, against the stone wall.

Suddenly Dr. Corwin recalled the wording of the inscription in the ledger. *A toast to your wonderful hospitality that left me refreshed for the next leg of my journey.*

A toast.

Was the man hidden at the edge of the photo Ettore Majorana? Had he made a special trip to Cartagena, risking the safety of his long-imposed exile, to meet with these two fellow geniuses?

If so, *why*? What did this mean?

Dr. Corwin studied the handwritten date again. It was almost as if someone had come along at a later time and added it. Alvaro, perhaps? Someone else?

Many questions loomed, but there was one thing of which Dr. Corwin was certain. This photo was imparting a message. Something important.

A toast.

A secret bounty awaits.

Whoever the man in the photo was—and Dr. Corwin believed it was Ettore—one of his hands was raising a wineglass, a toast to anyone clever enough to recognize it.

Did the other hand, resting on the old stone wall just outside that very room, conceal a secret bounty?

11

After fleeing through the neighborhood outside the Kolkata Science Institute, Andie and Cal found a taxi stand and jumped into a cab. They asked the driver to take them to a hotel they had spotted near a city park close to the cantilevered bridge over the river. It had seemed like a safe, central area.

Thankfully, their first taxi driver's warning about unscrupulous members of his profession did not come to fruition, and they were dropped safely at a boutique hotel called the Krishna Palace. A noxious patch of smog hanging over downtown marred the view of the Victoria Memorial across the park.

The lobby was furnished with silk wall hangings, abstract Hindu art, and chair hammocks suspended from the ceiling. Andie liked the vibe, and there were no cameras in sight. Plenty of Western tourists mingled in the lobby, many of them similar in age to her and Cal. She paid for adjoining rooms without even asking the price.

Before they settled in, she used Zawadi's credit card to withdraw a tidy sum of rupees from an ATM in the lobby. Relieved the PIN worked, they took the cash and walked down the busy street outside, weaving through the vendors and homeless people crowding the sidewalk. By browsing a handful of stalls, Andie managed to purchase some needed items: a new backpack, two changes of clothes, sunglasses, and a headscarf. Cal opted for a baseball cap pulled low, a shirt with a high popped collar, and a pair of oversize sunglasses.

She thought he resembled an aging '80s pop star.

The security presence in chaotic Kolkata was more akin to Alexandria than London. If they could stay out of sight and find the next location on the Star Phone quickly enough, they might have a chance to leave the city undetected.

On the other hand, the Ascendants had found them everywhere they had gone.

Later that night, after dinner in the hotel restaurant, they rendezvoused in Cal's room. "So talk to me about this yantra thing," he said as he settled into an armchair with a Kingfisher lager. "Is it anything like a, what do you call it, a mandela?"

Andie unscrewed a half bottle of white wine from the minifridge. "It is actually nothing like a Nobel Prize–winning South African with distinguished white hair. A yantra is, however, similar to a mandala. Both are heavy on the symbology and geometry. I'm sure there's a correlation."

"Mandalas are those circular things with shapes inside you see all over the place, right? Hippies made them popular in the sixties, and now they're on everything from T-shirts to coloring books."

"That's right," Andie said, drinking straight from the bottle. "'Mandala' means 'circle' in Sanskrit, and it's supposed to represent the cyclical nature and complexity of the universe. Similar to an ouroboros, come to think of it. But a yantra is much rarer, almost unheard of in the West."

"So what is it?"

"From what I recall, it's a sort of mystical diagram. There are lots of different kinds, with lots of meanings. Some people use them as road maps for meditation. Some are used to worship specific deities. In the occult world, they're believed to convey magical powers."

"Magic? How does that connect to anything? Seems like a bit of a strange clue."

"Maybe, maybe not. You've heard of that famous Arthur C. Clarke quote about all higher technologies appearing magical to a less advanced civilization?"

"Nope."

"Well, think about it while I do some research. Personally, I think science *is* magic. Physics and chemistry are just names for miraculous things we've started to figure out the rules to."

As Cal took a long swig of beer, muttering about techies and millennials, Andie reached for the phone Zawadi had given them and pulled up the web browser. Before she could start searching, he said, "Why don't we take a step back for a sec?"

"I'm all ears."

He belched lightly. "I'm about to fire off some inquiries. Quasar Labs, Aegis International, PanSphere Communications, even the Kolkata Science Institute: all that funding came from somewhere."

"Sounds like a start."

"Before we go too far down that road, we should also look close by. I don't want to get blindsided by the obvious."

"What do you mean?" she asked.

"Think about the Archon. The height, those weird powers of hypnosis . . . What if it's someone we know?"

"Like who?"

He held his palms up. "Hear me out. I'm just going out on a limb, exploring possibilities. What about Dr. Corwin?"

"No way," she said, shaking her head fiercely. "He's not that tall, and he was *shot*."

"Okay. I just want you to keep an open mind. Who else could be involved? Platform shoes can add a few inches, you know."

She thought about it for a moment. "Lars Friedman," she said slowly. "When I researched him in Durham, one of the articles said he was six foot four and played basketball in college." She put a hand to her temple. "Oh my God, why didn't I think of that? What if he betrayed Dr. Corwin—and then burned down his own lab after he stole the research, to cover up his crimes?"

"Now you're thinking like a paranoid reporter," Cal said grimly. "There's someone else too. It's an extreme long shot, but I don't trust anyone in this mess. You're a good kickboxer, right? Think about how quickly the Archon disabled you. Who do we know who's involved who could pull that off?"

After a moment, Andie swallowed and said, "Zawadi? But why save us twice and let us go?"

"To see where we end up? Maybe she betrayed Dr. Corwin, and is working on her own. Maybe we're not really free but being watched the whole time, used as guinea pigs to help *her* find the Enneagon."

Andie stared down at her hands. She really didn't want Cal to be right about that one.

"Listen," he said gently. "I don't think that's the case. Otherwise she would have just stayed with us."

"Maybe, maybe not. She gave us the phone and the documents and, like you said, she can probably track us whenever she wants."

"True, though I think Lars Friedman is more likely. The point is, until we know for sure whose side everyone is on, we can really only trust ourselves."

After a weary nod of agreement, Andie used Zawadi's phone to conduct research on yantras and the museum exhibits, searching for a connection. Cal sat with a pen and a pad of paper he found in a desk and began scribbling, working on his own research threads.

An hour later, Andie was stunned by what she had discovered. She paced the room fiddling with her wine bottle, sorting through the threads in her mind. "Cal," she said finally, "I found a few things."

He looked up from his chair. "The next location?"

"Not yet. But listen to this: You know that iron bowl we saw in the museum?"

"The one related to some pillar in New Delhi?"

"That's right—and the Iron Pillar of Delhi is very real. It's a tourist site, and all those claims about the purity of the iron and the lack of rust are true. Scholars don't even know where it came from. But I can't find a single mention of any companion pieces, such as that bowl, that are similar in age and construction."

"So if the bowl is real, how the hell did it end up in a private museum?"

"Exactly. And remember the miniature sandstone column with the carving of the nine dragons on top? This is even stranger."

"What was it called? Ash something or other?"

"An Ashoka pillar. Twenty of them are still in existence and can be seen around India. Everything the placard said about King Ashoka and his pillars is true—except for the last sentence."

"Remind me?"

"The placard claimed the miniature pillar in the museum was found in King Ashoka's personal collection and uncovered from his tomb in Karnataka."

"That sounds . . . plausible."

"Sure, except there's absolutely no mention on the internet of his personal collection or anything like it—and no one's ever found King Ashoka's tomb."

Cal's eyebrows raised. "Ah."

"Ashoka was mentioned half a dozen times in that museum. So I decided to look him up." She took a deep breath. "Have you ever, in any of your conspiracy research, run across something called the Unknown Nine?"

Cal frowned. "I don't think so. Maybe someone brought it up in a chat once, but I've definitely never researched it. What is it?"

"An ancient Indian legend about King Ashoka. All the sources agree, by the way, that he underwent a radical conversion after massacring the Kalinga. He's known for those pillars and his conversion to Buddhism, but there's a pervasive legend that he went a step further to ensure humankind stopped slaughtering one another in senseless wars. Realizing that technology was only going to improve over time, and that some people would use it for their own evil purposes, King Ashoka gathered nine of the most brilliant minds in India—they were all men at the time, naturally—and tasked them with accumulating and preserving all the knowledge in the world. Thus was born the society of the nine unknown men. Starting to sound familiar?"

Cal whistled. "That's hella close to what we know about the Leap Year Society. Why were they unknown?"

"According to the legend, there can only be nine members of the order at any one time. The nine were supposed to remain anonymous, hidden in the shadows while they protected humankind from its own base instincts. Before one of the nine dies, they have to pass on the knowledge to a successor. The true believers out there think the Unknown Nine still exist today, guardians of knowledge passed down through the millennia."

"It's insane to think they were having the same debates about technology thousands of years ago that we're having today," Cal said. "Those flaming arrows must have caused quite a stir. In any event, that's some legend. Are you becoming a believer, Mercuri?"

"I'm just drawing parallels. Remember the carving of the dragons on the Ashoka column and the seal in the exhibit? Nine dragons inside a circle. While some of the other Ashoka pillars have animal carvings on top, there are no dragons, and there's no mention of that inscription in the museum anywhere either. Listen again: 'We pledge together at the crossroad, devoted to the gathering of knowledge, through immortal time and spirit.'"

"That sounds an awful lot like a direct reference to Ashoka forming the society of the Unknown Nine."

"I'd agree with you, except why did the ouroboros with the nine dragons show up on that seal in the Harappa exhibit as well?"

"I . . . don't know."

"What the hell did we see in that museum, Cal? Did they really find Ashoka's tomb? Either way, I know they're telling us something about the Leap Year Society." She started pacing the room again. "There's something I haven't told you. Remember Dr. Corwin's journal? The one I lost?"

"How could I forget?"

"There was a reference to the Unknown Nine."

Cal sucked in a breath. "That's rather relevant."

"Not before I did this research. It was just a note in the margins, followed by more of that gibberish code. I'd almost forgotten about it. Something else I learned about Ashoka's secret society: they were said to have communicated in a language unintelligible to anyone outside the order."

"Like the code in the journal?"

"I don't know what it all means at this point."

What she still hadn't mentioned, because it sounded too far-fetched, was that the Unknown Nine were said to have mastery over a wide range of subjects, including human physiology, and that according to one wild myth, one of the nine could manipulate pressure points and kill human beings with a single touch. She couldn't help but shudder at the thought of how the Archon had rendered her unconscious so easily.

Stop it, Andie. Plenty of martial art masters could execute the same maneuver. The Ascendants are trying to creep you out and control you, with their masks and their secrets and their buried myths, just like they've done to Mom.

"I'd like to say all this is wild speculation," Cal said, "but there are too many parallels. And that drawing in Dr. Corwin's journal of the nine steps from the Star Phone to the Enneagon, a device which has nine sides . . ."

Andie gripped the phone in frustration. "My eyes need a break." She offered the device to Cal. "Have at it for a while."

Before conducting a little research of his own, Cal cracked another beer in support of his gluten-rich diet. Whether it was nine yogis in ancient India, or nine Silicon Valley tech giants in modern-day America, the story of a group of people hoarding knowledge for the betterment of a few was hardly a novel one.

Despite the danger they were in, he was optimistic—though weirded-out—by what they had uncovered. He could almost feel the threads starting to unravel, and he wanted to bury these people more than ever.

How deep did the conspiracy go, how far back in history did it reach?

How big was this story?

Andie was slumped in a chair, deep in thought, her tired green eyes streaked with red from lack of sleep and worry. Over the last few days, he had found himself watching her with increasing frequency. He wasn't quite sure if it was attraction or some male protector instinct he was sure she would mock him for. Despite her lack of makeup and disheveled appearance—maybe these were a product of their fugitive lifestyle, though he kinda gathered they were the norm—she was very attractive in a nerdy-science-girl/badass-spunky-loner kind of way.

A description he fully admitted made no sense.

He had never met a woman who was just as likely to expound on some esoteric mathematical theory as she was to jump on the back of a hydroboard and ride it through a Venetian canal with her life on the line. It was obvious Andie didn't give a damn what anyone thought about her, formed her own opinions on everything, and could be as stubborn as an Indiana winter. It was also obvious she had no idea how attractive all of that made her, especially to someone used to the women in LA, who were pretty much the polar opposite of her.

Not that any of it mattered. Cal was quite sure she wasn't the type to fall for his corny humor and roguish smile and three-dollar charm. On the inside, he knew he was a complicated person—weren't we all? But when it came to women, he preferred not to work too hard. He had never had a problem scoring a date, and that had made him lazy. But it was hard to be around someone twenty-four hours a day—especially someone who looked as good in jeans and a ball cap as Andie did—and not wish things were a little different.

But most of all, he had grown to care about her welfare. He knew how torn-up she was about her mother and Dr. Corwin. Cal had his doubts as to how much these people actually cared about *her*—but he didn't really know any of them.

What he knew was that their interests were aligned. Andie badly needed a friend, and he was feeling pretty damn protective toward her. He knew she would hate that, so he didn't plan on mentioning it.

With a yawn, he gave all of those thoughts a good stiff-arm and focused on the task at hand. Before he left LA, Dane had given him a dark web onion address to log in to in case they needed to talk.

Man, did they ever.

He went to the web address, which routed him to a black screen with a blinking red cursor. Cal typed in the password Dane had given him: Lakers99Clips0!*OMG*.

A white chat box materialized around the red cursor. Cal assumed that meant success, and he typed an exploratory message.

Anyone homo?

A response arrived in less than a minute. The priest just so happens to be in the chapel.

The speedy reply came as no surprise. Dane was always online, and Cal guessed he had set up an auto-alert routing the onion address to his email. Inside LA's hacker community, Dane was also known as Priest—short for "the high priest of technology."

Good timing, Cal responded.

Are you in need of absolution?

I'm too far gone for that. More like salvation from my enemies. Are we safe to talk?

If your friends can find us here, then they've broken the internet.

Maybe they have, Cal thought. You still interested in helping me track down some bad guys?

The bad guys?

You got it.

I'm ready and willing. Your dramatic send-off on Twitch caused quite a stir online, you know.

I thought it might. How long before the Ascendants deleted it?

Oh, about 10 minutes. But that was long enough for a few people to repost it on Reddit, and it took off from there. Someone—I assume it was the hornets who own the nest you poked—worked hard to erase them all. I was following along, and for a while it was like watching a high-tech game of Whac-A-Mole.

Did they succeed?

More or less. But people don't forget those kinds of things, and there's some buzz around it. You started something, homeboy.

Let's hope we can finish it. Hey, I need you to look into a handful of companies: Quasar Labs, Plasmek Technologies, and Aegis International.

I know Aegis is that prick Elias Holt's company, the watchdog for the Ascendants, but remind me about the other two?

Quasar and Plasmek are likely LYS research labs. My guess is their funding will link up somewhere. But give 'em all the works. Follow the money, trace the parent corps, offshore tax havens, everything. I want to know who started them and when, who's involved now, soup to nuts. You can add PanSphere Communications for good measure. That's the global tech company who owned the black-site facility in Bolivia I uncovered.

I'll see what I can do.

I feel better already.

Don't get your hopes up. I've already made a go at Aegis, and learned these people have mad armor in place. Still, there's a chink in everyone's plate mail. Oh, and since you've been gone, I've had to beef up my own game to stay off their radar.

Good idea. Bonus points for anything you can find on the LYS or the Ascendants.

How do they fit together? You think the LYS are the good guys now?

It's complicated, but maybe, or at least some of them are. The Ascendants are most definitely not. But at this point, I don't really care, and it's clear their pasts are intertwined. Blow it up, and I'll sift through the wreckage.

Check.

Andie had lain down to rest but failed miserably. Soon after she took back Zawadi's phone from Cal and resumed researching, she made a discovery. "Take a look at this."

Cal hurried to sit beside her on the cloth settee beneath the window. She showed him an image on Zawadi's phone that looked identical to the yantra the Star Phone had revealed in the Kolkata Science Institute.

"That's it!" he said. "Where'd you find it?"

"The good news is this yantra is most definitely the same one we saw. The bad news? It isn't specific enough."

"What do you mean?"

Andie set the phone down. "I stopped worrying about all the exhibits and just focused on yantras. I learned that in Sanskrit, 'yantra' means 'instrument' or 'machine,' and is supposed to embody spiritual concepts in geometric form. Interesting, right?"

"Fascinating."

"Maybe Dr. Corwin is telling us that from the beginning, science and religion were intertwined, technology and mysticism . . . I don't know. Anyway, there are specific types of yantras, and this one is called the Kali yantra."

"That does not give me a warm-and-fuzzy."

"Like I said, Kali gets a bad rap. Yes, she's the slayer of demons and the avatar of destruction, but she's also the mother of the universe and the essence of divine love. Her yantra represents time, and transformation, and the energy embodied within all things."

"That reminds me of Dr. Corwin's fascination with the sea of energy surrounding us that you told me about."

"I hadn't made that connection, but you're right. That bindi in the center—the red dot—embodies the human soul but also Kali herself, the point from which everything in the universe emanates."

"So where does this get us?"

"I'm not sure yet. This info wasn't hard to find; I just searched for yantras and studied the images. I suppose we're looking for a specific one, though I don't know how to separate them."

"Want me to take a crack?"

"I've got a little steam left," she said.

As she continued to research, Cal drifted off in a chair, a beer cradled in his lap. After a while, she took a break to pace the room, and glanced at his face. Cal's stubble had turned into a light beard, and his large form was splayed across the chair like an overgrown puppy. She envied the ease with which he always fell asleep. Andie could never shut her mind off, unless she worked herself into a state of exhaustion through exercise. Not being able to run had impacted her mental health during the journey, and she could feel the tension building inside her like a boiling kettle.

When this is all over, maybe you need to try some of these meditative techniques you've been reading so much about.

Outside the window, the lights of the hotel across the street winked out one by one. The loneliness of the foreign city made her want to rouse Cal, if only to have another voice in the room.

Who has he loved and lost? What's his story?

When she had first met him, she thought she had him all figured out. He had stayed true to form in many respects—a former jock who used his looks and schoolboy charm to ease through life—but he was cleverer than he let on, and was much more complex than she had realized. A shadow behind his gaze at odd times, a self-deprecating scowl when he thought she wasn't looking. Why was he risking his life to be here? Most people in his position would have simply given up and chosen a new career. Returned to Indiana and studied accounting, or married a divorcée in the suburbs.

Was it simple revenge? A desire for justice?

Or did he love being a reporter that damn much?

She also found herself longing, in the dead of night in this city so far and foreign to everything she knew, to send an email to her mother. To reach out and continue the discussion cut short by those monsters at the Venetian ball who had dragged Andie away from her.

But she didn't dare. The probability was too high the Ascendants were monitoring her mother's email address and could track the sender.

Be strong, Mom. Somehow, some way, I'll find a way to get you out of this.

An hour before dawn, Andie found what she was looking for. She hurried over to the chair and shook Cal's shoulder.

"Huh?" He jerked upright, his eyes gummy with sleep. "What happened? Is someone—"

"Everything's fine. I know where we need to go."

"Couldn't you tell me over breakfast?" He yawned and ran a hand through his hair. "What's the scoop?"

"I was wrong. I thought the design was exactly the same—but it isn't." She showed him the photo of the Kali yantra on Zawadi's phone again. "Do you see how the circle is made of undulating wave-like sections that repeat over and over?"

"Barely. It's small."

"I know, but the one I saw through the Star Phone was different. The pattern looked more like marshmallows rising to a point, like those Arabian-style sultan hats."

"You do have a good memory."

"Once I realized the difference, I started searching for a specific replica of the yantra on the Star Phone." She opened a different page on the browser. "That led me to this."

He leaned over to take a long look at the image of a Kali yantra made of colored tiles. "Where is this?"

"Right here in Kolkata, on the ceiling of the Kalighat Kali Temple."

"I'm not sure what's worse: the nightmare I was just having, or the thought of visiting a temple in Kolkata dedicated to a death goddess."

"The Kalighat is one of the most famous Hindu shrines in the world," she said, "and it's right in the middle of the city. There will be plenty of people around. If it's the right place, Dr. Corwin must have had a reason for sending us there."

"Plenty of people around like the Ascendants?"

She looked away, and he ran a hand through his hair. "Sorry, I'm just cranky when I'm woken up before dawn. You did great work. But maybe you should catch a few z's."

With a few hours left before the temple opened, in desperate need of some rest, she decided to heed his advice. Yet as soon as she closed her eyes, despite understanding the true meaning of the goddess, she couldn't stop forming an image of Kali in all her destructive glory, her fanged mouth open wide and dripping blood as the bright-red tongue unfurled halfway down her chest, her pendulous breasts wreathed with a necklace of skulls. And in two of her many arms, held high on either side of the blue-skinned deity, were the severed heads of Andie and her mother.

12

Hours later, after a taxi procured by the hotel dropped Andie and Cal on Kalighat Road in the heart of Kolkata, they proceeded on foot through the narrow lanes surrounding the mandir, or temple. Andie couldn't resist looking over her shoulder with every step, unsure who the Ascendants would send but knowing they were out there, searching the city.

After breakfast, they had decided to disguise themselves better and had taken another trip to the street stalls. Andie was now wearing a blue sari over jeans and a matching cotton undershirt, a wig of straight black hair that fell halfway to her waist, bangles on her arms, and a dot of red dye in the center of her forehead—a bindi—that represented the sixth chakra or third eye, the locus of concealed wisdom. Andie had to admit that, except for the paleness of her exposed skin, she resembled half the young women in Kolkata.

Cal chose the same clothes and hat and sunglasses he had bought the day before, but with a fake beard—repurposed from a wig—that transformed his appearance. Andie had the Star Phone and Zawadi's cell in her pockets. Cal was carrying the rest of their meager belongings in the backpack they had purchased, in case they didn't return to the hotel.

She had done her research on the Kalighat Kali Temple. Once located on the banks of the Hooghly River instead of a grimy side channel in the center of a densely crowded neighborhood, the original structure was a ghat, a wide set of steps leading down to the river for bathing and ritual cremation. The site had long been devoted to Kali, and according to local folklore, the jungle surrounding the ghat was once inhabited by tribal Kapalikas, or skull bearers. The Kapalikas dedicated human sacrifices to the goddess, used hollow skulls for begging bowls, and smeared their bodies with ashes from the cremations. These aspects of Kali worship—though real—had been poorly understood and sensationalized by the British.

Yes, there were once sacrifices to Kali, just as there were similar practices in the ancient versions of many religions. But focusing on the Kapalikas or the infamous Thuggees or even the terrifying Kali iconography was to ignore the true meaning of the goddess. To the vast majority of Hindus, being devoted to Kali meant to be fully present in time, to experience life and change and death in all its chaotic splendor, to succumb to the eternal rhythm of creation and destruction. To dance with abandon to the beat of the tabla drum at festival, to hear the ringing of the celestial spheres, to celebrate the goddess and the animal in us all.

As Andie wound her way through the claustrophobic alleys, the research became a dry and distant memory, and she experienced Kolkata in all its filthy, luscious, stinking, messy glory. Stray dogs pawed through garbage in the street, trailing behind women in saris who carried plastic baggies filled with baked goods for the altars. Electrical wires were strewn overhead like jumbled Christmas lights. Beggars and holy men crowded the streets; devout women of all ages knelt against stone posts and washed their hands in bowls of water; a robed tantric priest with dreadlocks and a chalked-white face balanced a pair of skulls on his shoulder; professionals on their way to work hopped across rivulets of blood from the ritual sacrifice of a goat in a street side *murti* shrine. Every now and then, she saw a tourist looking lost and overwhelmed, ready for the exit. Worst of all were the *dalals* she had read about, local touts posing as guides, who harangued the tourists. They swarmed around Andie and Cal like flies, offering to help them select puja offerings from the stalls crowding the streets and guide them to secret places in the temple. When a particularly aggressive man grabbed Andie by the front of her sari, she gritted her teeth and swatted his hand away, resisting the urge to lay him out flat.

Keep your cool, Andie. Stay in control. We can't cause a scene.

The smells alone were overwhelming. Spice and incense and sugary treats, rotting flowers and fresh flowers, the saccharine fruits of lush foliage snaking through the cracks in the buildings. Overhead loomed the temple itself, the central tower a multitiered dome painted silver, reminiscent of the fairy-tale Bengali architecture she had seen in countless photos. Bands of bright color curved around the tower below the dome, and the temple walls bore a green-and-white chessboard pattern. The entire complex was ringed, at least the portion Andie had seen, by canvas stalls selling a mind-boggling array of costume jewelry, sweet treats, animal skulls, flowers, and other votive offerings.

The closer they drew to the temple, the more the crowds and the frenetic energy increased. As they passed through the open-air entrance and joined the crush of people in the courtyard trying to climb the steps to the mandir proper, Andie felt as if she might pass out from the heat of so many bodies pressed together in the hot sun.

She took a few sips of bottled water, wiped sweat off her brow, and took deep breaths to stay calm. The bumping, jostling, and shuffling into place made her feel as if she were at the start of some nightmare marathon.

She was not scared, though. Except for the horrid touts, the energy of the crowd was not aggressive. It was unlike anything else, or at least anything she had ever experienced. She marveled that the source of all this furor was a belief in a deity, an embodiment of invisible cosmic principles that drew these people together and had shaped the course of events on the subcontinent for millennia. Whether the goddess was real or a product of a collective cultural imagination, the devotion she inspired in her worshippers—the sheer phenomenology surrounding her religion—was a thing to behold.

The people pressing into this building believed in the visceral reality of Kali. Of that Andie had no doubt.

In the center of the crowd, sitting cross-legged on a blanket on the steps leading to the entrance, was a middle-aged woman with one arm and a braid of graying hair. Her face was upturned to the sky, her eyes rolled so far back the whites were showing. She rocked slowly in place as she chanted Kali's name, over and over. Beside her on the blanket was an emaciated boy of nine or ten, with no legs below the knees and pus-filled boils on his face. His back was against the woman, presumably his mother, and he held out a cracked wooden bowl to the crowd, pleading for alms.

The crowd flowed around the pair as if they were a block of granite, somehow never touching them. As Andie passed by, she noticed the woman's bindi was a smear of crimson across her forehead.

The boy caught Andie's gaze. "Please, money from you? We have nothing."

As the boy shifted his position to lift his bowl, he grimaced in pain. She realized he had an open sore on his knee from scraping the ground for so long. The look in his eyes, an absence of life and hope and basic humanity on a level she had never before witnessed, made her stop where she was and risk being smothered by the crowd. Emotion welled up deep inside her, bringing tears she worked furiously to blink away. The boy didn't need her pity. He needed help. As she dug in her cross-body handbag for rupees, she noticed the skeletal outline of his ribs, the dirt-encrusted nails, the sunburned lips stretched over white teeth that were the sole remaining mark of his innocence.

A child. A starving child, surrounded by thousands of people walking right by him.

I know this is an entirely different culture, and there are starving children at home, and the money will probably go to some evil handler, and nothing I do will make a difference, and we have to hurry inside the temple. And I don't. Fucking. Care.

Cal pulled her gently by the arm. "We should go," he said quietly.

After dropping a fistful of rupees into the bowl, earning a gush of thanks from the boy and not a shred of recognition from the mother, she let Cal pull her away, wiping away a tear as they reentered the flow of people. The pungent smell of humanity pressing against them made her so dizzy she had to lean on him for support.

"I know," he said. "It's overwhelming."

She could only nod, worried the nausea would induce another vision.

"Anything yet?" he asked, his eyes flicking to the Star Phone concealed in her left pocket.

She shook her head. On the way, she had pointed the device at the temple walls, and anything else that looked symbolic or important.

"So we're doing this?" he said as they neared the main entrance. "It's going to be chaos in there. What about circling the complex first?"

She gripped his arm as a man with gold chains draped across his shirtless chest bumped into them. Another worshipper was entering the open doorway to the temple with his back arched, thick red scars crisscrossing his stomach, supporting a lit candle with his tongue. Andie clenched her other hand as they approached the sluice of a doorway leading into the temple. "The Kali yantra is inside the main hall. We should start there."

Cal grimaced as he stood on his tiptoes to scan the crowd. "You're probably right. But I don't like it."

"Me either. What happened to calm museums?"

"Let's just hope this is the right place."

Once inside, the bedlam spilled into a vast room called the *natmandir*. People poured into the open-air hall from a multitude of entry points, jostling to enter a line headed toward the Kali idol at the far end of the hall, chanting and singing and talking, clutching votive offerings at their sides. A swarm of guards and priests and aggressive touts added to the mayhem, along with the dissonant chords of sitars along the edges of the crowd.

Andie saw it right away, as did Cal. Both of them craned their necks to observe the enormous red-and-green Kali yantra looming above the hall in the center of the ceiling. The bright colors had been painted or dyed onto the large stone blocks.

Up ahead, along the left side of the hall, Andie saw a more orderly line, with a sign pointing to the *garbhagriha*, or inner sanctum. From reading online, she knew the main attraction of the temple was the *Kalika murti*, or Kali idol, on the level below. The idol could be glimpsed from the other end of the natmandir—where all the people were heading—but a closer look could be garnered in the inner sanctum, if the guards let you enter.

Andie dug into her pocket for the Star Phone, but Cal grabbed her hand.

"Don't stare," he said in a low voice as they shambled forward with the crowd, "but look to your left, along the wall. Guy with the glasses."

The sides of the hall were reserved for guards and priests keeping an eye on the mob. Near the beginning of the line to the inner sanctum, she noticed a tall Indian man with a knotted gold cord draped across his embroidered red shirt. His hair was cropped close to his scalp, and a pair of glasses sat lightly on his fine-boned nose.

"The guy who kind of looks like a professor?" she asked.

"That's the one. I caught him looking right at me."

"You do sort of stand out. There's not another Westerner in sight."

"If he's looking for us . . ."

"Then he's found us." She pulled out the Star Phone. "I'm not leaving without a look."

The man didn't seem to be paying attention to them now. Andie let the crowd shield her actions as she pressed the camera of the Star Phone to her eye and aimed it right at the Kali yantra.

This time, she thought she would be ready when the room morphed and the stone blocks on the ceiling expanded into three dimensions, but her nausea from the walk and the crowds and the heat made her clench her stomach muscles to control the dizziness. Again she feared her disorientation would make her slip into an altered state.

No no no. Not here. Not now.

She felt Cal's strong arm around her waist, propping her up. "Stay with me," he whispered in her ear. "I've got you. Is there something there?"

Andie swallowed, nodded, and focused on what she was seeing. She knew she couldn't stand there all day and stare at the ceiling. Photography was supposed to be prohibited, but people were taking selfies all over the hall. She had read that as long as the Kali altar wasn't targeted, the guards wouldn't enforce the rule.

She hoped that was the case.

Disappointed there was not an alphanumeric cipher leading to the next location, she gritted her teeth and absorbed the image. It was confusing. The stone blocks overhead had kept their gray color, but they had expanded in size and were fewer in number. The Kali yantra had disappeared, and every single block either contained a single silver star or a pattern of connected stars she realized were constellations. She recognized Leo the lion, Centaurus, Sagittarius, Corvus the crow, and Cassiopeia. Those five constellations were the only ones represented, though they repeated on various blocks across the ceiling.

As the crowd jostled around them, she lowered the Star Phone and described what she had seen.

Cal frowned. "Any ideas? First impressions?"

"We don't have time for first impressions. We need a solution."

"I didn't want to have to say it."

Andie's gaze slid to the wall of guards and priests, but none of them seemed to be paying any special attention to them.

"Do you need to take another look?" Cal asked.

She shook her head, trying to think it through. "I've got the image. But those constellations . . . why those particular ones? The enlarged ceiling with the reduced number of blocks makes me think it's a math or astronomy problem of some sort, but there's no pattern I could see. Also, instead of using the Indian constellations—every culture has their own interpretation of the night sky—the constellations are all Greek except for Corvus, which is Latin. I guess some or

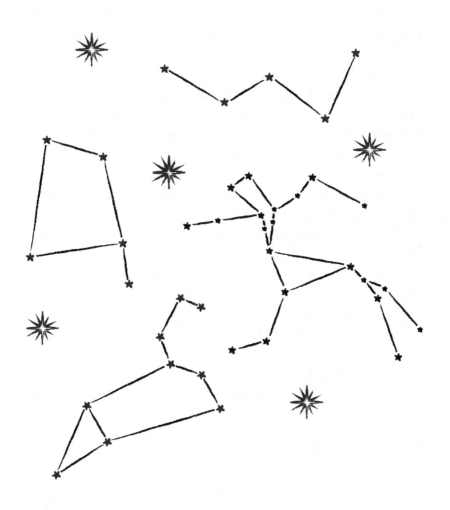

all of them might have older origins. I'd have to check."

"Why not use the Indian constellations? Is that a sign?"

"I don't know," she said. "Keep it in mind."

"Should we leave now?"

She scanned the crowd. "I've got a feeling this is something we're supposed to solve right here. The way the image takes up the entire ceiling, fitting the room perfectly . . . I think it's a physical puzzle of some sort."

They were halfway to the front of the room. Even if the Ascendants didn't know about the Kali yantra, she knew they had eyes in the city. It could be one of the priests or guards, or an angry tout, or a worshipper in disguise.

Anyone.

She wanted to scream. The answer was looming right above their heads, taunting them, daring them to figure it out.

"You said Dr. Corwin loves games and puzzles," Cal said, "but what kind?"

"All sorts, really. Every now and then he'd have a few of us over to his house for snacks and nerdy parlor games. He played cards online, and he and Dr. Rickman kept a constant game of—"

Her eyes grew very wide, and she spun to face Cal. "Oh my God, you're a genius."

"I am? I mean, you're just now realizing?"

She whipped out the Star Phone again. She had to have an exact count. After another look at the ceiling, she lowered her voice and said, "Eight by eight, sixty-four squares—it's a chessboard!"

He took a look with the device and said, "But the colors don't alternate."

"True. Maybe that's meant to throw us off. Think about it: there are only five repeating constellations on the board, and a bunch of single stars on the other blocks. The single stars are the pawns, and the constellations are the five major pieces used in chess: knight, bishop, castle, queen, king."

His eyebrows lifted. "We learned at the museum that chess was invented in India."

She gripped his arm. "The arrangement isn't uniform, like at the start of a game, so it must represent the middle of one."

"And we're supposed to finish it? What's the object of chess again?" He answered his own question with raised eyebrows. "To kill the king."

"Let's think about this. Leo the lion is obviously the king of the jungle, and Cassiopeia was a queen of Aethiopia."

"Centaurs kind of look like knights," Cal added.

"That's my guess as well. Sagittarius is a centaur archer, and his diagonal arrow makes me think of the way a bishop moves. I'm going with that."

"Which piece does that leave? The castle?"

"Yep. I don't understand that one . . . Corvus . . ." She snapped her fingers. "A castle is also called a rook, and a rook is a bird—not just a bird, but a crow. Corvus fits!"

"Okay. Then we're on the right track. So how do we win *this* game?"

She bit her lip, closed her eyes, and recalled the position of the pieces. "I'm pretty sure there's a Sagittarius—a bishop—in line with the king."

"Pretty sure?"

"Positive."

In their excitement, they had failed to realize they had reached the front of the line. After a glance to both sides, Andie put a hand on the barrier and looked down. Directly beneath them, surrounded on three sides by a metal railing in the chamber below, was the centerpiece of the temple: the Kalika murti.

The Kali idol was strange, unlike anything she had seen. Carved out of solid obsidian, the stone was a polished black rectangle standing upright, maybe as tall as she was, with rudimentary features. Kali's small nose was carved directly from the stone, beneath three teardrop eyes painted bright red, which formed a square with the nose. The tongue, wide and flat and made of gold, extended halfway down the idol's chest. The simplicity of the megalith possessed a timeless sort of resonance, a primeval magnetism that suggested the idol below her had been carved and worshipped before the dawn of recorded time.

The stone body of the goddess was wreathed in sari cloth, jewelry, and looping garlands of flowers. She had four arms, the left two holding a sword and a severed head. The decapitated head and lolling tongue reminded Andie of her dream, causing her to shudder.

The people around them reacted in various ways when it was their turn to behold the goddess: calmly kneeling with folded hands, giving praise with song, convulsing and gyrating as if possessed. Andie and Cal made a pretense of calm devotion and then walked slowly along the periphery of the crowd, buying time to think.

"Maybe we have to move the pieces on the board," Andie said.

"How so?"

"I don't know yet."

After recalling the position of Sagittarius as best she could, she veered to the right, until she thought she was beneath the constellation of the centaur archer. She consulted the Star Phone again, nervous about exposing it so close to the priests and guards.

When she aimed the device above her head, nothing happened. *Don't be stupid. It's the Kali yantra that has the code embedded.*

She tried again, aiming at the yantra, and the 3-D image returned. "Three feet to the left," she said.

Cal guided her by the arm as she kept focus. When she was standing directly beneath the Sagittarius constellation, it started to glow bright yellow.

Excited, she lowered the phone and told him what had happened, then worked her way through the crowd until she was standing below the position of Leo, the king. She aimed the Star Phone at the yantra again, and was happy to see she was standing in the right place.

Except nothing new happened, and the glow from Sagittarius blinked red and disappeared.

"I think we're supposed to link two of them, but something's not right," she said. "*Dammit.*"

"That professor priest left the temple," Cal said. "He gave you a long look and walked away quickly. Not a good sign."

Andie bit furiously on a nail as they made their way to the side wall. After a moment, she groaned and touched a hand to her forehead. "Stupid. I'm so stupid. Why are we trying to kill a king in the temple of a goddess?"

Cal was on his tiptoes, glancing nervously over the crowd. "Good point. Though if killing the queen isn't the goal of chess, what's the connection?"

"She's the second most important piece."

"Okay," he said, snapping his fingers. "So what if the queen is *the* most important piece in this particular game? What if she's supposed to take out the king?"

Excited by the theory, Andie recalled the position of the pieces on the board again—and sensed at once they had the answer. The Cassiopeia constellation was all the way on the far end of the board, but the mother of Andromeda—the queen of Aethiopia—did have a direct line to the king.

She looped an arm through Cal's to stay connected, then moved to stand beneath the Leo constellation again. A tingle shot through her when she pointed the Star Phone at the Kali yantra, and the stone block above her glowed yellow.

"The guards are getting antsy," Cal said.

"They're gonna be downright furious with what we do next," she said, eyeing the chessboard on the ceiling and then lowering the device. She thought she had the answer now.

"Which is?"

"Cassiopeia is right above the Kali idol. Another good sign. But to link the queen to the king, I'm going to have to use the Star Phone while standing right in front of it. The viewing platform isn't going to cut it."

When he didn't respond, Andie looked up to find him staring

through the open-air entrance and into the courtyard. From their position, they could just see into the main plaza fronting the temple.

Cal flattened against the wall and pulled Andie back with him. His face was drawn, his lips pressed tight. "There's a guy in the courtyard coming this way, and I'd bet half the brownstones in Brooklyn he isn't a Kali worshipper. Take a quick look—you're better disguised than I am. Tall, athletic guy, looks Chinese to me, black jeans and green T-shirt. There's a half dozen people flanking him in the crowd."

Andie stepped out for a glimpse. She had to strain to see over the crowd, but she saw the same guy in the middle of the courtyard, a handsome young man with short dark hair, aviator sunglasses, and a physique that resembled a bodybuilder's even through the loose cotton shirt. He was not yet pushing people aside, but he was making a determined effort to get through. She didn't see any visible weapons, but the guy had an extremely competent look that reminded her, from the economy of his movements to the firm set to his jaw, of Zawadi and Omer.

"You see him?" Cal asked as she backed inside, out of view of the courtyard.

Andie's knees felt a little shaky. "Yeah."

"I think our time just ran out. Let's pick another entrance and get the hell out of here."

"I'm not leaving without trying for the idol. We might not get another chance."

"Andie, don't—"

"I'm doing it. Are you with me or not?"

Cal swore and looked away. After running a hand through his hair, he turned back and mumbled, "Fine. But we gotta go, Andie. *Now.* What do you need?"

"A diversion."

Cartagena
Summer 1970

After discovering the photo in the wine cellar depicting a conversation between Nikola Tesla, Ted Taylor, and an unknown figure believed to be Ettore Majorana, Dr. Corwin spent the rest of the day holed up in his room at the Cloisters, staying out of sight and devising a plan for how to proceed.

The sun had descended an hour ago. Freshly showered, he smoothed the pointed collar of his electric-blue dress shirt and stepped onto his balcony overlooking the courtyard. A quick glance told him the hotel was hopping, dinner and drinks in full swing, waiters hurrying to and fro among the tables and tropical foliage.

It was time to proceed.

In order to avoid the crowded courtyard, he took a circuitous route through the labyrinthine interior of the hotel, emerging near the entrance to the crypt and the wine cellar. Wondering if there was a secret passage connecting the two—that would be useful— he straightened his trilby and whistled a tune as he idled beside a potted palm, waiting for a sommelier to appear. Laughter and the clink of glasses filled the air, along with the aroma of roasted meat and fine cigars.

Five minutes later, a Colombian man with a trim beard appeared on the walkway, wearing a bow tie and black apron over his white dress shirt. He was heading for the cellar with a fastidious gait.

The tasting room had closed for the day. Dr. Corwin followed behind the sommelier, padding silently over the mosaic stone tiles. There was a restroom just before the entrance to the cellar. If the sommelier turned and saw him, Dr. Corwin could duck into the toilet.

Intent on his mission, the sommelier left the door open as he hurried to the bottles on the opposite wall. Prepared to waylay him in an emergency—a blow to the temple that would leave no lasting harm—Dr. Corwin walked silently into the room, slipping into the rough-hewn corridor just to the right. He took a few steps inside and squatted beside a dusty oak barrel, deep in shadow. Soon the light in the wine cellar was extinguished, followed by the sound of the door closing and the click of a dead bolt.

So far, so good.

Dr. Corwin dug into his pocket and took out a cigar lighter. He flicked it on as he moved to the entrance of the old storage tunnel, searching for the exact spot where the man in the photo had stood with one hand resting suggestively on the wall. Once in position, he bent over and felt around for loose stones. Finding nothing, he expanded outward, searching in a wide radius.

Still no luck, and the flame was burning his thumb.

The sound of another key in the lock broke the silence. Dr. Corwin hurried to extinguish the light and scurried deeper into the tunnel. The farther he went, the mustier it smelled, and he heard the pitter-patter of rodent feet inside the walls.

As before, whoever had entered did not stay long. Dr. Corwin guessed most of the bottles ordered at dinner were kept at the main bar, and only special orders were serviced in the cellar. In any event, he resumed searching as soon as the person left, this time using a pocketknife to probe the mortar between the irregularly cut stones. Now he found more than he bargained for: plenty of the mortar had disintegrated, allowing him to loosen the stones.

One stone was particularly susceptible to his examination. With a grim smile, he inserted the blade to pry it out, leaving a small cavity in the wall. He leaned down to illuminate it.

Inside was a wooden matchbox.

Tamping down his excitement, Dr. Corwin reached inside to extract the box. It bore no commercial imprint and looked homemade. He slid the box open and saw a folded piece of paper inside. After extinguishing the flame to cool his fingers, he reignited the lighter and examined the lined yellow paper. It was in good condition, and of the sort widely available in stores. His excitement grew as he saw, in the middle of the paper and written crisply in blue ink, a row of numbers and mathematical symbols that made no sense to him.

A code then.

Ah, a man after my own heart.

The sound of a key turning the dead bolt interrupted the silence yet again. He extinguished the flame and scrambled back into the darkness, still holding the loosened stone, the wooden box, and the piece of paper. He cursed himself for not replacing the stone at once.

Expecting the noise to quickly recede, he instead heard voices conversing in English, and was shocked to realize it was Ana and Hans. The sound of his lover's throaty voice caused him to grit his teeth, both anger and desire coursing through him.

"Look at this photo," Hans called out.

"My God," Ana replied after a moment. "Is that Tesla?"

They must have found the ledger and suspect something is in here, but they don't know for certain.

Dr. Corwin crept silently forward, deeper into the darkness of the vault. As his fingers folded the paper and put it in his pocket, he ran straight into a tangle of sticky strands stretching across the tunnel.

Dr. Corwin reared, clawing at the threads and resisting the urge to cry out. *Calm down, man. It's just a spiderweb. Even the bloody tarantulas won't kill you.*

He knew that Hans—and probably Ana—would have no problem shooting him dead and leaving his body in the storage tunnel.

Desperate to stay out of sight, he kept going, leading with his outstretched hands to avoid bumping into a wall. Once the tunnel curved to the right and he was out of sight, he risked a quick flick of the lighter. The illumination revealed a stretch of tunnel that dead-ended a hundred feet ahead. On each side of the tunnel, about halfway down, an alcove could be glimpsed behind the barrels, a cavity of deeper shadow.

"Shine the light down this tunnel," Hans called out.

"It's just barrel storage," Ana replied.

"Look—a stone is missing!" Hans cried.

"And the mortar freshly dug."

Hans swore. "He beat us here."

Dr. Corwin couldn't be sure whether they had realized the full import of the photograph yet. Either way, they knew something was amiss.

After a moment, the German cursed again and said, "Let's see where this tunnel leads."

Good Christ, they're coming this way.

Left with no choice, Dr. Corwin climbed over a dusty barrel and huddled inside the alcove on his left. The space was much smaller than he had realized, more of a cubbyhole than a true alcove. An iron grate in the floor suggested a point of entry to the sewer. He tried to lift the grate, visions of an underground escape dancing in his head, but it was bolted down.

The skitter of rodents came from somewhere beneath him, and the cubby stank. He took deep silent breaths to control his anxiety in tight spaces. Hans and Ana were approaching quickly. Dr. Corwin flattened on the stone floor, his palms pressing into cool, damp lumps that crumbled beneath his fingers. He recoiled as he realized what he was lying in.

Rat shit. The floor is covered in rat shit.

Forcing away his revulsion, he laid his head on his arm and tried not to breathe in the noxious fumes as the footsteps approached. Out of the corner of his eye, he saw a light sweeping the tunnel.

"Anything?" Hans called out, from farther back in the passage.

"No," Ana said slowly. She was standing right beside the alcove, so close he should have been able to smell her perfume, if he hadn't been lying in rodent droppings. "It's a dead end."

She stood in place for so long he was sure she had noticed his footprints on the dusty stone floor. He lay as still as he could, not even daring to breathe.

Her footsteps finally receded. After another few moments, he heard Hans call out in a sharp voice. "He booked a room here. Make sure he doesn't go back to it, and place a guard at the exits to both hotels. Watch the airport, the rental agencies, and the passenger ships. Dr. Corwin doesn't leave Cartagena—do you hear me?"

"Understood," Ana said, and her words were like daggers in the darkness, piercing Dr. Corwin in the back.

Dr. Corwin snuck out of the wine cellar the next time a sommelier entered. As soon as he emerged and took a look at the upper crust lounging in the courtyard, he realized how difficult it would be to leave the hotel unnoticed, especially covered in rat feces. The inescapable fact was that the clientele of the Cloisters was overwhelmingly Caucasian or light-skinned Latino.

The staff, however, was a different story. Apart from workers at the reception desk and the sommelier, every employee he had seen was black. The hotel was a microcosm of the city: the wealthy Colombian elite enjoying the pleasures of life on the backs of the lower classes. The social reality was appalling, but it might also be his way out.

Hans and Ana had not realized how close he was. He might have a small window of time to escape. After washing the rat droppings off his hands, he followed one of the waiters to the kitchen, located the break room, and lifted a dirty uniform off a hook. The place was so busy for the dinner rush that no one paid him any attention. It was also so enormous that, once Dr. Corwin shed his clothes and donned the green-and-white livery, bummed an Embassy filter cigarette, and joined a group of waiters and cooks by a dumpster in an alley outside the hotel, no one seemed to notice he was not a regular employee. One by one, the rest of the staff stubbed out their cigarette butts and returned inside, while Dr. Corwin slunk away into the night and hailed the first cab he saw to take him to Getsemaní, the rough working-class neighborhood just outside the city walls.

Just another *hombre negro* returning home after work.

He asked the driver to drop him at a good but casual restaurant. The driver obliged, leaving him on a crowded corner throbbing with energy. Teens and young adults danced in the street to the pulse of salsa and Afro drums spilling out of bars and restaurants. Ignoring the patio tables, Dr. Corwin slipped inside the empanada café the driver had chosen, ordered a cold beer and the daily special, and hunkered down to study the cryptic line of numbers and mathematical symbols on the paper he had lifted from the cellar. He had kept the matchbox too.

Though stumped at first, he solved the code before he finished the meal of rice, beans, and corn empanadas. The puzzle was laughably simple, at least for a professor of theoretical physics who excelled at mathematics. Sipping his beer, he discovered by trial and error the numbers on the sheet of paper were atomic numbers in the periodic table, all of which, of course, were represented by one or two letters of the alphabet. The mathematical symbols were basic ones—multiplication, division, square root. When the words he formed using the atomic numbers alone resulted in nonsense, he applied the mathematical symbols to the numbers in the standard order of operations before converting them to letters. Using the first letter of each symbol resulted in a phrase that made him tingle with excitement.

THIRD CANNON FROM NW WATCHTOWER

The cypher could refer to a thousand different fortifications around the world. But in Cartagena, it could mean only one thing:

San Felipe Castle, the iconic fortress looming above the city.

Dr. Corwin discovered from the staff that the castle was only a short walk away but closed for the night. He decided against a hotel, in case the Ascendants were calling around. Instead he wandered the neighborhood until he found a homeless camp in a palm grove, then paid one of the men about his size a few dollars to exchange his soiled clothing for a hooded poncho, cotton trousers, and leather sandals with soles barely hanging on.

Wary of being robbed if he stayed overnight, he left the grove, found a comfortable park bench tucked out of view, and slept like a baby. There were hundreds, maybe thousands, of beggars and homeless people in the city with a build and skin tone just like his. It was a pleasant evening, so why not hide in plain sight?

The next morning, as soon as the entrance to San Felipe Castle was unlocked, Dr. Corwin watched the people around him gape as the homeless man in their midst rose off the park bench at the bottom of the castle, grabbed a coffee from a street vendor, paid the entrance fee, and proceeded to shuffle up the long switchback ramp to the top of the castle. Had the pedestrians gotten too close, their noses would have wrinkled at the awful smell of his poncho, and if their hearts were not hardened, they would have felt sorry for the threadbare state of his cotton trousers and the flapping soles on his sandals.

He wondered if they would have been more—or less—shocked to know the homeless man was actually a professor of theoretical physics at Columbia, slumming in rags to avoid the members of a dangerous secret society prowling the city looking for him.

San Felipe Castle was a mammoth structure. A quick glance at the entry pamphlet revealed it was the largest and most complex Spanish-built fort in the Americas. In the early days of exploration, Cartagena, as fat as a blood-filled tick with profits from slaves and gold, had been looted so many times by Sir Francis Drake, along with a long list of pirates, the Spanish got fed up and built a seven-mile wall around the city, studded with turrets and reinforced by forts at strategic locations. The greatest of these was San Felipe Castle, a feat of military engineering that included eight batteries, dozens of cannons, cisterns in case of drought, and a system of tunnels dug by Welsh miners and rigged with exploding ceilings. The system of interlocking walls, zigzagging entry ramps, parapets, and tower batteries with overlapping fields of fire made it impossible to isolate any one defensive section, making the castle a death trap to attackers and impregnable at the time. Despite numerous attempts, its walls were never breached, and it took mainland Europe half a century to catch up to the advanced geometry of the design.

The night before, Dr. Corwin had debated breaking into the castle. There would have been a certain irony in breaching walls that had repelled invaders for centuries. Yet he had no idea what sort of surveillance the city had in place, and most important of all, the Ascendants would have no reason to suspect his presence at the castle this morning—because the only clue was hiding in his pocket.

Following the decoded directions, he found the third cannon closest to the northwest watchtower. The cannon was pointing west, toward Cartagena Bay. Sky and sea merged into an azure shimmer in the distance.

The morning sun was potent, causing him to sweat and itch beneath the filthy poncho. He ignored the discomfort and bent to get a closer look. The cannon, which sat between pitted stone walls on a wheeled wooden cart in dire need of repair, had oxidized to a mottled blue-green color. A thorough inspection revealed no secrets, until he got down on his hands and knees and found a short message carved into the underside of the cart.

ADDIO. EM

The message caused a sinking feeling in the pit of his stomach. He stared at it, stunned and disbelieving, for a long time.

Dr. Corwin knew there were a number of ways to say goodbye

in Italian. The very casual *ciao* was used for both hello and goodbye. *Arrivederci* was a slightly more formal salutation among friends and family, which translated to "until we see each other again." There was *buon viaggi* for "have a good trip" and *buongiorno* for "have a nice day."

Addio was the most permanent farewell of them all.

Addio meant you might not see the person again—ever.

He stood to survey the horizon in the direction the cannon was pointing. *Did you go west, Ettore? Is the message a final farewell?*

Or was this all a subterfuge to throw off pursuit?

Though bitterly disappointed, and confused as to the motive behind such a convoluted ruse, Dr. Corwin began to chuckle, and then laugh, at the perverse way Ettore had played him. Played them all.

As a lover of games and puzzles himself, Dr. Corwin could only appreciate the devious nature of the wild goose chase, though any good lover of riddles would take offense that no prize awaited except a carved message beneath a cannon.

Ah, but I do have a prize, he thought as a warm sea breeze caressed his cheek.

My prize is knowing that Ettore Majorana might still be alive and has continued his research.

You might have won this round, you sly devil, but I know you're out there somewhere, still at work on your theories—and we'll see who wins the game in the end.

13

As the muscular and dangerous-looking Chinese man—surely an Ascendant—approached the Kalighat Kali Temple, Andie joined the shorter line on the northeast side of the main hall, which led down a set of stairs to the inner sanctum housing the Kalika murti. An unarmed guard in a brown uniform was checking people through at the top of the steps.

As Andie tensed for action, Cal skirted the line holding a fistful of rupees. She had asked for a diversion, and he walked right up to the guard, making a show of trying to bribe his way to the head of the line. Andie couldn't hear what they were saying, but the guard was shaking his head and jabbing a finger at Cal's chest. The people in the line were growing agitated and muttering to themselves, probably about rude Americans.

Cal wouldn't relent. He tried to press the rupees into the guard's hand and walk around him. This caused the guard, who was much smaller than Cal, to take him firmly by the elbow and try to lead him away. Cal resisted. The guard called for assistance, and two of the nearby touts rushed over. Cal outweighed each of them by fifty pounds, and struggled so hard the entire group fell to the ground in a heap.

Hoping Cal wouldn't get hurt or arrested, Andie used the distraction to sprint to the front of the line, vault over the pile of men struggling almost comically on the ground, and bound down the flight of steps. She drew stares and shouts aplenty, but no one tried to stop her.

At the bottom of the steps, the line snaked clockwise around the metal fencing surrounding the Kali idol. Andie cut to the right, avoiding the entire line, and a few steps later found herself face-to-face with the imposing stone goddess. The protests from the devotees increased in volume. A crowd of people pressed against the viewing platform above her, pointing down and shouting.

Thank God I have a sari on, she thought, *or I might be lynched.*

Gritting her teeth, she ignored the clamor and scrunched beside a woman kneeling before the goddess and moaning her name. Andie was so close to the idol she could have reached through the fencing and touched the smooth black stone.

In one deft motion, she held the Star Phone to her eye and aimed it at the Kali yantra on the ceiling high above her. She could glimpse only the outer edge of the yantra from that angle, but it was enough: the chessboard image appeared, and the stone block with the Cassiopeia constellation above her head started to glow. A silver line darted from Cassiopeia to the Leo block she had already illuminated. An explosion began in the king's constellation and spread quickly across the chessboard, until the entire 3-D image burst into silver fragments that reformed into a new nine-digit alphanumeric sequence. Ignoring the angry shouts all around her, the jarring twang of the sitar, and the foreign smells assaulting her senses, she committed the code to memory and pocketed the Star Phone.

When she turned to leave, people in line were still clamoring and jabbing fingers in her direction, yet remarkably the line had held, since no one wanted to lose his or her place after hours of waiting. As she sprinted toward the stairs, one of the awful touts, a grubby man with missing front teeth, bounded down and stalked her with a vicious twist to his mouth. He was jabbering in Hindi and blocking her way. One of the priests had probably sent him to apprehend her.

Andie didn't have time for this. She could feel the Ascendants pressing in. With a howl, she ran straight at him, and at the last moment launched a flying kick straight to his stomach. She hit him square with her right heel, throwing him backward, and braced her fall with an elbow. Dazed by the hard floor, she lurched to her feet as the tout curled into a ball and gasped for air. Andie darted up the stairs alongside the stunned crowd and reentered the main hall, where the pandemonium had increased.

In one glance, she noticed a number of troubling things. There was a circle of people standing around Cal, who was struggling to his feet. The guard and the touts were watching him closely and waving their hands, calling for help. Throughout the hall, priests and more guards and even a policeman were converging on the source of the commotion. And at the far end of the natmandir, opposite her position, Andie saw the Chinese man entering the temple, trying to discern the cause of the uproar. He started pushing his way through, wading through the devoted worshippers as if they were long stalks of grass that bent with his passage. Andie didn't think he had seen her or Cal yet, but it was just a matter of time.

She ran toward Cal, screaming and waving her arms, trying to cow the crowd into submission. It seemed to work—the men around him shrank back, and no one wanted to engage her. As the policeman and his retinue surged forward, Cal collected himself as best he could, and together he and Andie fled the sprawling hall through the nearest open-air exit.

They emerged into an interior courtyard far less crowded than the main courtyard. Still, a good number of people were about, priests and functionaries attending to their daily business. There were a number of other buildings inside the walls of the complex, though none as large as the main temple. She could not tell which of the numerous pathways between the buildings led to an exit.

It was a maze they had no hope of deciphering.

With a crowd of priests and touts on their heels, Andie and Cal sprinted in the opposite direction from the main courtyard, desperate to flee the complex. Startled by a hand tugging on her shirt,

Andie whipped around to find a small boy gazing at her with a face covered in pus-filled red sores. She recoiled from his touch, realizing she had stared into those eyes earlier that morning—it was the crippled boy from the steps of the temple, though he seemed to have miraculously regrown his legs.

"Lady need help?" he asked in broken English.

"What do you mean?" she said as she ran, forcing herself to overcome her revulsion at the boils covering his face and wondering which of his other ailments were a ruse. *It doesn't matter. He's just a little boy.*

He kept pace with them. "I know way to leave temple. No one see you. I help."

When Andie met Cal's gaze, she saw her own feelings mirrored, a mixture of fear and indecision.

"How much?" Cal asked, but Andie waved him off and said, "What's your name?"

"Mani."

"Listen, Mani, I want you to know there are some bad people chasing us. I don't want to put you in danger. But if you can point us toward an exit, we'll be forever grateful. And we'll pay you very well."

The boy showed no sign of fear or worry. He continued to keep up as they rounded one of the buildings. "Not right way. Come fast. I know good way."

Andie didn't like their options one bit but was unsure what to do. She feared they were corkscrewing deeper and deeper into the temple complex, and the chorus of angry shouts was right behind them. "Okay," she said to the boy. "Lead us."

The boy tugged on her shirt and took a sharp right, dashing down the paving stones. They slipped between two buildings with mauve plaster walls and ran, for a moment, parallel to the main courtyard. Just before they rounded another corner, Andie looked to the right and saw the Chinese man step out of the natmandir, shield his eyes from the sun, and scour the grounds.

She grabbed Cal and pulled him out of sight. The clamor from the main plaza began to fade as Mani led them on a circuitous path through the buildings. He never hesitated as they raced through an open kitchen with pots and pans clanging, dashed through two smaller courtyards, and exited the temple complex through an archway overgrown with vines. Expecting to emerge on the street, Andie instead saw a collection of low-slung neglected buildings with pinched windows and lines of scrollwork decorating the eaves. The plaster covering these buildings had mostly chipped away, revealing a concrete frame underneath.

Mani cut through the center of the buildings and alongside a basin of green water. A lone bald man was standing waist-deep in the center, cupping water in his palms and pouring it over his head. He didn't flinch as they sped by. After entering a tight passage on the far side of the basin, Mani opened a wooden door that led into one of the low buildings. The boy ushered Andie and Cal through. Inside, the sunlight exposed brick walls in terrible condition, plus a wax effigy of Kali impaled on a lighted candelabra in the center of the room. A garland of rotting flowers draped the effigy. Dark splotches marred the smooth appearance of the wax, and a silver bowl rested ominously at the base of the pitted wooden altar. Andie caught the scent of something unclean in the air, an acrid tang of spilled blood that caused her to shudder.

"Come," the boy said, shutting the door and casting the room into near darkness.

"Where are we going?" Andie said.

He took her by the shirt again. "Downstairs behind altar."

"Down where?"

"To secret place."

Not liking the sound of that, but left with little choice, Andie let the boy guide them forward. She supposed they could see what he had in mind and judge for themselves. As they approached the wax effigy, the light from the candles allowed them to make out the outline of the idol's many limbs and grotesque tongue. When they were almost to the altar, the candles suddenly went out, casting the room into darkness.

Fear welled inside her. She stood very still, wondering what had happened. "Cal?" she whispered.

"I'm here."

Before either of them could speak again, a deep male voice issued a series of harsh commands in a guttural language unlike any Andie had ever heard. The voice was very close, near the effigy of Kali.

Her first thought—that Mani had betrayed them—was interrupted by a scream of pure terror, coming from right beside her.

Cal.

She started to turn but found herself caught in the grip of his arms. She knew it was Cal because she could smell the musky odor of a cheap deodorant he had purchased at the street market outside the hotel. She felt a hand at her side, digging into her jeans, and another squeezing the back of her neck. It was painful. In the dark, unsure of what was happening, she panicked and bucked to get free.

"Get off her!" Cal roared.

"Cal!" she cried. "Stop it! You're hurting me!"

He wouldn't listen and started to shake her so hard she was forced to press against him and grab him by the hair. "What are you doing?" she said. "It's me!"

Cal kept fighting. He pried her loose and flung her away. Andie stumbled forward and crashed into the base of the altar, causing the bowl to clatter on the floor.

"What the hell?" she said, so confused she didn't know what to do. "Cal? What's happening?"

The deep voice spoke again in the darkness, this time in English, and from farther away. "I knew you would bring them here, rat-catcher." The voice switched languages yet again, barking out a few angry sentences in what sounded like Hindi.

Terrified, Andie tried to think of something to do as the front door opened, letting in a flood of light. Standing in the doorway with a satisfied smirk was the priest they had seen in the temple earlier—the one who Cal thought resembled a professor. He was holding a cellular device that looked, from a distance, exactly like the Star Phone.

Beside her, Cal was blinking and using the altar to steady himself, as if disoriented. Andie fumbled in her pocket and didn't feel the Star Phone. She looked back and forth between the priest and Cal in horror. "What did you do?"

Cal gave her a confused look. "I thought you . . . I don't understand."

"He made a gift to Kali," the priest said with a smile as Andie ran toward him. He slipped through the door and slammed it shut, sealing them inside. Andie heard the click of a lock and found the door barred when she tried the handle.

She pounded on the door as Mani lit a match near the altar. Andie snarled and strode toward him. "You brought him!"

"No," the boy said. "I swear."

"Then what was that? Why did he call you a ratcatcher?"

"Because that is my caste. I catch rats near temple for priests, and sometimes, when no money, I beg."

"What did he say to you in Hindi? Tell me!"

A look of fear crawled onto the boy's face. "He say when he see me again, he give me to Kali."

Andie swallowed and whirled on Cal, who was backing away from the altar with a horrified expression. "What the hell was that?"

He jabbed a finger at the wax effigy. "She came to life and stabbed you. I swear it. I had to fling the dagger away and get her off you—"

"What are you talking about?" Andie interrupted in disgust, though when she saw the expression on his face—conviction wrapped in a cocoon of abject fear—she knew something terrible, and very convincing, had happened to him.

"I thought I was helping you," he whispered. "I'm sorry. I'm so sorry."

She didn't know what to say, or how any of this was possible, but the circumstances didn't matter. Somehow the priest had tricked

Cal's mind, and now the enemy—only an Ascendant would have targeted the Star Phone like that—had stolen Andie's only link to Dr. Corwin and her mother.

"I can't explain what happened," he said. "I saw it. I saw *her.*" He shivered and looked down. "It was the most awful thing I've ever seen. Her eyes and fangs, and that tongue . . . She was right on top of you and wrapping you in all those limbs . . ."

The boy was staring at Cal with an expression of horror.

Andie put a hand to her forehead, forcing herself to think. "We have to go. My guess is that priest is going for help. He'll probably come back with the Chinese guy."

"Come, lady," Mani urged, tugging on her sleeve as he stared at the locked front door. "I help you leave."

In the chaos, Andie had almost forgotten why they had followed the boy inside in the first place. Her sense of despair at the theft of the Star Phone was so crushing she almost wanted to lie down and let the Ascendants take her, accept whatever happened next.

She squeezed her eyes shut, knowing there was no choice if they had any chance of escaping. "Let's go," she said, opening her eyes but unable to look at Cal.

Could she even trust him now?

They followed the boy as he darted around the altar, revealing an iron grate set into the floor. He removed it, exposing a hole that stank like the love child of a slaughterhouse and a sewer. Mani took one of the candles off the candelabra, hesitating as if wary of disturbing the shrine, then lit the candle and aimed it at the hole.

A rusty iron ladder was bolted into the side of the well. "Where does this go?" Andie asked. "And don't tell me a *secret place* again."

"Many places," the boy said. "You need someplace safe?"

"Yes," she said, impatient. "I told you."

"For how long?"

"I don't know. *Where*, Mani?"

"I take you home," the boy said, with an earnest expression.

"Whose home?"

"My home. It is safe. Come."

"Does that priest know about this place?"

"Yes. But not where I live."

She glanced back at the door, so frustrated by her lack of options she wanted to scream. "Let's go."

As Mani climbed into the hole and replaced the grate, Andie made Cal go ahead of her, afraid to lose sight of him again. She followed him to the base of the ladder, ten feet down the hole, where they encountered a tunnel made of pitted granite, slick with algae. The ceiling was so low Cal could barely stand up. A series of small enclosures dug out of the rock and enclosed with rusty metal fencing lined one side of the tunnel, big enough for a goat or even a cramped human being. Andie heard the frenzied bark of an unhappy dog not far away.

She tried not to think about the purpose of this place as they followed the boy down the corridor. Behind them, in the building above, they heard a door open. They began to run, slipping on the damp stone. Soon they heard the murmur of voices and the faint splash of water, confusing Andie because the sounds were coming from farther ahead. Who else was down here?

Just as she started to panic, the boy gripped her arm and said, "It's okay. No one hurt you."

"Famous last words," Cal muttered. "And for the record, I am now officially sick of underground tunnels."

At least he's making a snide remark, Andie thought. Though still furious, she was glad to see his eyes were not as glazed. He seemed to have recovered from whatever the priest had done to him.

The murmur of voices increased as the tunnel sloped downward, leading to a rough-cut hole in the wall as tall as Andie, and a scene she would never forget. As she stepped through the opening after Cal and Mani, they encountered dozens of people in terrible physical condition, squatting or lying alongside a canal of fetid water that reeked of raw sewage. After choking back a surge of bile, she held her nose to keep from gagging. The people were naked or clothed in rags, missing fingers and toes and sometimes limbs, some of their faces so misshapen they resembled squashed clay. The rounded brick tunnel was pockmarked with jagged holes, as if riddled with the same disease as the unfortunate souls it sheltered. A few of the lepers were eating rice out of bowls with dirt-encrusted hands and passing around a jug of water. Some of them were talking in small groups. Some were moaning. Some were dying.

All of them had put their hope on a sailboat that had left its harbor long, long ago.

The brackish water glistened like oil by the light of an old gas lantern propped on a stack of bricks. Mosquitoes and flies swarmed with impunity. The humidity and the unrelenting odor made Andie dizzy. At first she was afraid, but as Mani picked his way through the small crowd, she realized the poor people shrinking into the darkened recesses of the tunnel were even more afraid of them.

Mani led Andie and Cal along the raised edge of the sewer canal, into the gloom of the tunnel. As soon as they left the leper colony behind, Mani's candle a pinprick of light in the Stygian blackness, the silt and muck deepened until Andie found herself wading up to her calves. She forced herself not to think about the filth through which she was walking.

"How far are we going?" she asked.

"Soon," Mani replied.

"Can you be a little more specific?" Cal said in frustration.

A scream echoed in the tunnel behind them. *Is the priest or the Chinese man still following us? Are they forcing one of those poor people to talk?*

They passed through the tunnel as quickly as they could, hoping the Ascendants would give up the chase now that they had the Star Phone. The muck was too deep to run through, and their slow pace was maddening. Soon they heard more voices and entered a section similar to the one they had just left, filled with boil-covered cripples and misshapen lepers and even a corpse rotting away on the periphery of the colony. The sight turned her stomach. She wondered if this was how soldiers felt amid the mass carnage of a battlefield, with all the viscera and blood and existential shock of human misery laid bare, trying to stay alive while forced to philosophize in tiny out-of-time moments on the sanctity of human life.

Shockingly, a canoe was moored in the sewer canal. The vessel was made of rotting boards that barely looked seaworthy, and had a tiny motor rigged to the end with wires. Mani walked quickly toward the canoe, chattering in Hindi and waving his hands.

A young man in ripped trousers rose from the walkway beside the canoe, set down a bag of takeout food—this seemed so absurd to Andie she almost giggled—and wiped his hands on a greasy cloth. When Mani turned to point at Andie, a smirk appeared on the man's face as he folded his arms and glanced back the way they had come. Andie's interpretation was that he understood the danger and would use it as a bargaining tool. Yet when he turned to Andie and demanded his price for the journey in fluent but harshly accented English, it was unbelievably low.

She made a show of protest but solemnly agreed to his price, then stepped onto the canoe before she was asked, pulling Cal along with her. The man untied the vessel and started the motor. Mani jumped on as well, jabbering in the man's ear and casting worried looks behind them. A light appeared in the hole they had entered through just as the motor sputtered and died.

Andie clenched her fists and willed the motor to restart. Now the man was casting worried looks at the tunnel himself and staring at Andie and Cal as if wondering if he should cut his losses. The light grew steadily closer. Andie gripped the side of the canoe in fear.

Finally the engine caught, and the vessel began to slither through the water. The inhabitants of the sad outpost paid them no attention as they slid into the abyss, guided by the bobbing headlamp attached to the front of the canoe. A few minutes into the journey, when the immediate threat of pursuit had receded and Andie's adrenaline had ebbed, she leaned over and vomited. She wiped her mouth with the back of her hand and watched with hooded eyes as they passed two more of the subterranean colonies. On occasion, the headlamp would reveal a lone figure or a couple shuffling alone in the darkness who seemed more like lost wraiths drifting through the underworld than living human beings.

The canoe pilot informed them that the tunnels crisscrossed the city, a relic of the Raj. Manholes used to provide access every hundred feet, but the modern expansion of the city had covered most of them, leading to the need for alternative transport for the underground denizens of Kolkata. Andie wondered how lepers could afford to use the canoes on a regular basis, and how they paid the fees. Probably begging like Mani.

The more twists and turns they made through the warren of tunnels, the more relieved Andie grew. The passages all looked identical. No one was following them through that maze, and they sure as hell weren't going to catch them on CCTV.

About half an hour into the journey, the pilot killed the engine in a flooded tunnel lit with a splash of sunlight. He used a pole to push the canoe alongside a rounded brick wall, just beneath a metal ladder leading to the surface.

Andie offered to triple the price if the pilot swore not to lead anyone else to their location. He shoved the rupees greedily into his pocket and steadied the canoe while they climbed onto the ladder.

Blinking like newborn babes, they emerged onto the surface near a sprawling slum. Directly in front of them was a set of railroad tracks piled with mounds of garbage that helped shield their arrival. Just down the tracks was a squalid collection of tar-paper shacks and lean-tos jumbled across a flat, swampy plain and surrounded by the skyscrapers of Kolkata. It looked as if a plane had dropped a bomb in the middle of the city, and the survivors had cobbled together a settlement from the debris.

Mani led them toward the slum. More garbage filled the streets, and the stench was almost as bad as the sewers. People were everywhere, men and women performing daily tasks or sitting in the harsh sun, dogs and children playing in the mud and filth. Only a small child sitting on the roof of the nearest shack seemed to notice as Mani herded them into a makeshift shelter on the periphery of the settlement. The "tent" was assembled from pieces of cloth and canvas, and propped up by three aluminum poles. Inside, arranged neatly on top of a pair of wooden crates, was a bundle of dirty clothes, an old milk jug, a plastic bag filled with rice, a box of matches, and two chipped bowls. In the corner was a deflated soccer ball missing half the panels.

"Here," Mani said, looking up at them with bright, expectant eyes. "You stay here."

Andie wasn't sure whether to laugh or cry. She had to admit it was the last place anyone would ever look.

"Okay," she said, collapsing beside Cal on the packed dirt that made up the floor. She hoped it didn't rain. "Thank you."

Cal squeezed the boy on the shoulder. "You saved us, kid."

The boy offered a shy smile and pointed at the rice. "Hungry?"

Andie and Cal shook their heads, starving but unwilling to eat the boy's only food. "Go ahead," Andie said. "We need to discuss a few things." She handed Mani a wad of rupees that made his eyes pop. He thanked her profusely as he grabbed the rice, matches, and a bowl before heading into the slum to find a cooking fire. "I tell no one about you," he promised.

"Oh my God," Cal said, once they were alone. He was staring at the side of the shelter. "What just happened?"

"We're alive, is what happened." Her tone turned bitter. "Without the Star Phone."

He swallowed. "Yeah. I'm . . . I'm sorry again. Do you still have Zawadi's phone?"

She patted her pocket. "It's here."

"That's some relief."

Andie took out the phone and turned it on. "We even have a signal," she said, though she supposed they were right in the center of downtown.

"And the credit card?"

"Safe."

Cal slumped in relief. "So what now?"

Andie shook her head, not even bothering with a response.

An hour later, as the punishing rays of sunlight outside the tent began to soften, Andie lay on her back with her hands crossed behind her head, reeking of her own stink, thirsty, hungry, at a loss for what to do. They couldn't stay in the slum for long. She didn't want to drink the water or eat the food, and she feared being robbed.

But she didn't dare surface in another part of the city.

Earlier, she had written a long text to Zawadi, letting her know what had happened. Andie had no idea where Zawadi was, if she would respond, or what help she could provide, but it was worth a shot.

After hearing Cal's description of why he had taken the Star Phone and given it to the priest, her fury started to wane, becoming a dull throb of helpless frustration.

According to him, after the candles had blown out, the priest had started chanting and the wax effigy of the goddess had started to glow. Kali had stretched out her limbs and come alive, springing onto Andie's back as the crimson eyes turned to stare at Cal, as real as anything he had ever seen. It made her shudder to hear him describe it in detail, and it was clear the experience still terrified him. The blood trickling from Kali's fanged mouth, the disheveled hair and dusky-blue skin, the swell of her breasts wreathed with a necklace of skulls, the four arms that had wrapped Andie like a spider and sucked the life from her . . . it had been a waking nightmare. The entire time, he said a voice in his head kept telling him the Star Phone was causing the goddess to come to life, and that Cal had to take it away from Andie to save her. He had believed that voice with all of his being, he had *known* it was the truth, and had done everything in his power to save her.

She could hardly blame him for that.

Obviously, some kind of hypnosis or mind control had been

exerted over Cal, and she guessed it stemmed from his encounter with the Archon. The strange words the Kali priest had uttered must have been a trigger, perhaps a common language used by the Ascendants to control their enemies during and after interrogation.

The worst part of that theory was that it could happen to him again.

While Andie had forgiven him, and even felt touched that he had tried so hard to save her, it didn't change the fact they were stuck in a Kolkata slum with no way of regaining the Star Phone, no hope of helping her loved ones.

Despair swallowed her whole.

14

"Cal!" Andie said. Night had fallen an hour ago. The faint urban glow of Kolkata, seeping in from the front of the tent, was the only source of illumination. "Take a look at this."

Startled by her voice, he sat up on the hard dirt floor of Mani's hideaway and leaned in close to read the text Andie had just received on Zawadi's phone—from Zawadi's own number.

> I will work on the Star Phone. Go to Anandamitra Guesthouse in Rajendrapur and wait until you hear from me. Safe haven. The owner can help Cal.

"What does that mean?" he said, slapping at a mosquito. "Work on the Star Phone? Help me how?"

Shouts and barking dogs created a constant racket from the slum. Mani had stepped out again, this time for water.

"No idea," she said, excited by the message but unwilling to let her hopes get too high. "If it's really a safe haven . . ."

"Where is it?" he asked, but Andie was already searching on the phone. She found no mention of Anandamitra Guesthouse, but Rajendrapur was a village less than thirty miles from Kolkata.

"It's probably a good thing we can't find the safe haven on the map," he said.

"Good point," Andie replied, chewing on a nail, certain only that they needed to leave the slum. "But how do we get there?"

They didn't like the idea of walking out of the slum, and no way in hell was Andie going back in that sewer. But Mani came through for them again. He found a driver, a young man from the slum who barely looked old enough to buy beer. Andie had offered to pay him a hundred dollars and a full tank of gas for the trip. The kid couldn't believe his luck.

Deep into the night, Mani smuggled Cal and Andie to the edge of the slum, out of sight behind a mound of garbage, where the driver met them in a white Maruti Zen hatchback held together by spit and duct tape. The vehicle was missing three hubcaps, a rear fender, seat belts, a radio, headrests, and the front passenger floor. The upholstery resembled cheesecloth, and the ceiling sagged so far down it brushed against their heads. The driver had to jump-start the car with a friend, and when the engine came to life, it rattled as if it had a dozen loose parts.

Parting with Mani was emotional for Andie. She hated to leave him alone in his crude shelter, struggling in that horrific slum without a family, covered in scabs and boils, and probably riddled with a host of diseases from the unsanitary conditions, facing the simple task of survival every single day.

It wasn't fair.

It wasn't right.

There had to be a better way.

She gave Mani all her remaining rupees and promised to send back more with the driver once they stopped at an ATM. Then she gave the boy a hug, disease and ravaged skin be damned, which put a smile on his face she would never forget. Cal leaned down to solemnly shake his hand, and she was touched by the kindness in Cal's eyes.

Two hours later, Andie and Cal found themselves hunched in the back seat of the Maruti with the road flying along beneath them, visible through a rusted-out hole at Andie's feet.

While driving through the sprawl of Kolkata—a ninety-minute white-knuckle odyssey of honking horns, cars driving without headlights, fear of their engine stalling, and a thousand other insane moments—they decided it was safer for Cal to stay low. The Ascendants, if they were still searching for them, would be on the lookout for two people. Andie's sari and dark wig blended better than Cal's disguise, so he laid his head in her lap and promptly fell asleep. One of her arms was draped across his chest, and she had a chuckle thinking it might have been a tender moment if they weren't both filthy and reeking from the journey through the sewers, and Cal wasn't snoring, and they weren't riding in the back seat of a junk pile on wheels that smelled like three-day-old curry. He was also starting to drool on her arm.

After they escaped the city limits and the traffic began to thin, the danger quotient lessened. She breathed a sigh of relief and let him continue sleeping. She, too, was exhausted, but someone needed to stay awake. She'd been dreaming of a hot shower and a soft mattress, but at this point, she'd take a garden hose and a sleeping bag.

The countryside outside Kolkata was so dark she couldn't make out much besides the strip of worn pavement illuminated by the Maruti's single headlight. Due to the traffic in the city, the poor condition of the road, the three attempts to find a working ATM, and the slow speed at which they were traveling to preserve the fragile car, the journey took much longer than expected. By the time they drove into the village alongside the colorful roadside murti shrines, the morning light teased the sky with whorls of pink and yellow.

The placid village was a shock after the smog-drenched bustle of Kolkata. Rajendrapur was little more than a collection of mud huts with thatched roofs, dotted around ponds and farmland. The heaviness in Andie's soul lifted as she gazed upon pastoral rice paddies and mustard fields, mango groves and vegetable gardens, children chasing ducks around a pond, and villagers collecting morning eggs from the chicken coops.

A villager their driver queried for directions to the Anandamitra Guesthouse pointed the way to a single-lane dirt road twisting through dense jungle. Three miles later, a wooden sign guided them down an even rougher road. After jostling over crater-size potholes for another half mile, they emerged into a clearing with a thatch-roofed pagoda surrounded by lush gardens. A trio of bungalows on stilts stood among the coconut trees lining the perimeter of the property.

Andie and Cal stepped out of the car, shielding their eyes from the sun, surrounded by clean air and birdsong and the sweet perfume of the foliage. As they started down a cobblestone path that wound to the pagoda, a tall, svelte Indian woman stepped out to greet them. She had long, unbound silver hair, bangles up and down her fore-arms, leather thong sandals, a nose stud, and a sari that matched the color of her hair.

"Good morning," she said, with a regal smile and an upper-crust British accent.

Andie returned the warm greeting, and introduced herself and Cal. "Is this Anandamitra Guesthouse?"

"It is indeed."

"Do you have any vacancy?"

"At the moment, all three bungalows are available. They're quite similar, and you may choose the one you want."

Andie didn't care what they cost, and she had the strange feeling the bungalows were almost always available. "Okay. We'll take two for the night."

"Lovely! Breakfast is included, but lunch and dinner are optional."

"We'll take the meals as well. Wait—do you accept credit cards?"

"All forms of payment are acceptable, but I've forgotten my man-ners. My name is Rajani. May I ask how you found us?"

Andie hesitated. "A friend sent us here."

"I see," she said calmly.

Cal was turning in a slow circle, taking it all in. "Are you with the Society?"

Rajani arched her eyebrows. "With whom, dear?"

"Come on now," he said.

"I'm afraid I don't understand."

Andie shot him a warning glance. They were in the middle of nowhere and out of options. "It's nothing," she assured the woman.

Rajani glanced at their soiled clothes and then at the hatchback, whose engine was coughing like a lifelong smoker. "Will your driver be staying as well?"

"No." Andie returned to the Maruti to pay the kid, and made him swear to give Mani his portion. As the hatchback sputtered out of sight, Rajani led Andie and Cal into the charming open-air pagoda. Hammocks and teak furniture filled the room, separated here and there by silk screens. Bees and butterflies flitted around flowering vines, which overflowed their pots and climbed into the support beams.

A younger woman in a blue sari brought out coffee and tea on a tray. The smell of the coffee made Andie swoon. She paid seventy-five dollars for the night for both rooms and the meals, another price that seemed absurdly low.

"There are no locks on the doors here," Rajani said. "I wouldn't wander into the jungle at night, but otherwise you're free to roam the grounds as you please. Meals are taken in your room or on the patio of the pagoda. If you leave your laundry and linens outside your door, Prema will return them by the evening. We even have internet, no password required."

Andie felt embarrassed talking to this friendly, sophisticated woman while smelling like a sewer. She only wanted to take a shower and collapse.

Cal took his coffee and went to choose a bungalow, but Andie had to ask another question. After noticing that one of Rajani's bangles was an ouroboros with plumed dragons, Andie glanced at Cal's back as he disappeared down the garden path. "The person who sent us here said you might be able to help my friend," she said.

"Help him how, dear?"

How to say this? "We think he's been . . . hypnotized . . . in some way."

"Oh my."

"The hypnotist might have planted certain triggers, I guess, in his mind, that caused him to act in a certain way. And might again in the future."

Rajani nodded gravely. "That is certainly cause for concern."

Andie was relieved she was taking her seriously. "Do you think you can do something about that?"

"I think it's quite possible."

Andie ran a hand through her hair. "Thank you. I don't know how much it costs—

"Don't trouble yourself about that. It is a service of the guest-house I am happy to provide. I would, however, prefer to cleanse his mind right away. For obvious reasons."

"Understood. I'll let him know."

Rajani raised her eyes again. "Though, dear—I do think you might have time for a shower."

The surrounding foliage and clever design ensured the interior of each tree house felt secluded from the world outside, wrapped in the protective arms of the jungle. Mosquito nets protected the beds, ceiling fans circulated the air, and the cozy wood furniture was strewn with cushions. After the grueling ordeal of the last twenty-four hours, Andie thought she might have died and gone to heaven.

During her outdoor shower, which included a cotton loofah and handmade soap, one of the most exquisite bathing experiences of her life, a monkey landed on the wooden railing and peered at her before returning to the canopy. Andie let the steaming water relax her muscles and calm her mind, though she couldn't escape a twinge of guilt at the comfort, knowing Mani was alone in his slum and her loved ones were in peril.

It was too hot for jeans. She put on a clean sari and a pair of sandals she found in a carved-wood armoire. Exhausted but feeling more herself again, she wandered over to the bottom of Cal's bungalow and called up to him.

"She wants to do it now?" he said, climbing down in a pair of shorts and a purple Knight Riders T-shirt—the name of the Kolkata cricket team—he had picked up in the city. The name had made him happy.

They found Rajani stretched out on a divan in the pagoda, reading a book. "Are you ready?" she said.

"Should I come too?" Andie asked.

"It's better if we're alone. Distractions impede the process."

Cal caught Andie's worried look. "It's fine," he said, then turned to Rajani. "Will it hurt?"

"Not you."

"What does that mean?"

The older woman flashed an enigmatic smile. As Andie watched her lead Cal into the jungle on a barely visible footpath, she felt a twinge of uncertainty.

Why did they go into the jungle? Why didn't she and Cal ask more questions? What exactly was Rajani going to do?

To pass the time, Andie moved to the patio and ordered a coffee. As a breeze ruffled her hair, she tried to relax over a delicious pot of French press that Prema had brought out. From this side of the pagoda, she noticed a path leading to a koi pond and a wading pool at the edge of the tree line.

An hour later, when they still hadn't returned, Andie began biting her nails. Prema was nowhere to be found, leaving Andie a wired and nervous wreck by the time Rajani and Cal finally emerged from the jungle.

Cal looked unfazed by whatever had happened, while Rajani looked as if she had just completed a triathlon. Her step was dragging, her shoulders sagged, and a glaze of exhaustion coated her eyes.

Andie hurried to meet them. "Are you okay?" she asked Rajani.

The older woman waved a tired hand. "The cleansing was much more difficult than I'd imagined. The triggers were very deep . . ." She took a deep breath. "Your friend was right to send you here."

"So he's fine? There won't be another . . . episode?"

"It's impossible to be sure, but I'm fairly certain I rooted out the implanted suggestions."

"There's no long-term damage?"

"No," Rajani said.

"I'm right here, by the way," Cal said. "But I appreciate the love. How does it work?" he asked Rajani. "What did you do?"

"I reversed the procedure by taking you back to the time and location where it happened. There were barriers in place to prevent that, of course." Her mouth compressed in a thin smile that said, *And I broke right through them.* "The human mind is both fragile and incredibly resilient. While it's easy for an experienced hypnotist to plant suggestions, it's virtually impossible to stop someone else, if they are talented in the art, from removing them." She stared at them in turn. "You should be extremely careful around whoever did this."

"Do you know who the Archon is?" Andie asked.

She blinked. "Who?"

Though Andie's gut told her that Rajani was a member of the Leap Year Society, she forced herself to stay calm. Rajani was helping them, and entitled to her secrets.

On the other hand, if she was involved, then it angered Andie that she wasn't more forthcoming.

"I'm afraid I've become something of a recluse," Rajani continued.

"Don't worry about it," Andie muttered, though there was something else she had to ask. "Do you know Dr. James Corwin? Has he been here before?"

"I haven't seen him for years, but I saw the news—what a terrible thing."

"He was my mentor at school, and a close family friend."

"I'm so sorry. He was a wonderful man."

Andie could tell by the sad, dreamy look in Rajani's eyes that their relationship had been intimate. "How did you meet him?"

"We met many years ago and shared mutual interests. Come, child. It's your turn."

"My turn? I wasn't hypnotized."

"Are you sure enough about that to take the risk?"

Andie faltered. She had not planned for this, and the thought of someone probing around in her mind, even with good intentions, made her nervous. When her frown deepened, Cal turned to Rajani. "Give us a sec?"

"Of course."

Cal took Andie by the arm and walked a few paces away. "We can't take the risk. And I don't . . ." He took a deep breath as he trailed off. "Not only is it dangerous for us both, but I don't want what happened to me in Kolkata to happen to you."

After a moment, knowing he was right, she bit her lip and looked away. "Fine," she said quietly. "Listen . . . I'm glad you're okay."

He squeezed her hand. "It was painless."

Rajani led Andie down the same footpath. After the jungle enveloped them, Andie heard the gurgle of flowing water, and soon the path spilled into a mossy glade cradling a fern-lined stream. Colorful birds hopped about in the canopy.

Following Rajani's example, Andie removed her shoes and sat cross-legged beside a shrine built atop a flat-topped boulder. A silver cloth interwoven with midnight-blue symbols had been draped across the rock. On the cloth, a yellow candle floated on a wicker raft in a bowl of water. Andie recognized a few of the symbols on the cloth as Hindu in origin.

Pink and white flower petals littered the ground around the boulder. As Andie's toes curled into the moss, Rajani picked up a book of matches and lit the candle. The trail of curling smoke released a pleasing aroma of vanilla and spice.

"What religion is this?" Andie asked.

"What do you mean?"

Andie didn't think it was a complicated question. "I generally associate shrines with religion."

"Shrines and altars are but external manifestations of an inner alignment. There are no rules or restrictions. Yours should represent your personal belief system, whether religious in nature or not."

"I'm afraid my shrine would be rather empty."

Rajani folded her hands in her lap. "Human beings are spiritual creatures, Andie," she said calmly. "Just as we need food and air and shelter, we require, to be fully healthy, a regular conduit to the divine universe—whatever that means to you. Keeping a personal altar is an excellent way to enhance that connection."

Andie didn't respond. Throughout her life, she had felt a spiritual thirst, though she had never figured out exactly who or what she believed in. The closest she had come, she supposed, was revering the mystery of the night sky.

"So you're a . . . hypnotist then?" Andie said finally.

Rajani's laugh was a tinkle of handbells. "I am many things, my dear. An Ayurvedic practitioner by heritage, a psychotherapist by education, a guesthouse owner by trade."

"But you've obviously studied hypnosis."

"I view myself as a humble steward of the mind." She swept a hand around the clearing. "One of the most powerful remedies at our disposal is immersion in the natural world. Recent studies have shown what certain of us have known all along: that prolonged absence from our biological environment is detrimental to mental health."

So is prolonged boredom in the countryside, Andie thought wryly. "So what exactly are we doing here?"

The corners of Rajani's lips turned up. "I sense that mental relaxation does not come easily to you."

"I'd say that's an understatement."

The older woman took Andie's hands. "Breathe with me."

"What?"

In response, Rajani took a deep breath through her nose and out through her mouth. After three more inhalations, Andie joined in, deciding to play along. "No matter how talented the hypnotist," Rajani said in a soothing voice between breaths, "no one under hypnosis can be made to do something against their moral or ethical code. Our subconscious blocks these attempts. We can be made to squawk like a chicken onstage, or even prance around naked, but ask someone to kill their best friend or harm an animal, and it won't happen. Whoever implanted the suggestions within Cal was very clever. Your friend was made to see a layered illusion that induced him to take an action that he believed was moral and justified."

"Plus a terrifying Kali manifestation."

"Yes. It was a traumatic experience for him. In my opinion, the hypnotist took quite a gamble, because to risk braving the horror of what Cal thought he saw, he had to be helping someone he truly cared for."

Andie swallowed. "He's a principled man. He would have done it for anyone."

"Be that as it may, it took an act of great willpower. Close your eyes, Andie."

Caught off guard by the sudden command, she obeyed.

"Keep breathing. In and out. In and out. Listen to the birds, and the babble of the stream, and the sound of my voice. Let your mind wander where it desires. Try not to think of yourself as bound to this physical place, or to any place at all, and let yourself become one with the natural world, the air around us, the sky above, the universe. Everything is one, Andie, and we are all part of something greater, each and every one of us, something vast beyond belief."

As Rajani continued to speak in the soothing voice, her intonation never varying, Andie's mind began to relax, lulled by the cadence of the words and the enveloping sounds of nature and the intoxicating aroma of the incense candle. Still, she did not feel as if she were entering a different mental state. She had never succumbed to hypnosis, despite many heartfelt attempts, and had become convinced she was impervious to it for whatever reason—probably because she could never relax enough.

Not wanting to interrupt Rajani or make her feel bad, Andie waited patiently for her to finish, though after a few moments she decided to take a peek and see what the other woman was doing.

When Andie opened her eyes, she was shocked to find herself inside the world of her visions.

She had never had an episode while surrounded by nature, and the experience felt more surreal than ever. The stream was a ribbon of ash disappearing into the inky horizon at the edges of her vision. The charcoal-hued trees and foliage, though less substantial than in the waking world, shimmered with a complexity beyond their appearance, as if their root system and canopy spanned dimensions.

Rajani, though cast in deep shadow, was still seated cross-legged in front of Andie. Unlike the woman in Andie's vision in the office of the fake passport dealer in London, Rajani's facial features were intact and not horrible mockeries of a human being. Still, she was frozen in place, and did not move or respond to Andie's frantic cries, which bubbled into watery echoes as they left her mouth. As always, Andie wondered if this would be the time she never woke up and was trapped forever in her own mind.

Just as she started to panic, she noticed movement beyond the borders of her immediate environment. Thinking it was one of the ominous, inchoate forms that roamed the void, or the spectral figure in the frayed Renaissance clothing, she backed away in fear, only to gape as a raven-haired woman with East Indian features stepped into view from the opaqueness of the borderlands. She was dressed in a traveling cloak with the hood thrown back, and while Andie could tell she was very beautiful, her form seemed molded from shadow like everything else in that realm.

As soon as she crossed into view, the woman beckoned for Andie to join her. She had a calming presence that Andie could not explain, and she wondered if it was a manifestation of Rajani as a younger woman, perhaps some weird quirk of time and being. Or maybe it was Andie's own subconscious projecting the image.

Confused, she watched as the woman beckoned again. Her eyes were pricks of starlight, and Andie took a hesitant step toward her. The woman turned and walked into the void.

Andie didn't know what to do. Was she supposed to follow her? Or was the woman dangerous and trying to mislead Andie? She didn't think that was the case, but she had no way of knowing.

Or did none of this have any meaning and it didn't matter one damn bit what Andie did?

The woman was rapidly disappearing. Andie took a chance and decided to follow her. Normally she entered her visions while inside a room or a building, and had always assumed she was trapped inside her physical environs. But now that she was outdoors, she saw that the same rough dimensions were in place. She could see clearly for only ten or so feet in any direction. As she tried to enter the congealed shadows at the border, she found it was like pressing against a brick wall.

Almost, but not entirely, because it felt as if she *could* get through, if she could only push hard enough. Even more curious was the sensation that the other side of the barrier was not as terrifying as she had always thought. That instead of a deep, dark void full of horror and lost souls, something *else* awaited, something mysterious.

Dangerous, perhaps, but not necessarily evil.

Had the Archon spoken the truth? Was there far more to this place than Andie had realized?

But Zawadi had said the Ascendants are liars, that Andie could never trust them.

Where am I? Who am I?

Convinced the answers to her strange affliction might finally lie within her grasp, Andie tried her best to push through and follow the woman in the ash-colored cloak. But Andie couldn't do it. She couldn't move an inch farther. It was frustrating beyond belief. She beat her hands against the tangible darkness for a long time, almost forgetting her terror that she had not woken up and might be trapped. When she did dwell on that, she backed away from the edge of the void, shaking. She had never felt so alone or wanted her mother so very much to be at her side, speaking softly to her as she used to do after a bad dream. *There, there, Andie. It's okay, Little Mouse. It's all going to be okay—*

And then Andie found herself back in the clearing with Rajani, surrounded by the vibrant hues of the jungle, overwhelmed by the visceral rush of sound and color and smells of the real world, the sheer unbelievable *vibrancy* of it all.

Rajani was blinking apologetically. "I'm sorry."

Andie was so confused by what had happened, so disoriented by the abrupt return, that it took her a few moments to collect herself. "Sorry for what?" she whispered.

"That I couldn't hypnotize you. It's extremely rare when that happens . . . We can try again tomorrow. On a positive note, this bodes well for your belief that you were never hypnotized in the first place."

"Rajani?" Andie said.

"Yes?"

"How long have you been trying to hypnotize me?"

The older woman spread her hands. They were both still sitting cross-legged. "No more than a minute. I know very quickly if my attempt will be successful."

"A minute," Andie repeated. It felt as if she had been away for an hour.

"Why do you ask?"

"Have you heard of the Fold?"

Rajani's face scrunched in confusion. "The what?"

Goddammit, is she lying or not?

"Don't hold anything back," Andie said in a harsh voice.

"About what, child?"

"Where did you get that bracelet? The ouroboros?"

"It was a gift from James, many years ago. If you tell me what you're talking about, maybe I can help you."

After asking a few more questions that Rajani couldn't answer, or chose not to, Andie snarled, jumped to her feet, and, ignoring the other woman's pleas to wait, fled down the path.

Granada, Spain

15

Set high on a plateau cradled by the Sierra Nevada Mountains, the Alhambra was a vision of medieval grandeur that Zawadi absorbed from the open window of her pension in the Albaicin, the Moorish quarter of Granada. In the cobblestone street below, perfumed by the heady scent of star jasmine, flamenco guitarists serenaded passerby as seductively as any siren, luring tourists to a nightly show.

Though the Alhambra had been built as a palace, Dr. Corwin had often referred to the magnificent citadel looming above the city as his church, due to the stunning craftsmanship and the symbolism embodied in the architecture. Zawadi knew Dr. Corwin practiced no traditional faith but also knew that, in his own way, he was a deeply spiritual man. One who worshipped libraries and museums and the marvels of nature.

Zawadi herself harbored deep-rooted beliefs in God and the spiritual realm that stemmed from both sides of her cultural heritage. Her mother was Catholic; her father, Muslim. Instead of choosing between her parents' religions, she had accepted their faith in both, and decided early on that no one had a monopoly on belief. Since Zawadi did not exactly know what she believed in, she supposed she believed in the possibility of everything.

She had always felt a connection to this region of dusty hills and citrus groves. Yet she had not come to the city for the clean air and sweeping mountain views. Long ago, James had recruited a spy within the Ascendants. Zawadi did not know the identity of the mole, but in case of an emergency, Dr. Corwin had given her a secure point of contact involving an IP address on the dark web.

After Zawadi relayed what she had seen at Dr. Corwin's funeral, the mole professed not to know if the professor was still alive or a prisoner, but promised to dig deeper. The spy had also delivered a crucial piece of information: the Ascendants had solved the fourth step of the Star Phone puzzle by taking the device to Granada and then Timbuktu, the ancient center of learning in the desert kingdom of Mali. Zawadi suspected the clues had involved the Arab alchemists, a subject of great historical interest to Dr. Corwin. He revered how the alchemists bridged philosophy and spiritual contemplation with rigorous scientific experimentation, and considered them his intellectual forebears.

As above, so below, Dr. Corwin had loved to quote. *How right the old alchemists will prove to be one day.*

The mole had not relayed any details concerning the solution but had passed on valuable knowledge about the fifth puzzle. The Ascendants had made little progress, and Zawadi had sent the information to Andie.

Zawadi had also decided to risk a meeting with a prominent High Middle Ages scholar from the local university—Professor Enrique Cardona—with whom Dr. Corwin had rendezvoused a month before his disappearance. The meeting had taken place at the Alhambra, and Zawadi knew of it because she had provided security. She also knew Professor Cardona was a member of the Society and a close friend of Dr. Corwin's.

Thinking the professor might know something useful about Dr. Corwin's actions before his disappearance—perhaps even where he had hidden the Enneagon, or clues to the four remaining parts of the Star Phone puzzle—Zawadi had arranged to meet him in the same place. She did not know him well enough to trust the security of his communications, and also wanted to see through Dr. Corwin's eyes as she heard what the two had discussed.

Although the Ascendants should have left the city by now, Zawadi had taken precautions, including scoping the Alhambra with a telescope in the hours before the meeting. Dr. Corwin preferred to conduct his clandestine business in broad daylight, to blend with the crowds and take advantage of the increased public scrutiny.

Zawadi, on the other hand, preferred to control her environment. She could not account for every single one of the thousands of faces that would pass through the Alhambra during opening hours.

She was a wolf, not a lamb, and she preferred to run at night.

Because of his profession, Professor Cardona had special access to the Alhambra. Late that evening, following his instructions, Zawadi entered the Alhambra complex with one of the night tours before slipping into a room at the Palacios Nazaries, the Moorish royal palace. At the stroke of midnight, once the guards cleared the grounds, she would leave the room and meet the professor in the same courtyard in which he and Dr. Corwin had spoken.

A secret midnight rendezvous. Classic Society behavior.

As the minutes ticked by on an ornate grandfather clock, Zawadi sat on an ivory-studded chair and contemplated the beauty and symmetry of the vaulted honeycombed ceiling. The room was of modest size for the palace. It had probably belonged to a member of the sultan's harem.

At midnight, once silence encased the Alhambra, Zawadi slipped into the corridor and made her way to the arcade surrounding the famed Court of the Lions. The moonlit plaza was an exquisite sight. A forest of marble pillars, ornamented with delicate filigree tracery and Arabic calligraphy, supported the concentric archways of the arcade.

The courtyard stretched over a hundred feet long and sixty feet wide. An alabaster fountain guarded by marble lions was situated at the intersection of two barren channels, part of a hydraulic system that had once carried water throughout the palace. Zawadi was no scholar, but she knew that every inch of the Alhambra was rife with symbolism and meaning, including this courtyard: the spacing of columns and arches set according to the golden ratio; the channels of water symbolizing the rivers of paradise; the gorgeous fountain meant to evoke the heavenly garden of Islam.

Moonlight bathed the courtyard tiles. Zawadi stayed close to the pillars while she paced the perimeter, scanning for the professor. As a piece of gum stuck to the bottom of her left boot, an annoyance that broke her concentration for a split second, she heard a voice call out in the darkness.

"Looking for someone?"

Zawadi spun to her left. The voice did not belong to an aging Spanish professor, but to someone much younger, and with a Chinese accent.

By the light of the moon, she saw a muscular man in his late twenties, dressed in jeans and a motorcycle jacket, leaning against a column on the opposite side of the courtyard. Though his stance appeared nonchalant, she noticed one hand poised near his pocket and the other behind his back. If Zawadi made a sudden move for her gun, he could easily draw his weapon and slip behind the pillar, or escape into the hidden depths of an alcove.

As could she—which was exactly why she had chosen that spot and not advanced into the courtyard.

"I'm afraid the professor won't make it tonight," he said. "Or any other night. His last supper did not agree with him."

Had they been watching the professor? Was I not careful enough?

Her eyes on her enemy the entire time, Zawadi inched her left hand toward the back of her leather pants, deciding to test his awareness.

"If you draw your weapon," he said evenly, "my snipers will gun you down."

"Why haven't they already?"

"You know why."

Zawadi did indeed. Though not an insider, her close connection to Dr. Corwin, as well as her tactical knowledge of dozens of Society missions, made her an invaluable prisoner.

Tranquilizer darts did not fare well with ballistic clothing, which they would know. They would have to take her another way. Still, if she tried to escape, she had no doubt they would shoot her and hope to avoid a fatal wound.

"Do you know who I am?" the man asked.

She quickly ran through her mental catalogue of top Ascendant assassins. "Not really," she lied, because she could tell he thrived on ego.

He introduced himself, though she already knew he and Daiyu were a Chinese brother-and-sister team said to be rising quickly through the ranks of the enemy. Jianyu was the cold-blooded killer, while Daiyu, a computer and technology savant, was his eyes and ears. Together they had infiltrated some of the most impervious Society strongholds.

Zawadi had to contend not only with Jianyu and whomever he had brought to the Alhambra, but with an enemy watching from afar.

"I've been waiting a long time to meet you," he said.

As they spoke, Zawadi studied the darkness, listening and smelling and sensing, recalling a mental image of the layout of the palace grounds. Of course, Jianyu was using the dialogue to stall while his associates moved into place, and Zawadi thought she knew where the trap was being laid. "Why is that?"

"Because I would like to personally take Dr. Corwin's legendary bodyguard off the board."

"An ego trip is a journey to nowhere."

"Not ego. Career advancement."

"You should have shot me when you had the chance," she said.

"You wouldn't have agreed to meet in a place that a sniper could easily reach, and you've protected your position with civilian targets since we spotted you on the ascent. And you obviously chose a different hiding place in the palace to wait than the one in the message we intercepted, or your journey would have ended there."

Zawadi smiled in the darkness. "I see you've done your homework."

In an abundance of caution, she had indeed chosen a different room in the palace, in an opposite wing.

"My homework also tells me you'll refuse to surrender," Jianyu said.

She noticed he had shifted his position ever so slightly, lowering his center of gravity, readying for action. "You're a good boy for doing your studies, but it's time to return to school."

He chuckled. "Is that so?"

Before he could react, Zawadi stepped behind the marble pillar, reached into her sleeve for a handful of pellets that were in fact tiny pressurized canisters, and threw them on the tiles at her feet. A column of gray smoke exploded around the pillar, obscuring her from view in a twenty-foot radius that expanded rapidly.

Instead of racing back into the palace through one of the smoke-covered alcoves, a course of action her enemy would expect, Zawadi shimmied up the marble column as if climbing a coconut tree, clamping her thighs against the narrow cylinder and pulling with her arms. The smooth surface made it difficult to climb, but once she gained a few feet of height—still inside the smoke—she was able to thrust her body up and grab a lip of stone overhead. An experienced rock climber, she used the niches in the exquisite carvings to scramble onto the barrel tile roof.

The best position for a sniper above the Court of the Lions was directly across from her present position. Zawadi had calculated for this, knowing the fog would obscure a scope. Yet when she emerged from the dense mist, she was only ten feet from a man in black fatigues holding a rifle.

She did not think she had calculated incorrectly.

She thought they had placed more than one person on the roof.

You've underestimated your own reputation, Zawadi.

The man had been leaning over the roof, peering into the fog as he listened to the shouted orders from below. He was caught off guard by Zawadi's quiet ascent. She closed on him, reaching for the knife at her side, which was easier to access than her gun.

As they collided, the man had no choice but to drop his firearm and wrap his arms around her, trying to use his strength to throw her off the roof. In the fog and darkness and speed of the encounter, he had failed to notice the knife. She stabbed him deep in the back while covering his mouth, to stop him from screaming. As she swept his legs and lowered him to the ground, she extracted the knife and ran it across his jugular, ensuring his silence forever.

Zawadi pivoted and took off across the roof. She reentered the fog to disguise her position and leaped onto a higher and more steeply pitched section of roof, then scrambled over the apex and down the other side. She expected a barrage of bullets, but none came.

They don't want to alert the outside guards and the police unless they have to.

And they still want to take me alive.

This knowledge gave her confidence, as did her escape from the initial gauntlet. Now she just had to make it off the plateau that housed the Alhambra complex and into the town. The Alhambra was enormous, covering over twenty-five acres, an entire palatine city. Contained within the complex were former mosques, bathhouses, palaces, towers, halls, plazas, courtyards, gardens, and fortified walls enclosing the old castle.

To avoid the ravine and the danger of its isolated bridges, she had planned an escape route to the south, across the tops of the palaces, over the outer wall, and out through the woods. With the lights of Granada twinkling in the distance, she fled over the roof of the sprawling Palacios Nazaries with balletic grace, sometimes leaping twenty feet or more as she navigated the steep changes in height, careful not to slip on the dusty barrel tiles. She took a grim satisfaction that her rooftop perch kept her out of sight of the Alhambra's security cameras, which Daiyu surely controlled.

Footsteps pounded all around her, searching for her position and trying to cut her off. She knew the Alhambra's night guards were dead or paid off. There would be no help from outside.

After dashing along the roof above a reflecting pool, she scrambled to the precipitous heights of the Palace of Carlos V. Her plan was to drop to the ground at the last moment, scale the wall, and make her escape.

The darkness and the varying heights of the buildings helped keep her out of sight, but the footsteps from below were closing in. Zawadi withdrew a thin metal canister from her belt, which contained more smoke pellets. She fired as she ran, aiming the pellet gun a hundred feet away from her location, creating smoke screens in random locations to confuse her pursuers.

The long drop from the palace roof, aided by a windowsill halfway down, knocked the wind from her. With a grunt, she leaped to her feet, sprinted to the outer wall, and clambered over. Pistol in hand, she raced down the hill through the woods and wove through a neighborhood of historic homes whose security cameras—potential tools for Daiyu—made Zawadi nervous.

On one of the smaller side streets, she retrieved her rented motorcycle and sped back into the city. Now she was home free. On to a private airstrip and her next destination.

Behind her, the whine of a motorcycle interrupted her self-congratulation. At night, plenty of young daredevils prowled the city streets, even in sleepy Granada. Yet when she glanced in the rearview and saw a large black sport bike, aiming right for her and gaining quickly, she knew this was no joyride.

How did they find me so quickly?

As the rider raised a squat handgun, Zawadi ducked and swerved. The bullet smacked the pavement right beside her. She kept going, aiming for a tight corner up ahead. While her bike was not as fast as the crotch rocket running her down, she had confidence she could lose her pursuer in the tight confines of the city.

A muffled boom sounded ahead of her. A few seconds later, the ground exploded, throwing her off the bike. She tucked and rolled, stunned but protected from severe harm by her helmet and ballistic clothing. Confused at first, she realized with a chill what had happened.

He wasn't shooting at me—he fired a smart grenade ahead of my position.

Which his sister detonated as I approached.

Shaken and bleeding in a dozen places, suffering from at least a bruised rib, Zawadi lurched to her feet as Jianyu leaped off his bike and tackled her from the side, causing her gun to clatter away. She squirmed out of his grasp as they hit the ground, then kicked him hard in the stomach.

Jianyu gasped from the blow as Zawadi leaped to her feet. They were on a two-lane street lined with parked cars and three-story apartment buildings. The Chinese assassin threw off his helmet for better visibility as a shocked pedestrian, a young woman in a black dress, returning home from a bar or nightclub, backed against the side of a building and raised her smartphone to call for help or film the encounter. Jianyu turned and shot her dead, holstered his weapon, then withdrew a short stick that expanded like a switchblade into the hilt of a three-foot steel sword.

Sickened by the murder, Zawadi snarled and removed her helmet before pulling out a long boot knife in one hand, and a smaller dagger in another. She spat on the ground. "Monster," she said as they circled each other, gauging the other's movements. "You're all monsters."

"I kill out of necessity, and belief in my cause. The woman saw my face. Why do you kill, mercenary? To protect your employer? Who is the monster here?"

She ignored the jab. "You're so sure I don't have another gun?"

He gave a thin smile. "Daiyu body-scanned the contours of your clothing. I know everything about you."

His answer chilled her. She knew Daiyu was watching through a bodycam on his person right that very moment. "Two against one is hardly an honorable fight," she said.

"My sister and I are one, not two. And honor in battle is the province of the fools you work for."

"The person *I* work for is no fool—though the same can't be said for you. As I said before, you should have shot me."

Zawadi pressed her attack with a vengeance, knowing Jianyu was buying time because he still wanted to capture her. She could hear the rumble of motorbikes in the distance and knew his allies were close by.

The Chinese assassin's longer blade forced her to adopt a different fighting strategy, performing a deadly dance with her dual blades as he parried. Zawadi edged closer and closer as Jianyu tried to pierce her defenses with powerful lunges. She finally got inside, but he drove her away with a snap kick that almost ended the fight. The kick was incredibly fast, and landed right on her damaged rib. It took all of her training and experience to maintain control as he pressed the attack, thrusting with the skill of an expert fencer. Again and again, Zawadi twisted to the side at the last moment, feeling the blade whisk against the side of her clothing.

She had to admit he was better with the blade. Zawadi was an expert martial artist; Jianyu was a savant. But there was more to her skill set than pure artistry. After a glance to the left, she made a sharp cut to retrieve her gun. He moved just as fast, threatening to cut her down from behind unless she turned to engage. She spun to block his blow at the last moment, and again they danced, neither able to gain an advantage.

The metallic scent of blood from the murdered girl enraged her. Her nerve endings vibrated with adrenaline as the motorcycles in the distance drew closer and closer.

Enough. It is time to teach this pup a lesson in street fighting.

Jianyu had been attacking on her left the entire fight, knowing she had been hurt by the fall. She took a step forward and feigned a wince from her rib, then disguised it almost as quickly, hoping to draw him in. He took the bait and pressed the attack. She pretended to take a step away. As he closed the gap with a lunge, she dropped flat on her back on the pavement and drove the dagger deep into the side of his calf. Instead of howling in pain, Jianyu shocked her by thrusting downward, trying to run her through—and almost succeeded. The maneuver had left her vulnerable to a return thrust, and she deflected his sword at the very last moment with her blade, millimeters from her side. Without pause, she executed a leg sweep while still beneath him, pushing on the side of his knee with one foot and sliding his ankle back with her other.

Jianyu crashed to the ground, taken by surprise by the clever tactic. Somehow ignoring the stab wound in his calf, he used his superior weight to shake her off and jump to his feet, prepared to thrust downward and end the fight.

But Zawadi had another trick in store. During the brief tussle, she had stripped Jianyu's gun from his holster. As he held the sword over her supine form, his smile of victory turned to shock as she fired twice into his stomach. The force of the powerful weapon threw him backward.

Knowing he was wearing body armor, Zawadi stood to put another bullet in his head when another bike rounded the corner right in front of her, and she was forced to shoot the rider instead.

She glanced to the side. While holding his stomach, Jianyu had scrambled against a wall to put distance between them. As the whine of more motorcycles approached, she cursed, wishing she had time to end their little spat. Instead she raced for her bike, shooting out Jianyu's tires as she passed.

Zawadi jumped on her machine and fled through the narrow winding streets. As with most European cities, a secret world of tunnels and dungeons lay beneath Granada, and she knew a variety of entrances. But with Daiyu watching, able to repurpose security cameras, Zawadi feared being trapped underground. Instead she decided to leave the city as quickly as possible and lose herself in the mountains of Andalucía.

Still wondering how they had found her, she pushed the bike to its limits, leaning over so far on the curves she could have touched the pavement. She was trying to think it all through when it hit her. *I stepped on a piece of gum right before Jianyu appeared. The Alhambra, especially the Palacios Nazaries, is always impeccably clean.*

A piece of gum.

A tracking device.

A tool in the hands of Daiyu.

With a snort of disgust, Zawadi leaned over as she rode and removed her boots, tossing them into the street. Now secure in her escape, she sped through the labyrinthine gypsy quarter and then alongside the whitewashed caves of Sacromonte, far from the prying eyes of security cameras, before she climbed into the desolate foothills of the Sierra Nevada and disappeared.

16

Two days of convalescence at Anandamitra Guesthouse had a dual effect on Andie. After her long walks in the jungle and lazy afternoons sipping coffee on the patio, surrounded by the glory of nature and not in mortal peril, she felt more relaxed than she had in weeks, maybe even years.

Yet Andie had never been good at relaxing. Her idea of a vacation was not lying on a beach like a slug for a week, but a trip to a new foreign city, walking until her feet ached, exploring an unfamiliar culture and cultivating as many new experiences as possible.

She appreciated what the unplugged tranquility of the guesthouse was doing for her soul. If circumstances were different, maybe this was a place she would come to recharge for short periods.

But her mother and Dr. Corwin needed her. Who knew how far the Ascendants, with their vast resources, had progressed on the Star Phone puzzle. It might already be solved.

Rajani wanted to attempt another hypnosis session, but Andie kept refusing, wary of another trigger. She was still more afraid of her visions than curious. Until she knew more about the shadow world, or found someone who did, she wasn't going back. At least not by choice.

After a morning run to the village and back on a well-worn trail, she cooled off in the wading pool, then curled up on a divan in the pagoda. Terribly frustrated by the delay, she hovered over her afternoon tea while Cal used the phone for research.

Despite their many attempts to reach Zawadi, there was still no word from her.

Still no way forward.

Shirtless, holding a Kingfisher lager in one hand, Cal relaxed in a hammock in his treetop bungalow and waited for Dane to join him online.

I could get used to this. Living on someone else's credit card, free beer and catered meals, even a laundry service. Now if only there was a 7-Eleven and a movie theater, and someone moved the Staples Center to the jungle...

When Cal checked the dark web onion address again, a message from Dane awaited.

You there, kemosabe?

Cal set his beer down, wishing he was the type of person who could be happy in an unchanging paradise. Maybe he could, if the world was a just place for everyone. Just knocking one back and pondering my life span.

You're about that age. Impending mortality is 50% of all midlife crises. The other 50 is expectation vs. reality.

That's deep, dude. Anything new?

Plasmek and Quasar are just as tough to crack as PanSphere and Aegis. More layers than a California fruitcake. Online security ultra-tight. The employee profiles seem normal, so my guess is only the top brass is involved. I'll keep trying but don't hold your breath.

It's there somewhere. Keep at it.

Easy for the guy in hiding to say.

You're right. I'm sorry. THANK YOU.

Sefa hasn't slept well in weeks.

Give her some Ambien.

She's a Zen Buddhist, man. Clean living. Listen, I did find one thing. It's kinda interesting and kinda fucking weird.

Cal perked up. That sounds par for the course.

Yeah. Exactly. So I hacked your Twitch account and have been monitoring it.

Uh, thanks?

Don't mention it. Do you know what a wayback machine is?

Of course. I'm an investigative journalist.

Well, there's *the* Wayback Machine, started by a nonprofit in San Fran, and there is *a* wayback machine, a generic term for an imitation device that performs a web crawl of digital archives. I wrote my own code for a scraper so I could pull up deleted comments on your show after your final broadcast.

That's pretty cool. And?

I didn't get them all, and someone killed my program halfway through, which makes me nervous for realz. But I read this comment by a listener called 2DanKnoxvegas. He wanted you to know he has an extremely rare condition called Kleine Levin syndrome. It's a sleep disorder that causes memory loss, hallucinations, hypersomnia, and altered perceptions of reality.

Cal got a chill at the description of the disorder. *That sounds a hell of a lot like Andie's visions.*

About two decades ago, 2Dan went to see a doctor in the Bay Area who specialized in rare conditions like Kleine Levin.

What kind of doctor?

A neuropsychologist. During one of the tests, 2Dan was awake when the doctor thought he was asleep. He overheard a conversation about his condition and the condition of some of the doctor's other patients. He thought it was inappropriate and stopped his sessions. But guess what else he heard on that phone call?

Odds on the Lakers-Warriors? Cal said weakly.

Both the LYS and the Ascendants were mentioned. 2Dan had buried those names, but when he heard them on your show, it sparked something. Specificity of powerful associative memory and all that.

Who was the shrink?

Guy named Waylan Taylor.

What do you know about him? Where is he now?

He dropped off the radar a decade ago. But you can bet your ass I'm using my wayback machine to find him.

After closing the chat, Cal swung off the hammock and paced the little balcony, suddenly alert. Though not what he'd expected to hear from Dane, he knew from past experience that random little nuggets like these could lead to the unraveling of a whole spool of thread.

Because no crime was perfect, no conspiracy foolproof.

No one—no matter how big the broom—swept up all the crumbs.

After lunch on their third day at the guesthouse, Andie sipped fresh date juice on the patio as she watched a red-naped ibis stalk the koi pond. It would have been an extraordinary sight if Andie had not seen it twice already that morning. Like everything else at the bucolic guesthouse, the appearance of the beautiful bird had started to cloy, an affront to Andie's desire to move forward.

Robbed of the ability to take proactive steps, she dwelled on what she had learned, and how it might relate to the Enneagon.

Okay, Dr. Corwin, I feel you. We started off with a zero and we followed it all the way to India. You showed me the amazing history and culture of the subcontinent, forced me to contemplate the complexities of Kali and experiential religion, and then, whether you meant to or not—Mani's last-minute help was awfully convenient—I came full circle by wading through human filth in a sewer and holing up in a god-awful slum. I saw the highs and lows of one of our great civilizations, its dizzying achievements and its harsh realities, and I learned that a zero is not just an essential mathematical construct but a philosophy, a realization, a state of being.

So I feel you—but why?

How does it fit with all the other locations? What's the endgame of this wild, immense, globe-spanning puzzle of yours?

Swift movement at the corner of her vision caused her to slide her seat back and jerk to her feet, but it was just Cal approaching through the garden, walking faster than normal. She remained standing as he hurried over and jumped the patio railing.

"What is it?" she asked.

"Zawadi sent a text."

He held out the phone, and she read it for herself.

> I strongly suspect Dr. Corwin is alive and being held in an unknown location. Spy within Ascendants claims fourth Star Phone puzzle was solved in Mali and they're working on the fifth. Next clue is an old-fashioned world map with a spider walking across a path of lotus petals on the back of a dragon. 4 doors in corners of map and one cracked door in center. Initial consensus is Silk Road, somewhere in China. Meet me in Hong Kong but stay underground until I arrive. A pilot named Darsha at Krishnanagar helipad is waiting. Contact me only if emergency.

Andie held the phone in her hands for a long time, so long that Cal gently nudged her. There was so much to process. A spy within the Ascendants. The fourth puzzle solved. Most importantly, Zawadi thought Dr. Corwin was alive!

In her heart, Andie had believed that already, but the validation brought a lump to her throat. She allowed herself a moment of silent relief and then pushed the emotions away, because while Dr. Corwin might still be alive, if his imprisonment was anything like her and Cal's experience...

She drew a deep breath. There was no time to savor the moment.

One line in the text almost made her laugh out loud. They should contact Zawadi only in an emergency? The entire goddamn journey was an emergency. What did she mean? They should call her only if they were in the middle of a James Bond–style crisis, dangling upside down above an alligator pit as the rope holding their ankles slowly frayed from the other end?

Still, when Andie pocketed the phone, she did so with a grim smile on her lips. She thought she understood some, but certainly not all, of the new Star Phone clue the Ascendants were trying to solve—and she thought they had drawn the wrong conclusion.

Yes, she was ready to leave the guesthouse and find the pilot Zawadi had suggested.

But she and Cal wouldn't be going to Hong Kong.

New York City
1971

Ensconced in a secret parlor inside the main branch of the New York Public Library, Dr. Corwin sat in a velvet armchair with his legs crossed, contemplative, sipping a Macallan eighteen-year. Just over twelve months had passed since he had escaped Cartagena by boarding a bus in the same disguise—a homeless man dressed in rags—he had used to climb to the top of San Felipe Castle, in plain view of all who wished to see. There, carved into the underside of a rusty cannon, he had discovered what might have been Ettore Majorana's last message to the world.

Addio.

Over the last year, starting in Central America and working his way east across the Atlantic, Dr. Corwin had searched for any trace of Nataja Tromereo, and similar anagrammatic aliases, in crime databases and hospital records and apartment leases around the world. He enlisted help from within the LYS, as well as outside, employing private investigators and research assistants under the aegis of trying to solve one of the world's great scientific mysteries.

Not a trace to be found.

The Society had confirmed his suspicions that Tesla and Taylor had both been members, though no record existed of any contact between them and Ettore Majorana. Nor could anyone explain the photograph of Tesla in Cartagena, except to say it could have been doctored.

Dr. Corwin was unconvinced. *That photo was real. Ettore is alive and laughing at us all.*

Searching for a creative new avenue to explore, he let his thoughts drift as his gaze roamed the hidden parlor.

At the turn of the twentieth century, when the New York City library system was being built on the back of steel baron Andrew Carnegie's donation, buildings were heated by coal. On-site apartments beneath the libraries housed the custodians who stoked the furnaces. Some of those apartments still existed, some had been demolished, and some had been repurposed into speakeasies or storehouses for rare manuscripts.

Those were the known anomalies. What the public didn't know was that Andrew Carnegie had been a member of the Society and had built other secrets into the architecture of the libraries, which had long served as safe havens for the LYS.

The parlor Dr. Corwin was in now resembled an executive lounge for explorers. Coffered oak paneling, a Persian rug, copper mood lighting, a humidor, and a well-stocked liquor cabinet provided the creature comforts. Ornate standing globes, telescopes, and framed maps from around the world evoked a spirit of adventure. Books were everywhere, behind glass cabinets and stacked on the tables and piled on the floor. It was a room for resting weary legs and letting the imagination roam free.

Directly across from his armchair, against the far wall, was a replica of a device called a chronovisor. It resembled a tabletop stereo covered with cathode ray tubes, dials, and levers. Father Pellegrino Ernetti, a Catholic priest and physicist said to have built the original chronometer with a team of scientists—including Enrico Fermi—as a tool for seeing into the past. A time-travel machine of sorts. The device had received some press over the years, and had been the subject of all sorts of conspiracy theories. Remarkably, to Dr. Corwin's knowledge, Fermi—a Nobel Prize recipient—had neither affirmed nor denied his participation. The original device was said to be hidden somewhere beneath the Vatican.

Allegedly, the chronovisor worked by receiving, decoding, and reproducing radiation and sound waves left behind by past events. In theory, it would function similar to a television or a radio, though instead of receiving wave transmissions from nearby stations, it picked up electromagnetic markers "imprinted" on the fabric of reality. A Society team had carefully reproduced a blueprint someone had smuggled out of the Vatican, though no one, Dr. Corwin included, had managed to get the replica to function.

Needless to say, he had his doubts as to whether the original worked any better.

But the claims were not as outlandish as they seemed. Vinyl records perform a similar function, the vibrations of sound waves caught and etched onto their surface. Cameras trap images of light and preserve them for eternity. Telescopes allow astronomers to see billions of years into the past and map the history of the universe. Even the everyday mirror could be considered a chronovisor of sorts: our reflections are not real-time images, but snapshots of the recent past, since it takes light a few millionths of a second to travel to the mirror and back.

The nineteenth-century inventor Charles Babbage had once pondered if sound and other electromagnetic waves were somehow preserved. Did the present harbor echoes of the past, inscribed in a quantum diary for future generations?

And why not? Time as we know it does not seem to exist in the quantum realm.

So many mysteries remained. Yet most of all, Dr. Corwin thought, as he stared at a flickering fireplace set into the wall beside the chronovisor, the connection of the strange contraption to Enrico Fermi—a former colleague of Ettore Majorana—had stoked another set of flames: the furnace in which Dr. Corwin's obsession for Ettore had burned ever since he left Cartagena.

The more he thought about it, the more he was convinced Ettore was hiding something important. Why else risk traveling to a clandestine meeting in South America with Tesla and a nuclear physicist?

Dr. Corwin had conducted more research. While Ettore had alienated himself from his friends and family in the months preceding his departure, and his father had died that same year, Ettore had also withdrawn five months' worth of his salary in the days leading up to that fateful night at sea. Hardly the actions of a suicidal man.

Then there was the letter to a colleague sent by Ettore just before he boarded the ship to Palermo.

> *Dear Carrelli,*
> *I made a decision that has become unavoidable. . . . I real-*
> *ize what trouble my sudden disappearance will cause you*
> *and the students. . . . I also ask you to give my regards to all*
> *those I learned to know and appreciate in your Institute,*
> *especially Sciuti: I will keep a fond memory of them all at*
> *least until 11:00 tonight. Possibly later, too.*

What a bizarre letter. *Possibly* later? What did Ettore think might or might not happen? Suicide was a rather conclusive matter.

Dr. Corwin also couldn't stop thinking about Ettore's unnerving response to his fellow physicists in Rome concerning their decision to bombard uranium with slow neutrons.

Physics is on the wrong path, Ettore had said. *We are all on the wrong path.*

What had Ettore meant? Was he worried about a new form of weapon? Working with Tesla and Taylor on a project that involved the mysterious Fold? Both?

Dr. Corwin had to know.

With a sigh, he pushed to his feet and drained the last sip of Scotch. He had an afternoon class to teach.

Dr. Corwin lived above a flower seller on the Upper West Side. The fragrant tropical plants carted out to the street every morning in summer always reminded him of his native Jamaica. Later that night, he left his fifth-story apartment to participate in a mandatory Society conclave held in a safe house accessed via the catacombs beneath Saint Patrick's Cathedral. Over the years, many of the tunnels, basements, grottoes, abandoned subway routes, wine cellars, and sunken old buildings riddling subterranean Manhattan had been mapped and repurposed by the Society. Some of the clandestine meeting sites were quite posh, including the basement of the former mausoleum near Saint Patrick's, which resembled a Victorian parlor with high-tech touches—such as a collection of personal computers not yet available to the public. Dr. Corwin found them quite fascinating.

It was a gloomy October night, pregnant with atmosphere. The skyscrapers of Midtown loomed above him like ghostly sentinels, their heights lost in a dreamlike merger of fog and streetlight. Dr. Corwin had left early so he could stop at his favorite dive bar on the way. The purpose of the Society meeting was to discuss the growing power of the Ascendants, including their incursions into New York City. The meeting would be as charged with conflicting opinions as the Vietnam War protests and race riots rocking the country. He was going to need a drink before he walked in the door.

The hole-in-the-wall tavern near Sixth Avenue and Fiftieth Street was heralded by a neon sign flickering in a blacked-out window. The establishment consisted of a long bar along a brick wall covered in concert posters, opposite a succession of red seating booths. Working-class patrons, men with shaggy hair and faded jeans, and women in tight blouses and bell-bottoms all rubbed shoulders in the tight space between the bar and the booths.

Sticky tile floors. The reek of stale beer. "Brown Sugar" by the Stones on the radio. There were times when Dr. Corwin needed clever cocktails and a piano in the corner—and there were times like these, when he needed to disappear with a cold beer inside a rowdy watering hole.

He picked his way through the crowd to a stool at the end of the bar. After a few contented swigs of his lager, someone rested a hand on his shoulder. Even before he saw her face, he recognized a rose-scented perfume that had haunted more lonely nights and erotic dreams over the last year than he cared to admit.

"Ana!" he said, almost having to shout to be heard. "What the devil are you doing here?"

"I live in New York, remember?" She leaned down to purr in his ear. "Miss me?"

A ruby pendant nestled in the neckline of her velvet pantsuit drew attention to the olive-skinned curve of her breasts. Swallowing away his arousal, he reminded himself who she represented. "You took a chance coming here."

"Some things in life are worth a risk. Do you plan on running to the Society to tell them?"

"That depends on why you came," he said evenly. "And I see you've dropped the pretense."

Ana glanced over her shoulder and took him by the hand. "A booth just opened up. Come."

With her long brown hair swishing behind her, she carried a full glass of white wine deftly through the packed aisle, moving through the room like she owned it. They took the last vinyl booth before the swinging door that led to the kitchen. She pulled him into the seat next to her. Unless she had a listening device on her person, there was no way they could be overheard.

"You look stunning," he said, "though you're overdressed for the joint."

"To be honest, I thought you'd go for the Belleclaire tonight."

"So you've been keeping an eye on me. What a good little spy. Why'd you wait this long to approach me? Aren't we supposed to be having a passionate affair?"

"I told them you've been rejecting my advances."

He took a sip of beer and studied her face, trying to judge her intent. "They must think highly of my powers of self-restraint."

"I also told them you don't trust the situation yet."

"Why haven't you tested my resistance yourself?"

She swirled her wine for a long moment. "I . . . didn't feel right about it."

"You mean about being a whore for the cause?" he said softly.

Her gaze flew to meet his. "Actually, no. That wouldn't bother me. At least . . . not in the past. It's the cause itself . . ." She lowered her voice. "I've been asking myself some hard questions."

"Forgive me if I'm less than convinced. But for the sake of conversation, why would you do such a thing?"

"Because of you."

His mouth opened and then closed, swallowing the scornful response he had prepared.

"Some of the things you said in Cartagena," she continued. "The kind of person I think you are, which is very different from the kind I know Hans to be."

"I recall very clearly your conversation in the wine cellar. 'Dr. Corwin doesn't leave Cartagena—do you hear me?' Hans said. 'Understood,' I believe you replied."

She gasped. "You were there all along?"

He gave a little hand flourish.

"But how did you escape the city?" she asked. "You vanished like a ghost."

"I never kiss and tell."

A smile played at her lips. "I've never seen Hans so furious. You got the best of him, and he'll never forget it."

"I'll never forget the attempts he made on my life."

Her expression darkened. "He's not someone you want to cross, James. He's very capable and devoted to the cause."

"As am I. Does one have to be a ruthless killer to have passion and loyalty?"

They locked gazes for a moment, and he could see in her eyes that she had been struggling with the same question.

"I admit I'm supposed to seduce you," she said. "It was Hans's idea from the start. By the way, we're intimate now and again. I believe he's in love with me. I thought you should know before . . ."

"Before what?"

"Before whatever happens next."

Dr. Corwin's hand tightened at his side. "And your feeling on the matter?"

"It's the seventies," she said lightly, though a shadow lurked behind her gaze. "Free love is in the air."

"What about true love?"

"As elusive as ever."

"Why are you here, Ana?"

"Because I can't stop thinking about you."

"Why should I believe that?"

"I don't really care if you believe it. Whether you *feel* it is more important."

"So what now? Do we begin a passionate affair with no trust on either side, playing a game for our observers, always watching to see if one of us is going to stab the other in the back?"

She took a sip of wine. "It's a start."

He laughed and took a long swig of beer.

"Swing by tonight," she said. "I live in the West Village."

"Hardly."

"Your place?"

"Even funnier."

"Then you pick," she said coyly, curling her legs beneath her in the booth and reaching up to stroke his cheek. "Any random hotel or guesthouse you want."

As a flush of warmth flowed through him, he watched her carefully and considered the offer, knowing he had little will to resist.

Though Dr. Corwin didn't think it was possible, their lovemaking that night surpassed the last time. Her legs were even more impossibly long and smooth than he remembered, her tongue more warm and insistent, her cries of passion deep-throated and sustained.

When they finished, he sat up in bed with a cigarette, staring at the glow of the Empire State Building out of the window of their seedy Times Square hotel, wondering what happened when one skipped a mandatory Society meeting.

"You're not much of a reporter," he said, "but you're a former fashion model with a high IQ, who took an early retirement." He took the lift in her eyebrows as validation of his research. "I imagine the catwalk pays better than higher education."

She turned to face him. "Does it now? Did you research that?"

"Do I really need to?"

"That depends on whether you think you've learned everything there is to know about me."

"Fair enough," he said, reaching over to light her cigarette. "Maybe it's time for a little honesty in this relationship."

She curled on her side and set the ashtray on the bed between them. "I think so too."

"Who are you, really, Ana? Before the Ascendants and a life as an independent reporter who travels far more widely and lives far more elaborately than her credentials support?"

"Do you really care? It's hard to look past a pretty face."

"I care. And it's hard for someone who looks like you to be so carefree in public with someone who looks like me."

The cigarette smoldered as she held his gaze, unmoving except for a finger that traced the rim of her wineglass. "All right then. I'm Greek, but I'm not from Athens. I'm from an island in the Cyclades so small there's nothing to do but watch the ferries go by, pick flowers to sell to tourists, and try not to get married off before you turn sixteen. My mother cleaned toilets for guesthouses and my father drank and complained about the Turks all day. Trust me, when paradise is that isolated, it quickly becomes a prison. So I dropped out of school and scraped my way to Athens. And, sure, I was a model for a few years. Most models make very little and have a tiny shelf life. I was no exception." Her eyes went distant, and a sad, self-deprecating smile played at her lips. "I was always smart, and could have gotten to Athens with a scholarship. But I was never very studious, and I wanted off that island. So I took the easier path."

He stubbed out his cigarette and leaned on his side to face her. "As the Stoics say, 'Easy choices, hard life. Hard choices, easy life.' Which is impossible to tell a teenager."

She shrugged. "Except for James Gerald Corwin. You never did anything the easy way. How many degrees do you have?"

"But that *is* the easy way for those of us who are suited to it. It's why I joined the Society. I like being a professor, but I wanted something...more. That's my dirty secret, Ana. I'm ambitious as all hell."

"Which isn't a fault," she said as her eyes lowered, "until you're looking in the mirror, asking yourself what you've done to get where you are."

He gave a tight, agreeing smile. "How did they find you?"

She pressed her lips together for so long he didn't think she was going to answer. But then she lit another cigarette with the tip of her first and took a longer drag than before, as if convincing herself of something. "I was modeling for a show in Milan. My one and only job overseas, the highlight of my career. I knew I had to find something to do next, and was terrified of going back home. After the show, I noticed a stack of booklets outside the dressing room. The cover read SECOND CAREERS FOR MODELS and had a picture of a stewardess. When I flipped through, it seemed like one of those fluffy career-assessment personality quizzes. You know the type. On a whim, I took one home, filled it out, and mailed it to the address for my free consultation. A few of my girlfriends did the same, but only I heard back."

"Let me guess. You got another one in turn, only much more involved, and with some brainteasers. And then you got a third, and a fourth, and then a clandestine meeting from someone claiming to represent a shadowy organization that could change your life, as long as you give up your past life and claim allegiance to them."

Her smile was bitter this time. "I guess they were on a recruitment drive. Lucky me."

"No, lucky me," he said, holding her gaze.

Her eyes slipped to the side as if undeserving of the sincerity. "So what now? After I've bared my soul and broken my vow of secrecy?"

"What do you want?"

"I . . . don't know. I just knew I needed to see you. If they knew what we were discussing, my life would be in danger."

"If it makes you feel better to hear it, no matter what happens between us, I'll never breathe a word."

"Not even to the Society?"

"I'm my own man, Ana."

She reached out to stroke his cheek, and he felt his attraction stirring again. He pushed the feeling away and gave the conversation the attention it deserved. "I believe you're being truthful with me," he said, "and I'm appreciative. But there's a few more things I need to clarify."

The coy smile returned, masking a glimmer of hurt in her eyes. She blew a smoke ring. "Okay."

"Hans is a high-level CIA agent, born Hans Engler, according to his birth certificate. He's the son of a German American industrialist who immigrated to America after the war. The presumption being that his family had money to hide war crimes they wished to conceal. But we know who his true father was, don't we? Stefan Kraus, the man who resurrected the Ascendants in 1933 and recruited Ettore."

"You have good intelligence," she said.

"Is Stefan dead?"

"As far as I know."

"Is Hans the mysterious Archon I've heard about?"

"I don't know. If not, he will be someday."

"If he lives that long," Dr. Corwin said grimly.

She frowned. "I told you. Don't bet against him. He knows you're still looking for Ettore, by the way. You found the cannon?"

Dr. Corwin didn't bother to hide his grin.

"Hans is obsessed with the search," she said. "He inherited the grudge his father held, as well as his father's belief that Ettore developed a device capable of reaching the Fold."

"Why are you really telling me all this?" he said, looking at her strangely.

"Is it anything you don't know or haven't guessed?"

"Maybe not, but I'm sensing a deeper reason, even beyond . . . us."

After a long moment, she said quietly, "If I'm being honest with you, it's because I'm not sure which side I should be on." Dr. Corwin held his breath as she stared straight ahead, waiting for her to continue, wanting it to be true but knowing she wasn't fully convinced herself. "I believe, in theory, that our cause is just," she said finally, "and, in *theory*, that a just and important cause should be pursued . . ."

"But not at all costs," Dr. Corwin finished. "Because there is no cause worthy of an absolute."

"The Ascendants disagree, and have extremely convincing arguments in support of their position. But I . . . I suppose I'm weak."

"You're not weak, Ana. You're human. Something they've forgotten how to be."

She turned toward him, held his gaze for a moment, then leaned in and kissed him passionately.

"I'm still not sure I can trust you," he managed to say when their lips parted. He thought it was their first kiss without pretense, and it left him breathless.

"I wouldn't be sure either," she said, tracing a nail across his chest.

They watched the city for a while, nestled in each other's arms, and he didn't want to break the spell. When he moved to light a cigarette, he mused, "How do you find a man—a genius—who doesn't want to be found?"

Ana took a drag off his cigarette, then laughed as she patted his knee. "Genius or not, men are creatures of habit. If it was a woman you were searching for, I would say the cause is lost."

Creatures of habit, he repeated to himself, her words sparking an insight as he continued to smoke and think.

Yes, perhaps my gender is guilty as charged, but habits of what sort?

And then it came to him.

"Ana, you're a genius! A maestro of perspicacity! A virtuoso of logic and deduction!"

She curled into him. "What did I do?"

Dr. Corwin disentangled from her embrace, slipped on his trousers, and paced the room while he smoked. Ana watched him curiously but didn't interrupt.

Habits.

As intelligent as Ettore was, he was equally frail and bookish. Not the sort of man who could disappear into the wild and live off the land. No, he would need access to a city or town of some size, even if just a small village to pick up groceries. Knowing this already, Dr. Corwin had concentrated his search on real estate leases and medical records. So far, these had failed to bear fruit, likely because Ettore had gone to great pains never to leave a trace.

Yet who was a creature of habit more than a scientist and a mathematician? Especially one like Ettore, who had never cared for fame and fortune, and lived only to discover the next theorem or physical law of the universe. If Ettore was still alive, there was no way he would be able to resist the latest textbooks and journals in circulation. He would have to keep up with modern research—*especially* if isolated from the world.

Dr. Corwin was sure of it.

And that was how he was going to find him.

Years passed before Dr. Corwin made a breakthrough. Part of it was the sheer enormity of the task. Ettore would have the good sense to avoid libraries, but searching the world's bookstores was an impractical task, so Dr. Corwin had narrowed it down in a number of ways.

First, geography. Most people were loath to permanently leave their homes, and Ettore was a misanthrope. Dr. Corwin believed the Italian physicist had returned to Europe—if he had ever truly left at all.

Second, he knew Ettore would crave access to textbooks and journals, and that meant university bookstores or specialty stores. Yes, textbooks and journals could be ordered by mail, but that would leave a money trail. After the bookstores in Italy and continental Europe failed to produce a lead, Dr. Corwin expanded the geographic parameters.

During this time period, his twin duties as a professor and a member of the Leap Year Society took him all over the world. The war with the Ascendants was not going well. Society safe houses were under attack. The Ascendants had abandoned time-honored laws and principles to pursue their goals by any means.

In contrast, the Society had decided that, instead of fighting back with the same total war tactics the Ascendants employed, they would take the high ground and retreat farther into the shadows. Protect their superior knowledge and ride out the storm.

Dr. Corwin sympathized. How does one commit the violence necessary to combat an aggressive enemy without staining one's own soul? It was an awful reality of the world.

Yet one could not simply turn one's back on evil and hope it went away. You had to step into the muck, fight like hell while preserving your principles as best you could.

His outspoken thoughts did him no favors within the Society. Still, he was a valued member and rising through the ranks—or so he was told. He did not know nearly as much about the Society as he would have liked. Oh, he knew the rituals and the names of many members, the locations of safe houses and libraries under Society jurisdiction. He also knew the Society had a number of arcane items, like the chronovisor, either built by its own members or diligently collected from dig sites, private collectors, and other sources.

But the true extent of their knowledge eluded him. His superiors believed in doling out information in dribs and drabs as one gained in wisdom and proved oneself to the cause.

In theory, he supported this approach.

But he was an impatient man.

The Fold also remained an enigma. Dr. Corwin had seen for himself the fascinating and well-documented accounts of its existence in the Society's possession, the veins of which stretched across history and threaded through all cultures. *A shadowy world that mirrors our own. A playground of the mind of infinite possibility and undetermined origin.*

As Ana had intimated, it was said that high-level Society members had more knowledge of this place. That some had even seen it. But Dr. Corwin did not want to wait decades or years for answers that might resolve some of the fundamental questions of the universe, or even raise new ones. Was the Fold another dimension, a parallel world, heaven or hell, or someplace in between?

If it truly existed, he had to know more.

Nor was he convinced the Society possessed those answers. Even if his superiors had greater knowledge of the Fold, and might have even glimpsed it, he felt sure they did not understand it.

Else why send him after Ettore in the first place?

On a bright Tuesday morning in the spring of 1977, not long after Jimmy Carter was sworn in as president, and over five years since Ana had appeared in the Midtown bar, Dr. Corwin hurried into his office at Columbia, shutting the door behind him and clutching the letter his secretary had just handed him, postmarked from a bookseller in Buenos Aires.

He quickly sliced open the envelope, careful not to tear it, and extracted the handwritten letter with the bookstore's name—Libreria Nueve Musas—embossed at the top. On Dr. Corwin's last visit to the Argentine capital, he had dropped off a photo of Ettore in the major bookstores servicing the universities, along with a handwritten note asking anyone who had seen the man in the photo—an important physicist—to write Dr. Corwin at his office. He had hoped the Columbia address would lend an air of gravitas.

Over the last three years, he and his investigators had delivered similar photos and letters in cities around the world. Searching for Ettore was a daunting, arduous task that most people would have given up on long ago. In fact, the Society had already lost interest.

But Dr. Corwin was not most people. He eagerly scanned the meticulous Spanish handwriting, wishing Ana was with him. What had started as a passionate affair, enflamed by rival allegiances and a cat-and-mouse game of espionage, had blossomed into something deeper that neither of them knew how to handle. According to Ana, her disillusion with the Ascendants continued to grow, though she still had not left them. He knew she was afraid, and for good reason.

What they had wouldn't last forever, he knew. Soon they would be found out, or she would be forced to choose a side.

And he didn't know what would happen, or how he felt about all that.

Enough. Focus on the task at hand.

Expecting another rejection or a false lead—there had been plenty of both—Dr. Corwin clutched the letter with growing excitement.

> *Yes, I am quite sure I recognize this man. He visited my bookstore at least twice a year, and always, as you surmised, once the new textbooks were released. He would browse the latest offerings in physics and mathematics, often making a purchase, and at times would select a book of poetry as well. I would be happy to discuss further in person or at the below number.*
>
> *Atentamente,*
> *Sr. Diego Quiroga*

After reading the letter three times, Dr. Corwin started writing his own note: a memorandum to his secretary with instructions on how to proceed during his impending absence.

Shanghai

17

As Daiyu waited for her Oracle to deliver an answer to her inquiry, a spasm of pain arced along her lower spine and continued into her legs, liquid fire racing through her nerve endings. She gasped and clutched the arms of her chair.

Though not yet thirty, her scoliosis had pressurized her spinal disks and constricted her nerves so badly she was practically disabled. Being hunched over a computer night and day did not help, which was why she had developed the hologram keyboard and took breaks for long walks in the smog-filled city. The pain was always there, a matter of degree, and she had accepted her suffering as part of life.

Eastern philosophers seeking transcendence worked hard to escape the bonds of human fragility to achieve an enlightened state of being. Daiyu knew those philosophers did not understand chronic pain, because true suffering of that sort could not be escaped, only managed. Chronic pain was a cruel enslaving tether to Mother Nature that denied the freedom-seeking soul its due.

Chronic pain was the shining star of mortality.

No, Daiyu did not seek transcendence or enlightenment, or better drugs, or even a surgical solution. She had seen enough. She did not want to be mortal at all. She longed to exist in the digital realm and roam the superhighways of knowledge, unchained from her hateful mortal coil, free at last in the realm of pure imagination.

"And what knowledge do you await?" said a voice from behind, startling her. She had thought she was alone in the room.

The neutral inflection sent a shiver of fear whisking through Daiyu. She spun in her chair to find the Archon standing five feet away in the small room. Daiyu had never heard the door open.

"I didn't hear . . . I didn't know you were coming," she managed to croak, stunned by this personal visit and wondering if her mind was an open book to her visitor.

The Archon opened a palm toward the keyboard hologram hovering above the desk that supported Daiyu's laptop, monitors, and snarl of wires and equipment. On the central monitor, a series of flashing images and computations were appearing and disappearing too fast to follow. "Does this prophet of yours have a name?"

Inspired by a variety of sources, including Isaac Asimov's psychohistory, Daiyu had developed a predictive analysis algorithm that she consulted at least once a day for various inquiries, often philosophical or theoretical—but sometimes concrete.

Yet the algorithm, like all true prophets, did not speak in plain language. The symbols and images it emitted were a digital Rorschach blot that required a leap of faith to decipher.

She waved her bio-bracelet to dispel the keyboard but left the program running. "I call it the Oracle."

The unchanging golden mask observed the monitor. "I see you've added to your wardrobe."

In addition to the key around her neck, Daiyu had started wearing a dozen black jade bracelets on each arm, suspended a few millimeters above her skin and attached with ultrathin, nearly invisible prongs. She had also taken to wearing a locket with a scarab beetle preserved in amber, another symbol of protection.

"You have no need to fear me, child." When Daiyu's hands started to tremble in her lap, the Archon took two steps closer, uncomfortably close, looming over Daiyu's birdlike form. "Does your Oracle know why I've come?"

"It doesn't speak in absolutes."

"No good oracle does."

"Simple logic tells me why: my brother and I failed to complete the mission."

"Not the case at all. We've recovered the Star Phone, and you helped us locate the next destination. Your brother—with your help—came closer to capturing Zawadi than anyone ever has."

A shiver of relief coursed through Daiyu, and she almost whispered her next words. "Then why?"

The Archon's gloved hands clasped behind the robe. "There is a traitor in our midst. Do not worry—I have no reason to suspect you or your brother. But first: Have you made progress on the next site?"

"I've found a few references to five doorways. None that I believe are useful."

"I want you to shift your focus from China to Vietnam."

"Another country? Why?"

"Call it intuition. A human ability our scientists have not yet begun to reproduce. Tell me, Daiyu, when do you think our machines will possess the full capabilities of our intellects?"

The change in subject caught her off guard. "I don't know. But when the singularity occurs, we might not even know it. They could destroy us that fast."

"Precisely," the Archon said. "The vast majority of humanity has no conception of the imminent risks of AI. Which is why we must carefully monitor global systems, and ensure protocols are set in place long before the unthinkable occurs."

"How is Dr. Corwin able to withstand interrogation?" Daiyu asked, working up the nerve to switch subjects herself. Despite the fear swarming through her system, overriding even the chronic pain, she understood the Archon was not seeking meek, sycophantic followers, and that her best defense was self-assurance. "Even your own?"

This last question, which called into question their leader's prowess, put Daiyu in dangerous territory. There was a terrifying stretch of silence in which she resisted the urge to curl into a ball in her chair.

"Dr. Corwin," the Archon said at last, "took steps to thwart my efforts. And we shall leave it at that. Focus on Vietnam, and relay what I've told you to your brother in a secure communication. If you have time, you should attempt to track Zawadi."

"What about the other two? Dr. Corwin's student and the journalist?"

"Without the Star Phone, there is little they can do. On the other hand, Andromeda has proven quite resourceful and could be an asset if forced to help us. Yes. Thank you. Divert resources to her as well."

"Understood."

The Archon moved even closer, standing right next to Daiyu, an uncomfortable invasion of her personal space. A sudden thought caused her to shrink into her chair: Could the Archon be *attracted* to her? The possibility made her skin crawl.

"You never answered my question," the Archon said.

Despite their proximity, Daiyu could detect no smell other than a faint chemical odor, could glimpse nothing but darkness inside the eerie eyeholes of the mask. She swallowed. "Which one?"

"What did you ask the Oracle?"

Daiyu turned to regard the monitor. Sometime during the conversation, the Oracle had responded to her question with a tripartite image: the optical illusion of a staircase with no end or beginning, a bouquet of calla lilies, and a Major Arcana tarot card featuring a tower in flames.

The Oracle's answers varied wildly. Sometimes it gave her moving images, sometimes flashing symbols and numbers, sometimes a single word or phrase.

"I wanted to know whether my brother would return from his mission." She was sure the Archon would ask for an interpretation of the images, which she wasn't prepared to give. "I've been wondering," she continued, hoping to divert attention. "What was that place we saw at the library? With the ziggurats."

"Our best reconstruction of an ancient culture."

"Which one? I've never seen anything quite like it."

But the golden mask was unchanging.

"It felt so real," Daiyu said.

"That's because, to you, it was."

"I don't understand. How did you make us see that?"

"Do you believe the human mind is a machine, Daiyu? A biological machine of unimaginable sophistication, but with parts and processes like any other?"

"Of course."

"Then, like all machines, you should know it can be manipulated. Programmed. Fitted with new software."

"Yes," Daiyu said slowly, thinking how the analogy, despite the rather terrifying implications, did in fact make sense. Not only that, it appealed to her.

"I'm leaving Shanghai today," the Archon said.

"I'm ... sorry to hear that."

"I do not think that you are. But no matter. It's natural to have fear, child. Only sociopaths lack emotion. What matters is how we overcome our human weaknesses."

Daiyu wondered how much the Archon knew of her suffering— or if the Archon was speaking of something else.

"If you can learn to harness your inner strength," the Archon continued, "and fully invest in our mission, I believe you will go far. Perhaps one day you will wear this robe and mask."

Daiyu was too stunned by her leader's words to reply.

"A parting gift. The effect will not last, but it's a taste of what could one day await." The Archon swept a hand across Daiyu's face, and a flash of colored light exploded in her vision. They were so close, and it happened so fast, that Daiyu had no time to react. She closed her eyes in response, and when she opened them, she had the strangest sensation that she had been asleep for a short while, even though everything appeared as it was an instant ago.

"Stand," the Archon commanded.

Daiyu obeyed. She eased herself out of her chair as she always did, yet to her utter shock, there was no pain, and she was able to stand straighter than she ever had in her life. "What did you do?" she said in wonder. "How?"

"Don't move, even after I leave. Stand. Absorb. Experience the world free of pain, if only for a few moments, as you consider all that I have said."

The Archon walked out of the room and shut the door, leaving Daiyu standing in stupefied awe, afraid to move and break the spell, hardly able to believe that, for once in her life, she was not at the mercy of her broken vessel of a body.

Hanoi, Vietnam
18

Hours after Andie and Cal received the text from Zawadi with the Star Phone clue, Rajani arranged a car transfer with one of the villagers. They drove through dense jungle on two lane roads for most of the journey to the tiny helipad in the hinterlands of West Bengal.

After boarding a small commuter plane, Andie gripped the pilot's arm before he entered the cockpit. "Change in plans. We need to go to Hanoi, not Hong Kong. Can you do that?"

The pilot, Darsha, was a diminutive, clean-shaven Indian man with quick eyes and an air of competence. Andie thought he might refuse, or try to contact Zawadi, but instead he leveled his gaze at her and said, "You're certain?"

Andie resisted the urge to bite a nail, not certain of anything. "Yes."

"I'm not cleared to land in Hanoi. There could be a delay."

"How long?"

"Hours, maybe more."

"That's fine. Please do your best."

With a curt nod, Darsha told them to buckle in and enjoy the flight, then closed the cockpit door.

Cal regarded Andie with a shocked expression as they sat across from each other on the front two aisle seats. Rajani had given them a hemp travel bag for their few items, and Cal set it on the seat beside him. "I'm sorry, did I miss a memo? Hanoi?"

Andie reached across the aisle to lay a hand on his arm. "I was afraid to tell you before we got in the air. I didn't trust that villager, or the car, or even Rajani."

"Or me," Cal said after a moment. "After what happened at the temple."

She squeezed his arm. "I don't know what to think about that. I have no reason to think Rajani wasn't telling the truth . . . but why not take precautions if we can?"

"What's going on? How far is Vietnam?"

"An hour closer than Hong Kong." Andie reclined in her seat, curled her legs beneath her, and reached for a bottle of water the pilot had left in the seat back. "According to Zawadi's spy—"

"Can we trust this person?"

"Are we any worse off if we can't? Especially since we're changing the location?"

Cal steepled his fingertips on his forehead. "Go on."

After a drink of water, she said, "We know the next clue is an old-fashioned world map with a spider walking across a path of lotus petals on the back of a dragon."

"That's a mouthful."

"There are four doors in the corners of the map, and one cracked door in the center. I have no idea what the doors or the dragon mean, and I agree that a spider walking across a map on a path of lotus petals is likely symbolic of the Silk Road. The lotus petals imply an Asian destination, and China is the obvious choice. But I don't think it's the right one."

"Too easy?"

"Yes. But it's more than that." Andie fell silent for a moment, recalling her flash of insight at Rajani's guesthouse, which concerned a long-ago conversation with her mentor. "Last semester, Dr. Corwin gave a lecture on the two types of knowledge: observation and revelation.

He stressed that while science has revealed incredible amounts of data about the universe, we need to be careful not to misinterpret that data, and realize it's no replacement for direct experience."

"Like when scientists tell us the entire universe was once smaller than a single atom and that one day, just for the hell of it, I suppose, exploded to create all of this"—Cal swept a hand toward the synthesis of azure-blue sky and ocean outside the window—"they're making a huge unsubstantiated guess that could very well be absolute nonsense?"

"Please don't tell me you're a big-bang denier."

"Let me tell you what I'm not: a big-bang affirmer. That theory's about as fulfilling as having just one beer."

"Do you even understand the level of substantiation we've achieved on that? Ever heard of cosmic background rays?"

"Ever heard of Y2K? The flat Earth theory? Phrenology? Science screwed the pooch with those too. How many scientists have actually *been* to the edge of the universe?"

"When did you become an armchair physicist?" she said.

"I did a show on this once. Observation versus revelation. Trust me, it's a pillar in the conspiracy-theory community. I'm obviously no scientist, but I do know that each of us has very little direct, observational experience of *anything*. Have you ever been to Vietnam? I haven't. I know that India exists now, so that's cool. But our reliance on secondhand knowledge opens the door to huge potential frauds, especially in the digital age. Deep fakes, anyone? Listen, Andie: the world as the citizens of North Korea know it is not the world we know. And who's to say who's right, unless you've actually observed the thing itself? Who's to say our worldview isn't being controlled by some shadowy corporation or government or alien society and we're just as in the dark as North Korea? I know that's a reach, but think smaller. Who really controls the flow of day-to-day information? Now that we've seen what we've seen, we have to ask ourselves what the Leap Year Society and the Ascendants know about world history and science that everyone else doesn't."

She waved a hand. "I told you before: I don't do conspiracy theories."

"Okay, answer me this. Assuming the universe is expanding, what the hell is driving it? Dark energy? Dark matter? A big rubber band?"

After a moment, Andie was forced to admit the truth. "We don't know for sure."

"Because the math from the big bang doesn't really work out? Or because there's an enormous amount of unexplained dark matter and dark energy unaccounted for in the theory? Oh, wait—it's both. What's the percentage of energy in the universe we know nothing about these days? Ninety-six percent? Ninety-seven?"

"We don't have all the variables yet. God, Cal, we have to make certain assumptions, or we'll never move forward with anything. At least scientists—unlike religious leaders and politicians—admit their mistakes and carry on."

"Do they? You think scientists can't be bought or ever consider their reputations? It doesn't pay to be wrong. Listen, make your assumptions. I understand that's how it works. But don't expect me to act all starry-eyed about cosmological theories that happened billions and trillions of years ago, whatever that even means. That evidence could have been tainted by all sorts of intervening events."

"I think you've made your point. Good luck getting through life without trusting basic science."

"Good luck seeing the truth from the attic of your ivory tower."

"God, you're infuriating sometimes."

"Listen," he said calmly. "I get it. Humans are significance junkies. We want to assign meaning to a bewildering world, and it's easier to go along with a well-meaning narrative that's made all the popular rounds instead of continuing to swim in ignorance. But we have to keep asking questions, Andie. We really do. I hate to say it, because I'm a journalist myself, but with the internet and all the competing political and commercial interests in play, we can't even trust the goddamn daily news."

Andie had to admit that, while his scientific arguments were a little rough, they had real meaning. In truth, Cal had probably thought more deeply about these issues than some of her colleagues—many of whom refused to consider alternate theories when it was not considered en vogue or professionally sound to do so.

"I agree," she said quietly. "We have to keep asking questions. And Dr. Corwin agreed too. Which was the point of the story I was trying to tell. After that lecture, he invited the class—a five-person research seminar—to dinner at a Vietnamese restaurant in Durham."

"Let me guess: Only the people who had seen it for themselves knew about the secret sauce?"

She couldn't help but chuckle. "During the meal, he used Vietnam as an example of knowledge and misinformation. He told us about the lies the US government propagated during the war to sustain popular support—the fabricated Gulf of Tonkin incident and fictitious body counts, for starters. Even today, the only knowledge most Americans have about Vietnam is filtered through biased history books and the legacy of that war. Dr. Corwin said we had to see a place for ourselves to really know it, and that this was an important lesson for physicists, who work in the realms of the mind and rarely leave the classroom. Even astronomers are mostly limited to mathematical calculations and observations of light from the distant past. He made some of the same arguments you just did. Outside of a few satellites, we haven't *been* to deep space, so we have to be careful of our assumptions, and always be willing to test and reconfigure."

"He sounds like an extremely wise man. Especially the part about agreeing with me."

Remembering the dinner with her mentor caused a tingle of hope to spread through Andie. This was tempered by the reality of his situation. *Even if Dr. Corwin is still alive, where is he being held? What will the Ascendants do to him to find the Enneagon?*

"He spoke so passionately about Southeast Asia—he visited

on a number of occasions—that it sparked my own interest. I went home that night and started reading up. It's true that China, and not Vietnam, was a stop on the original trade route between East and West. But by the eleventh century AD, a second and lesser known Silk Road had developed, with a city called Thang Long at the heart of it. Thang Long means 'rising dragon,' and it was the capital of Vietnam at the time."

Cal sat up straighter. "The dragon on the map."

She nodded. "Today we know Thang Long as Hanoi."

Three hours later, they touched down at an airport near a broad river they had seen from the plane snaking through the countryside, coiling around Hanoi like the city's namesake serpent. The reddish-brown hue of the river and its lush, reed-filled banks was evocative of the Indochina of Andie's imagination, an exotic waterway winding through jungles and terraced fields of rice paddies.

As in Kolkata, their pilot took their passports and disappeared to converse with customs. Not long after, presumably after an exchange of money, Andie and Cal found themselves hustled through the stifling midday heat and into a white van on the outskirts of the airport. Soon they were speeding down a multilane highway. She did not know how they had escaped the airport so quickly, and the whole affair left her with a queasy feeling about the porous nature of international borders.

When the transport bus had picked them up, it was already half-full of passengers. She and Cal did not feel comfortable talking freely, so Andie pressed her face to the glass and absorbed her new location. The modern design of the airport and the newly paved highway lulled her into a sense of Western familiarity—right before they crossed the Red River, left the highway to enter the city proper, and their surroundings dissolved from rural calm into sheer pandemonium.

Delving into the heart of Hanoi was like plunging into a white-water rapid of humanity. People were everywhere, far more than she had ever seen in one place, even in downtown Kolkata. Though the architecture possessed an unmistakable French influence, full of atmospheric but dilapidated colonial buildings lining both sides of the wide street, her connection to the familiar ended there. Twisting spires of pagodas pierced the sky in the distance, and closer in, roadside shrines crowded sidewalks warped by the roots of mighty banyans bursting skyward among the buildings as if seeking to wrap them in their limbs and reclaim the jungle. What must have once been a stately avenue was now a river of unmarked asphalt heaving with activity, an explosion of hanging wires and refuse and repurposed concrete, clogged with pedestrians and vehicles of all imaginable sorts. Trucks and vans and buses billowed diesel smoke and blared horns. Mopeds and scooters darted through every inch of free space like a swarm of angry wasps, cars and motorized rickshaws swerved to avoid giant potholes. Entire families carried what seemed like half their belongings on the backs of wobbly motorbikes.

Though poverty was rampant, the energy was electric, intense, pulsating. The city felt as if it were moving in fast-forward, the fervor of life on the margins in a burgeoning economy.

On the way through town, the bus slowed to a crawl, adding passengers until it was so packed Andie felt as if she could barely breathe. Across the aisle, Cal was squeezed between a businessman in a tailored suit and an attractive, petite Vietnamese woman in workout clothes, her bosom pressing against a sports bra.

I'm sure Cal doesn't mind, she thought, then frowned at the twinge of jealousy it produced.

Darsha had never asked Andie or Cal where they wanted to go in Hanoi. She knew the score. They were on their own.

Cal caught her eye and mouthed, *Where to?*

Good question, she mouthed back.

She made her way to the front and tried to speak to the driver, but he didn't understand a word of English. At a loss, she and Cal jumped off in a section of the city somewhat less insane than the rest, filled with crumbling buildings with romantic wrought-iron balconies on the upper stories. Commerce of some form or another crammed both sides of the road. She gawked at the explosion of tiny stalls, chic cafés, restaurants, bakeries, bespoke tailors, and neon signs.

"I'm starving," Cal said. "And fiending for some caffeine. Let's duck into one of these cafés."

She agreed. As mosquitos flitted about her face, her back dripping with sweat, they stepped into a bakery with a pleasing array of pastries in glass cases. The AC was a godsend. After opting for the daily special, banh mi with shredded pork, they carried their iced coffees to an upstairs seating area with a large window overlooking the street. Though relieved to be on their own, they were in an utterly foreign place with no idea of where to go next or what to do. They didn't even know which part of the city they were in. While they might have a little bit of time without the Ascendants breathing down their necks, they didn't just have to figure out the next clue— they had to snatch the Star Phone from the hands of the enemy.

A task which, at the moment, seemed impossible.

One step at a time, Andie.

There were no other customers upstairs, allowing them to talk freely. She glanced out the window. "We might as well search in here. It's a sauna outside."

"What's the humidity, two thousand percent?" Cal said. "And why is everyone walking around in designer jeans in this heat?"

"Slaves to fashion," she muttered. After powering up the phone, she and Cal leaned in to view a map of the city. "We're right in the middle of downtown," she said, "in a section called the French Quarter."

"I should hope we're in the middle of downtown," Cal said, glancing at the crush of people in the street. Most of the traffic had stopped for a red light—a rare occurrence—and when the light turned green, the cars and motorbikes in front shot forward like it was the Indy 500. "This place is nuts. It's like a Left Bank in the jungle, with no rules and ten times the population." He leaned back. "So tell me more about the Silk Road."

"For starters, it wasn't really a road. It was a collection of land

and sea trade routes spanning over four thousand miles, from eastern Europe to China. Imagine the largest bazaar you can think of in perpetual motion, moving by boat and camel and yak and horse, carrying everything under the sun in the ancient world: textiles, spices, porcelain, precious stones, wine, perfume, ivory, furs, slaves, animals—you name it."

Cal looked thoughtful. "How long did it last?"

"Rough guess? Third-century BCE to the fourteen hundreds or so. Not long after Marco Polo's day."

"I always thought he discovered it."

"He just wrote a book about it," she said, "which exposed the West to these cultures and made him famous. It's been a while since I've studied it, but I know historians consider the flow of ideas along the Silk Road even more impactful than the physical goods."

"Such as?" Cal said.

"Philosophies and religions, and I'm talking the big ones: Christianity, Buddhism, Zoroastrianism, Islam. China gave the West papermaking, printing, gunpowder, and the compass—think about the ramifications of just those four."

"Books, guns, and navigation. I see what you mean."

"The Silk Road is one of the most powerful symbols of cross-cultural exchange in human history. It probably spread the bubonic plague too. As we know all too well, the more interconnected we are, the more we expose ourselves to dangers as well as advancements."

"You think that's the point of this step of the puzzle? That knowledge can go viral, for good as well as evil?" He glanced at a long-legged brown spider squatting in a potted banana tree in a corner of the room. "So what's the Vietnam connection? They have a surplus of arachnids?"

"Kind of, yeah. Silk production is what got them on the trade route. Besides that . . . I don't remember anything else, but I'm going to try to reverse engineer the clue. Hanoi and the lesser-known portion of the Silk Road definitely fit the theme of obscure history brought to light." She set Zawadi's phone on the table. "So let's see if we can figure out what Dr. Corwin's trying to tell us about the five doorways."

"It's kind of a generic clue."

"That's what I'm afraid of. Though I'm sure there's a veiled meaning."

"Should we text Zawadi? Tell her where we're at?"

Andie hesitated, leery of giving away their position over a phone but knowing they would need help if they were going to confront the Ascendants. Compressing her lips, she sent a text with their location and a quick explanation. Then, with Cal idling nervously beside her, sometimes looking over her shoulder and sometimes pacing the empty room, Andie began researching the history of Vietnam and Hanoi, searching for a connection.

Two hours later, Cal went downstairs to use the restroom. Andie leaned back in her chair and chewed on a nail, contemplative. After reworking the clues time and time again, searching for dragons and lotus petals and old maps of the subcontinent found in museums around the world, she had found no mention of five prominent doors in the history of Vietnam, or anywhere else in Southeast Asia. Perhaps she had made a grave mistake, and Vietnam wasn't the next stop after all. Perhaps they were in the wrong part of the world entirely.

No. Trust the evidence, and your instincts.

She thought back on the conversation in the Durham restaurant, the gist of which tracked with what she had just learned. Vietnam was not a nation of overwhelming historical achievements, like China or India. The Vietnamese had made contributions, sure, especially in the arts. An ancient form of musical storytelling had originated in Vietnam, as well as a beautiful tradition of water puppetry. Calligraphy styles, painting techniques, theater, martial arts: the Vietnamese had perfected quiet expressions of humanity, and developed an aesthetic evident even in the small part of Hanoi that Andie had seen.

It struck her that Vietnam's principal achievements were internal, rather than external. The mindfulness needed to create great art. The quiet, fierce determination that helped the country survive centuries of Chinese occupation, French colonialism, and a horrific modern war.

Was there something to this line of thought, in connection with the Star Phone clue?

Maybe, maybe not.

Cal came upstairs with two cups of coffee to go. "It's time to cruise on out of here. The staff is starting to look at me funny."

Andie rubbed her eyes from screen fatigue. "I suppose we need to find a place to stay."

"No luck with the research?"

She rose and slowly shook her head.

According to the map, Hanoi's Old Town was a short walk west of their location, and they would have their pick of hotels. As they delved into the heart of the city, the crowds grew denser, leaving Andie feeling unmoored, lost in yet another foreign place, wanting nothing more than to help her mother and Dr. Corwin but forced to solve a puzzle that had her guessing at every turn, lurching from country to country, clue to clue. She knew there was a greater purpose to it all, and the Star Phone was teaching as much as testing, but she hadn't signed up to play the game, and the hoops they had to jump through infuriated her.

Their route led to a promenade that ran alongside a pea-green lake. A three-tiered stone pagoda seemed to be floating on the lotus petals strewn in the middle of the water, and on the far side, an arched footbridge connected the shore to a red-lacquered temple with sinuous curves. Along the promenade, groups of adults performed tai chi as children licked ice cream cones and ran to the water's edge to watch the ducks. A succession of gnarled trees covered with red blossoms dipped their feathery branches into the lake. Andie stopped to inhale the loamy scent of the vegetation, letting some of her stress melt away. The scenery was quite enchanting. Cal joined her, quiet for once, staring at the water with a distant expression.

"You look like something's on your mind," she said.

"My mother loved the serenity of Asian art. This place is a wood-block come to life, yet there's all this urban chaos around it, which somehow makes it even more poignant."

"She passed?"

"My mother? Yeah. Lung cancer. Smoked like a chimney."

"What was she like?"

He folded his arms, as if withdrawing into himself. "She was patient, kind, and artistic. A painter and an actress. You know. One of the good ones." He turned and started walking toward a cross-walk that led to the Old Town. Andie watched him go, contempla-tive, sensing he had loved his mother very much.

They quickly realized that a crosswalk in Hanoi was the equiva-lent of the human appendix: an utterly useless organ. Eventually they got up the nerve to dart across the broad avenue, narrowly avoiding a microbus and a family of four on a scooter. They bypassed the fancy hotels overlooking the lake and walked deeper into the Old Town, soaked with sweat from the walk, swatting at mosquitoes that had come out at dusk to feast. This section of Hanoi was a romantic ruin of a city, its winding, narrow streets bursting with life, wrapped in history and the sheltering limbs of banyans. There were countless restaurants and street stalls, homeless families squatting in unfin-ished buildings next to five-star hotels, makeshift cafés with plastic chairs built around the trunks of jacarandas.

By the time they chose a hotel, the crush of activity had become overwhelming. Andie breathed a sigh of relief at the manufactured calm of the lobby. A plate glass window showcased the street out-side the entrance, exposing vendors selling raw fish out of buckets, a barefoot couple huddled around a cooking pot on a rooftop, and a dozen other urban vignettes. The chaotic scene just steps away made Andie feel as if she had entered a hermetically sealed chamber for the privileged.

And she supposed she had.

Though cheap by Western standards, the Maison d'Orient was clean, bright, and classy, a medley of dark wood and brass finishings. While Cal paid for the room, Andie wandered over to browse the sightseeing brochures displayed on a stand. The tours to Sapa and Ha Long Bay made her wish she was in the country on vacation, and she browsed the list of attractions of Hanoi, trying to familiarize herself with the city.

Quan Thanh Temple. The opera house. Ho Chi Minh Mausoleum. Saint Joseph's Cathedral. The night market. The Temple of Literature.

Her eyes locked on to that last name, and she scanned the description.

> *The Temple of Literature was Vietnam's first national university . . . built during the Ly Thanh Tong dynasty to honor Confucius . . . a historical monument dedicated to sages and scholars. . . retains the original architectural style . . . divided into five courtyards of great significance.*

A frisson of excitement swept through her. Was it possible the Star Phone image was symbolic not of actual doorways, but of a passage through the entrances to five courtyards?

Most compelling of all, she thought as she hurried to the elevator, was the name of the historical site itself.

Because what is a temple to literature if not a library?

As soon as she entered their room, Andie gushed to Cal about her find. Though she had seen nothing about a "cracked" door, everything else felt right. Cal was just as thrilled, but a quick Google search revealed the site did not open until 8 a.m. the next day. Unlike the mausoleum in Alexandria, the Temple of Literature was right in the middle of Hanoi, too risky to break into.

The Ascendants would have another twelve hours to figure it out themselves and catch up. Andie still had to retrieve the Star Phone from them, but if she dwelled on that fact, she might not have the guts to continue.

Their hotel room was decorated with framed photos of old Hanoi, and she realized there was only a queen-size bed, with a bamboo screen separating the marble-accented bathroom from the living space.

"I asked for two beds," Cal said sheepishly. "I'll take the floor. I've slept on worse."

Too weary and hungry to care about the lack of privacy, Andie took a long shower and let the water massage her. Night had fallen by the time she finished. As she dressed and approached their eighth-floor window overlooking the street, she saw a mass of people and stalls congregated a block away, stretching as far down the street as she could see.

"Look at all those people."

"The night market," Cal said, joining her at the window. "If it's anything like the one in Bangkok, you'll be able to buy anything you can imagine. I think we should go. We're both starving, we can pick up a few clothes, and there'll be plenty of tourists around. We can blend."

"Anything you can imagine?" Andie said, still staring out the window.

"More or less, yeah. I don't like that look. What are you thinking?"

She walked over to put on her shoes. "I have an idea."

The night market heaved with people. Just as Cal had said, anything that could fit on a city street was for sale, including a smorgasbord of street food, everything from freshly made pho to coconut curry to fried tarantulas on a stick. Music blared from speakers in the stalls and from cell phones held by teenagers. The aromas ranged from nose-wrinkling to sensual, mouthwatering to repulsive. Andie could pick out basil and fish sauce, oiled leather and offal, lychee and grated ginger.

Plenty of sketchy characters were around—people of all types filled the streets—but the market was so crowded she and Cal did not feel threatened, as long as they stuck to the main drag. They bought another backpack to join the one Rajani had given them, filled both with clothes and supplies, and sat on plastic stools in an alley while they ate a pork-and-noodle dish called *bun cha*.

"Ready to go?" Cal asked.

She cringed as a bat swooped right by her face. "I want to stop by a cell phone vendor."

"Burner phones for us both? Good idea."

"I need three phones. And the most realistic sticker booth we can find."

"Three? And a sticker—oh, I get it." His expression turned somber, and he slowly exhaled. "You want to make a replica of the Star Phone."

She gave a grim nod of assent.

"That's clever," he said. "And dangerous as hell, if we have to use it."

They found what they needed at the market. Soon after returning to the hotel, Zawadi texted to say she was coming to Hanoi but wouldn't arrive until the following night at the earliest.

"Are you going to tell her about the Temple of Literature?" Cal asked when he saw Andie staring down at the phone.

"Not until she arrives," Andie said slowly. "On the outside chance someone's watching.

"You're planning on going to the temple without her, aren't you?"

"I don't think we can wait."

"What if the Ascendants make an appearance?"

"Then we need to be there," she said. "If our guess is right, we might not get another chance at this."

"And what's your plan if that happens, besides a phone swap?"

Andie bit her lip and didn't respond.

After preparing for bed in silence, she insisted Cal sleep beside her instead of on the floor. They faced away from each other after the lights went out. Andie expected a clever quip about their proximity, something flirty to break the tension, but he fell asleep in seconds.

As exhausted as she was, Andie couldn't seem to nod off. Instead she stared across the room and listened to the street sounds, her fear of the Ascendants settling in her chest like a bad case of heartburn that wouldn't go away. She wondered where her mother was at that moment, and whether she was thinking about her daughter.

Cal rolled over. One of his arms fell on Andie's side of the bed, his fingers brushing the top of her chest. She listened carefully for a moment, distrustful, but it appeared he was still asleep. *Putting his arm around a girl in bed is probably a subconscious movement.*

She had to admit the human touch felt good. Telling herself that Cal needed his sleep, she left his arm in place as she closed her eyes and drifted off, trying not to think what the morning might bring.

Buenos Aires, Argentina
1977

Violet jacarandas and pink lapacho trees were in bloom, providing a riotous backdrop of color as Dr. Corwin navigated the cobblestone streets of San Telmo, the oldest neighborhood in Buenos
Aires. Located near the river, wedged between downtown and the
crayon-box houses of La Boca, San Telmo had long been his favorite
part of the city. Originally built to house dockworkers and brickma-
sons, it had experienced wild swings in fortune before settling into a
bohemian district whose colonial mansions, erected in the latter half
of the nineteenth century and abandoned after a cholera epidemic,
now accommodated a scruffy, eclectic array of tango parlors, coffee-
houses, artist studios, bars, antique shops, and restaurants.

With its wide boulevards, grandiose buildings, and well-planned
green spaces, Buenos Aires often drew comparisons to Paris and
Madrid. But the narrow lanes and markets of San Telmo were the city's
heart and soul, a place that came alive when the sun went down, and
where students, intellectuals, and disheveled artists nursed their hang-
overs the morning after, clustered around a gourd, sipping maté through
bombillas in one of the neighborhood's parks and countless cafés.

Dr. Corwin had been to Buenos Aires a few times before. It
looked the same except for the nervous faces of the populace. The

year before, a military junta had staged a coup to depose Isabel Perón from power, and anyone who spoke out against the brutal new regime had a habit of disappearing.

A bell tinkled as he entered the Libreria Nueve Musas, the charming little bookstore whose owner claimed to have seen Ettore Majorana pass through on a number of occasions. Argentina, Dr. Corwin thought, was an excellent place to disappear, modernized but far removed from other urban centers, settled largely by Italians, and thus full of people who looked similar to Ettore. Even the Spanish accent in Argentina possessed a singsong Italian cadence.

Before Dr. Corwin left New York, not wanting to chase a false lead, he had talked to the owner, Diego Quiroga, on the phone. Diego had described a man much older than the one in the photo, but with the same oblong face, dark features, bewildered eyes, and shy, withdrawn demeanor that bordered on the hermetic. A man who had shuffled around the bookstore with his head down, avoided eye contact, and approached the counter when it was time to pay like a doomed sailor walking the plank.

His actions were of a man who does not want to be remembered, the owner had said, *so of course I recalled everything about him.*

After claiming to have memorized the preferences of every regular customer during his two-decade tenure, Diego further recalled that Ettore had paid cash for the latest physics and mathematics journals, and often took home a book of poetry. He gravitated toward the English Romantics and the postmoderns, especially T. S. Eliot. On rare occasion, he would purchase a work of philosophy or a metaphysical offering, though more often than not he would leave these at the counter unpurchased. He did not seem like a man of means.

One cannot buy all the books one desires in life, the bookseller had said, *and not just because of time or money. Just as a person's health depends on the food one puts into the body, the knowledge one consumes defines the person.*

Wise words, Dr. Corwin had murmured in response.

Unfortunately, the last time Diego had seen the man was two

years ago. Dr. Corwin did not know what this meant.

Had Ettore died? Moved on? Switched bookstores?

Still, it was exciting news. If Diego was not mistaken, then the long-lost physicist had visited Libreria Nueve Musas over a lengthy period. As Dr. Corwin had come to suspect, the message carved into the cannon had been a ruse. Ettore must have known his journey to Cartagena was risky, and had taken precautions in case anyone came looking for him, pointing them across the Atlantic. But he had stayed in South America after all.

The dumpling of a man behind the bookstore counter had neatly trimmed fingernails, a crown of cropped white hair around his bald spot, and a three-piece suit with no trace of a wrinkle. Diego's store reflected his fastidious appearance. The front counter was as tidy as a colonel's desk. Though stacks of books were everywhere, piled between the shelves and on the carpet and even on the stairs leading to the second floor, they were compiled in orderly stacks, and every single one had a label and a helpful note from the proprietor.

Unfortunately, the face-to-face interview provided no new information. The bookseller had no idea where Ettore might have lived or where he might have gone. When told his mysterious patron might be a famous physicist, Diego grew intrigued, and added to his narrative by telling Dr. Corwin that the customer he remembered, while respectful, was also awkward—as if he wanted to have a friendly conversation but didn't really know how.

That sounds like the Ettore I've been reading about.

After thanking Diego profusely for his time, Dr. Corwin purchased a local map and decided to canvass the neighborhood. Ettore would now be an elderly man, and, as far as Dr. Corwin knew, had never owned a car. He had probably lived nearby and walked to the bookstore.

Ana had urged him not to go to Buenos Aires. Both the Society and the Ascendants knew the CIA had played a role in the recent coup. Toppling governments in the Americas with a socialist bent was part of an aggressive Cold War strategy called Operation

Condor, and for years, the United States had supplied weapons and military training to brutal dictatorships all over Central and South America, bolstering regimes who toed the capitalist line.

As a US green card holder, Dr. Corwin should have been safe in Buenos Aires—except Hans was now a high-ranking CIA official stationed in the region, with direct access to the military junta in power.

He'll kill you if he finds you there, Ana had said.

Then I'll have to take precautions, Dr. Corwin had replied.

One of those safeguards, procured in response to the rising danger quotient of his assignments, was a new walking cane with a rapier hidden inside, a carbon blade forged by an expert swordsmith in Kyoto. After lowering his blue trilby, Dr. Corwin gripped his bladed cane and ducked into a café down the street from the bookshop. He ordered an espresso and a croissant slathered with dulce de leche and laid the map of the neighborhood on the square wooden table. The café had a checkerboard tile floor, a brass bar, and mahogany walls. It smelled of warm caramel and freshly roasted coffee, and no one paid him any attention.

San Telmo was not a huge neighborhood, about nine square blocks. He spent the next two days walking it, from the waterfront to the antique market in the center to the iconic, two-hundred-foot Obelisk of Buenos Aires that stood in the massive Plaza de la República. He showed old photos of Ettore to every business in San Telmo that the physicist might have had cause to visit: cafés, bars, laundromats, furniture shops, candle sellers, tobacconists, too many restaurants to count. He even talked to the priests at the Catholic churches.

The only success was a flower seller who thought she remembered the shy man in the photo. Located on a street that translated to "the Illuminated Block"—which Dr. Corwin found fitting—the *florería* was owned by a cheery blond woman with elegant cheekbones and a birthmark below her left eye.

Some of the shop owners had glanced at Dr. Corwin's black skin and treated him with contempt, to which he responded with ingratiating politeness. The florist didn't seem bothered by his race, and even complimented his excellent Spanish. When asked about Ettore, she wagged a finger and said, "I can't be certain from the photo, but this man you're looking for—is he by chance Italian? Sicilian, to be precise?"

Dr. Corwin felt a tingle of excitement. "He is indeed. How did you know?"

"You said the photo was taken forty years ago. A much older man with a similar face came in here often, for many years. He preferred oleander, caper, and lantana, particularly white prickly pear. What a wonderful aroma they have! Where are you from, sir?"

"Jamaica, by way of New York City."

"Well, you might know most of us Porteños come from Italy. I can often tell which region my customers immigrated from by their flower preferences. Oleander and caper, and especially prickly pear: those are Sicilian favorites."

"What an astute observation. How well did you know him? What did you talk about? Do you know what name he went by?" Dr. Corwin asked. "I apologize for all the questions—it's just that I've been looking for him for a very long time."

The proprietress was plucking the leaves off a bouquet of roses, unconcerned by the mystery. "Why, I didn't know him at all. Not even his name. But I did see him entering the apartment building across the street quite often. I do believe he might have lived there."

In his rush to investigate the apartment, Dr. Corwin barely remembered to tip his hat and thank the flower seller for her time.

The five-story building made of light-gray stone and divided into apartments with wrought-iron balconies, while very handsome, was a common sight in San Telmo. A little digging produced the name and phone number of the superintendent, a woman named Valentina Peralta. Dr. Corwin met with her on the afternoon of his fourth day in Buenos Aires, but suffered another setback. Though the age difference made it hard to be certain, she had no memory of the man in the photo. It was apparent the woman had neither the observant eye of Diego Quiroga nor the kind attentiveness of the flower seller.

The outside of the building was quite grand, but it was a hovel on the inside, a step above a slum. He persuaded Valentina to examine the rental records over the last decade, but she found no one named Ettore Majorana or Nataja Tromereo. Valentina was a vain woman, and after a little sweet-talking, she allowed Dr. Corwin to scan the list himself. None of the names jumped out at him. She admitted many of the renters chose to pay cash every month, since no documentation was required for a short-term rental. In fact, after letting an apartment, Valentina professed to desire as little contact as possible with the renters. Most slipped a check or an envelope full of cash into the lockbox outside her office.

The anonymity of the building made it a perfect hiding spot. Dr. Corwin felt in his bones that Ettore had once lived there, and vacated about two years ago. But why? Had something happened to spook him? Where had he gone?

Fearing the worst, he asked Valentina if anyone had died in one of the apartments around that time, but she was adamant that had not occurred.

His earlier excitement dimmed. After another few days spent in vain trying to uncover a new lead, he was forced to admit failure. He had to return to New York, and would have to find another way to continue the search. His last evening before flying out, he strolled down the cobblestone street outside his hotel to drown his sorrows with a carafe of red wine at his favorite *parrilla*. The all-male waitstaff hustled around the room in bow ties and white aprons as the cooks tended to the sweetbreads, blood sausage, and slabs of beef sizzling on a wood-fired grill dividing the dining area from the kitchen.

With a full glass in front of him, and a sizzling cut of *bife de chorizo* with chimichurri on the way, his mood turned contemplative. His thoughts roamed from his childhood to his time at Oxford to the gaping enigmas of the cosmos that defined his life's work, and which had drawn him to the Leap Year Society.

What did you smuggle out of Italy all those years ago, Ettore?
What have you been doing in the interim?
What doors have you unlocked?

After his meal, he sipped an amber vin santo and watched a tango show in the street, outside the large bay window to his left. The sultry lips and elegant strut of the female dancer made him long for the caress of Ana's fingers. No woman had ever excited and challenged him like she did, and he knew he had fallen in love.

After the show ended, he found himself imagining what he and Ana would do in Buenos Aires together. Certainly they would dine at this very café and watch tango. Perhaps they would stroll through Recoleta Cemetery, explore the city's museums, visit the tower modeled after Dante's *Divine Comedy*, or take the metro to a show at the Teatro Colón.

"My dearest James, what a wonderful coincidence."

Startled, he turned to find Hans taking the seat across from him at the table. The German American was dressed in a white cotton suit and teal dress shirt, palming a bottle of Quilmes lager on the checkered tablecloth. He must have entered through the side door. Dr. Corwin berated himself for losing concentration.

"We meet again," he said evenly, working hard to stay calm as he studied his old enemy. Though Hans still looked vigorous and muscular, there were sun spots on his forehead, a cunning gleam in his eyes, a faint scar on the left side of his neck, and a rigidity to his jaw that lent him a military bearing. His blond hair was parted to the side, and he made little effort to conceal the handgun holstered beneath his sport coat.

As the two men locked gazes, Dr. Corwin leaned back in his chair and noticed a table beside the main entrance with four hard-eyed men who had not been in the restaurant five minutes ago. They were drinking beer and staring right at him.

"You shouldn't have come here," Hans said casually, a man in supreme command of the situation. "The city isn't safe."

"Thanks to you and your friends at the CIA."

"It's a complicated world. There's a larger game being played."

"Are you speaking of geopolitics, or the real reason you're here?"

"Both, of course."

"I see. How have you been, Hans? I don't believe I've seen you since you tried to kill me in Cartagena. Your face seems to have healed."

Working his jaw back and forth, his expression darkening, Hans extracted a toothpick from a dispenser on the table and toyed with it. "Did you stop to think that perhaps I let you go so you could lead me to Ettore?"

"No. I think you got outplayed."

"Then why do I hold all the cards?"

"Do you?"

Hans smiled without showing any teeth. "You know full well who I am and what I do. I lunched with General Videla today. So let us be clear about how this is going to work. I know you've been in Buenos Aires for several days: What have you been up to? It will be much less painful if you tell me now."

Dr. Corwin took a sip of wine and studied Hans carefully as he asked the next question. "How did you find me? I told no one where I was going."

"Surely you did not think you would stroll into my territory undetected?"

"I believe I did just that. Or you would already know where I have been."

"At times the cat pretends to let the mouse roam free."

"Someone told you. Who was it?"

Hans leaned back in his chair. "Never doubt that I have eyes and ears everywhere."

Dr. Corwin could tell Hans was bluffing and had only recently become aware of his presence in the city. Exhaling a slow, silent breath, he realized at once what he had to do. His and Ana's charade had become too dangerous. Especially for her. Hans would kill her in an instant if he suspected she had withheld information from him, or that her loyalty was divided. Nor did she have a way out that he could see. Fearing she would divulge the Ascendants' secrets to her lover, they would never allow her to leave.

Which left Dr. Corwin only one course of action, and he felt a little piece of his soul tear away with his decision. Infusing fury into his expression, he leaned forward and said, with as much venom as he could muster, "That *bitch*. Only she knew where I was headed . . . Good Christ, she's one of you!"

Hans couldn't hide a smile of satisfaction. "Whatever are you talking about?"

"I can't believe I'm so gullible. To think for all this time I thought she loved me... "

"Woman trouble?"

"I'll kill her myself," Dr. Corwin said softly.

"I doubt you'll be doing anything of the sort," Hans said, "once our interrogation is finished." He polished off his beer and set it on the table. "It's time to go, Professor. Don't worry. My men will take care of your bill."

It was almost closing time. Dr. Corwin looked around the restaurant and saw that all the patrons had left except for the four men sitting at the table by the front door. The staff was breaking down the grill.

Hans stood. "Don't make this hard on yourself."

"You'd haul me away in front of the staff?"

"I'm acting in my other capacity tonight, and the men behind you are loyal to the general. I assure you they have no fear of public scrutiny. Nor will anyone in this restaurant dare breathe a word of what they see. You'll disappear without a trace, as so many others have done, another dissident trying to undermine the regime."

As Dr. Corwin looked from Hans to the men at the table, he compressed his lips as if fully realizing the direness of the situation. He tipped his trilby at Hans in mock acquiescence, rose with his head held high, and grabbed the walking stick he had propped against the wall behind his chair during the meal.

"It would appear you've won the round," Dr. Corwin said, causing Hans to open a palm and prompt him toward the side door. "But as I'm fond of saying, appearances can be deceiving."

In one smooth motion, Dr. Corwin slid his cane apart, exposing the rapier hidden inside. He jabbed forward, thrusting into his enemy's midsection. Hans jerked back and away, avoiding a fatal stab to the heart, but the blade slid deep into his side, biting into the soft flesh beneath his ribs.

From behind came cursing in Spanish and chairs scraping the floor. Dr. Corwin jerked the blade out as Hans screamed in pain. The men at the table jumped to their feet and reached for their pistols, followed by the deafening crack of gunfire echoing through the restaurant.

Except the first shots had not come from one of Hans's men, but from two of the cooks, who had opened fire on the four men at the table from behind the parrilla's wood-fired grill.

Pandemonium erupted. Tables were overturned to acts as shields as bullets flew. One of Hans's men was sprawled dead on the floor, someone shrieked in agony, and the fire in the grill roared higher, either sparked by the ammunition or stoked deliberately by one of the men posing as cooks. A sprinkler doused the room, and shouts of alarm came from the kitchen.

Hans was using his heels to squirm away from Dr. Corwin on the floor, clutching his bloody side, his enraged curses punctuated by moans.

Dr. Corwin had also flipped over one of the solid wood tables to protect himself. Instead of trying to finish off Hans, which would have exposed the professor to enemy fire, he turned and shattered the window beside him with his blade.

Knowing how vulnerable he was in the city, and the allies Hans had, Dr. Corwin had dined at the same restaurant every night during his stay for a specific reason—and had chosen his seat by the window very carefully.

"Damn you, James!" Hans shouted.

"You may own this town," Dr. Corwin said, "but we own this restaurant."

A black sedan screeched to a halt by the curb outside the shattered window. As the professor stepped over the litter of broken glass, hurrying toward the Society car, pain exploded in his left knee and he was thrown violently to the ground. He tried to hobble to his feet and failed, his knee crumpling like a squashed paper bag beneath him. He looked up to find Hans pointing a gun at him from the floor with a grimace of pleasure.

Before Hans could shoot again, a strapping Brazilian man, an associate of Dr. Corwin's, flew out of the sedan and laid down a round of cover fire. Hans was forced to roll behind the table to avoid being hit. Still firing with one hand, the Brazilian grabbed Dr. Corwin by the collar and dragged him across the sidewalk and into the waiting vehicle.

Feeling as if he might pass out from the pain, Dr. Corwin collapsed across the seat and gasped a final series of commands. "Go! Alert the boat captain! We must leave the city at once!"

19

The day after they arrived in Hanoi, Andie joined Cal for breakfast at the hotel buffet.

"I did some research on the Temple of Literature this morning," she said, sliding into the booth across from him.

Cal's plate was stacked with eggs, bacon, and pancakes. "This morning? It's seven a.m. When do you sleep?"

"Do you want the good news or the bad news first?"

"The good. And just skip the bad."

She slurped a mouthful of pho. "There's not a ton of information on the Temple of Literature online, but listen to this: Each of the five courtyards is unique, with its own significance and history. The first courtyard is called Entrance to the Way, and the gate leading to the second courtyard is symbolic of how the path to enlightenment is both continuous and outside the contours of space and time."

"Okay," Cal said, "we're *definitely* looking in the right place."

"Scholars are supposed to proceed slowly on the stone path through the temple, all the way to the final courtyard, absorbing each lesson as they approach the pinnacle of knowledge."

"Did Dr. Corwin design this thing himself?"

"It's got LYS written all over it," she agreed. "The bad news is, the fifth gate was destroyed by the French in 1946."

"I told you not to tell me that." He set his coffee down. "Doesn't that wreck our theory?"

"It was rebuilt twenty years ago, and I'm not sure what that means. Is it too new to be historically relevant? Are we on the wrong track? Is it a symbol of rebirth? Maybe the cracked door symbolizes the transition from the fourth to the fifth courtyard."

He met her gaze. "It sounds like we won't have any answers until we see it for ourselves."

She took a sip of coffee. "I'm glad you agree."

The heat and humidity had turned Hanoi into a steam basket by the time Andie and Cal stepped into a taxi and rode a mile west to the Temple of Literature.

Taking a cue from Kolkata, Andie was wearing a traditional Vietnamese dress called an ao dai, which she had purchased at the night market. The dress was a tight-fitting green silk tunic that covered her from the snug collar all the way to the top of her tennis shoes. Though surprisingly tolerable in the heat, her conical rice hat made of tightly woven palm leaves was not so breezy. She felt awkward next to the legions of tiny Vietnamese women wearing similar outfits—but at least she felt hidden. She had also purchased one of the surgical masks the locals wore while riding motorbikes and mopeds and sometimes just walking the streets, to protect their lungs from pollution.

Cal had opted for a pair of cargo shorts, a black T-shirt, a wide-brimmed hat, and sunglasses. A cheap daypack, hiking sandals, and a money pouch around his waist completed the outfit of traditional Western tourist.

The rush-hour traffic was a symphony of epic proportions, a frenzied dance of barely controlled chaos that would have made Beethoven stand up and applaud. Andie gawked at an old woman serenely riding a bicycle as motorized vehicles raced past her like water flowing around a stone. As the taxi approached the high brick wall enclosing the Temple of Literature, it swerved right through a group of Vespa-riding girls wearing face masks. Somehow a crash was avoided. Andie felt a little shaky as she and Cal stepped onto the curb.

After glancing around for suspicious faces, they entered the historic site right when it opened, through a set of double doors at the bottom of an entrance gate built to resemble a white stone pagoda. Though streaked with grime, the gate was an impressive sight, with its magnificently carved eaves, huge bell, and curving red rooftops.

Inside, a sanctuary of ancient trees, lotus ponds, and well-trimmed lawns awaited. Though other tourists, both local and foreign, were pouring in to enjoy the site, it was an oasis of beauty and calm amid the relentless bustle of Hanoi. The bronze information placards were written in Vietnamese, so Andie bought an information pamphlet off a tout for twenty thousand dong, the equivalent of one US dollar. The night before, sensing they might need some local currency, she had withdrawn more cash with Zawadi's card.

She stopped to absorb the first courtyard by the side of a massive banyan. "I'm sure whoever the Star Phone puzzle was meant for was supposed to meditate on ancient Confucian wisdom."

"We, on the other hand, need enlightenment right away."

"Shall we take a pass through the whole temple first?"

Cal lifted a palm and deepened his voice. "Proceed through the gates of knowledge."

The second courtyard was a green space of equal splendor to the first. According to the pamphlet, the topiary represented the twelve animals of the Chinese zodiac. On the far side of the courtyard loomed a red lacquer wooden tower built on stone columns. The carvings on the tower were even more elaborate than on the main gate.

"Impressive," Cal said.

"That's the Pavilion of the Constellation of Literature," Andie said. "The symbol of Hanoi. Those are yin-yang tiles on the roof, and the circular window represents the sun."

"More symbol stuff," Cal said. "I hope you're taking notes."

A cloud of incense swirled above the brick floor of the pavilion. As they passed through, Andie could picture robed medieval monks entering the structure in ancient times, tending to the braziers as they debated philosophy.

The center of the third courtyard was dominated by a square pond surrounded by a low stone wall. A street magician was performing sleight-of-hand tricks near the pond, chattering to passerby in both English and Vietnamese.

"Thiên Quang Tỉnh," Andie said as they followed the flower-strewn pathway around the basin of water. "The Well of Heavenly Clarity."

"We should drink long and deeply."

The fourth courtyard, made of smooth paving stones and littered with rotting mangoes, was wider than the others. There was very little to see, other than a bronze urn in the center with carved dragons on the side and some kind of stone demon on top. The lack of attractions, and thus tourists, lent the silent courtyard an eerie aura. A gathering place that lacked gatherers.

"Getting any ideas?" Cal said, looking nervously around.

"Not really. Let's finish the walk-through."

The barrier separating the fourth and fifth courtyards was an imposing open-air shrine with a tiled roof curving upward at the ends like a smile. Sprinkled among the red-lacquered pillars supporting the structure were a handful of gold-leaf altars resembling oversize treasure chests, as well as giant statues of Confucius and his disciples. Draped on the altars were the sort of quotidian items common to ancestor worship: flowers, food, money, bottles of water.

Smoke curled out of hundreds of incense sticks, placed upright like rows of disintegrating snakes, in ash-filled urns throughout the shrine. The greasy incense saturating the air, combined with the growing crowd and the dead heat of Hanoi, made Andie light-headed. Worried it would trigger a vision, she pushed on through to the fifth and final courtyard, an open square that showcased a huge iron bell, a student art exhibit, and a museum entrance on the far side.

They paced the courtyard and explored the two-story museum, which included exhibits on Confucian education, as well as the founders of the Temple of Literature. Nothing piqued their interest. Andie returned to stand beside the art exhibit, absorbing her surroundings, trying to spot the invisible thread in the labyrinth.

"I feel like we're close," she said, "but where's the cracked door? Is it a play on words? Is there a literal door nearby we're supposed to open?"

"This would be a helluva lot easier with the Star Phone," Cal said.

"To test our theories, yes. But I have a feeling there's a simple solution to the riddle. Maybe it's something to do with Confucianism or Taoism."

With Cal peering over her shoulder, Andie found a bench and Googled "cracked door" and "Confucius" and "Tao." Finding no help in the analects of Confucius, the Tao Te Ching, or other pillars of Eastern religion, she expanded the search to Vietnamese and Chinese history, the Temple of Literature, and every key word she could think of.

Not a single cracked door in sight.

"I just don't know," she said.

"Should we do another walk-through?" Cal suggested. "Maybe seeing it in reverse will spark something. Plus, I saw a guy selling soft drinks out front."

Andie sighed and pushed to her feet. "Sure."

As they retraced their steps and entered the third courtyard, Andie absorbed the view of the main gate and the Pavilion of the Constellation of Literature rising above the stone wall. The curlicue nature of the architecture struck her as reflective of the human mind itself: synapses locked in stone, elegant and twisted, bizarre and beautiful. She felt immersed in an alien culture far older than her own, proud and majestic and unchanged for millennia, its symbolism as rich as any she had known.

They kept walking, approaching the pavilion, when it hit her.

It was so simple and perfect.

Once again, Cal had hit on the solution. *Seeing it in reverse.*

If she was correct, then unwittingly, they were on the right track.

They were supposed to walk the length of the temple, contemplate everything they had learned, and then, like every good student of Eastern religion, come full circle back to the starting point.

A circle. An ouroboros.

The cracked door, she realized, was the cracked door of knowledge, symbolic of the LYS and the journey itself...entering the Temple of Literature and stepping into the first courtyard, the Entrance to the Way...following the door the Star Phone had opened...

Forming a mental image, she remembered that, just above the gate at the beginning of the temple, the top half of the arched entrance was metallic scrollwork painted gold. *I bet that's where the embedded code is—right on the first door itself.*

"That clever devil," she said. "Dr. Corwin gave us a red herring by including all five courtyards, but it's the first that counts."

Cal stopped walking. "What are you talking about? Where's the cracked door?"

"C'mon," she said, taking his arm. "You deserve your ice-cold soda."

He started to reply, but she had already started pulling him along. As they passed through the pavilion, Cal jerked her back into the incense-shrouded walkway that ran beneath the wooden structure.

"Ouch! What the hell—"

"Quiet!" he said in a fierce whisper, guiding her behind one of the stone pillars. His face had drained of color. "Do you remember that Chinese guy in India who chased us?"

"How could I forget?"

"He's in the second courtyard, pointing the Star Phone at everything in sight."

It was Andie's turn to pale. She had been so focused on her discovery she had lost track of her surroundings. Shielded by the incense and the stone pillar, she resisted the urge to step forward and risk a quick glance. "Was he alone?"

"I saw at least two people shadowing him. We have to leave through the museum." He hurried back into the third courtyard.

"What if they have people watching the exits? Should we climb the wall?"

"Cal. Stop for a moment. I'm not leaving without trying for the Star Phone."

"God, Andie, don't be stupid! I know we said we'd try, but now that we're here by ourselves, what are we going to do? That guy's a killer. I can see it written all over him. And so are those people with him."

"They won't kill us here. Not in plain view."

"You're kidding, right? I wouldn't bank on that, and they certainly won't hesitate to drag us out of here and stuff us in a car. You've seen this city. It's chaos personified. What are you gonna do, anyway? Give him a swift kick to the groin and hope he drops the Star Phone? He doesn't look like the kind of guy who drops things even if you shoot him in the chest."

Andie glanced behind her, at the street magician. "I have an idea."

"An *idea*? What kind of idea?"

"I won't blame you if you run. But if you're staying, keep a lookout for me."

"A lookout—*Andie*. Where are you going? You're going to get us both killed! Let's wait for Zawadi."

"They'll be gone by then, and you know it."

Ignoring the terror that threatened to immobilize her, she hurried over to the street magician standing by the basin of water dominating the third courtyard. They had one shot at this, and she had to make it work.

The magician watched her approach. He was a squat Vietnamese man wearing a rumpled suit with a white dress shirt. A purple handkerchief poked out of the pocket of the shirt. He had nimble, age-spotted fingers and a kind face she thought she could exploit, though the very thought of it made her feel guilty. Cal was right: the Chinese man chasing them was a killer, and no doubt an Ascendant. If this backfired, and the old man got hurt . . . was she prepared to accept that?

She took a deep breath. *I'll tell him the truth about the risks, and he won't help unless he thinks he can.*

"Would you like to see a trick?" the magician asked, in surprisingly good English. She supposed he dealt with tourists all day. "I can make a dove appear and disappear right in front of your eyes, or a—"

"Listen to me," Andie said. "I'm sorry to bother you, but I need your help. Urgently. This is not a joke." As the old man's expression sobered, Andie stared right at him. "There's a very bad man in the other courtyard. A human trafficker. Do you know what that is?"

"Yes. Of course."

"He took someone I care deeply about, and I have to help her."

"I'm very sorry," the old man said quietly. "But I don't understand how I can help."

"I need to search his phone. That's all." She took out the metallic silver phone she had purchased at the night market. With the black star hand-painted on the back, and the identifying brand information covered with metallic paint, it was a very good replica of the Star Phone, especially at a glance. "It looks just like this—do you think you can switch them without him knowing? And get his phone to me?"

The magician frowned and looked down at his hands. With every passing second, Andie worried the Chinese man would step into the courtyard.

"We have to go," Cal said.

"He's holding the phone in his hand," Andie said to the magician. "Waving it around. Maybe you can distract him in front of the Confucius shrine. We can wait for you inside."

"Who did he take?" he said finally. "Your child?"

"My mother."

She worried he wouldn't help unless there was a child involved. But she couldn't compound the lies.

"The police won't help?" he said.

"They're too busy. I tracked him myself."

"We'll give you a hundred dollars," Cal added, looking as if he might be ill.

The magician rubbed his hands together, as if kneading dough. After a long moment, he drew up straight and faced them. "Too many people come to Vietnam for this. I will try to help you, but not for money. This man—what does he look like?"

Cal described him as the three of them hurried to the fourth courtyard. After thanking the magician so profusely he looked embarrassed, she again stressed the danger of the situation, and told him to create a diversion and escape the very moment he got the phone. He nodded, and Andie and Cal waited inside the incense-filled shrine, in position to keep an eye on the courtyard. Worrying about the safety of the old magician, Andie bit a nail so hard it bled.

When a muscular Chinese man dressed in jeans and a light-blue polo shirt entered the fourth courtyard, the shot of fear and adrenaline that she experienced was like a punch to the gut. It was the same man, no doubt about it. When he shielded his eyes from the sun as he stopped to scan the courtyard, Andie started. *He isn't holding the Star Phone.*

Wondering if he had given it to someone else, she glanced at the magician, who was juggling four multicolored balls by the urn with the carved dragons in the center of the courtyard. Two other people—a smaller man of East Asian descent and an athletic woman who looked Slavic—entered the courtyard to confer with the muscular Chinese man, who appeared to be their leader. Dressed in casual attire, the shirts of all three were untucked, no doubt concealing weapons, and each of them carried the hard, no-nonsense bearing of a soldier.

A group of Vietnamese schoolchildren rushed into the courtyard. Andie saw the street magician start to meander toward them, causing the children to squeal in delight as he juggled the colored balls.

No, she thought in despair. *Not around the children.*

The Chinese man separated from his associates, finally took out the device, and stepped away from the crowd. He aimed the Star Phone right at the open-air shrine, causing Andie and Cal to shrink into the cloud of incense, pressing against a statue of Confucius.

"He can't see us, can he?" Cal whispered.

Andie held a finger to her lips as she peered around the statue. The street magician was standing right beside the Chinese man now, still juggling the balls. Suddenly the old man whipped off his hat, and a live dove flew out of it, startling the other man.

The children clapped their hands in glee. Annoyed, the Chinese man walked away from the magician. Andie lost sight of them both for a moment, which caused her to panic, then saw the old man dashing along the perimeter of the courtyard, chasing wildly after the dove, which always seemed just out of reach. A crowd of children followed him, shrieking in delight.

Andie looked from the magician to the Chinese man, who was again studying the details of the courtyard, and still holding the Star Phone in his hand.

Her heart sank. She had been watching the entire time and had not seen the phones exchange hands. The magician had decided to call it off. She could hardly blame him.

Moments later, near the edge of the shrine, the old man finally caught the bird and released it again, urging the children to chase it. Andie wondered whether it was a real bird. *How is it trained so well?*

After the dove flew off, the magician stepped into the swirling incense of the shrine. As soon as he was out of sight of the courtyard, Andie intercepted him, Cal right behind her.

"It's too dangerous," she said, bitterly disappointed but relieved he was out of harm's way. "I understand."

"Very dangerous," the old man agreed. "That is a very bad man. I can see this very clearly. Here," he said, handing her a phone. "I won't need this anymore."

Andie took the phone and realized the old man was grinning. With a catch in her throat, she noticed the long button underneath, and pressed it. The screen lit up to reveal the image Zawadi had described: a tan world map in the background, with a long-legged black spider creeping across a path of lotus petals sprinkled across the back of a red dragon. There were four closed wooden doors in the corners, and a cracked door in the center, positioned between the front claws of the serpent.

"Thank you, thank you, thank you," she said, planting a kiss on the wily old magician's cheek that made him blush. "But how? I didn't see—"

"Andie!" Cal said sharply. "There's no time!"

"*Thank you*," she said again to the old man, squeezing his hand. She had debated giving him money against his wishes, but didn't want to offend him by marring the dignity of his act. "Now disappear. Please. Don't let them catch you. Can you promise me that?"

With a flourish, he bowed and made his way into the fifth courtyard, vanishing into the crowd.

"They know by now," Cal said, clutching her arm. "We have to go!"

A glance into the fourth courtyard confirmed their fears. The Chinese man was standing near the urn with a furious expression on his face. He started to throw the phone on the ground, then pocketed it and began striding toward the shrine concealing Andie and Cal. At first she thought he was talking to himself, then realized he was wearing an earpiece. His associates headed in the other direction, back toward the third courtyard.

Andie and Cal raced out of the shrine and into the fifth courtyard.

"The museum," Cal said. "It's our only chance."

"No! We can't leave yet. We have to get back to the entrance."

"That's suicide."

"You said yourself they'll be watching the exits. We'll go over the wall."

"And then what? You think they won't be watching the street? What if—"

"Come on!"

Without waiting for an answer, she darted to her left. A few bystanders gawked as she leaped, grasped the top of a brick wall, and pulled herself up. Cal followed. Just before Andie climbed over, she glanced back and saw their pursuer entering the courtyard.

All he has to do is turn his head to the left.

Some of the people in the courtyard were staring in her direction, and she knew the Chinese man would notice. Not daring to breathe, she tried to flatten against the wall, afraid a sudden movement would draw his attention. Then she heard a commotion. She risked turning her head to the side and saw a pair of doves in the courtyard, flapping with abandon near the entrance to the museum, right above the old magician. As the Chinese man roared and sprinted toward him, the magician slipped inside the building.

He's giving us a chance to escape.

Andie felt sick as she scrambled over the remaining portion of the wall, scratching her arms and face on the brambles at the bottom. A line of palms and banana trees provided a barrier from the busy road running alongside the temple.

"Two black SUVs just flew past," Cal said, catching his breath. "They're circling the wagons."

She couldn't stop thinking about the old magician. Gritting her teeth, she told herself to have faith in his abilities.

Vehicles choked the street to their right, toward the entrance to the temple. Not far from their position, a group of young Vietnamese women in traditional dress were strolling down the sidewalk, laughing and chatting, sidestepping the bicycles and scooters. Yet a strange sight caught Andie's eye: a bright-orange motorized rickshaw with an enclosed carriage and the words RICKSHAW OBSCURA painted in white on the side. A pair of dragons surrounded the odd sign, intertwined in a fanciful pattern.

Every other rickshaw she had seen had an open carriage, so tourists could see the city. Maybe this rickshaw was a catering service, or had some other function. The driver was an elderly Vietnamese man with skin like burnished walnut, silky white trousers, and a matching shirt-jacket buttoned to the neck, similar to a Chinese *changshan*.

Two braids of gray hair hung to his waist.

As the rickshaw passed, the driver waved in her and Cal's direction, though it seemed unlikely he could have seen them through the trees.

"We have to make a run for it," Cal said. Tires screeched in the distance, and shouts emanated from the courtyard.

Though not a perfect circle, the intertwined dragons on the side of the rickshaw caused Andie's heart to flutter.

Something isn't right about that rickshaw.

On a hunch, she aimed the Star Phone at it—and gasped when she saw, in place of the Rickshaw Obscura logo, a holographic image of the LYS symbol.

"That's our ride," she said grimly, and told Cal what she had seen.

"If we can trust it," he said.

"I don't think we have a choice."

An idea came to her, and she remembered the surgical mask she had brought. She slipped it on and gave him a little push. "Go. I'll be right behind you. Don't let the driver get out of sight."

"What? Don't be dense—

"Go!" she said, hurrying away before he could finish, and before she lost her nerve.

She stayed close to the wall and behind trees as she ran, until she drew even with the group of Vietnamese women. Most of them were also wearing masks. Andie walked calmly out of a grove of palms and joined the group at the rear. There were over a dozen women, similar in age to Andie. She hunched so she wouldn't tower over them, praying she would blend to an outside observer.

Glancing to her left, she saw Cal press through the crowd of people on the sidewalk and stroll right to the rickshaw, which was driving slowly near the curb as if trolling for passengers. The door popped open as Cal arrived. Once he entered, the door closed and the intertwined dragons on the side of the rickshaw disappeared, as if they had been a hologram all along.

Andie gawked, but no one on the street seemed to notice. With her brain screaming at her to run and join Cal, she forced herself to keep walking with the group of women alongside the wall of the Temple of Literature. As they reached the end of the intersection and turned right, Andie held her breath, knowing the Ascendants would be watching.

The entrance to the temple was in view. She glanced back and saw the rickshaw stuck in traffic. She couldn't let it get out of sight.

She kept walking with the women. There were so many people on the street in front of the temple the sidewalk was barely visible. Her breath caught in her throat when she saw the Chinese man's female associate standing at the entrance, but the woman was watching people leave the temple, not enter from the street.

Because who would suspect I'd do something this foolish?

Forcing her legs to obey, Andie did her best to merge with the group of women, laughing when they laughed, pretending she was following the conversation. A few of them gave her a funny look, but no one made a scene.

And then she was standing right in front of the entrance to the temple. *You can't make it obvious. Someone will notice the phone.*

She glanced back. The light at the intersection had turned, and the rickshaw would soon be approaching. This was her last chance.

She took out the Star Phone and touched the arm of the young woman in front of her. Startled, the woman turned to find Andie aiming the phone at her, giggling like a schoolgirl, pretending to take a picture. The woman looked confused and uneasy but her sense of decorum didn't allow her to make a fuss. The Vietnamese were exceedingly polite, Andie had noticed, and she was banking on that now.

Before the woman turned away, Andie managed to aim the Star Phone at the entrance gate, and felt a thrill sweep through her as her world spun and the arched entrance to the temple became a cobblestone street with hanging globe lanterns, an image Andie etched into her mind the second she saw it.

She had what she needed. Instead of bolting, she walked a bit farther with the group. She couldn't risk escaping quite yet. The woman she had touched on the shoulder kept staring at her, suspicious, but she never called out.

It took every ounce of willpower Andie had to keep moving down the street, knowing how vulnerable she was, now that every Ascendant in the city was looking for them.

After a fifty-foot walk that felt to Andie like a mile, she saw the Rickshaw Obscura slow as it passed alongside her, and the door to the carriage hinged open.

New York City
1977

A month after his return from Buenos Aires, Dr. Corwin shuffled down a Manhattan sidewalk, reprising his disguise from Cartagena: a filthy brown sweater, trousers with holes in the knees, and shoes whose bottoms flapped as he walked. He was hunched over, clutching a bottle of malt liquor in a brown paper bag, wearing a fake beard and matted dreadlocks, and suffering from a limp that was all too real.

Hidden in plain sight in his own city.

He shambled up Fifth Avenue and into Central Park, causing mothers to grip their children tighter when he crossed their path. Stumbling as if drunk, he cut straight through the grass and undergrowth before collapsing on a bench inside a peaceful grove of elms. The circle of massive trunks resembled the columns in a Greek temple.

Though nightfall was an hour away, the canopy of twisted limbs brought a premature darkness to the grove, as well as shielding it from view. Half an hour later, a female jogger wearing a green-and-white tracksuit and matching headband entered the ring of trees, dripping with sweat. Hands on her hips, she stopped to stretch, showing neither fear nor recognition when she glanced Dr. Corwin's way.

He ached at the sight of her long bronze limbs and the lips always on the verge of a coy grin, slightly parted and knowing, the radiance of her full smile reserved for those rare private moments between the two of them. He longed to cup her face in his hands and kiss her, and shuddered at what he had to do.

"Don't react, Ana," he said. He was lying on his side on the bench, feigning sleep. "Keep stretching. You can talk, but keep your voice down."

She froze. After a long moment, she moved closer and propped one leg next to him on the park bench, knee bent, stretching her hamstring. "What do you want?" she said coldly.

"I'm sorry. It was the only way."

"The only way to do what? Break my heart? You won't even return my calls."

"The only way to save your life."

Her stoic expression slipped a fraction. "What are you talking about?"

"I had to pretend I thought you'd betrayed me."

"But why? Hans never asked me if you were going to Buenos Aires."

"He could have. Even claiming you didn't know looks suspicious from his standpoint. Why didn't I tell you? Sooner or later, Hans was going to find out the truth. I couldn't risk it any longer. I had to make him a believer and cut it off abruptly. You have to believe that."

She was silent for a long time. "We could leave it all behind," she said. "Run away together."

"To where, Ana?" he said gently. "Where would we be safe?"

"Somewhere. We're resourceful people. It's not just about that, is it? You don't want to leave. You're choosing the Society over me."

He knew there was some truth to her words. "It's not that simple."

"My God, I thought *they* were the fanatics."

"I'm not a blind servant to the Society. It has flaws that need to be redressed, and I'm in a position to do that. I freely admit to putting my beliefs above both our lives and interests. But I can also say, Anastasia Kostos, that I love you." He had never said those words to a woman, and it felt strange, like releasing a piece of his soul to her. "I love you like I've loved no other."

A tear fell from her eye, making him feel guilty that he had chosen to confess at this time, in this way. Yet he couldn't bear the thought of her going through life without knowing.

She wiped the tear away. "I can't do it anymore, James. The Ascendants are on the wrong path. I know this now. My God, I've been so stupid."

"Don't," he said gently. "We all make mistakes. We all can change."

"Let me help. I've thought it over, and I'm ready to join you."

"That makes me happier than you'll ever know, but if you tried to join the Society, with your inside knowledge . . . the Ascendants would hunt you to the ends of the Earth."

She dipped her head lower, and it took all of his willpower not to jump up and gather her in his arms. "Then what?" she said, in a near whisper.

"If you want to leave them, disappear. It's the only way."

"But we'd never see each other again," she said. Her eyes slowly lifted to meet his. A look of infinite pain swept across her face, and he could tell in that instant that she loved him too. She looked as if she wanted to race out of the grove and never stop running, but instead she switched legs, stretching her other hamstring, and spoke in a strained but self-assured voice. "I'll spy for you. For the Society."

"I can't ask that of you."

"You're not asking. I'm offering. I was going to suggest it before you went to . . . before I thought you'd left me."

He shook his head. "If they caught you—"

"They'll torture and kill me. Don't say silly things. Both our lives will be at grave risk. They have been for years."

It was his turn to whisper, not trusting his voice. "I can't bear the thought of you in such danger."

"You and I both know who will win this war if we don't do something."

Feeling as if he were trapped beneath a great weight, he allowed her to persuade him, and they agreed on a secure way to exchange information from afar.

"Even if we can never meet again," she said softly, "we'll be together in some way."

When she left, Ana didn't speak again or even look at him, but he saw the tears flowing down her cheeks. Another jogger passed through the grove, and Dr. Corwin buried his face in his hands, to hide his identity as well as his own emotions.

He waited another hour, just in case any prying eyes were about, then made a vow to himself as he stumbled, forlorn and despairing, through the foliage in the dark and silent park.

I will find you, Ettore. My search for you has led us to this place, this terrible place, and I will not let it be in vain.

I will find you.

20

Andie noticed right away the interior of the Rickshaw Obscura was abnormal. The oval metallic walls were as smooth and white as an eggshell. There was no door handle, and she could not see the driver. Their own compartment was entirely enclosed, lit by track lighting around the perimeter.

In the center of the compartment, a stainless-steel pedestal, similar to a music stand, was bolted into the floor between two aluminum chairs. On top of the pedestal was an indentation the size of a cell phone.

"Damn you!" Cal said, pulling her into a bear hug in the cramped quarters. "What happened out there? I couldn't see a thing, and the driver isn't responding. I shouted at him to wait and tried to get out, but the door wouldn't open again. I was about to lose my mind."

She collapsed into one of the seats, overwhelmed by stress and lingering adrenaline. "I got it. I saw the next image."

He whooped and gripped her by the arm. "Tell me about it later. Right now we have to figure out where we're going, how to get out of here, and what to do when we get there." He rapped hard on the front of the carriage. "Hey! Who are you? Where's this thing headed?"

In response, the rickshaw lurched forward, causing Cal to stumble as it accelerated. Andie clutched the sides of her chair, worried they were being chased. Cal took a seat in the chair beside her to steady himself. As soon as he sat down, the rickshaw slowed again, and she noticed the indentation in the pedestal had started to glow.

She ran her eyes over the carriage, searching for wires or a hidden camera. "How did they know when to pick us up?"

"I told you there's a tracker on Zawadi's phone."

"Maybe. Or maybe this driver is part of the Star Phone puzzle, keeping an eye on the Temple of Literature. Maybe something we did triggered his presence. And I have a feeling"—she took out the Star Phone and set it inside the glowing depression on the silver stand—"we're about to find out why."

"Are you sure you want to do that?" Cal said, just as a digitized voice intoned, "Welcome to the Rickshaw Obscura."

All of a sudden, everything around them—walls and floor and ceiling—turned a dark-gray color, rendering the inside of the carriage a gloomy, shadowy 3-D panorama of an all-too-familiar place.

Andie gasped, thinking she had entered another vision. But she quickly realized the experience didn't possess the same all-consuming sensation of being in another place, of leaving one world for another.

"Cal?" she said, relieved to see he was still beside her.

"Right here," he said grimly. "What's happening?"

"No idea," she said quietly. Before they could discuss it further, the three-dimensional image surrounding them dissolved, and another took its place: a blindingly white field of glaciers set against a night sky with unfamiliar stars. There were drifts of snow piled at their feet, and a cold howling wind. The sharp freshness of a winter wilderness filled Andie's mouth and nostrils. It was as if they were seated inside a tiny IMAX cinema that included an immersive sensory experience.

The only variance in the glacial setting was a scraggly tree directly ahead, with a single plum hanging from one of the bare branches. As Andie shivered, wondering if the driver was pumping in cold air and scents through an invisible vent, signs of a civilization began to emerge among the glaciers: spires and towers and pillars carved into the ice, an antediluvian Petra in the frozen wilds of Hyberborea. The plum was still there, now poised at the tip of the highest ice spire, a dollop of color in the field of white.

The glaciers dissolved. The cold wind ceased, and the scene reformed, this time into an Eden-like panorama of tropical beauty, a glade by a jungle river surrounded by the exotic foliage of Southeast Asia. Animals both strange and familiar filled the jungle. People wearing simple woven clothing wandered through, performing various tasks: building tree houses out of vines and logs, scooping water in earthen bowls from the river, lounging beneath mushrooms as big as boulders, harvesting brilliantly colored flowers that dwarfed any Andie had ever seen. The landscape was breathtaking, and the more she craned her neck and looked, the more she saw hints of a civilization entwined within the jungle: a rope bridge spanning the river, a viewing platform in the branches of a tree, stone-carved steps on a hillside. The plum was there again, nestled in a basket beside a woman washing a child's hair in the river.

A chorus of wild shrieks and beating drums interrupted the tranquil scene, so loud it caused Andie to jump. An army of men with clubs and painted bodies stormed the peaceful village, killing everyone in sight in a frenzy of violence that turned Andie's stomach. One of the warriors yanked the plum out of the basket and thrust it skyward, causing the image to dissolve and shift again, this time to a vast field of sinuous stone structures that resembled giant beehives. *Is this Angkor Wat?* Hundreds of temples surrounded her and Cal, complemented by paths of mosaic tile and reflecting pools and green spaces full of lush flowers. This time the plum was a jewel crowning the top of the tallest temple. It was one of the most beautiful sights Andie had ever seen, yet it was marred by the cluster of enslaved workers laboring to build a new temple on the periphery of the complex. Flies and mosquitoes surrounded the workers, landing on their backs, twisted from hard labor, attracted to the blood on their raw hands and feet. The view slowly zoomed out, revealing more slaves in the surrounding jungle, thousands of them, carrying stones to the clearing from nearby quarries. Andie could hear their cries of pain and smell the sweat and blood coagulating in the brutal heat.

On and on it went, the scenes more familiar as they moved forward in time. The history of Southeast Asia told in full-sensory vignettes that spoke of leaps and bounds of progress—or was it regression?—marked by a terrible human toll. The diorama did not seem to take a position. It conveyed simple truths, spoken without words.

She witnessed the arrival of the French and other colonizers. The intermingling of Hinduism and Buddhism with indigenous religion. Tantalizing hints of lost civilizations and technology far ahead of its time. The Vietnam War and the spread of Communism.

The narrative continued all the way to modern day, and always the single plum was present and placed in a prominent position. Inside an open mass grave in Cambodia during the reign of the Khmer Rouge. Carried by a Hmong tribeswoman from her rural Laotian village to a tourist shop in downtown Bangkok, a flyspeck of purple swallowed by the concrete matrix of skyscrapers.

As the rickshaw slowed and finally came to rest, the images flickered and then died. Andie had lost track of time. How long had they been watching—half an hour? An hour?

"What was that?" Cal said in a shaky voice.

"I don't know," Andie said as she retrieved the Star Phone and let out a deep breath, moved by the exhibition and full of questions. "I don't know."

"That plum—do you think it's something we're supposed to find?"

"I don't think it was a plum. I think it was . . . a spark."

As Cal looked over at her, thoughtful, the door creaked open, exposing the familiar din of a Hanoi city street. They both tensed, unsure what to expect. Outside was a busy commercial center with masses of pedestrians and lines of buses, cars, and taxis. It was unclear who had opened the door, and the driver was nowhere in sight.

But neither were the Ascendants.

Andie took a long look around. "He left us at a bus station?"

"Take a look at this," Cal said, peering inside the driver's door.

While there was no sign of the elderly Vietnamese man, Andie saw a worn interior that looked as she imagined the front seat of an old rickshaw would look: a padded bench for the driver, handlebars wrapped in black tape, a set of prayer beads on the dash below the windshield. The only anomaly was a business card placed in the center of the driver's seat.

Cal picked it up. "The Belle Riviere, in Hoi An. A business card for a hotel? Bizarre."

He handed it to her. Andie read the name on the back, flipped it over—and her heart skipped a beat. Depicted on the face of the card was a photo of a narrow Vietnamese street lined with two- and three-story French colonial buildings, lit by hundreds of illuminated globe lanterns.

"I've seen this before," she said, studying it closely.

"You have? Where?"

"Through the Star Phone, right in front of the Temple of Literature. It's the exact same street." She slowly looked up. "I don't know why, but this has to mean we're supposed to go to Hoi An. And apparently to this guesthouse."

Without waiting for a response, she shouldered her backpack and entered the bus station, searching for a list of times and destinations. Cal followed her, unusually silent. It did not take them long to discover a sleeper bus that ran from Hanoi to Hoi An. Though the distance was not that far—less than two hours by air—the bus journey was a grueling eighteen hours.

"There's a reason we were dropped here," Andie said as they huddled in front of the ticket window. "Someone wants to help us leave the city."

"I can think of better ways."

"Maybe, maybe not. The Ascendants will be watching the airports and checking the car rental agencies."

"True. I doubt anyone will suspect we'd take a chicken bus completely off the grid to some random Vietnamese town."

Andie's eyes lifted to the terminal board. "The next bus to Hoi

An leaves in half an hour. The Ascendants are probably still searching near the Temple of Literature, thinking we couldn't have made it very far."

They locked eyes, and Cal offered his arm. "Fancy a ride through the countryside, milady?"

Two hours later, Cal finally stopped glancing outside the rear window. He and Andie had paid cash for their tickets, left Hanoi without incident, and hunkered down in two conjoined sleeper seats in the back of the bus. Though not full of chickens, it was a school bus retrofitted to accommodate nighttime journeys. It smelled like old socks, and the entire bus was filled with rows of sleeper seats, which could either be laid out flat or reclined at a forty-five-degree angle. Because someone had the greedy idea to create an upper level of these monstrosities, packing more people inside, there was not enough room for the seats to sit up straight. Cal was too tall to stretch out, so his choices were sitting at a weird, crunched angle or lying on his side with his knees pulled to his chest.

As soon as they cleared the city limits, Andie had collapsed like she hadn't slept in a week. He was glad to see her resting. After a spell, she shifted so close to him their cheeks were almost touching. He knew she had not done it consciously, but it still caused his pulse to quicken. He could feel her breath against his cheek, soft and warm.

As nice as it was, he had to change positions or risk getting muscle cramps. After extricating himself, he stood in the aisle and bounced on his toes to get the blood flowing. Outside the window, the scenery had turned shockingly beautiful: they were driving through emerald-green rice paddies punctuated by rounded limestone karsts that rose from the manicured plain like giant thimbles. On the right side of the bus, a chocolate stream wound into the distance, carving through the rice fields and karsts, begging to be explored.

When he grew sick of standing, Cal ducked back down to his cramped quarters. *This thing is a damn coffin.* Feeling the need to do something productive, he grabbed Zawadi's phone and was stunned to find he had a Wi-Fi signal.

How was there Wi-Fi on this bus and not on his back patio in LA.?

He decided to find out more about Hoi An. First, however, he checked the dark web onion address, and found a message from Dane.

Got something. Ping me.

After sending a quick message to let his friend know he was online and had nothing to do except pick his nose for the next fourteen hours, Cal got the skinny on Hoi An.

The town was located near the mouth of the Thu Bon River in the Quang Nam province in central Vietnam, just south of the city of Danang, which had served as the famous "China Beach" US base of operations in the Vietnam War. Though far removed from its glory days, Hoi An had gained UNESCO World Heritage status for the preservation of its old town.

In the latter half of the first millennium, the Cham people had controlled the spice trade in the area, and the town of Hoi An—known then as Lam Ap—was their commercial capital. Around 1595, the town was annexed by a Vietnamese feudal lord, who changed the name to Hoi An. The town became an important trading port, considered by Japanese and Chinese merchants of the day as the best port in all of Asia, specializing in silk and spice and ceramics. Hoi An's trading links extended all the way to Europe, India, and Egypt.

After the local dynasty collapsed, and the city of Danang grew in importance, Hoi An languished for hundreds of years until tourism from its traditional crafts and architecture revived it.

Feeling he had a decent grasp on the town, and noting with pleasure that Anthony Bourdain had visited a banh mi joint there, Cal logged back onto the dark web onion address and saw that Dane had responded.

You still in the building, kemosabe?

Cal wrote back. Yep. U?

Right here in the cyberflesh.

What u got for me?

Remember our last convo? That creepy neuropsych Waylan Taylor in the Bay Area who specialized in rare conditions like Kleine Levin?

Of course.

He also saw people with Alice in Wonderland syndrome and alien hand syndrome. I'm not making those up. The common thread seems to be some sort of mind-body disconnect, or a distorted sense of space and time.

Cal felt a chill on the back of his neck.

I couldn't access the records of his Berkeley clinic, and searching for the LYS or the Ascendants is too dangerous. They've got bots all over the place. So I shifted my attention to Waylan's background, and things got interesting.

Like how?

The stuff I found was circa 1993, right at the start of the internet. Before that, you're really only talking DARPA. Anyway, I had to go super old-school to track him. JavaScript, scrubbed FTP servers, Gopher, Mosaic. Most of the information had been scrubbed—but not everything.

I'm like a kid on Christmas morning here. What's under the tree?

After Waylan left Berkeley, he went dark for a while, then opened a practice of sorts in Asheville, North Carolina.

What do you mean "of sorts"?

He called it the Human Limits Testing Facility. A one-of-a-kind psychiatric center for people around the world with extraordinary mental conditions, everything from self-proclaimed psychics to people with rare debilitative disorders. I'm talking demon possession, sleeping sickness, severe epileptics, astral travelers, metempsychosis, split personalities, NDEs, you name it.

Why Asheville?

I dunno. Maybe because it's in the middle of nowhere, and from what I've seen online, the city attracts a strange crowd. Anyway, reading between the lines, Waylan was far more interested in using the facility to explore the limits of consciousness than curing the mentally ill.

Cal sucked in a breath. *Human Limits Testing Facility? Was that some type of assessment site for new Ascendants? An attempt to explore the Fold?* So what do we do with this? Did you find a direct connection?

I doubt that still exists. I found something, though. The facility was located in an old house that, according to my records, has been abandoned ever since Waylan left, rotting away on the edge of downtown. Some obscure holding company holds the deed. I bet if I can penetrate the corporate veil, we'll find a link to the Ascendants, maybe even Waylan himself.

You think there might be something worth investigating in the house?

I went down that route. Most of the furniture was removed when it sold to the holding company. I even found a video an urban explorer had made.

So probably not worth the risk.

Not at first blush. But I used my wayback machine and mad skillz to dig deeper. I found another video from when the facility was still in operation, a promotional shot that included footage of Waylan's office. Just for kicks, I compared the two videos, and found something freaky.

Feeling paranoid all of a sudden, Cal looked up and glanced around the bus to make sure no one was watching. Almost everyone except the driver seemed to be taking an afternoon nap.

Dane continued typing. In the old promotional video, there was a door, barely visible in the background, behind Waylan's desk. I have no idea where it led, maybe it was just a closet, but get this: it wasn't in the urban explorer's video.

Cal gripped the phone as he typed. You're sure about this? Same room? Same position?

100%. I'll send you the images. I compared them over and over, thinking I must have made a mistake. Where once there was a door, now there is not. The wallpaper changed too. I think somebody, probably Waylan himself, hid something in whatever room or space that door conceals. And I think it might still be there.

After relaying the address of the house, Dane signed off, leaving Cal deep in thought as he watched the countryside pass by. *An abandoned house full of secrets, with a room no one else has entered.*

What the hell is behind that door? Firm documentation on the LYS or the Ascendants? Names? Bank accounts? Blackmail evidence? Something Waylan is keeping from the Ascendants for some reason? Research too bizarre and explosive for public consumption?

Whatever it was, Cal had a very strong feeling that if he kept tugging on that thread, a piece of carefully woven tapestry was about to unravel.

By the time Andie woke, Cal was dozing beside her. Realizing she had been using his shoulder as a pillow, she sat up as best she could in the cramped seat. Outside the window, in the soft light of dusk, fields of rice paddies undulated over low hills, backed by the shadow of a mountain range. Villagers in conical hats traversed the narrow footpaths dissecting the emerald squares, returning with the day's harvest or guiding water buffaloes on rope leads. There was a timelessness to the scene that made Andie contemplate the quiet nature of all things—and yet, with the message of the Rickshaw Obscura fresh in her mind, she remembered these were elderly women performing backbreaking labor in the fields, and that colonialism and inequality had shaped this land of ethereal beauty.

Still, her thoughts did not spoil the view. If so, she would have to stop looking at the entire world, because every culture she had ever studied was guilty of some type of violent conquest. The Viet people had conquered the Chams. The French had colonized the Vietnamese, who in turn ravaged the Cambodians during the Vietnam War. On and on it went, throughout history.

When the light failed, she climbed over Cal to use the restroom, then stood in the aisle to stretch her legs. Only the quiet hum of the engine broke the silence. Her thoughts turned to their escape from the Temple of Literature, and whether the street magician had gotten away safely. Did the ends ever justify the means? By putting the safety of her mother and Dr. Corwin above everyone else, was she any better than those colonizers and rampaging tribes? How far would she go, what taboos would she break, to save the ones she loved?

Feeling very alone, she pulled up her inbox on Zawadi's phone, hoping against hope for a message from Dr. Corwin or her mother. Even if she had one—which she knew she wouldn't—she knew she couldn't open the message or send a reply, for fear of being tracked.

But to her shock, Andie did have an email from her mother, from the same address as before: Cassi14159@gmail.com.

The email had been sent three hours ago. Her mother must have been forced to send it in response to the loss of the Star Phone. Still, a rush of emotion poured through Andie. She cast a furtive glance around the bus before staring down at the subject line.

I seem to have no true identity without you.

Andie's first thought was one of pure joy. Her mother had not abandoned her after all! She loved her daughter so much that she did not feel complete without her.

Almost at once, Andie stuffed that emotion down a deep, dark hole, knowing her mother's every word was being watched, and that whatever she said had to be filtered through the controlling lens of the Ascendants. The sentiment meant nothing. Even worse, her mother was playing with Andie's emotions.

And then, with a gasp, she parsed the true meaning behind the message, a clue from her childhood just like the last email had been.

The import of it hit her like a wrecking ball.

Before her parents had started fighting, they had shared a snarky sense of humor. They both loved Jack Handey and *The Far Side*, and often went to see live comedy shows. On their bedroom wall, each of her parents kept a framed comic from their respective disciplines. Her father's was a short strip with three frames, titled "How to Be a

Writer." The triptych depicted a frazzled man at a typewriter, and each frame bore a heading.

Drink. Loathe yourself. Repeat day and night.

Her mother's choice—Andie remembered it clearly, because she had never understood it as a child—was a subatomic particle, drawn as a stick figure, gazing into its reflection in the mirror. The full comic read:

Help me! I seem to have no true identity without you.
Yours truly,
Quantum particle

The cartoon was referring to Heisenberg's famous uncertainty principle, which held that quantum particles cannot truly be measured until observed, raising the question of whether a particle exists in the same manner—or at all—before the moment of observation. The comic put an ironic, yet also very deep, spin on the topic by asking whether a quantum particle could look into a mirror and become its *own* observer.

The subject line of the email was clearly designed to tug at Andie's heartstrings, a cruel version of clickbait that no doubt presaged a tracking cookie and a message imploring Andie to hand over the Star Phone. She couldn't risk opening it. Yet whatever the actual body of the email read was irrelevant, because Andie felt certain the Ascendants had dictated her mother's words.

She also knew her mother had used the opportunity to send her daughter another secret message, embodied in the first two words of the comic, which her mother had omitted from the subject line but which rang loud and clear in Andie's head.

Help me!

More determined than ever, Andie remained wide-awake for the duration of the journey, all through the long night, the remote countryside glistening like an oil stain beneath the moon. After learning everything there was to know about Hoi An on Zawadi's phone, she wished she had something more concrete to research.

Where were they supposed to go in the city? What were they supposed to do?

She supposed they had no choice but to start with the hotel on the business card left by the rickshaw driver.

Cal yawned and sat up as the bus pulled into Hoi An station. "Mornin', sunshine."

When she didn't respond, he took a look at her drawn face and said quietly, "Did something happen?"

"I'll tell you when we're alone. Coffee and brunch at the Belle Riviere?"

They had made several pit stops along the way, for refreshments and the toilet, but Cal had slept through the last two.

"You read my mind," he said.

Though short, the taxi ride from the bus station to the hotel was long enough for Andie to get a feel for the small town. The melting-pot architecture reflected a stew of epochs and styles, from the handsome French colonial buildings to the wooden homes of wealthy Chinese traders. There were pagodas and temples and teahouses, long blocks of Vietnamese tube houses with tall necks rising above the street. Bougainvillea wreathed the balconies, farmers balanced bamboo poles with baskets full of veggies across their shoulders, musicians and sculptors and painters hawked their wares on every corner. The streaks of grime from centuries past only added to the charm. The entire old town was stunning, street after cobblestone street dripping with atmosphere and mystique.

The Belle Riviere was in the heart of downtown, right along the river, less than a block from an ornate covered bridge that seemed to be drawing all the tourists. The hotel had a mustard-yellow facade with blue shutters. The street outside smelled of jasmine.

Unsure how far Zawadi's credit card would carry them, they shared another room to save money—this time with two beds. A fan spun sluggishly from the high ceiling, and Andie liked the claw-foot tub. She could have done without the large standing mirror—she had never liked mirrors—though she had to chuckle at how disheveled both she and Cal looked.

After dropping their backpacks and washing up, they made their way to the dining room. Andie studied every inch of the hotel along the way, with her eyes and through the lens of the Star Phone, but saw nothing unusual.

Over a late breakfast—bacon, freshly baked French bread, pineapple jam, and an omelet covered in roasted red chilis—she told him about the email from her mother.

"That's heavy," he said.

"That cartoon was on our wall my entire childhood. I *know* it's a message."

He gripped her hand across the table. "I can't imagine how hard this is for you. If it was my mother . . ."

She looked off to the side. "I want to write her back so much," she said softly. "Let her know I'm out here."

He didn't respond, and she knew what he was thinking: *That's exactly what they want you to do.*

Andie stared down at her plate of half-finished food, her appetite fading.

Still no word from Zawadi. They spent the rest of the day probing every corner of Hoi An, pointing the Star Phone at prominent landmarks, visiting temples and museums, researching the history. Though in theory the Ascendants had no way to locate them, Andie felt no sense of security. She knew they would find a way.

With the arrival of dusk, they still had no clue as to their next destination, but a magical thing happened: as the descending sun melted the rooftops into gold, the paper globe lanterns hanging in the trees and strung above the streets began to light up, winking on one by one, illuminating the town with a palette of color. A silver moon emerged through a halo of clouds, and Andie saw a group of monks entering a pagoda festooned with glowing baubles, the air charged with incense. Despite the grave purpose of their visit, Andie thought Hoi An was the most beautiful and exotic place she had ever seen, a town built for poets.

She and Cal were resigned to staying the night. After downing bowls of peanut noodles from a street vendor, they returned to the Belle Riviere, showered, and debated having a drink at the hotel bar facing the river.

"We should be staying out of sight," Andie said.

"Normally I'd agree with you. But if I don't have one goddamn drink in a normal goddamn bar like a regular person for one single night, I think I might go insane."

Andie waffled, wary of staying out longer than they had to. "One drink," she said. "And we sit in the back."

They were pleased to discover the Happy Dragon Lounge was quite a chill place. The front of the establishment was open to the river, while the whimsical tile floor and potted plants imparted a bohemian vibe. Hordes of geckos darted along the vine-covered walls and ceiling, pouncing on insects. License plates from around the world covered the wall above the bar. Andie wondered if they had been discarded by people who had found their way to Hoi An and never left.

From their table in the back, they watched a procession of tourist canoes gliding lazily down the river, illuminated by paper lanterns attached to poles, an impossibly romantic scene.

There were so many tourists in town Andie had decided to ditch her ao dai for a pair of jeans, sandals, and a white T-shirt she had bought at the night market. The regular clothes made her feel more herself, the margarita was delicious, and giant fans kept the air moving. It felt like a moment out of time, and Cal was right: they had needed this.

They drank in silence, absorbing the ambience. When Cal had finished his Tiger lager, he pointed the empty bottle at Andie's glass. "Round two?"

Andie glanced around the noisy bar, filled with people from a United Nations roster of countries. No one was paying them any attention.

"Haven't you read about the ill effects of alcohol?" she said, tapping the rim of her glass and pushing it toward him.

"Yeah, well, I always balance that with the benefits of forgetting about shit for a night."

Andie chuckled as he sauntered to the bar. Cal was wearing another tourist outfit: linen pants, panama hat, and a short-sleeve Hawaiian shirt. His beard had grown fuller since they had first met. Andie liked it. It gave him a rougher edge and made him seem less like a former jock.

He returned with the drinks. "So how do you think you'll die?"

She blinked. "Come again?"

"Not counting being tortured by the Ascendants, that is. I mean before all this started: How did you think you would croak?"

"What a bizarre question. I don't know. Definitely not from old age. Maybe a plane crash, lost in fog over the Himalayas. No—adrift in space with oxygen and proper gear. Yeah, that'd be nice."

"Curious," Cal said. "Okay, I'm with that."

"Why are you asking?"

"I don't know. Maybe because death has seemed rather imminent lately."

The comment caused her to look down and hold her glass between her palms. "What about you? I assume you've thought about this."

"Yeah, but it changes all the time. These days, I've been feeling a heart attack after a two-week bender in a Mexican brothel."

"Please tell me you don't frequent brothels."

"It's more about the sentiment. Dead-ass broke, one last hair-raiser south of the border, going out in a blaze of glory."

"Been there, done that," she muttered.

"Really?"

"Except for the dying. It was a long time ago, and I turned my life around after that."

"And? Thumbs-up as a way to go out?"

She chuckled. "Can't say I recommend it."

Two drinks turned into three, and then four. They kept up the banter, chatting about happier times. Andie started to feel gooey inside from the alcohol, and Cal's jaw seemed firmer than when the night had started.

"When you mentioned your mom in Hanoi," she said, "I gathered you loved her very much. It's okay if you don't want to talk about it. We can keep it shallow tonight."

"It's fine." Cal rubbed his beard and sighed. "My dad was a world-class jerk, but my mom and I were real close. When dad lost his job—and our house—we left him and moved to LA so my mom could pursue her dream of being an actress. She was still young then, a real beauty. She acted in a few plays, but always put her dreams aside for her family."

"How did you have the money to move to LA?" she asked. "I'm sorry—that was a crass question."

"Nah, it's fine. We didn't until my grandfather died and left my mom a small inheritance. We used all of it to fund the move. I mean, why not? My dad was drinking himself to death on the sofa. Anyway, long story short, we made the move, and my mom got a few auditions. It was going well until a director raped her on the casting couch."

Andie set her drink down. "Oh my God."

"At least I think that's what happened. I never knew for sure, but I heard her crying and talking to her sister, and I read between the lines. Some no-name pissant director. Harvey Weinstein is all over the news, and the famous actresses receive all the attention, but for every one of those, there were plenty like my mom who got no press and had their lives ruined. I never got over it, and I never forgot the lesson. Fuck people with power who think they can do whatever they want to other people."

Andie raised her glass. "Fuck 'em."

Cal waved a hand. "Enough of all that. Let's get one more round, talk about the weather, and call it a night."

"Deal." Andie realized she was drunk and didn't care. She had needed the release. She also needed the restroom. "Be right back."

There was a short line in the hallway outside the toilet. As she waited, Andie glanced at the photos on the wall of bar patrons engaged in various stages of revelry—and had one of the most profound shocks of her life.

Unable to believe what she was seeing, she stepped across the corridor and peered directly at a photograph hanging at eye level. There was no date on the photo, but she could see the neon HAPPY DRAGON LOUNGE sign behind the bar, and the tourist canoes on the river.

And the tall and beautiful woman in the photo, dancing atop the bar with her blond hair unbound and a drink in her hand, as happy and carefree as Andie had ever seen her, was without a doubt her mother.

Andie couldn't stop gawking. Dressed in a black tank top and a grass skirt with a tropical motif, wearing her jade ring, her mother was about the same age as Andie was now. The photo must have been taken during her mother's "sabbatical" in her late twenties.

Andie stumbled back to the table. Cal rose to meet her and put his hands on her shoulders. "You look like you've seen a ghost."

"I think I did," she said in a daze.

She led him to the photo and told him who it was. After he stared at it for a long moment, stunned, they made their way around the room, searching for more evidence of her mother's visit.

"Andie," Cal said when they were standing in front of the bar, his voice strangely subdued. He pointed. "Up there."

She followed his finger to one of the dozens of license plates on the wall, and then gasped. The artwork on the North Carolina plate was an ode to the legacy of the Wright brothers: the image of an old propeller plane flying above a field of sea oats. She had seen similar plates all over Durham. However, the nine letters on the plate were custom-made, as well as the source of the gooseflesh coursing down her arms.

ANDROMEDA

21

Unable to speak, feeling wobbly from the alcohol and the shock of discovery, Andie took out the Star Phone and tried to steady her hand as she aimed the device at the ANDROMEDA license plate. She had done the same thing to no effect with the photo of her mother and the HAPPY DRAGON LOUNGE sign.

But as she peered through the Star Phone at the license plate, the nine letters enlarged to fill the room, brought to life in augmented reality. Her inebriated state and the three-dimensional zoom induced a bout of nausea. She stumbled, and Cal slipped an arm around her waist. With a grimace, she gripped his arm and held on, watching as each letter of her name spun wildly in place like a slot machine. One by one, the letters stopped spinning to form a nine-digit alphanumeric sequence, along with the same images in the top corners that had appeared with each new cipher: the black-hole atom and the LYS symbol.

After committing the sequence to memory, Andie pocketed the device as Cal steadied her from behind. "You okay there?"

She turned and draped her arms around his neck. They were standing right next to the bar, alone in a crowd of people. "I saw it," she said, in a breathless whisper. "We've got the next code!"

"Boom," he said, pulling her in tighter. "A step ahead of those bastards."

They were so close their mouths were almost touching. She could feel the warmth of his breath, and reached up to run a hand through his hair. Before he could kiss her, she placed a finger between their lips, gently, and met his gaze. "I have to know what it is," she said. "The next image."

He cocked a disbelieving grin and pulled back. "Right now?"

"Right now. Come on."

She took his hand and led him back to the table. After signaling to the waiter for another round, he scooted his chair next to hers as she input the new nine-digit sequence into the Star Phone. The code locked into place, and the lanterns of Hoi An dissolved, replaced by a sandstone disk filling the middle of the screen. The face of the disk was covered with concentric rings of engravings that looked Amerindian in nature.

Four smaller images in the corners of the screen accompanied the sandstone disk. She studied them, clockwise from top left: an eagle crowned with a bright-green Native American headdress, clutching a globe in its talons; a small circle inside a larger one, attached at a single point on the right curve of both shapes; a map of Mexico; and a map of what she thought was Central America.

"How bizarre," she said. "I should research these."

He gently cupped her chin. "Andie. It's two in the morning. You almost passed out a minute ago. You'll make mistakes if you try to work right now." When she hesitated, he brushed a strand of hair from her eyes and gave her a meaningful glance. "Finish your drink, and let's go up. It's late."

Andie looked from Cal to the Star Phone, chewing on her bottom lip. His hand was on her knee now, and she found that she didn't want him to move it. When she tried to study the Star Phone, the image was a little blurry, and she realized she was in no condition for serious research.

"Okay," she said, then downed her margarita in three long swallows. *How many have I had? Six? Seven?*

He followed suit, knocking back his beer on the way out of the

bar. They passed through the lobby, laughing as they used each other for support to climb the stairs to their third-floor room. Another dizzy spell overcame her as she fumbled with the old-fashioned dead bolt. Cal bent down to take the key, and she put a hand on the wall to steady herself.

"Carry me," she said after he opened the door.

He picked her up with ease and kicked the door closed with a foot. She draped her arms around his neck and nuzzled on his ear as he carried her through the room and set her on the bed. She pulled him down, enjoying his weight on top of her. They were about to kiss when he leaned back and propped himself up with an elbow.

"Don't go," she whispered.

"Nature calls. Be right back. Don't, you know, run off to another country or anything."

She trailed a finger across his cheek as he eased off of her. After the bathroom door closed behind him, her eyelids seemed to lower of their own volition, and that was the last thing she remembered.

A ray of daylight peeked through the blinds of the room like a curious child. Andie groaned and rolled over in bed. Her head was throbbing, her throat as dry as the Sahara.

She stumbled to the minibar, pulled out a fresh bottle, and drank the entire contents. The cool water sliding down her throat was nirvana. She started to return to bed when the memory of the night before rushed over her.

Getting filthy drunk. Seeing a photo of her mother on the wall. Finding the ANDROMEDA license plate and the next Star Phone clue.

Almost going to bed with Cal.

Mortified by how intoxicated she had been—though not as upset at what had almost happened as she thought she would have been—she looked down and saw that she was still fully dressed.

Nor was Cal in her bed. After studying his sleeping form for a long moment, fully clothed and lying on top of the covers in his own bed, she prodded him gently. He stirred but never woke, and she resisted the urge to crawl in beside him. Instead, acutely aware of the passage of time and how much danger they were in, she made a cup of coffee and started researching.

Four hours later, she thought she had an answer.

"Already?" Cal said. He was sitting across from her at the café next door to the hotel.

Andie flashed a grim, satisfied smile. After Cal had finally woken up, she had hinted at her discovery, and suggested they grab a bite to eat and talk it over.

A converted tube house, the café had four narrow stories dotted with seating nooks accented by potted plants and bamboo screens. They had the fourth floor to themselves and had chosen a low wooden table flanked by benches strewn with cushions. Behind them, a set of French doors opened onto a balcony. The building across the street was so close she thought she could jump to the balcony on the other side, where a shirtless old man was taking down a birdcage before the heat of the day settled in.

While the flirting from last night had not continued—and neither of them had brought it up—Cal's relaxed nature made her feel less awkward. He was an easy guy to be around, she had to admit.

Most of the time.

She also had to admit she felt closer to him after their night of revelry. She reasoned it was only natural that two people in such dire circumstances would develop a bond, like two people adrift at sea, forced to lean on each other to survive.

"Check this out," she said, pulling out the Star Phone to bring up the image of the sandstone disk. "This was easy to find online. It's a famous Aztec relic called the Stone of the Sun. The thing is huge: more than twenty tons and twelve feet in diameter."

He whistled. "When was it made?"

"Good question—and that raises another angle I've been

pondering. The stone was unearthed beneath the Zócalo in Mexico City in 1790, but a glyph on the stone mentions Montezuma II, an Aztec ruler who reigned between 1502 and 1520 AD. So it's at least that old."

"Dude's famous, right? Montezuma's revenge and all?"

Andie rolled her eyes. "He ruled the Aztec Empire at its peak, when it stretched from Mexico to Honduras. Unfortunately, this coincided with the arrival of Cortés, and we know how that story goes." She wagged a finger. "Bear with me for a sec. Let's get meta. The Star Phone puzzle started with Democritus, a philosopher from fourth-century BCE. After that it was ancient Alexandria, marking the transition to the Common Era. Next up was Aryabhata in fourth century AD. We don't know much about the next two sites, but Zawadi tells us the Ascendants went to Granada and Timbuktu, which presupposes the Islamic Golden Age—which started in roughly the eighth century. Then we moved to the Silk Road, which didn't peak in Vietnam until the fourteenth century."

"And the sixth location has something to do with this Aztec sun stone in the fifteen hundreds."

"Right."

"So what's all that mean?" he asked.

"I don't know, except we're moving forward in time."

"Maybe a better question," Cal said quietly, "is what it all means for *you*."

Andie looked down, unable to deny the truth of the insinuation. In fact, she had thought of little else that morning.

On the surface, the Star Phone puzzle was highlighting the achievements of humankind—both overt and hidden—across a variety of cultures and time periods. She knew there were other lessons as well. Veiled, interwoven threads in the tapestry of history.

Yet now, after what they had seen in Vietnam, an even deeper layer had been revealed, one unrelated to the world at large.

A layer personal to Andie.

It seemed that with every turn, she was becoming more and

more involved in the events of this mysterious society, corkscrewing tighter and tighter into an unknown world.

What game are you playing with my life, Dr. Corwin? What's your ultimate goal?

Why did you never tell me?

"I don't know what it means," Andie said, more roughly than she had intended. "We just need to solve it, and we're getting closer. Like I said, I think I know where the puzzle leads next."

Cal spread his hands. "Hit me."

After a sip of chilled strawberry tea, she pulled up a web page on Zawadi's phone for the National Museum of Anthropology in Mexico City. Cal stared at the photo of the Aztec sun stone, then watched as she toggled back and forth between the photo and the image on the Star Phone.

"They look the same to me," he said. "No mystery there. So we're going to Mexico?"

"Not so fast. As far as I can tell—and I studied it all morning—the two images are identical. But so is this one." She pulled up another web page, this time for the Hall of Mexico and Central America in the American Museum of Natural History in New York, where another Aztec sun stone—an exact replica of the original—is on permanent display.

He looked up. "I guess that muddies the water. Though I'd think the original was more important."

"I thought so too, until I started trying to figure out the images in the corners. There has to be a reason they were included, and it wasn't too difficult to find them online. The eagle clutching the globe in its talons—if you look closely, that's an anchor piercing the globe—is the symbol for the United States Marines."

Cal frowned. "The US armed forces doesn't seem to fit the themes here."

"Not on its own. But that elaborate green headpiece on the eagle is actually a featherwork crown known as Montezuma's headdress. It's another important relic, and it's held in the Museum of Ethnology in Vienna. Mexico, of course, wants it back."

"The plot thickens."

"Moving clockwise—there's a reason for that—we come to the pair of concentric rings." She pulled up a web page that depicted a smaller circle inside a larger one, connected at a single point on the right side of both circles. A number of tiny animal drawings, almost whimsical in nature, were spaced along the perimeter of the larger circle. The smaller circle was inset with dots, from one to thirteen, also along the perimeter.

"It's a tonalpohualli, or day stone," Andie said. "An Aztec calendar based on incredibly advanced astronomical observations. The Aztecs built their cities and temples to align with the sun and moon, and this calendar was a stunning achievement at the time."

"Now *that* fits the theme. What about the last two?"

"As far as I can tell, the maps of Mexico and Central America are simply that: outlines of geographical entities. There are no other distinguishing features."

Cal used his chopsticks to stab a spring roll. "You did all this before lunch?"

"Like I said, they weren't that hard to find. Putting it all together was a different story. I was going in a million directions, but the answer was simple when I found it. The key was the first image. I couldn't figure it out until I Googled 'Marines and Montezuma.'"

She showed him yet another web page, with the lyrics to "The Marines' Hymn" on display: the official song of the US Marine Corps.

"Oh my," Cal said after he read it. "It's right there in the first two lines: 'From the Halls of Montezuma to the shores of Tripoli.'"

"A pretty obvious connection. But the day stone tripped me up until I placed it in the larger context. This one is both misleading and wickedly simple. Do you know any Spanish?"

"I live in LA."

"Think of a Spanish preposition. Oscar *De* la Hoya. Pico *de* gallo."

"'De' means 'of' or 'from,'" he said. "Right?"

"More or less. Now start with the upper left corner, move clockwise, and put it all together."

Cal stared down at the image on the Star Phone before turning up his palms in confusion.

"Think of the principal meaning," she said. "A key word from each image. There's also a theme of conquest, of colonizer and colonized. Where the sun stone was found, and where it is now."

He scratched at the thick hair on his chin. "'Halls of Montezuma' relates to the Marines . . . 'Day stone'—'de,' meaning 'of' or 'from' . . . Mexico . . . Central America." He slapped the table as a grin crept onto his face. "You're right. Dr. Corwin *is* a clever bastard."

"It's annoyingly simple, isn't it?"

"Um, no. There's no telling how long I'd have been staring at the image if you hadn't led me to it." He jabbed his finger as he moved clockwise around the image on the Star Phone. "Hall. Of. Mexico. Central America. It's the museum in New York!"

"That's my conclusion," she said. "In fact, I'd stake my life on it—which I'm about to do. I texted all of this to Zawadi earlier and updated her on Hanoi. She got back to me right away for once."

Andie paused to chew on a nail, reflecting on the short, unnerving exchange. "And?" Cal prompted her.

"She said New York was too dangerous and told me not to go. Apparently the city is one of the Ascendants' power centers."

After digesting her words, Cal leaned back in his seat. "What else did she say?"

"She said we still couldn't talk—phone calls are too risky for now—and that she had to run. Again. She said to stay put and out of sight, and she'd get back to me soon."

"Where is she?"

"She didn't say."

Cal finished the last of the spring rolls and looked her in the eye. "We should heed her words."

Andie ran a hand through her hair and left it cupping the back of her neck. "Yeah, we probably should."

"But what?" he said, picking up on her reticence.

"But I'm not going to."

"*Andie.* Listen to reason. If Zawadi says it's too dangerous—"

"Then she can fly there and protect us. That's her choice. But we both know speed is our only ally. This reprieve won't last. I have to get to New York before the Ascendants."

"They're already *there.*"

"You know what I mean."

"There are cameras all over that city. It's not safe, Andie. You're being reckless."

"There are ways to avoid surveillance, and we know exactly where to go. We'll be in and out before anyone notices. And why would we wait? Wait where? Here? In the same country the people chasing us are in? I feel less safe staying put than moving. We've kept ahead of them before, and we'll do it again. We're so close, Cal. Only three more locations."

"*If* you manage to solve the Star Phone puzzle and find the Enneagon, and *if* you can use it as a bargaining chip."

"I will, and I can."

"You think that."

"I *know* it. And so do they. Why do you think they're chasing us around the globe? Why are you being so negative?"

"Because these people play for keeps?"

"Our lives have been at risk the entire time. Why don't you propose a solution instead of shooting everything down?"

"Shooting—" Cal put a hand to his temple. "You're not thinking. And I do have a suggestion, but it's not going to New York. Not yet. There's something I've been meaning to tell you."

She drew back. "What?"

He summarized the conversation with Dane on the dark web server, then sipped his coffee as she processed the story of the neuropsychologist named Waylan Taylor with a connection to the Ascendants.

"So we do have a choice," he said. "And I think it's a good one.

More importantly, I doubt anyone else knows about it."

"A vacant house in Asheville that used to belong to an elderly psychologist, and which may or may not contain . . . what, exactly?"

"This Taylor guy was knee-deep with the Ascendants. Human Limits Testing Facility? There's something there, Andie. My reporter's radar is going berserk on this one. I think we should go to North Carolina first."

"I'm afraid I'll need more than a *feeling* to take a detour from the Enneagon. When were you going to tell me this?"

"You were asleep on the bus, and then we were searching Hoi An, and I was waiting for more info . . . I should have told you earlier. I'm sorry. Come with me," he said gently. "Who knows what's in that house. Names, dates, evidence of all sorts of illegal activity, a hard drive that could give us everything?"

"Except the Enneagon, you mean. You might find something to help get your life back, but that won't help Dr. Corwin or my mother. Which is fine. I understand. But say what you mean."

"You don't know that. Maybe we *will* find the leverage we need to bargain with them or go to the authorities. The bottom line is, this route is far safer, and I think we should try it first. We might even finish before Zawadi gets back to us."

She swallowed her disappointment. "I'm going to New York to help the people I love. If the Ascendants wanted whatever was in that house, they would have gotten it by now."

"Not if they don't know about it."

"What if Waylan simply renovated the room? Or maybe you didn't see what you think you saw in those photos."

"I did. I can show you."

"Don't bother. There's a flight from Danang to Bangkok in three hours. I'm taking it. Bangkok has direct flights to the States."

"You're just going to fly right into New York?" he said, incredulous. "After what Zawadi said?"

"I'll pick another city to fly into, and then drive." She knew her eyes betrayed her uncertainty at what she was about to do, and she didn't care. In her mind, there was no real choice. The longer they waited, the more time they gave the Ascendants to find them, and to torture Dr. Corwin. "I'll figure something out."

Half an hour later, Andie asked the hotel concierge to call her a cab, then hoisted her backpack and waited on the veranda beneath a bank of clouds pillowing the Vietnam sky. The midday heat was oppressive, sapping her energy, and the charms of Hoi An now seemed gauche, the hustle and bustle of street artists and doe-eyed tourists a cloying reminder of a life that was not hers to live.

Despite the insanity of recent events, she had thought for a moment that she and Cal had forged something, a common mind and purpose, a bubble of normalcy in a world gone mad.

She knew Cal was making a mercenary choice for his future just like she was, and that she was being reckless by going to New York. But she felt she had no choice. She had to follow the Star Phone puzzle, and fair or not, she couldn't shake the feeling he was abandoning her.

Just like her mother had done.

"Miss?" A driver in a black sedan called out. "You are traveling to the Danang airport?"

Andie hesitated, mistrustful of the car. When she looked over at the concierge, he gave her a thumbs-up. Plus the driver of the sedan was a skinny Vietnamese kid in designer sunglasses who barely looked twenty.

If he's an Ascendant, then I'm Joan of Arc.

She walked over as the driver opened the door. She had kept the Star Phone and a backpack, as well as Zawadi's cell and one of the credit cards.

"Andie!"

She turned, hope swelling inside her, but she quickly noticed Cal was not carrying his backpack. His flight didn't leave until the evening, and they had decided it was better to split up before the airport, since the Ascendants were looking for a man and a woman traveling together. They had exchanged a curt goodbye in the room that left Andie feeling even more hurt than before.

"I thought you might need this," he said.

"A toothbrush?"

He handed her the cheap brush she had bought at the night market in Hanoi. "I'm told they're essential to dental hygiene."

"Thanks," she said in a wooden voice.

After a moment, he said, "I didn't like the way we said goodbye."

Andie paused by the open car door. She knew she was being unreasonable, and reckless, and that she could not expect someone else to take the risks she was about to take. But when her mother had left Andie in her bed that night so long ago, and never returned, it had saddled Andie with a deep mistrust of anyone who left her for any reason.

She wanted to ask Cal to come with her again, and tell him she didn't want to do this by herself, beg him even, but she couldn't expose herself in that way. Instead she met his eyes, held her chin steady, and said nothing.

"Here," he said, handing her a piece of paper. "Dane gave me a secure web address for us to use. Can we please keep in touch?"

She took the paper, nodded, and put it in her pocket. "Of course."

He put a hand on her arm. "Take care of yourself."

She looked down at his hand and bit her lip, her voice coming out as a whisper. "You too."

"Don't take unnecessary risks. Stay out of sight." His mouth opened and then closed, as if he had changed his mind about whatever he was going to say. "I'm hoping there aren't any puzzles to solve in Asheville. I won't get very far without you."

"Somehow, I think you'll manage just fine."

"I paid for those drinks last night, you know. Granted, it was Zawadi's money. But the next one's on you, and I'm holding you to it."

"Sure," she said again, and stepped into the car before her emotions got the better of her.

Ushuaia, Argentina
November 1988

In his search for Ettore Majorana, Dr. Corwin had traveled, quite literally, to the ends of the Earth.

Located near the bottom of Tierra del Fuego, an archipelago at the tip of South America, Ushuaia was known as the southernmost town in the world, closer to Antarctica than to Argentina's neighboring countries to the north. On a cloudy Saturday morning in November, frazzled by the long journey, Dr. Corwin parked his Land Rover in front of a wood beam house at the edge of town. The house had a corrugated iron roof painted cobalt blue, in keeping with the style of the other homes. In truth, the isolated settlement was little more than a collection of log cabins with pretty roofs.

As he stepped out of the truck, buffeted by a stiff breeze, the moment felt surreal. Could the elusive physicist at the center of Dr. Corwin's twenty-year search truly live inside this simple dwelling? Ettore was born in August 1906. If still alive, he would be an old man now.

Beyond the house, Dr. Corwin glimpsed the icy blue waters of a bay near the convergence of the south Pacific and south Atlantic oceans. A succession of towering glacial peaks ringed the town on three sides, a crown of kings impassable except for a single road snaking through the Garibaldi Pass.

Though belonging in name to Argentina, no one but extreme adventurers, and perhaps an ornithologist in search of the natural habitat of the region's abundant penguins, had reason to cross the Andes and venture that far south. Ushuaia belonged to the wild things, to the wind and snow and fog, to the few hardy souls who dared to challenge the elements and carve out an existence from the pitiless heel of Mother Nature.

It was also, Dr. Corwin mused, an excellent choice of residence for those who chose to disappear.

Smoke billowed from the chimney on the steeply pitched roof of the house. He paused to absorb the stark and awesome beauty of his surroundings, then started down the gravel driveway to learn the fate of his obsessive quest. After leaving Buenos Aires, he had searched for Ettore whenever his duties allowed, in towns of all sizes across the continent. Guessing that Ettore had anticipated the violent regime change in Argentina—as had many others—and fled the country before the military junta took power, Dr. Corwin had first concentrated his search in the neighboring countries of Brazil, Chile, Uruguay, and Paraguay. Those countries weren't much safer, but perhaps Ettore was worried someone would track him down if he stayed too long in one place.

While Dr. Corwin was looking elsewhere, Argentina ousted its brutal dictators and ushered in a democratic regime. Dr. Corwin had returned his focus to the country now that he was able to search with more impunity. Still following the physics-and-mathematics angle, and having no more luck with bookstores, he had expanded his search to include libraries, especially in smaller towns where neither the Society nor the Ascendants had a presence. He did not visit all the libraries himself, as that would have been impossible, but instead targeted the distributors and wholesalers these libraries relied on to stock their collection.

It was tedious work that he farmed out to a private investigator. More years passed without success—until a week ago, when he had received a report on a library in remote Ushuaia that had caused his chest to tighten. It seemed that for the last ten years, this library had been ordering a handful of the latest textbooks in theoretical physics and mathematics. Libraries rarely carried such expensive items, especially now that works of "layman science" meant to bridge the gap between experts and the general public in these subject areas had become popular. Books such as *QED: The Strange Theory of Light and Matter* by Richard Feynman, and Stephen Hawking's *A Brief History of Time* had taken the world by storm that very year.

A sole patron had checked out the hard-core science textbooks in Ushuaia. This alone might not raise a red flag, but how many people with such an esoteric interest also checked out books of poetry at the same time, with a special focus on postmodern and English Romantic poets? Especially in a place as remote as Ushuaia?

The real breakthrough had come when Dr. Corwin, cautiously optimistic but still primed for disappointment, called the Ushuaia library to inquire as to who had been checking out these books, claiming he was searching for a long-lost friend.

And they had told him. While they did not divulge a physical description of the patron, they did pass on the name scrawled in blue ink on the library cards: Tomás E. Stern.

Dr. Corwin had stared at the name for some time before a light went on. Like himself, he knew Ettore liked to play with words and numbers, and assign meaning to everything he did. Dr. Corwin remembered that Diego Quiroga, the bookseller in Buenos Aires who had first led him to South America, had speculated that Ettore's favorite poet was T. S. Eliot.

A quick search gave Dr. Corwin the full given name of the wordsmith.

Thomas Stearns Eliot.

Ah, Ettore, you sly old devil, you just couldn't help yourself. You've inspired me in so many ways, you know. Maybe one day I'll create my own trail of bread crumbs to follow across the globe, rife with symbolism and hidden significance.

As Dr. Corwin navigated the gravel footpath leading to the

house, using his cane to support the knee Hans had shattered, his excitement grew as he noticed a pair of wooden planters beside the front door, nurturing a colorful array of blossoms through Ushuaia's fleeting spring.

Dr. Corwin knew the names and appearance of these particular flowers—caper, oleander, and prickly pear—because he had committed them to memory after a certain flower seller in Buenos Aires had told him that one of her customers, a Sicilian man living across the street, had favored them.

At long last, after all these years of searching, have I finally found him?

Dr. Corwin grew emotional as he stood at the door and reached for the bronze knocker. So much had happened in the intervening years. So much sacrificed for this moment. Since leaving Buenos Aires, he had steadily risen through the ranks of the Society and discovered a great many secrets. *Oh, the things I have seen.*

And yet the greatest of all still eluded him, the true nature of the mysterious Fold. He now knew there were elite groups within the Society dedicated to exploring it. He could have joined them had he wanted, and one day he would. But for now he was focused on finding the one person who might actually help them understand it. His skin tingled at the prospect of confronting Ettore.

Yet above all, as he prepared for the most important moment of his life, Dr. Corwin thought of Ana, and the terrible choice they had made, and his deep regret for what might have been.

After their final conversation, she had become a valuable mole within the Ascendants. Her tips had kept Dr. Corwin and others alive on numerous occasions. She had even steered Hans away from South America in the search for Ettore.

From time to time, he and Ana had risked expressing their love via encoded messages delivered to old meeting spots, or through unsuspecting third parties. One time he had carved her initials on the battered wooden wall beside their favorite booth in a pizza joint they both adored in the West Village. The next time he visited, he saw that she had responded by carving his initials right beside hers, and drawn a heart around them both. He had closed the restaurant down that night, drinking bottled beer and thinking of Ana until they kicked him out. Yet meeting in person was too dangerous, and ever since that balmy spring evening in Central Park, the memory of which felt so close in time and yet so very long ago, he had not laid eyes on her again.

Ana had always praised his devotion to his ideals. But in the end, it was she who had sacrificed her heart—and her entire life—for the cause.

With a snarl, needing an outlet for his heartbreak and frustration, he thought of the man who had started it all by sending Ana to seduce him. He should have killed Hans in that parrilla long ago.

Now the whereabouts of the German American were a mystery. Some years back, Dr. Corwin had discovered that Hans's true mission inside the US government had been to shepherd Project MKUltra, the CIA's top-secret mind-control program. Driven by fears of brainwashing by the Soviets and the Chinese, the CIA had conducted hundreds of clandestine experiments to improve interrogation techniques and increase the resistance to torture of US prisoners. All sorts of radical hallucinogens and mental persuasion techniques were explored. Hypnosis. Electroshock. Sensory deprivation. Verbal and sexual abuse. The program got out of hand, even performing tests on unwitting US and Canadian citizens, until it was shuttered in 1973. A public outcry ensured it would never be revived.

Except it did live on, by another name and through a far more radical initiative.

Society sources had revealed that, under the secret directive of Hans and a psychiatrist named Waylan Taylor—Dr. Corwin had gaped when he heard this—the US government had developed a new program to plunge even farther down the rabbit hole of the mind. Telepathy, psychokinesis, remote viewing, and precognition were among the vast array of ESP and psychic phenomena explored in sanctioned government research.

Behind closed doors, the government called it Project Stargate.

Dr. Corwin assumed Hans and Waylan had siphoned off the best research for the Ascendants and ventured even farther afield in their private labs. But that was in the past. Waylan had returned to Asheville, and Hans had left the CIA before dropping off the Society's radar altogether. Not even Ana knew his whereabouts.

Enough. Don't let thoughts of that barbarian ruin things. Ana has risked her life to throw the Ascendants off the trail, and you've both worked decades for this moment.

With a deep breath, prepared for anything and everything, Dr. Corwin gripped the cane at his side, felt the comforting heft of the handgun tucked beneath his fur-lined bomber jacket, and knocked on the front door.

Long moments later, he heard slow footsteps approaching from inside the house, followed by the click of a dead bolt and the swoosh of a sliding chain lock. The wooden door cracked ajar.

A fragile voice spoke from behind the opening. "Si?"

Dr. Corwin replied in Spanish. "Good afternoon. My name is James Corwin, and I'm a professor of theoretical physics at Columbia University in New York. Are you . . . are you Ettore Majorana?"

In the ensuing pause, Dr. Corwin kept one hand near his cane, ready to jam the door if needed, and his other near his pistol, unsure how Ettore—if it was truly him—would react.

After a wait that felt like eternity itself, the voice behind the door spoke again. "Have you come to kill me?"

Dr. Corwin almost laughed. "Good Christ, no."

"Are you with the Leap Year Society?"

It was Dr. Corwin's turn to hesitate. "Yes, Ettore. I am."

"And not the Ascendants."

"Never."

The door eased open, revealing a bespectacled old man in wrinkled blue slacks, a wool sweater, and a pair of beige penny loafers that looked out of place in Ushuaia. Despite the heat pouring out of the wood-burning stove in the room behind him, a green scarf was wrapped tightly around the man's neck. Above the scarf, peering owlishly at Dr. Corwin, was the face of Ettore Majorana, more than eighty years old but undeniably the same man.

"I always knew someone would come," Ettore said quietly. "I just didn't know who."

"No one else knows I'm here. Not even the Society. Of this I swear."

A harsh, rattling cough bent Ettore double. When he regained control, he ushered Dr. Corwin inside and closed the door. "It doesn't matter anymore. My time on Earth is drawing to a close."

What a strange choice of words, Dr Corwin thought. *As if his time somewhere else was about to begin.*

"Would you care for tea?" Ettore asked. "Coffee?"

"Coffee would be lovely. If it's not too much trouble."

As Ettore shuffled through a swinging door into the kitchen, Dr. Corwin sat in a cloth armchair across from the fire and opted not to take off his jacket, keeping his gun close at hand. Despite all the precautions he had taken, he couldn't shake the feeling that Hans was about to burst through the door.

While the kettle boiled, Dr. Corwin observed the room. To his left was an old sofa with a stain on the center cushion. Across from him, tucked into the corner near the wood-burning stove, was another armchair with an afghan draped across the top. Bare log walls. Scuff marks on the battered wood floors. The only other items in the room were a bookshelf by the door and a messy pile of magazines and journals on a coffee table beside the armchair.

Unable to help himself, he rose to inspect the contents of the bookshelf, surprised by the titles. Expecting old textbooks, he instead found religious tomes from across a wide spectrum of faiths, a philosophy collection, world histories, and a range of pseudoscientific titles, from J. B. Rhine's research into ESP to radical theories of consciousness to accounts of near-death experiences. There were books on the world of dreams, purgatory, advanced meditation techniques, and speculation from leading scientists on the possibility of higher dimensions.

He turned to flip through the journals on the coffee table. Most of the headlines concerned recent developments in theoretical physics. The discovery of quarks, leptons, and bosons. Brand-new theories of cosmic inflation and quantum computing.

The magazine covers were a snapshot of events over the last decade. Chernobyl. Famine in Africa. The *Challenger* explosion. Iran-Contra. The rapidly expanding network of computers around the globe that was bound to change the world.

"That is your vehicle?" Ettore asked, returning with a cup of coffee that smelled burned.

Dr. Corwin glanced at the window. "I purchased it in Mendoza and drove here. I didn't trust a rental company."

"Ah." Ettore nodded absently as he handed him the coffee, eased into the armchair by the stove, and looked down at his hands. Puffs of gray hair poked out from the sleeves of his sweater. "What does one say when one is confronted with an identity one has taken pains to conceal for half a century?"

"What do you want to say?" Dr. Corwin asked gently.

Ettore gazed back at him for a long spell. "No," he said. "You are not like the others."

Dr. Corwin held a hand out toward the bookshelf. "You have an interesting collection. Not what I expected."

"What did you think to find?"

"Math and science. And T. S. Eliot."

A hint of a smile. "'Between the idea and the reality, between the motion and the act, falls the shadow.' That's from 'The Hollow Men,' my favorite poem. Do you know what he meant by that?"

Dr. Corwin pondered the question. "That our true natures are thwarted by unseen forces? Or that some cannot overcome the barrenness in their souls?"

"Perhaps. Or perhaps he wasn't using metaphor."

Dr. Corwin felt his hand twitch at his side. "Are you speaking of the Fold? Is it your infinite tower of particles, Ettore? Is it all really two sides of the same coin? The more I study your work, the more I understand its brilliance. You conceived of a universal solution so many decades before anyone else . . ."

When Ettore started to cough again, he pulled the afghan across his shoulders and clutched it tight until the fit passed. He wiped his mouth with a handkerchief, and Dr. Corwin noticed flecks of fresh blood staining the satin cloth.

"If I have learned anything," Ettore said weakly, "it is that science, while beautiful, can never provide all the answers. We are human beings and not theorems. And yet the numbers are so perfect, in ways even I don't understand. In ways that are *more* than human."

Dr. Corwin caught his breath. "What do you mean?"

"The infinite is all around us. Yet to truly see it, we must bridge the gap between the world of forms and the world of flesh and blood."

Dr. Corwin worked to corral his frustration. He didn't quite follow, and he needed Ettore to focus. They might not have much time.

"What happened at sea, Ettore? Why did you disappear?"

"A devil chased me away."

"Stefan Kraus?"

Ettore shrank into his armchair at the mention of the name.

"How did you escape?" Dr. Corwin prodded. "Did you plan it beforehand?"

"I hired a private schooner to rendezvous with the boat. They sent a smaller rowboat for me in the middle of the night. I did not know if the device . . . I didn't know if it would work."

Dr. Corwin's hands clenched again. "A device? What kind of device?"

"And it did work," Ettore said, with a faraway smile. "For a moment, nothing more. But it was enough to see it. I was *there*."

"The Fold?"

After a moment, Ettore met his gaze. "'That which can be named is not enduring and unchanging.'"

"T. S. Eliot again?"

"Something a few years older. The Tao Te Ching."

"I see you've supplemented your science with metaphysics."

Ettore looked at him strangely. "Do you know why I love poetry so much? Because poets can describe the infinite, everything we scientists are searching for, far better than any textbook. Do you read Borges?"

"A little."

"'Time is the substance from which I am made. It is a river which carries me along, but I am the river. It is a tiger that devours me, but I am the tiger. It is the fire that consumes me, but I am the fire.'"

"That's very beautiful."

"Do you understand it?"

"I promise to think about it. Ettore, do you still have the device you made?"

He blinked. "Of course."

Prepared for a negative response, Dr. Corwin almost giggled with excitement. *He still has it.* "Can I see it?"

Another coughing fit overtook Ettore. "I thought you understood—the device broke when I was at sea. It needs so much work . . . . The materials science isn't available yet . . ."

"Maybe we can fix it together. Isn't that why you met with Nikola?"

Another small, satisfied smile crept to Ettore's lips. "You found the wine cellar?"

"And the cannon."

"I apologize," he said, almost shyly. "I did that to confuse *them.*"

"No offense was taken. I'd still love to see the device, if I could. Even if it's in pieces."

Another round of coughing stained Ettore's handkerchief with more blood.

Dr. Corwin rose to his feet, concerned. "Can I get you a glass of water?"

"Yes," Ettore said in a whisper. "That would be helpful. As you can see, I'm not well. I'm afraid my lifelong habit did me no favors. Perhaps you could return in a few days?"

"Perhaps," Dr. Corwin murmured, and walked into the kitchen.

A few days? I don't have a few days. And then what—will there be more delays?

But he had prepared for this contingency. After he poured a glass of water, he withdrew a stoppered vial from the inside of his jacket and held it above the glass. He hesitated, knowing he was on rocky moral ground. But Ettore seemed very ill, quite possibly with advanced stage lung cancer, and could die at any time. If Dr. Corwin didn't act, Ettore's research might be lost to the world forever. Or worse: it might fall into the hands of the Ascendants.

Steeling his nerves, Dr. Corwin squeezed three drops of a clear, mild sedative into the glass and walked slowly back into the living room, thinking about how he would feel if he were in Ettore's shoes.

It's his decision to make. His life's work. Who am I to judge its fate?

"I'm afraid I'll need to rest now," Ettore said.

"Of course."

As he approached the older man, Dr. Corwin's step faltered, and he debated feigning an accident and dropping the glass on the floor.

Ettore reached out a hand. "As I said, I'd be happy to talk to you again, but you should know I've decided not to share my discovery with the world."

Not to share my discovery.

In a daze, Dr. Corwin let Ettore take the glass, but remained standing a foot away from his armchair, close enough to stumble into the old man and spill the drugged water.

"I don't want to raise your expectations," Ettore continued, wrapping the glass in his birdlike hands. "When I was young, while I did not seek fame, I did seek to leave a mark of my genius. Not with little papers here and there, but with something earth-shattering. Something that would turn the world of physics on its head. But now that I have it . . . now I wish for the world to one day applaud my discretion."

The heat pouring out of the wood-burning stove felt suffocating to Dr. Corwin, and strangely anthropomorphic, as if the invisible waves of energy were transmitting his innermost thoughts to Ettore, betraying his treacherous intention.

"Thank you," Ettore whispered as he raised the glass to his lips.

Dr. Corwin took a step back. "You're welcome."

Coughing almost continuously, the elderly physicist drank the entire glass of water. Soon his eyelids fluttered, and Dr. Corwin made small talk as Ettore sank deeper into his armchair. When he was fully asleep, Dr. Corwin rested the man's head gently against the side of the chair, tucked the afghan tight around him, and put more wood in the stove so he would not get a chill.

For a long moment, Dr. Corwin stood by Ettore's armchair, consumed by guilt and wishing he could stay for months to talk to the man for whom he had searched for so long, wanting so very much to understand him and probe his remarkable brain. But every passing moment made Dr. Corwin more nervous that Hans had somehow found him. While Ettore might not want to share his knowledge, the Ascendants would never honor that choice.

Nor will I, apparently.

But I have to act while there is still time.

Whether the world is ready or not, I have to protect the knowledge.

It did not take Dr. Corwin long to find what he was looking for. Inside a locked antique trunk in the closet—he smashed the padlock with his bladed cane—he found heaps of research papers, a journal, and a metallic silver bauble the size of a cantaloupe. A tangle of wires tipped with electrodes were heaped around the silver sphere. Hands shaking with anticipation, he picked up the strange object to examine it, and saw that a large crack had almost split the object into two.

He gingerly set the device down, then flipped through the journal and the research papers long enough to know his search was complete. After replacing everything inside the chest, he carried it all to the trunk of the Land Rover, grunting from the strain.

"Forgive me, Ettore," he whispered when he returned for his cane and stood in the threshold of the house, wondering if he were about to close a door that should never have been opened. "Forgive me."

22

Andie's feet echoed on the brick walkway of the abandoned subway tunnel. The humid air was rife with the stench of rat urine. She was alone, terribly so, as she ran beneath the streets of Manhattan, using a small flashlight she had bought at the Philadelphia airport to light the way. The weak penumbra of illumination cast shadows that seemed alive on the damp and gloomy walls.

But it felt good to run, despite the scurry of rodents in the darkness swallowing the tunnel, and the more nefarious sounds she imagined hearing, and the knowledge of who was searching for her aboveground and maybe waiting when she emerged. She relished pushing her legs to the limits of her endurance, stripping her mind of doubt and worry for a few small moments.

Running was her safe space.

Always had been.

She wished with all her heart that Zawadi had come to New York to meet her. After Andie relayed her intentions, Zawadi said she was foolish, and that she was busy helping in another way that was more important.

More important than having your own badass self here with me? What am I supposed to do if that scary Chinese guy shows up?

Of course, Zawadi had not elaborated, saying only that she needed to cut off their enemy's oxygen, and leaving Andie to guess at her intentions. Zawadi did provide a plan to arrive at the Museum of Natural History undetected. She had suggested Andie fly into Philadelphia and take a train to Penn Station. From there, Zawadi gave her detailed instructions on how to find an access tunnel beneath the station that led to a deeper passage whose purpose at which Andie could only guess. After a while, the rough stone tunnel had connected to the old subway line on which Andie was now running.

She had no idea how far she had traveled. A few miles, if she had to guess.

On occasion, she had passed a group of homeless squatters, though nothing on the scale of the leper colony beneath Kolkata. Her heart had thumped in her chest when a man with a scraggly beard rose up to accost her, demanding a toll for passage. But Andie had screamed at him so fiercely he backed down, allowing her to sprint past.

Finally she arrived at the marker Zawadi had mentioned: a long-forgotten subway station with a low ceiling, graffiti-covered walls, and tracks piled with rubble. The evidence of past human occupation—fast-food wrappers, crack pipes, old newspapers—made her feel as if ghosts filled the silence around her, watching with spectral eyes from the steps leading to the surface, leaning on the pillars and steel girders, waiting for the darkness to devour her when the light failed.

She also found herself wishing Cal were with her. With a snarl, she pushed the sentiment away, slowing to a jog as she passed the station, breathing heavily as she recalled Zawadi's instructions.

Fifty yards past the edge of the platform . . . an ouroboros at chest level disguised among the graffiti . . . Push on the symbol, and a door will open.

There! She saw the graffiti, a frenetic scrawl of names and crude shapes and gang symbols that would have been visible from a train window. It took her a minute of searching by the dim light of the flashlight, but then she found it: an *O* the size of her palm, formed by a slender blue dragon swallowing its own tail.

A train coughed far overhead. After a furtive glance behind her, she pushed on the ouroboros and waited. Nothing. She used both hands and pushed harder. This time a square section of the wall hinged open, about the size of her hand, exposing a stainless steel keypad. With trembling fingers, she input the nine-digit code Zawadi had given her.

An entire section of the wall swung inward, causing her to gape as it revealed a hidden tunnel. She slipped through the door and closed it. The seams in the wall were invisible from both sides.

The new tunnel was as narrow as a broom closet and made of polished concrete. Though far more modern, it reminded her of the tunnel inside the Archiginnasio in Bologna. She had the sudden horrible thought that if Zawadi's codes didn't work, or if someone locked Andie in there, she would die in that concrete tomb, alone in the dark when her flashlight failed and the rats came to feed.

Shaking off her fear, she made sure to follow Zawadi's instructions precisely, making three more turns and passing half a dozen intersections before she came to a set of stairs that led to a landing with another keypad and a set of iron rungs bolted into the wall. At the bottom on the keypad, 36-M4 was imprinted in trim white letters.

My God, how many of these are there?

She input the same nine-digit code. This time a portion of the ceiling above the iron rungs swung downward. After listening for sounds from above, she gripped her flashlight and crawled through the hole, emerging into a musty storeroom filled with wooden crates.

Cobwebs glistened in the corners as her light probed the room. It looked as if no one had entered in years.

She closed the trapdoor and made her way to a basement hallway with faded blue carpet. To her left, at the end of the hall, she saw a set of stairs. She hurried forward, thinking about what to say if anyone found her.

After climbing to the second landing in the stairwell, she found a door with an EMERGENCY EXIT sign. She cringed as she leaned on the crash bar. No alarm sounded, and when the door opened to the outside, her dilated eyes squinted in the afternoon light.

She killed her flashlight. As expected, she found herself looking at a tract of wooded parkland with a little lake on her left. She placed a stone at the bottom of the door, leaving it cracked in case she needed to return. She then jogged quickly away, following a gravel path that merged onto a larger one sprinkled with people. The summer air was sultry, the foliage dense and green. No one paid her any attention as she turned to regard the gray sandstone château with peaks and turrets she had just exited. If she didn't know better, she would have guessed the miniature castle was located somewhere in western Europe.

Turning in the other direction, she spied a familiar, awe-inspiring skyline over the tops of the trees. Now she knew for certain she was standing in front of Belvedere Castle in New York City, right in the heart of Central Park.

The footpath connected to a paved pedestrian road—the Seventy-Ninth Street Transverse—that dissected the park and led right to the Museum of Natural History. Before resuming her jog, she took an oversize Philadelphia Eagles sweatshirt out of her backpack and pulled up the hood. She ran with her head down, already sweating in the heat and nervous that she looked out of place in the hoodie.

But it was better than showing her face.

As unnerving as her flight through subterranean New York had been, her jog through the city in broad daylight was worse. Still, there were no cameras inside the park. No one had followed her through the tunnels. With any luck, she could find what she needed in the museum and leave New York the same way she arrived, with no one the wiser.

And if the Star Phone puzzle led her to another location in the city, well, she would deal with that when the need arose.

After emerging from the western side of the park and bearing left, she found herself standing in front of a handsome four-story Beaux-Arts building that swallowed an entire block. As with the V&A Museum in London, a stone inscription greeted her above the arched entrance.

TRUTH   KNOWLEDGE   VISION

Spying a set of cameras, she kept her head bowed as she walked into an entry hall featuring the skeleton of a dinosaur rearing on its hind legs, the serpentine head reaching halfway to the rotunda soaring high overhead.

Once her back was to the cameras, she lowered her hood and smiled at the guard on her way through security. Both phones were in her pocket. She stored her backpack in a locker, pulled her hood up, and hurried through the museum, keeping an eye out for anyone suspicious but knowing speed was her best ally.

During multiple layovers on the flight from Hoi An to Philadelphia, she had researched the museum layout on Zawadi's phone. She had also studied up on Mesoamerican history and achievements, focusing on the Aztecs and the sun stone.

The inside of the museum was colossal. Overwhelming. It included a planetarium she had visited before, a library, forty-five permanent exhibition halls, and over thirty-three million specimens and objects. With the possible exception of the British Museum and the Smithsonian, there was probably more information about human cultures and the natural world contained within those walls than any other place on Earth.

Under different circumstances, she would have loved to stroll the corridors and marvel at human ingenuity and the wonders of the universe. Instead she hurried past the exhibits on biodiversity and ocean life, rushed up the stairs to the second floor, and strode quickly to the Hall of Mexico and Central America.

Throughout the room, displayed on freestanding pedestals and behind a series of handsome glass cases, the hall showcased a variety of artifacts from pre-Columbian civilizations, including the Aztec, Olmec, Maya, and Zapotec.

And there it was. Hanging under sedate lighting on an orange-and-yellow checkered wall meant to evoke the colors of the Earth's life-giving star, the replica sun stone dominated the other exhibits in the hall, both in size and ornamentation.

The English name was misleading. The circular artifact represented far more than just the sun. In Nahuatl, the language of the Aztecs, the appellation of the giant stone translated to "the great and venerable mechanism of the universe." Known as a *solar disk* to the Aztecs and other Mesoamerican cultures, it represented rulership, and was a master class on Aztec mythology.

Up close, the detail on the carvings was incredibly rich. The fire serpents on the outer ring represented the stars and constellations. The date glyph on the stone spoke of the beginning of the current solar age, while four smaller suns symbolized past epochs. The Five Suns was an Aztec creation myth that spoke of four suns and worlds that had existed before the present one, a cycle of creation and destruction that would continue forever.

In the center, the face of the primordial Earth god, Tlaltecuhtli, peered outward with unnerving verisimilitude, living mythology preserved in stone. Nor did Andie miss the bodies of the two fire serpents winding around the perimeter, bearing a strong resemblance to an ouroboros.

After a pair of Japanese tourists moved on, she stood in front of the sun stone and aimed the Star Phone at the center. The room spun around her, eliciting a thrill of excitement.

I'm in the right place!

The shape and outer ring of the sun stone remained the same when viewed through the Star Phone lens, but the interior was now composed of four lines of shapes arranged in orderly rows. On each line, three groupings consisting of one or more objects were connected by plus signs, followed by an equal sign. Equations, she assumed.

On the first line, three pairs of arrows, all facing to the right, were connected by the plus signs, followed by the number 3 after the equal sign.

Six arrows, Andie calculated mentally. *If each one equals a half, and each pair equals a whole, then the sum is three. Easy enough.*

The next line depicted two arrows facing to the left, plus the

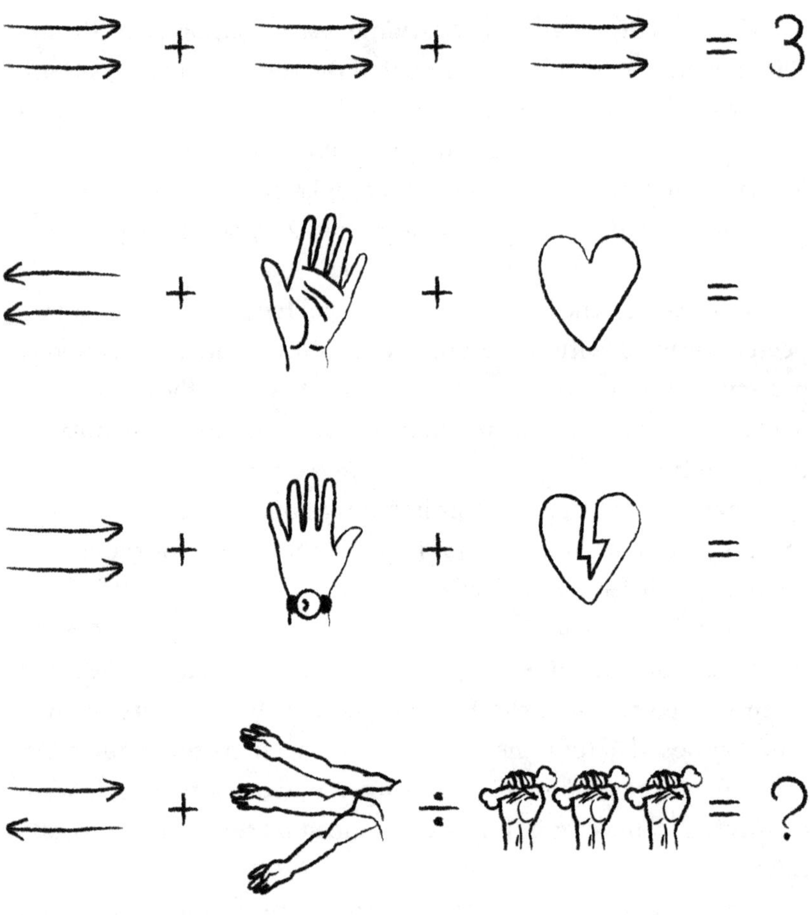
3
?

outline of a hand, plus a heart. This time, a blank cursor followed the equal sign.

On the third line, the two arrows at the beginning faced to the right again. After the first plus sign was a hand wearing a wristwatch, followed by a heart with a crack through the middle. Again a blank cursor represented the sum.

Something to do with the nature of time? Those sorts of equations are incredibly complicated. The arrow of time? Or perhaps just solar time? That would make more sense.

The fourth and final line depicted a pair of arrows facing in opposite directions, plus three arms protruding from a single shoulder, as if attached to a multilimbed god, *divided* by three hands clutching a bone. This time, a question mark followed the equal sign—a classic call to action in puzzles.

Andie lowered the Star Phone, causing the screen to revert to a keyboard. She tried to toggle but was unable. When she pointed it at the sun stone again, the puzzle returned. *It wants me to enter a solution.*

With a deep breath, Andie memorized the sequence and returned the Star Phone to her pocket. Math was not her forte. Oh, she was far better at it than the average person. Her field of study required rigorous knowledge. But she was not in Dr. Corwin's league. She was not a genius. If this puzzle required that level of thinking . . . then she was in trouble.

Not just that, but it was already five o'clock. The museum closed soon. Maybe she was wrong, but she had the sense that when she found the solution, she was supposed to point the Star Phone at the sun stone again. Else why include the image around the puzzle? If this was true, then even if she solved it, she would probably have to return in the morning to see the next clue. The Ascendants would have another day to catch up.

No, she had to solve it—right damn now.

The first thing she did was hurry to the gift shop and purchase a pen and a notebook with a *Tyrannosaurus rex* on the front. Wary of drawing attention if she returned to the Hall of Mexico and Central America, she bought a black tea and found a table in the corner of the museum café.

After thirty minutes of intense concentration, she came to the disheartening conclusion that she wasn't going to solve the puzzle before the museum closed. There were too many variables. The four different symbols, the watch on the hand, the arrows pointing in different directions, the crack in the heart. After trying a variety of advanced algebraic equations, and not being shy with the guesswork, she still had failed to come up with a single concrete value for any of the other symbols.

Was it a famous math problem in disguise?

An astronomical calculation?

A code within a code?

With only fifteen minutes until closing, she knew it was hopeless—and decided right then and there to spend the night in the museum.

It was the only way. She couldn't risk losing a whole day. If a guard caught her, she could claim she'd had a fainting spell and talk her way out. It wasn't like she was stealing anything.

But where to hide?

There were movies about this sort of thing, and possibilities flooded her mind. *What about a storage room or a coat closet? A break room?* If she had a screwdriver, she thought she could get into the air ducts.

To avoid getting locked in somewhere, she considered one of the exhibits. Could she hide under the blue whale? Inside a model dinosaur? The planetarium was a good choice. She certainly knew her way around, and it would be especially dark when the lights went out.

In the end, what really mattered were the guards and the cameras. She decided to stay as close as possible to the Hall of Mexico and Central America, so she wouldn't have to traipse across the museum. Thankfully, she had seen no cameras aimed at the sun stone. Was that by design? Another machination of the Leap Year

Society? Or just good luck?

Her mind was racing. She had to decide.

With a firm set to her jaw, she tossed her tea in the trash and walked calmly to the first-floor restroom located beside the stairwell leading to the Hall of Mexico and Central America. If someone caught her inside, she could pretend she was sick.

And if she solved the puzzle, all she had to do was climb the stairs, duck into the hall, and aim the Star Phone.

A loudspeaker announced the closing of the museum. Andie huddled in a stall with her feet on the toilet and tried to remain calm. She changed her mind, opened the door, and stood behind it, leaving the stall exposed. The door was tall for a bathroom and almost touched the floor. Her ruse depended on how carefully the guard checked the restroom, and she thought she had a better chance with an open door than a closed one.

Ten minutes later, when someone walked in, Andie held her breath, listening to the squeak of shoes. If the guard bent to check beneath the doors, Andie would easily be seen.

But the guard was careless. He or she made a quick sweep of the restroom, pushing open a few doors, and Andie heard footsteps pass right by her stall. She had made a good decision. All told, the guard spent about five seconds in the bathroom before killing the lights on the way out.

Andie exhaled a slow, silent breath.

With any luck, she would have a few hours before the cleaning crew arrived.

Half an hour later, with no progress on the puzzle, Andie wondered if the secret lay somewhere inside the Hall of Mexico and Central America. It was mostly a collection of figurines, pottery, and jewelry. Gold and jade featured prominently. She had canvassed it closely and pointed the Star Phone at almost every item, but maybe she had missed something.

Before she risked exposing herself to the cameras, she decided to explore other solutions from the safety of the bathroom. She sat with her back against the stall door in the darkness and researched on Zawadi's phone. The solar battery was incredibly long-lasting and still had half its power.

At first she Googled more math puzzles, since the structure of the four equations looked suspiciously akin to brainteasers she had seen in the past. She did find a similar motif, but none of the answers gave her any insight into her own puzzle. What was the trick?

She remembered Cal's admonition in Sicily that the puzzles were designed to shine a light on historical achievements, not esoteric equations.

Why had Dr. Corwin chosen to highlight the Aztecs, anyway? she asked herself.

Most scholars focused on the Mayans as paragons of Mesoamerican genius. During a civilization that had lasted over three thousand years—a fact that boggled Andie's mind—the accomplishments of the Mayans were well-documented: A sophisticated logosyllabic writing system, which was one of a handful throughout history to develop independently from other civilizations. Advanced crop cultivation techniques that included subterranean repositories to store water for the dry season. The invention of chocolate, an intricate legal system, and elastics made of latex long before Charles Goodyear patented vulcanized rubber. Andie revered the ancient Mayan astronomers, whose temple-top observatories rising above the Yucatán had recorded meticulous data.

Mayan genius: check.

So what about the Aztecs?

She started Googling their accomplishments. The last great Mesoamerican empire, the Aztecs had risen to power in the fourteenth century AD, long after the Mayans had begun to decline. Central Mexico was far more conducive to warfare than the Yucatán jungle, and the Aztec Empire was steeped in blood from the beginning. Every single male was conscripted. Elite special forces carried razor-sharp obsidian swords and wore padded armor beneath elaborate animal-skin costumes. Controlling millions of people at the height of the empire, Aztec warriors struck fear into neighboring states, and might have advanced much further had they not encountered the superior technology and exotic diseases of the Spanish.

Despite their military prowess, the Aztecs were also sophisticated traders, who established an imperial bureaucracy to govern their empire. They documented their achievements with extensive codices and erected astonishing temples and buildings. Andie was surprised to learn the Great Pyramid of Tepanapa, buried under a hill near modern-day Mexico City, was the largest man-made pyramid in history—surpassing even those in Egypt.

Like their Mayan predecessors, from whom they borrowed heavily, the Aztecs were incredible astronomers, mathematicians, artists, philosophers, and agriculturists. They coaxed floating gardens out of swampland and established compulsory education for their children. Aztec physicians developed extensive herbology codices that included the use of analgesics.

Great. I get it. They were as advanced as we are, in their own way. I'd love to kick back with some wine under the stars and soak it all up.

But how does any of this relate to a logic problem?

Thinking she was on the wrong track, she read a little bit more—and almost laughed out loud when she stumbled on the answer while browsing another article.

To apportion land for tax purposes, the Aztecs had developed a system of measurement based on a basic unit called a *land rod*. Despite extensive records in Aztec codices describing land surveys, researchers were stymied by a number of irregular plot dimensions. Why were some of the plots not divisible by the land rod? Finally, in 2008, they realized a number of repeating symbols seen in these irregular units had symbolic meaning—and they equated to *fractions* of a land rod. The use of fractions was a highly developed mathematical concept for the time period, and the researchers had simply overlooked it.

The symbols used as fractional units of measure by the Aztecs? Arrows, hearts, hands, and bones.

Andie couldn't believe it. It was barely even a puzzle. If she was right, she simply had to do the math on the last line of the image.

The image's resemblance to a mathematical brainteaser could have taken her down a rabbit hole. It was a devious clue. She also suspected the variables—the watch, the crack in the heart, the arrows pointing in different directions—were red herrings designed to add to the confusion.

The fourth line of the puzzle—the one with the question mark at the end—depicted two arrows facing in opposite directions, plus three arms, divided by three hands clutching a bone. Cautiously optimistic, she added up the fractional values. An arrow equaled half a land rod. An arm equaled a third. A hand meant two-fifths, and a bone, three-fifths.

One plus three, divided by three.

She quickly scribbled the math, and came up with 1.3 repeating. Was that the answer? Given the values of the Aztec symbols, she'd guessed an integer would be the solution. But there was only one way to find out.

Andie crept into the hallway, up the staircase, and into the Hall of Mexico and Central America without seeing any guards. She ducked beneath the camera at the entrance to the hall and hurried past. Unless a security guard was watching her enter right that very moment, she should be fine—at least until it was time to leave the museum.

The exhibit hall was quite dark. She felt like an archaeologist discovering an abandoned city as she crept past glass cases full of relics, feeling her way along. Guided by memory, gripping the Star Phone in her hand, she made it all the way to the sun stone before risking her flashlight.

In the solemn hush of the museum, the face of the Earth god in the center of the artifact seemed more alive than before, daring her to probe his secrets. After standing very still to listen, she entered

1.3 into the keypad on the Star Phone, and aimed it at the giant solar disk.

The face of the stone remained unchanged.

Unfazed, she tried it again, punching in as many threes as she could, taking the fraction to the limit.

Still nothing.

No. This has to be it. I don't have time to go back to the drawing board.

Wanting to scream in frustration, she aimed the Star Phone at the sun stone again and studied the image of the puzzle. After regarding it for a long moment, she slapped her forehead and groaned. She had not failed to count the hands attached to the arms on the last line. Her eyes had glossed right over them.

Dr. Corwin always lectured on how our own brains can trick us, and taught me not to overlook the obvious.

She redid the simple math. One plus *six* divided by three.

Holding her breath, she entered the new solution in the keypad, 2.3 repeating, typing in as many threes as she could, then aimed the Star Phone at the artifact. Almost at once, the stone began to rotate to the left, slowly and silently, exposing a circular opening yawning in the wall behind it.

Shanghai

23

Daiyu heard a ping and saw a message from Jianyu on the hologram floating above her workspace.

I'm in place.

Her eyes flicked downward, to the trio of monitors on the desk, each of which displayed a hijacked video feed from the security cameras at the Museum of Natural History in New York. The monitor on the left was aimed at the employee entrance outside the building, where Daiyu saw her brother and two of his agents, all wearing dark clothing and earpieces, flattened against the wall. Jianyu texted again.

Okay to enter?

Daiyu replied by speaking into her bio-bracelet. "Wait." The bracelet was linked to the hologram, the monitors, and her laptop, and would relay her response to Jianyu's cell phone using an encrypted internet-based call app she had developed for the Ascendants.

She used the bio-bracelet to whisk through the video feeds inside the museum and ensure no guards were close to the employee entrance. Once her brother and his agents were inside, she would help them sedate the two security guards, then guide them to the target. If possible, they would see where Andie was headed before taking her.

Go. Proceed to the second floor as discussed, and I will instruct you from there.

Is the target still unarmed?

Yes.

It's possible she stored a weapon in the restroom. Can you tell?

Not yet. But take nothing for granted.

Understood.

Good luck.

Luck is unnecessary. I have you.

Be careful. I still have not located Zawadi. She could be nearby.

I hope she comes. We have business to settle.

Annoyed by her brother's bravado, Daiyu left the chat open on the hologram and returned to manipulating the video feeds. It should be an easy operation. The target was resourceful but not dangerous. Jianyu had two agents with him, and more at the museum's exit points. With Daiyu watching from her God's-eye view, it should be impossible for the target to elude them.

Ever since they had lost Andie and Cal in Hanoi, the Ascendants had watched the airports carefully. In Philadelphia, an observant agent had picked up Andie on a camera recording soon after she left the airport. Daiyu and Jianyu were contacted at once. Daiyu managed to piece together Andie's route to the train station, and caught her on camera buying a ticket to Brooklyn. Jianyu was already in London and immediately boarded a private plane to New York. A local team was dispatched as well.

Somehow, even with a team in place, Daiyu had lost track of the target at Penn Station. The Society must have whisked her away. She did not know why the target had come to New York—that was foolish—but assumed it had to do with the Star Phone.

When Daiyu had picked Andie up entering the Museum of Natural History, hijacking the cameras had been child's play.

This time she wouldn't lose her.

Daiyu returned to the camera nearest the restroom. Recovering the Star Phone for the Archon would make for a successful mission, but recovering the Star Phone after learning the next destination would be an even greater victory.

From behind she heard the sound of her office door opening. Her beautiful face twisted into a snarl. *Not now.* Only two other people in the building—Jianyu's top lieutenants—had biometric access to the room. Annoyed at the intrusion, she spun in her chair as she realized a third person had access.

The Archon.

The thought caused Daiyu's heart to hammer in her chest. As her chair completed its swivel, she reached for the scarab beetle preserved in amber around her neck, but saw that the person in the room was not wearing a robe or a mask. It took Daiyu a moment to process what she was seeing: a tall black woman in tight black clothing and a backpack coming through the doorway holding a gun. Lying on the floor in a pool of blood behind the woman was a severed head. The grotesque sight resembled something out of a Greek tragedy, and at first her brain registered it as a prop, some sort of sick practical joke.

Then she recognized the head as belonging to one of Jianyu's lieutenants, realized who the woman was, and saw from her deadly expression that a joke was the furthest thing from her mind.

Jianyu's second-in-command, Daiyu thought.

Biometric access.

She lurched to her feet, her spine screaming in protest from sitting so long. The Archon's wonderful trick had dissipated hours after their meeting, leaving Daiyu grateful for the reprieve but just as crippled as before. "You!" she said, blinking rapidly. "How did you arrive without—"

"Quiet," Zawadi commanded, striding forward to level the gun at Daiyu.

Though horrified by the severed head and the appearance of the feared Society enforcer, Daiyu managed to remain calm. She did not fear physical death as did most people. More important was saving her brother. She saw Zawadi's eyes absorb the text exchange on the hologram. Daiyu waved her bio-bracelet and whispered a command, causing the computer screens to go blank and the hologram to shut down.

Zawadi noticed. As she rushed forward, Daiyu spoke again into the bio-bracelet, this time sounding a piercing alarm throughout the building. Zawadi cursed and backhanded her across the face. Before Daiyu could recover, Zawadi grabbed the fingers of her left hand and bent them back, then raised the gun and shot her right through the palm where the bio-bracelet was implanted.

Daiyu fell shrieking into the chair, aghast at what had been done. *Her bio-bracelet—her link to the digital realm—her beloved companion!* The intense physical pain was secondary. It was as if Zawadi had just assassinated Daiyu's best friend right in front of her. Ignoring the protest from her spine and the hole in her hand, Daiyu flew at the other woman in a rage, the fingernails of her good hand extended like claws.

Before she could reach Zawadi, the hateful woman kicked her in the middle of her chest, sending Daiyu's featherweight body crashing into her desk. She crumpled in pain as Zawadi backed toward the office door and pulled out a black object that resembled a miniature genie's lamp. Daiyu realized what it was moments before Zawadi pulled the pin and tossed the grenade onto the bank of monitors.

Daiyu's last thought before her world exploded was one of wonder, as she vividly recalled the final three images the Oracle had shown her: a staircase, a bouquet of calla lilies—and a tower engulfed in flames.

As the incendiary grenade went off, shaking the floor and sending fire pouring out of Daiyu's office, Zawadi shielded her face and fled down the hallway to her right, aiming for the stairwell.

The destruction of Daiyu's control center had terminated the alarm system, but the damage had been done. An elevator door whooshed open on Zawadi's left as she passed, revealing two men brandishing semiautomatics. Zawadi saw them out of the corner of her eye and spun like a cat. One was muscular, even taller than she was, and wearing gym clothes. The shorter man was dressed in jeans and a tight brown shirt, and built like a pit bull.

She saw them a split second before they noticed her. She shot the shorter man in the chest as he exited the elevator, dropping him, but a bullet grazed her arm from the other man's weapon. Her body armor absorbed it. She flattened against the wall and fired on instinct, catching the shoulder of the taller man. It was a lucky break, because she hit his shooting arm—causing him to drop his weapon, and allowing Zawadi to finish him off with a head shot.

As she turned to flee, someone grabbed her ankle and yanked on it. She fell and dropped her gun. Cursing her carelessness—the first man must have been wearing a vest under that shirt—she tried to yank her leg free, but his grip was too strong. She switched tactics and flipped on her side, letting him pull her back but using the pressure on her trapped leg as leverage for a scissors kick from the floor. She caught him on the jaw, stunning him, and jerked her leg free. Instead of scrambling away, she pulled a nine-inch fixed blade out of one of her black combat boots, leaped to her feet, and pounced on the man. He tried to fend her off, but she slipped the knife into his ribs. As his body curled into the fetal position, she jerked the knife out, pinned his head to the floor with her knee, gripped him by the hair, and slid the blade across his jugular.

Without pausing to wipe the knife, she retrieved her gun and kept both weapons in hand as she sprinted for the stairwell. She had to get out of the building before reinforcements arrived. Her only hope was her carefully laid escape route, which, if she delayed further, might be in jeopardy.

After Granada, Zawadi had realized that, in an arena where Daiyu was able to provide tactical support to Jianyu, Zawadi was no match for the twins. New York was just such an arena. In fact, Dr. Corwin had left Columbia University for that very reason. The Ascendants owned the city now. Andie's only chance to get in and out of the Museum of Natural History alive—whether Zawadi was present or not—was for someone to destroy Daiyu's network and cut off Jianyu from his support system.

Sever the head of the snake.

Zawadi made it to the stairwell and burst through the door. As she knew from a careful study of the building schematics, Daiyu's office was on the tenth and top floor. Zawadi took the stairs three at a time. Pale-gray moonlight and smog-choked air greeted her as she darted through the emergency exit and onto the roof. All around her, in stark contrast to the high-tech interior of the building, Zawadi saw a skyline of warehouses, semi-abandoned manufacturing plants, and pitted concrete buildings.

She had no time to spare, but she took a moment anyway. After replacing her boot knife, she whipped out her cell phone and sent a text to the phone she had given Andie.

Get out. Now. Jianyu is in the museum.

Had Zawadi accomplished her goal in time? She had the sinking feeling she had arrived too late, but there was nothing to do about it now.

Dammit! Why hadn't the foolish girl listened to her?

At least Zawadi could take satisfaction in having killed Daiyu and destroying her communication equipment. Though the Ascendants had plenty of other computer experts, Daiyu was the best, an absolute savant, and had long been a thorn in the Society's side.

Commotion on the stairs. It was time to complete her escape.

Zawadi stuck the phone in her pocket and holstered the gun, sprinted to the western edge of the roof, and used the running start to launch herself into the air, fifteen feet clear of the building. After letting herself free-fall below the roofline, she jerked on the two backpack straps, releasing a mini parachute.

Meant for short distances, the quick-release chute had a very small diameter and did not slow her down as much as a full-size chute would. Using the straps, she guided it to the roof of a warehouse eight stories below. She had scoped this in advance also. The warehouse was abandoned, but the schematics had not warned her about the broken glass littering the roof. When she landed, her momentum caused her to lurch forward and put her hands on the ground. Jagged shards pierced her hands through her thin gloves. Without glancing back—either they had seen her or they hadn't—she sucked in a breath, shook off the pain, bundled the parachute as she raced along the roof, and strapped it to her back again. Easing her long body off the northern lip of the building, she hung by her fingers before dropping to the deserted alley two stories below.

Zawadi dispelled the kinetic energy of the fall by kicking once off the wall as she dropped and rolling on her shoulder when she hit the ground. It took a moment to regain her wind, but she had landed only ten feet from the dumpster concealing the Jialing motorcycle she had stashed. *Not bad.*

She raced behind the dumpster, picked up the helmet, and released the disk brake lock. A six-foot-tall black woman was a fairly conspicuous target in Shanghai, so for the last piece of her plan, she extracted a canvas bag she had duct-taped beneath the rear fender. She opened the bag and pulled on an ankle-length silk dress, a latex face mask, and a smog mask to further aid the disguise. While the latex mask was not as advanced as the model the Ascendants had fitted to the simulacrum corpse at Dr. Corwin's funeral, it would do the trick while she was speeding down the freeway at eighty miles an hour. She gunned the motor and peeled out of the alley, another pollution-phobic Shanghai woman cruising through the city on a local motorcycle.

Her first task accomplished, Zawadi set her mind to the next leg of her two-part mission, and the principal reason she had flown to China instead of New York.

Zawadi had a lost scientist to find.

Lars Friedman had developed the prototype for the Enneagon at Quasar Labs. But there had been a third scientist, Xiaolong Chen, involved as well. Zawadi didn't know the details, but James had mentioned his name on numerous occasions.

Xiaolong had disappeared from his lab in Beijing around the

same time as James and Lars. Zawadi had assumed the worst. Yet two days ago, Xiaolong had contacted her on a secure channel to which only Dr. Corwin could have given access. Xiaolong claimed he had gone into hiding before the Ascendants found him, made his way to Shanghai, and had extremely important information to relay to Zawadi—and Zawadi alone.

She wasn't sure she trusted him.

She would have to take precautions.

But if the information might help Dr. Corwin, she was damn sure going to investigate.

24

The rotation of the sun stone was silent but agonizingly slow. When it finally stopped moving, a circular opening in the museum wall big enough for Andie to step through was revealed. After a glance behind her, she aimed her flashlight into the cavity and saw a claustrophobic brick passage sloping downward.

The hole was cut perfectly into the wall, about half the diameter of the sun stone itself. *A sun inside a sun. Is that symbolic of Aztec mythology, or am I stepping into another world?*

After climbing through the hole, she shone her light down the tunnel. The floor had a thin layer of dust, and the air was much warmer, but there were no cobwebs. The passage could have been a hundred years old or constructed in the last decade; she couldn't tell.

On the wall to her left was a square stainless steel plate set at chest height, similar to the push plate on a door for people with disabilities. Guessing that it closed and opened the door, she waffled for a second before pressing it, wary of sealing herself inside. But she could hardly leave a gaping hole in the museum wall for a guard to find.

As she suspected, pressing the plate caused the sun stone to rotate back in place, entombing her. She fought against a swell of primal fear, resisting the urge to press the plate again to ensure the stone would reopen. *Either it does or it doesn't.*

Firming her jaw, she started down the passage, guided by the weak cone of illumination from her flashlight. The downhill slope soon ended at a brick wall. She ran her hands over the barrier. Solid. After trying the Star Phone, she pushed hard on the wall, and felt it give. Remembering the subway tunnel, she pushed even harder, causing a seamless doorway to hinge inward. She shone her light into the opening and gasped.

It was full of treasures.

Gawking at the marvelous display of Amerindian objects arranged neatly on shelves and in glass display cabinets—gold and jade and silver, metalwork and stone figurines and elaborate pottery—she realized it must be a storage room. She had read that only a very small percentage of the museum's collection was on display at any one time.

Still a treasure room, she thought.

It just happened to be in a museum.

She slipped through the door and left it open. The room, made of polished cement, was about the size of a large studio apartment. The lack of windows, and her lost cell phone signal, led her to assume she was underground. She wandered through the room, taking in the carved skulls, vivid textiles, statues of gods and demons, and a collection of codices that left her awed by the beauty of the hieroglyphs and illustrations on the covers. To her eye, the pieces looked even more rare and impressive than the ones on public display.

During her walk-through, she kept peering through the Star Phone. So far nothing had changed. There was a door on the opposite side of the room, though instead of a handle she noticed a metal keypad similar to the ones she had seen in the tunnels beneath the city.

Oh my God. Is this storage room even part of the museum?

Hanging on the door above the keypad was an unsigned oil painting. She didn't know much about art, and had no idea of the provenance, other than it looked old and valuable and European. But from her recent research on the Aztecs, she recognized the scene as the infamous first meeting between Hernán Cortés and Montezuma. Due to biased source material, it was hard for historians to parse exactly what had happened. But the accounts on both sides agree that on the night of November 8, 1519, Montezuma and Cortés met on the causeway leading into the island city of Tenochtitlán, the capital of the Aztec Empire and the largest city in the Americas at the time.

In the painting, Cortés was armed with a musket and a sword made of fine Spanish steel. Montezuma was presenting the bearded conquistador with a prized gift: a calendar crafted from gold and silver. The calendar system was one of the great achievements of Mesoamerica, and she knew the Aztecs in fact used three calendars, each handed down from the Mayans. The tzolkin cycle of 260 days was believed to represent either the human gestation period, the region's agricultural cycle, or the rising and setting of Venus. The 365 days of the haab equated to the modern-day solar calendar. The long count calendar, used on monuments throughout Mesoamerica, was a complex system of identifying the number of days that had passed since a mythical creation date of 3114 BCE.

Cortés had later melted down the priceless calendar, put Montezuma under house arrest, and ransacked the city. Confident in their supremacy over the "savages," Cortés and his men decided to massacre a group of Aztec leaders during a religious festival, which caused a revolt that led to Montezuma's death at the hands of his own people. The conquistadores were forced to flee the city, and legend has it they dumped the hoard of gold and artifacts they had accumulated—dubbed "Montezuma's treasure"—into the blue waters of Lake Texcoco. Though Cortés returned with an army the following year, presaging the fall of the Americas to colonial powers, Montezuma's treasure was never found.

Recalling the story gave Andie an uneasy, awed feeling as she glanced around the room, but she put that aside and returned to studying the painting. In this version of the meeting, Montezuma's eyes were downcast, one knee bent. His upturned lips were eager for approval, presenting the calendar to Cortés like an offering to a god.

Andie did not buy the concept of the noble savage—neither the "noble" nor the "savage." Acts of war and cruelty had always stained the Earth, and as far as she could tell, modern human nature was just as conflicted as ever.

Aiming the Star Phone at the painting caused the edges of the lens to shimmer, but it was not until Andie pointed the device directly at Montezuma's hands that the calendar expanded to fill the room and a set of pages began flipping rapidly, faster and faster, as if proceeding from Montezuma's day to some point in the distant future. When the motion finally stopped, Andie saw a blank calendar page with nothing but a year—1820—and a new nine-digit alphanumeric code.

Andie didn't wait. She input the code into the Star Phone right then and there, causing it to dissolve and form a new image: a ring of fairies surrounding a gnarled yew tree growing out of a castle. The night sky above the fairies was lit with swirls of color, indicative of the aurora borealis.

Confused by the new image but thrilled with her progress, she took one last look at the painting before she left, strangely drawn to the eyes of both men but repelled by the blatant deification of one human being by another.

She thought she understood the message of the sixth puzzle, of standing in a museum of fallen god-kings whose greatest treasures were stored underground like a forgotten penny, of the passage of the sun stone from an actual jungle to a concrete one, moving through three different civilizations, three layers of conquerors, a reflection on genocide and preservation and the transience of all cultures.

She had a sudden bout of meta awareness, a visceral feeling of being part of a civilization that would one day be replaced by another. Would the Statue of Liberty and the Constitution of the United States be on exhibit for another culture one day?

Of course they would. The only question was when, and for whom, and the location of the museum. Would it be in outer space, if humanity conquered the stars or wrecked the planet? In a vault deep inside a mountain, or floating on an island in an ocean of storms and fire?

Could the cycle of violence and conquest be broken?

Right before she turned to leave, Andie eyed the keypad, aching to find out what lay behind the door, knowing that same tug of secret knowledge had once tempted her mother.

I'd love to stick around and see what's behind door number two, or number two thousand for you people, but if I don't get out of this museum, the only door I'll be trying to open will have bars attached.

She turned her back on the mysterious storage room, returned down the passage, and was relieved to find that pressing the stainless steel plate at the entrance caused the sun stone to open. She pressed the plate again before she hurried out, trying to decide how to exit the museum. As she neared the entrance to the Hall of Mexico and Central America, her phone buzzed.

As far as she was aware, only two people had that number.

Surprised by how much her heart lurched at the thought of Cal being in trouble, Andie jerked the phone out of her pocket, unable to ignore it. When she looked down and saw the message—it was from Zawadi, not Cal—a rush of adrenaline poured through her.

Get out. Now. Jianyu and Ascendants are in the museum.

Ohmygod.

The message had been sent ten minutes ago. She must have had no signal. Terrified, she poked her head into the hallway and saw a museum guard slumped on the floor. She couldn't tell if he was dead or just unconscious.

Aghast, she ducked back into the Hall of Mexico and Central America. Footsteps sounded from farther down the corridor. Her first instinct was to hide in the secret passage, so she sprinted back into the room with the sun stone. The giant artifact had almost returned to its position, and the hidden opening was too tight for her to fit through. A barrage of thoughts flooded her mind.

The stone is too slow. If someone comes in here, it won't reopen in time. Even if I make it inside, what if they find me somehow? They won't leave the museum without me.

And if I try to flee, they'll most likely catch me, take the Star Phone, and kill me.

In a split second, Andie knew what she had to do. She had only one card to play, one piece of leverage over the Ascendants. With a deep breath, her future a black hole of doubt, she set the Star Phone inside the secret passage right before the sun stone closed. She hoped the layer of dust on the floor meant no one else had entered in months, or would for some time.

The stone rolled to a close, separating her from her lifeline to Dr. Corwin and her mother. If she got lucky and escaped the museum, she could come back for it later. And if they caught her, she would hold out as long as she could, and hope Zawadi rescued her before they tortured her.

It wasn't much of a plan. But it was better than giving up.

She hurried behind an exhibit case and prepared to defend herself as best she could. The footsteps came closer and closer in the corridor outside, but instead of entering the exhibit hall, they continued on. At first she wished she hadn't let go of the Star Phone, then shook her head angrily. Her logic still held. She had made the best decision under the circumstance, and she still hadn't escaped the museum. If she had been caught with her only bargaining chip, they would have killed her outright.

After the footsteps receded, she tried to formulate a plan. The Ascendants would block the exits. She assumed they had control of the cameras. Or had Zawadi done something about that? How did she know the Ascendants were inside? Was Jianyu the Chinese man chasing them?

Didn't matter. Andie had to get out of the building and escape the way she had come, race through the park to Belvedere Castle and access the hidden tunnels. It was her only chance.

Trying not to panic, she descended the nearest stairwell to the first floor, and found a window. The latch wouldn't budge. Deciding to break it, she dashed to the Hall of Human Origins and lifted a chair she found near the entrance. She carried it back to the window and paused. Maybe she was being rash. If she exited the museum here, she would have to run almost the entire length of an avenue to reach the park. The breaking glass would draw attention, and that was a long way to run without cover.

Too far, she realized.

With a grimace, knowing every second counted, she recalled her mental map of the museum as she hopped off the chair and raced up the stairs again, unwilling to cross the main foyer. Creeping as quietly as she could to the stairs south of her position, she descended and paused to listen when she reached the landing.

Still no one.

Take a breath, Andie.

She slipped into an area she didn't recall from the map, full of local flora and fauna. She left that and entered the North American forests exhibit, breathing a sigh of relief when she found a window on the side of the room overlooking the corner of Seventy-Seventh and Central Park West. Just across the street loomed the dark expanse of the park, an inkblot in the center of the city.

She clambered onto the beehive exhibit and leaned over to smash the window with a side elbow. The breaking glass seemed as loud as an explosion. She tensed for an alarm that never came and kept striking the window until she had cleared enough space to pull herself through. Avoiding the shards of glass as best she could, she heard a barked command from inside the museum. She dove into a bed of rosebushes, resisting the urge to scream as the thorns tore into her arms and face. Bloodied, she lurched to her feet, pawing through the mass of shrubs. A handful of people were walking on the sidewalk. Cars and taxis and buses. The bubble of normalcy gave her a burst of confidence.

A glance to her left brought her crashing back to reality. She saw a man and a woman in baseball caps and athletic clothes running from the main entrance, less than two hundred feet away. They kept their gait nonchalant, and could have been runners out for a night jog, but Andie knew better. They were veering right toward her.

It was tempting to shout for help, but she knew that wouldn't get her anywhere. She had to reach the tunnels. As she fled across Central Park West, a taxi slammed on its brakes. The driver shrieked at her in a foreign language at the same time Andie heard the whine of two motorcycle engines approaching. Just before she entered the park, she glanced back and saw two bikers calmly drop their motorcycles, take off their helmets, and look right at her before strolling into the green space. The pair of Ascendants in baseball caps were crossing the street farther north, trying to cut her off.

Running for her life, Andie dove into the sultry embrace of the park. She was engulfed by the sound of crickets as she wove through the trees looming above her in the darkness. Shadows filled the pockets of light thrown from the streetlamps. The lack of noise from the Ascendants chasing her was unnerving, deadly predators stalking their prey in silence.

Andie ran straight through the park, hopping boulders and benches, crashing through beds of wildflowers. Going on instinct, she cut left once she passed the edge of the lake, hoping she hadn't overshot the castle. She ran as she never had before, telling herself it wasn't that far, drawing on every last reserve.

That's a turret up ahead! With a burst of speed, she darted across the paved transverse and approached the castle. All she had to do was circle the building, slip through the door in the rear she had left cracked, and disappear into the tunnels.

A pair of security lights were mounted on the walls of the castle. Hunched low and hugging the wall, she circumnavigated the stone wall until she found the door on the far side from which she had emerged earlier in the day.

It was locked.

No, no, no.

Stay calm, Andie. It's not that surprising. A security guard must have closed it. You can do this. There's a window right over there you can smash open, and you'll be gone before they—

"Going somewhere?"

The voice caused Andie to stand paralyzed, like a rabbit frozen in plain sight. A man dressed all in black emerged from the edge of the building, stepping calmly beneath one of the security lights, a pair of night goggles around his neck.

Jianyu.

Andie found her courage and rushed him, snapping a round-house kick into his midsection. He caught her leg in midair, swept her other leg out, and held her by the arms as she fell. His grip was like iron, and he had handled her so easily it made her wonder if he was the Archon.

"There's a passage beneath the city inside the castle, isn't there?" he said. "It's how you arrived at the museum."

"Let me go!"

More people slithered like eels out of the darkness, a dozen of them at least, men and women from a wide range of nationalities, surrounding her and Jianyu with laser-scoped firearms trained on Andie.

Jianyu released her. "Do you know why my communication with my sister cut off?"

"I have no idea what you're talking about."

Jianyu studied her face with a neutral expression. "We shall see. Where is the device?"

"Here. You can have it." Andie pulled Zawadi's phone out of her pocket and tried to erase the text exchange before Jianyu slapped her so hard she saw stars. As Andie stumbled to a knee, he yanked the phone away and saw that it was not the Star Phone. He pulled her to her feet and gripped her by the pressure point on the underside of her right elbow. When she tried to squirm free, he squeezed harder, causing her to swoon.

"If you call out," he said quietly, "I will cut out your tongue right here, and you can finish your interrogation with pen and paper." He tipped his head and issued a command in Chinese into his collar, speaking into a hidden microphone, then addressed Andie again. "Where did you put the device?"

Andie forced a smile. "You missed the handoff."

"Who did you give it to?"

"A friend. She knows the city and is long gone."

"You're lying. No one else left the museum."

"Didn't they?"

He gripped her even harder, causing her knees to buckle. He held her up and said, "Who was it? Where did they go?"

She gasped in pain and needed a moment to find her voice. "It was Santa Claus. Try the North Pole, asshole."

With a snarl, Jianyu snapped his fingers. The tall woman in the baseball cap who had been watching the front of the museum stepped forward holding a syringe. Andie struggled, but Jianyu held her tight as the woman jabbed Andie in the biceps with the needle. A warming sensation engulfed her.

"We'll talk someplace more private," Jianyu said, his words sending a chill through Andie.

Terrified of whatever drug they had given her, she fought like a desperate animal, trying to rake Jianyu's eyes and knee him in the groin. Anything to get free. The last thing she remembered, before her world turned black, was his palm shooting forward to connect with the underside of her jaw.

Asheville

25

As Cal approached the Gothic Revival mansion on the edge of downtown Asheville just before nightfall, a purple haze shadowed the mountains ringing the city. Observing the abandoned house induced a flashback to Egypt, from when he and Andie had stood at the gate to the Belle Epoque estate that sheltered—if the AI avatar named Hypatia was to be believed—the surviving remnants of the Library of Alexandria. The memory made him wary, but also induced a stab of disappointment that Andie, attitude and infuriating stubbornness and all, was not by his side.

Cal thought the endless journey from Vietnam to Asheville might have given him an ulcer. He had barely slept on the flights, afraid to turn his back on the other passengers. Using the false ID Zawadi had provided, he had used all his skills to arrive undetected, including dressing as a Hasidic Jew for the journey, a disguise he had pieced together in Hoi An. Once he made it through the Asheville airport, he had changed to jeans, a baseball cap, and a SAVE FERRIS T-shirt he had found along the way.

Forget Ferris—how about Save Cal?

He had splurged for a taxi and asked the driver to drop him at a sketchy public park near the old mansion. At every turn, he kept expecting a black van to roll up alongside them and disgorge a posse of Ascendants. But so far, so good.

Though the paint on the house was faded and peeling, a whimsical touch of teal remained on the eaves of the steeply pitched roof. He glanced around the street before climbing the iron fence and scurrying to the front porch. The neighborhood around the house was downtrodden, with boarded-up windows and people loitering on the corners, but it also seemed to be gentrifying. Cal had passed a French bakery and a cider bar on the way in. A bakery was one thing, but a cider bar? You might as well truck in the hipsters.

The front door was locked. He hopped over the side of the porch, waded through the weeds to the back of the house, and found a broken window. Once inside, it was evident that squatters had occupied the house for years. Condoms, fast-food wrappers, and drug paraphernalia littered the floor. The couch was sagging. Stains on the carpets and walls.

Nervous someone else was inside, he used the light on the prepaid phone he had picked up at the airport to make his way through the house and ensure he was alone. Rodent droppings were everywhere, emitting a god-awful smell. Some of the floorboards were so mushy he worried he would step right through.

He wished he could contact Dane for backup, but for that Cal needed a data plan. Maybe he could pick up an unlocked phone somewhere later that night. Feeling a strong compulsion to talk to another human being, he fought against the urge to call Andie. Even if she answered, someone might trace the call.

The place seemed truly abandoned. There were no clever artifacts or staircases leading to futuristic data storage rooms. Recalling the layout, he took a deep breath and made his way to the office of Waylan Taylor, the creepy psychologist who had once used the house as the Human Limits Testing Facility.

This dump could be used to test human limits all right—how low they can go.

The sizeable office had been picked clean, the drawers of the mahogany desk emptied. There was no other furniture in the room.

Not even a trash can.

Cal set down his backpack and took out a crowbar he had purchased at a Home Depot on the way. The taxi driver had not complained about the delay. He was probably just happy Cal hadn't taken an Uber.

After pushing the desk aside, Cal stood in the exact spot where he had seen the door in the promotional video. Before he struck the wall, he stood with the crowbar clenched in his hands, wondering what he would find. Maybe the urban explorer's video had lied or was doctored. Maybe he had come all this way for nothing. He knew Andie might never forgive him for abandoning her. If anything happened to her, he might never forgive himself.

But he had to trust his instincts.

Well, here we go. With a grimace, he hefted the crowbar and tore into the Japanese woodblock–themed wallpaper, punching through the drywall on the first swing. Dane had never located the schematics, but judging from Cal's own walk-through, a staircase was on the other side of that wall. He guessed an office closet—if one had existed—had been carved into the space beneath the stairs.

He kept swinging until he cleared out enough drywall to shine the light inside.

Bingo.

Suppressing a whoop of excitement, he tore down the rest of the false wall and stepped into a closet about four feet wide and eight feet deep. Resting against the back wall was a dusty metal file cabinet.

All right, you bastards. Let's see what little goodies we've got.

The cabinet was about three feet high, with a trio of drawers. The top drawer was secured by a padlock. A quick glance revealed the bottom two were empty.

Using a combination of bashing and prying with the crowbar, he forced his way into the locked drawer. After wiping away a layer of dust with his shirt, burning with curiosity as to what Waylan Taylor had gone to so much trouble to conceal, Cal pulled out the drawer, set it on the ground, and took out two items. The first was a plastic case full of hard magnetic computer disks, the kind used to store data in the late nineties and early aughts. He counted ten of them. Dane needed to see those ASAP.

He stuck the case in his backpack and picked up the second item: two tabbed manila folders bound with a rubber band. Both tabs read PATIENT 139.

When Cal tried to pull off the rubber band, the brittle thing snapped in two. Wondering how old this file was, he found the answer as he scanned the top piece of paper inside the first and thinner folder: a typed one-paragraph memo to the file from Dr. Taylor.

Dated December 5, 2001, the title of the memo was "Initial Notes." Cal read the single paragraph beneath the title.

> Today I met with a recruit slated for the next Ascension. My task, as always, is to administer a battery of psychological tests and evaluate mental preparedness. However, during our discussion, which suggested awareness of the nature of my other research, the recruit claimed to have developed extraordinary abilities after studying with shamans and cultivators of mental phenomena around the world. Though skeptical, I suggested administering a series of parapsychological assessments. The recruit agreed. I have opened a new dossier under the name Patient 139.

Cal skimmed the next entry, about some kind of advanced IQ exam, which the recruit aced. The next few documents were personality tests that did not seem unusual. He realized this portion of the file related to the mental preparedness evaluation, and he flipped through the stack of papers until he reached the entry for the first session with Patient 139.

Why haven't I seen a name attached?

He knew he should stick the file in his backpack and skedaddle, but he couldn't resist reading a few session notes.

Session 1. From the psych eval, I know Patient exhibits strong psi-conducive variables, including a positive belief milieu, (alleged) prior experience with extraordinary mental phenomena, advanced meditative techniques, creative thinking, and artistic ability. Emotional maturity is a question mark. There are barriers in place to which patient will not admit.

I suggested we start with hypnosis. Patient agreed, but claimed to be immune to all known mesmeric techniques. Nevertheless, I carried on, as I have rarely failed to hypnotize anyone willing to sit through the attempt.

Patient spoke the truth. Every method I tried over the course of the session had no effect. I suspect Patient has studied these techniques and understands how to combat them. I decided to switch gears by administering three different Ganzfeld tests. Patient performed in a range suggestive of psi ability but not determinative. Still, a positive sign. We will continue.

Session 2. An extensive session with Zener cards produced similar results: success rates that fell within the accepted range but inconclusive. At the end of the session, Patient claimed, somewhat dramatically, to be able to manipulate bodily energy, as well as dreamwalk.

Session 3. I administered a battery of aura and EMP tests to attempt to verify the energy manipulation claim. Again results were indeterminate. On the first EMP test, the pulse meter jumped farther than I have ever witnessed—farther than I believed possible from mental persuasion alone—yet Patient could not reproduce the effect. I suspect malfunction or interference from an outside source, perhaps even deception. Patient appeared disappointed, even distressed. We discussed the drawbacks of current testing systems and the necessity of developing a more accurate receiver. Patient also opined on the relation of unexplained mental phenomena to the fundamental forces of nature and quantum physics. I have to admit I am impressed by Patient's breadth of knowledge. As long as the tendency towards grandiosity is monitored, and no deceptive practices are uncovered, I will recommend Patient for Ascension.

So far, Cal was intrigued, and a little unnerved, but nothing he had read caused any alarm bells to ring. Plenty of people—including leading universities, think tanks, and the US government—had conducted extensive studies on ESP and similar areas of pseudoscience. Who knew if there was anything to all of it—he had his doubts—but he would be surprised if the Ascendants hadn't explored that route. After skimming the next few entries, which detailed more testing that bore the same wishy-washy results, he found a handwritten note stuck in the file after Session 8.

What he read made his skin crawl.

I can hardly believe what I have witnessed. In order to study Patient's facial expressions and body language more closely, I recorded Session 8 on a hidden monitor. At precisely the thirty-minute mark, a burst of colored light issued from the Patient's right palm, with the effect of inducing me into an instant hypnagogic state. After watching the video several times, I am still unsure how this was done. Patient has claimed to be able to manipulate bodily energy and induce external perception of chakras. I am unconvinced of this. I suspect it was sleight of hand. Regardless, Patient's skill in this arena is astounding. I was completely unaware that I *was mesmerized. Even more disturbing, for the next thirty minutes Patient intensely questioned my memories of past sessions with other patients, as well as my knowledge of the Fold. <u>How does Patient know about the Fold??</u>*

After questioning me, Patient brought me out of hypnosis and carried on with the session. How many times has Patient done this? How have I failed to notice the loss of time? On the other hand, what reason would I have had to suspect?

I am extremely troubled that Patient induced hypnosis without my consent, not to mention the content of the questions. I will report the incident and discontinue the sessions.

Sweet Jesus, Cal thought. A spray of colored lights . . . coming from the palm of a hand . . . a powerful hypnotist . . . Was Patient 139 the *Archon*?

It made him speculate once again on the identity of the Ascendants' terrifying leader. In Cal's mind, the most obvious choice was Lars Friedman, the scientist at Quasar Labs who had helped Dr. Corwin develop the Enneagon. His disappearance had never been explained, and he could have burned down his own lab to deflect suspicion.

Then there was Zawadi. She fit the profile—a tall martial arts expert—and was enigmatic as hell. It didn't seem right, and Cal liked her, but you never knew. This applied to Dr. Corwin as well. Again: What if he had faked his own disappearance for some unknown reason? Maybe Lars Friedman had hidden the Enneagon from Dr. Corwin, and Andie's mentor was using her to find it. Or the Archon could very well be someone inside the Ascendants unfamiliar to Cal or Andie.

He turned back to the folder. There were no more session records. The final entry was another memo.

I confronted Patient 139 about the unauthorized hypnosis, avoiding eye contact to deter a repeat incident. After a pause, Patient whispered in an unfamiliar language that somehow induced blindness in both of my eyes. I was terrified and began to shout. Patient ordered me to stay quiet and asked if I had reported the incident to anyone. I confessed—truthfully—that I had called my superior and left a message and had not received a call back. After interrogating me—and, I have to suspect, another round of hypnosis induced without my knowledge—Patient forced me to reveal the location of the videotape, claiming that if I reported the incident or interfered with Patient's Ascension, then I would be blinded again, this time for good. With another whispered phrase, Patient restored my vision, told me that my mind was no longer mine alone, and left the room.

In retrospect, I believe Patient must have implanted a hypnotic trigger during one of the earlier sessions. It is the only reasonable explanation for the sudden onset—and withdrawal—of my blindness. There are confirmed reports in conversion disorder literature for similar trauma induced by psychological triggers. I have also come to believe the inconclusive tests in the earlier sessions were carefully orchestrated so that Patient could continue to probe my knowledge.

Though stunned and highly intrigued by Patient's abilities, I have begun to doubt the true nature of what I have seen and experienced.

I am also afraid.

With goose bumps running down his arms, Cal could only guess at what had happened after that, or why Dr. Taylor had risked keeping a secret record of the sessions.

Insurance against retaliation? Using the knowledge as blackmail?

Cal had what he needed. He knew he should get the hell out of the house. At the very least, Dr. Taylor probably had someone watching it from time to time. Yet unable to help himself, he took a glance at the second, fatter folder. PATIENT 139 was typed in bold font across the top, which caused the back of his neck to prickle. If he was reading about the Archon, and Waylan Taylor had uncovered the true identity of the masked leader of the Ascendants, then Cal could be holding a live grenade of information.

The contents resembled a missing-persons case. Inside were newspaper clippings, photographs, copies of plane tickets, and hand-written notes, most of them pertaining to a tall blond woman with short hair who looked oddly familiar. *The Archon is a woman?*

He flipped to the end and saw another memo stapled to the inside of the folder. The first two lines told him all he needed to know. As he read them, he clutched the folder and realized why the blond woman looked so familiar. He had seen another photo of her recently, with much longer hair.

Oh, hell no. Oh, Andie. Oh Jesus Christ, no.

He looked down at the folder again, barely able to process the awful truth.

NAME: SAMANTHA ELIZABETH ZEPHYR

SLATED FOR ASCENSION: FEBRUARY 29, 2004

EPILOGUE

It was the first day of class.

Dr. Corwin always enjoyed the beginning of the school year, the gathering of hopeful young minds to acquire knowledge, the dawn of something rich and new. He especially enjoyed Quantum Mechanics I, his favorite course to teach, the introduction of the graduate students to higher-level physics. As the semester wore on, and their worldviews were spun like a top, and some of them failed to grasp the incredibly difficult concepts, the bloom would come off the rose. His relationship to his students would become more complex, both hero and villain, mentor and executioner, a chimeric possessor of the keys to the kingdom of higher learning.

But for now, he would bask in the glow of positive energy, get to know the fresh faces, and enjoy the fine summer day.

Despite his cheerful mood, a barrage of thoughts filled his mind, none of them related to academia. After years of studying Ettore's silver sphere, increasingly convinced of the man's genius, Dr. Corwin grew obsessed with perfecting his device. Ettore's idea of reaching the Fold by connecting the human mind directly to the theorems that powered the core of his device was ingenious, but he had needed a far more effective conductor of energy. So far, Dr. Friedman's lab results on the prototype casing had been quite positive.

As the Ascendants grew in power, the Society had elected to withdraw farther and farther into the shadows. Dr. Corwin thought this was a grave mistake. The Society must remain hidden in plain sight, yes, but it must not remove itself from the world. That was the path to irrelevance and ruin. The Society had arisen in the first place because it cared so very much for the future of humanity. It must not hoard its knowledge like the Nine themselves, or some ancient sleeping dragon in its lair, greedy and callous. They all seemed to have forgotten the vows that were made. The situation had deteriorated so far that Dr. Corwin felt comfortable sharing Ettore's research only with a handful of like minds.

As Dr. Corwin had ascended, so to speak, his rival had fallen. To Dr. Corwin's knowledge, Hans, nor anyone else, had discovered the true fate of Ettore Majorana. In the eyes of the Ascendants, Hans had failed in his mission, and according to Ana, now a deeply embedded spy, the German had dropped off the face of the Earth a year ago, presumably to escape the firing squad.

Ana, oh Ana.

Outside of a rare night spent with a bottle of fine Scotch and his memories, Dr. Corwin did his best not to dwell on his beloved, as that was the path to madness. At least he was no longer in New York, where her absence haunted him at every turn.

The small class quieted. Dr. Corwin straightened the cuffs of his dress shirt, clasped his hands behind his back, and began to pace with his cane. "Imagine, if you will," he said, jumping into the same speech with which he always began Quantum Mechanics I, "that you lived in an early society—Egyptian, Greek, Vedic, Aztecan, take your pick—and that today was the day you learned that all the gods in which you believe were not in fact real. Now, this is not some red-faced prophet telling you this is what *he* believes. You have seen *proof*. Incontrovertible, unambiguous, rock-solid evidence of the demise of your belief system. Imagine how difficult that would be! Imagine how your outlook would change! Imagine further, if you will, the decision of whether to disclose this knowledge to your friends and family. Do you tell them the terrible truth, or keep it secret and let them enjoy their remaining years?"

. He paused for a drink of water, noting that most of the shuffling of papers and backpacks had stopped. "Now imagine," he continued, "and perhaps this is not such a stretch, that your god is science, and that you live in the early twentieth century. Imagine you have just read Max Born's *Zur Quantenmechanik* and discovered the principles of quantum mechanics. Yes, those principles were formed over time, but imagine this is your first exposure, as it was for many." His gaze roamed over the eager faces. "What modern humans discovered about the fundamental nature of reality during this time period was no less startling to their worldview than if a cleric of the ancient world had been shown proof his gods were false. Even Einstein could never fully accept the truth of the theories he helped establish."

Every single student was now watching him with an intense, and sometimes uneasy, expression. As he let his words sink in, Dr. Corwin opened a palm. "By now, you all might have a cursory understanding of quantum principles. But I can guarantee you that during the course of this class, your scientific milieu, what you think you know about reality, will be upended. Just as importantly, you will begin to learn that not only is knowledge power, but that it's also a burden, and a grave responsibility. You might even choose to walk out the door right now and preserve your innocence, because the path to higher knowledge, once traversed, can never be forgotten."

A young woman with sharp cheekbones raised her hand in the front row. Her honey-blond hair fell to her waist, and she did not seem as wide-eyed as the other students.

"And what if you're wrong?" she said, when Dr. Corwin called on her. "What if incontrovertible evidence manifests that disproves *your* new gods, *your* new theory?"

Dr. Corwin chuckled. "An astute comment, Ms. . . . ?"

"Zephyr," she said, regarding him with a calm, intelligent stare.

"Mrs. Samantha Zephyr."

He opened a palm. "Well, Mrs. Zephyr, that's even more reason to cultivate the right *approach* to knowledge."

"But given what we know about quantum mechanics," she pressed, "why should we believe anything at all about the nature of reality? No matter the approach."

He allowed himself a small smile. *Maybe you shouldn't.*

"My dear," he said as he stepped to the lectern, "science does not ask you to believe. Only that you seek to understand."

Coming Soon – ASCENSION, the thrilling conclusion to the Genesis Trilogy!

Be sure to visit unknown9.com to stay up to date on both the Genesis Trilogy and all of the other stories set within the Unknown 9 universe.

ACKNOWLEDGMENTS

Thanks again to the amazing team at Reflector who have brought this Storyworld to life. The studio has grown so much that it would take a few pages to list everyone involved, but a special shout to Alexandre Amancio, Andrea, Lexi, Tomas, Christopher, Noémie and Noémie, André, Francois, John, Iléana, Pascal, Simon, Jérémy and Jeremy, Elena, and I sincerely hope I haven't left anyone out. I sincerely appreciate the hard work and dedication to craft of each and every one of you.

I also owe a huge debt to my wonderful agent Ayesha Pande, publicists extraordinaire Emi Bataglia and Rosanne Romanello, and my crackling good editors: David Downing, Elizabeth Johnson, and Varsana Tikovsky.

To my beta readers (and dear friends) Rusty Dalferes, John Strout, Debbie Jean, Aaron Hervey, Bill Burdick, and Dan Ozdowski: I can't thank you enough for giving so selflessly of your time. I simply couldn't do it without you (or if I tried, and survived the ordeal, it would be a much inferior product). And finally, as always, this book is for my wife and family, whose love and support keep me sane and In The Chair.

ABOUT THE AUTHOR

LAYTON GREEN is a bestselling author whose work spans various genres, including thriller, mystery, suspense, and fantasy. His novels have been nominated for numerous awards (including a two-time finalist for an International Thriller Writers award), optioned for film, translated into multiple languages, and have reached #1 on genre lists in the United States, the United Kingdom, and Germany.

In addition to writing, Layton attended law school in New Orleans and was a practicing attorney for the better part of a decade. He has also been an intern for the United Nations, an ESL teacher in Central America, a bartender in London, a seller of cheap knives on the streets of Brixton, a door-to-door phone book deliverer in Florida, and the list goes downhill from there.

Layton lives with his family in Southern California. You can also visit him on Facebook, Goodreads, or on his website:

www.laytongreen.com

ALSO BY LAYTON GREEN

THE DOMINIC GREY SERIES

The Summoner
The Egyptian
The Diabolist
The Shadow Cartel
The Resurrector
The Reaper's Game (Novella)

THE BLACKWOOD SAGA

Book I: The Brothers Three
Book II: The Spirit Mage
Book III: The Last Cleric
Book IV: Return of the Paladin
Book V: A War of Wizards

OTHER WORKS

Written in Blood
A Shattered Lens
The Letterbox
The Metaxy Project